Praise for *Home from the Sea*:

"Lackey's way with character description is phenomenal. I greatly enjoy being one of those people who is able to visualize books in such detail that it's almost as though I'm watching a movie, and Lackey does not disappoint in this regard. Every time I was interrupted whilst trying to read this book, when I came back I momentarily forgot I was reading at all. This book was fantastic, and I can't wait to start the series at the beginning."
—Bookshelf Bombshells

"Lighter in tone with more emphasis on romance than some of the previous titles, this fairy-tale homage offers a variant view on the usually tragic love between humans and selkies, and should attract both series fans and Lackey's sizable following."
—*Library Journal*

"With a nod to the Nordic tale 'East of the Sun and West of the Moon,' the latest *Elemental Masters* historical fantasy is a thrilling tale, due to the brave heroine who will fight for those she cherishes and to keep what is rightfully hers."
—*Midwest Book Review*

And for the previous novels of the *Elemental Masters*:

"This is Lackey at her best, mixing whimsy and magic with a fast-paced plot."
—*Publishers Weekly*

"Richly detailed historical backgrounds add flavor and richness to an already strong series that belongs in most fantasy collections. Highly recommended."
—*Library Journal* (starred)

"Fans of light fantasy will be thrilled by Lackey's clever fairy-tale adventure."
—*Booklist*

"I find Ms. Lackey's *Elemental Masters* series a true frolic into fantasy."
—Fantasy Book Spot

"Lackey has delivered an [...] *Masters* series. . . . The story [...] ven together and as usual, [...] delightful."

"All in fine fairy-tale tradit[...] historical detail, and just a hint of romance to [...] things."
—*Locus*

MERCEDES LACKEY

Home from the Sea

The Elemental Masters,
Book Seven

MONTROSE REGIONAL LIBRARY
320 SO. 2ND ST.
MONTROSE, CO 81401

DAW BOOKS, INC.
DONALD A. WOLLHEIM, FOUNDER
375 Hudson Street, New York, NY 10014

ELIZABETH R. WOLLHEIM
SHEILA E. GILBERT
PUBLISHERS
www.dawbooks.com

Copyright © 2012 by Mercedes Lackey.

All Rights Reserved.

Cover art by Jody A. Lee.

Cover designed by G-Force Design.

DAW Book Collectors No. 1588.

DAW Books are distributed by Penguin Group (USA) Inc.

All characters and events in this book are fictitious.
All resemblance to persons living or dead is coincidental.

If you purchase this book without a cover you should be aware that this book
may be stolen property and reported as "unsold and destroyed" to the publisher.
In such case neither the author nor the publisher has received any payment for
this "stripped book."

The scanning, uploading and distribution of this book via the Internet or any
other means without the permission of the publisher is illegal, and punishable by
law. Please purchase only authorized electronic editions, and do not participate
in or encourage the electronic piracy of copyrighted materials. Your support of
the author's rights is appreciated.

First Paperback Printing, June 2013

1 2 3 4 5 6 7 8 9

DAW TRADEMARK REGISTERED
U.S. PAT. AND TM. OFF. AND FOREIGN COUNTRIES
—MARCA REGISTRADA
HECHO EN U.S.A.

PRINTED IN THE U.S.A.

To Occupy.

ACKNOWLEDGMENTS

Profound thanks to Dr. Colin Dival of York University for invaluable information on the British rail system in the late 1800s. Not only did Dr. Dival make sure I actually sounded like I knew what I was talking about, he saved me from some very embarrassing errors!

1

BETWEEN the howling of the wind, the pounding of the rain on the roof, and the tumult of the ocean, Mari Prothero knew there was no point in listening for anything else. The damp, chill wind found a hundred little cracks and chinks to whistle through, and only near the fire was it at all warm. At least the wind wasn't sending the smoke down the chimney instead of up.

This was the sort of day that the wives and daughters of fishermen dreaded. It had begun with a red sky, always a bad sign, but by the time the sun was up to give the warning of rough weather to come, Mari's father Daffyd Prothero was already gone fishing. And not out in his little river coracle for salmon, no. Out in his bigger boat—still a coracle—out on the wide ocean, for herring. Whether meant for the river or the ocean, coracles were still unchancy boats, being little more than great round dishes made of wood and hide or canvas. Granted, the

ocean coracles had sails, but still! You had to be a mad
sailor as well as a fine one to take one on the ocean in
the teeth of a storm.

Oh, thought Mari Prothero, her heart full of anxiety,
and my da is both . . .

She bent over the fire and stirred the coals, adding a
little more sea-coal and a little more driftwood on top.
Flames sprang up, blue and gold and green, colored by
the salts in the wood and the coals.

By midmorning the threatening sky had made good
on its promises, and there was a full-throated storm
churning the ocean. The wind howled about the cottage
walls on the hill above the beach and wailed about the
chimney.

And had Daffyd Prothero come scudding in ahead of
the storm? *Of course not. Because he's mad.*

Mari'd had to latch the shutters tight on the seaward
side, and even so, wind-driven driblets of rain crept over
the sills whenever the rain drove hard against the windows. The drafty air inside smelled of the ocean and the
storm, and not the lovely hot pie and bread she had bak-
ing.

She sat down again and picked up her work. She had
her shawl wrapped tight about her, her flannel skirt and
petticoat tucked in around her legs, so she was warm
enough. Tucked into her chair at the hearth, if her da
hadn't been at sea, she'd have been content enough. Such
a storm! The fire burned bright, and the lantern was near,
and even so it was hard to see to mend the net in her
hands. Not that her hands didn't already know the work
so well she probably could do it in the dark. She could
knit in the dark, and had most of the winter, for there
were always socks to knit as well as nets to mend. But
net-mending required concentration and knitting didn't,

and she was trying not to think about her da off on the unforgiving sea.

By now, oh surely, even the salmon fishers were in off the river. But not her da; no, she knew him. He'd be out in the storm, stubborn as any donkey, pulling in fish where no other man could. And even when he had as much as the boat could carry, he still wouldn't come home. First he'd be off to Criccieth to sell half of it, and on a day like today, he'd get the best prices, there being no one else fool enough to be on the water. Only then would he come home to sell in Clogwyn, perhaps to trade a few for a salmon or maybe a treat from the baker. Everyone wanted Daffyd Prothero's herring; they were always the fattest, the tastiest.

A gust hammered the shutters and she flinched. A lash of rain battered it, sending a fine mist of droplets through tiny cracks in the wood. Oh, how she hated days like this one. It never mattered that he always came home unscathed, with herring or salmon or trout in his bucket, with whatever else he fancied they needed in a bag over his shoulder. It never mattered at all, because every time one of these storms blew up, someone generally did not come home, and Mari always dreaded the day it would be her da who didn't.

Tears stung her eyes; she gulped them down past the lump in her throat. She sniffed, wiped her cold nose on her handkerchief, and ordered the tears to go away, telling herself that he was probably in Clogwyn by now. At that moment her nose told her to check on the pie in the oven. The Prothero cottage was superior to most—for they had an oven built into the side of the fireplace, unlike most of the Clogwyn cottagers, who had to make do with hearth-cooking or buying bread from the baker. That was not the only way in which the Prothero cottage differed; most made do with a pounded and limed earthen floor, but the Prothero cottage boasted a wooden floor, and today she was mortal glad of it, for an earthen floor would have been mud by now. She put down the net and string, wrapped rags around her hands and carefully pulled down the cast-iron handle of the little door at the side of the fireplace. The rabbit pie was not quite done yet; the rabbit was a trade from yesterday, and its skin was drying over a rafter in the loft. The bread was done, though, and she fetched it out with a bit of plank. It smelled divine. She hoped her da would be here in time to eat it warm.

Outside, this cottage looked like all the others down in Clogwyn: weathered stone, tiny windows, slate-shingled roof. Thatch was for inland; it wouldn't last here, so close to the ocean. Inside was where this cottage differed from all the neighbors', with an ancient wooden floor made of ship's planks gone black with age, glazing in the windows as well as shutters, ships'-timber beams on the ceiling and the oven built into the hearth. Only the houses of prosperous farmers and the baker and shopkeeper were as fine as this. There were not one but two handsome dressers on either side of the door, one displaying copper pots, the other the bits of pretty china that Prothero women had gotten over the generations. Off to the side of the fireplace was the larder, with shelves full of preserves in glass and pottery jars, little casks and bags, and the keg of beer her da bought once every few months. Floor to ceiling, those shelves went, on two sides of the larder. On the third, the window side, was the sink. Opposite the fireplace there was a loft with a mattress where Mari slept; her da took up the bed in the bedroom beneath it. She preferred the loft, except when storms raged. It was a bit unnerving to listen to the wind howling right above you. But it was always warmer than the bedroom beneath it, and in summer, you could open the little window and let the cool wind off the sea come right in, and the gentle sound of the waves would sing you to sleep.

She put the bread on the table and covered it with a towel. No use going to the landward window to look for her father either; with the rain lashing outside, she wouldn't see him when he came—

If he came—

No. She wouldn't think that way. He always came home. He swore he always would. She had to believe him.

"He'll be home," whispered a giggly little voice. "It'll ne'er be water that kills Daffyd Prothero."

Mari shivered and did not look in the direction of the voice. She knew what she would see if she did. A small woman, translucent, with seaweed hair and knowing eyes and not a stitch of clothing on her, only seaweed, sitting on the edge of the water-barrel.

For the thousandth time, she wondered, was it a touch of the Sight that made her see such things or a touch of madness? Mari had seen her before, many times, and others like her, and heard her, too. Always, always around or about water.

She had seen such little creatures all of her life. And there had been the great black horse that came up out of the river, looked startled, bowed to her and went back down again. And the golden-haired beauties she had seen beneath the moon, walking or dancing together on the surface of the water as if it were a floor, and the great herd of red-spotted white cattle that she had seen one night, going down into the waters of the lake as though they were merely going down into a valley.

She knew what all these things were supposed to be, of course. When she was too little to bide in the cottage by herself, and her da thought she needed a caretaker, she'd gone to dame-school in the village. That was where the old woman who pretended to teach the village children letters and numbers had told them all tales between her naps. They were the Fair Folk, the Pharisees, the Tylwyth Teg. The black horse was the water-horse, of course, the cattle were Gwartheg Y Llyn, the Fairy cattle, the beautiful women Gwragedd Annwn, the water-elves. The black horse Ceffyl Dwr, who carried people off to drown, or just to frighten them, was the oddest, because he'd not offered to harm so much as a hair of her head. She wasn't sure who the little women were; they never figured in the old woman's stories. Mari had been seeing creatures supposed to be Tylwyth Teg for as long as she could remember.

But those were just stories. Nobody believed them but children and old women. Half the time Mari was afraid she was going mad; the other half, she was afraid she really was seeing them, even though they had never harmed her.

Quite the contrary. Even though she tried to pretend she saw nothing, heard nothing, they helped her. They showed her where to find sea-coal and driftwood washed up after storms, where the best shellfish and kelp were, and a spring with the sweetest water. Once, one had led her to a gigantic lump of greasy gray stuff with a strangely sweet smell. She brought it home and her da had taken it to Criccieth and come back with silver coins he put with the others he kept under the hearth-stone. "Amber-gris," he'd said it was, and that the men in towns that made perfumes would pay dearly for it. She hadn't told her da she'd been led to it. She'd only tried that once, when she was still in leading-strings. Something about his face when she'd babbled about her "friends" as that tiny child made her shut up about them and not say another word since.

But that hadn't stopped her thinking. The more she was alone, the more she thought about it.

Was she mad? Had her mother run mad before she died? Had it not been a rogue wave that had taken her, but her running into the waves?

Or was this something devilish? The creatures had never offered her anything that wasn't wholesome but . . . but . . . when she sat in the chapel of a Sunday morning and listened to the preacher, she had to wonder. When her da sat all hunched over and silent and looking as if he had a guilty conscience, she had to wonder.

And if it was the Sight, well, wasn't that dangerous too? Those tales were also of those with the Sight, who had eventually Seen things they shouldn't, and been blinded, or carried off, or cursed for what they had Seen. Though that seemed the least likely of the three . . . still . . . in no interpretation was there likely to be a good end.

The shutters shuddered, and she flinched. Oh, how she hated these spring storms!

And just as she thought that, she heard the thumping of her father's boot on the door, which meant he had his arms full, and she ran to open it and let him and a gust of wind and water into the warm, safe house. Her heart filled with happiness again.

He had a welcome bag of sea-coal and herrings strung on a bit of cord. She relieved him of these things, and he stripped off his old oilskin and went to the fire, shivering. Then she got out the pie, cut him thin slices of warm bread spread with butter and jam and poured a glass of beer. A glass of beer with his supper was one luxury he allowed himself. In this much, her da was a very careful man, for instead of spending extra money on luxuries, there were carefully hoarded silver coins under the hearthstone. She knew why; he worried that he might be sick or hurt and not able to fish. "For a rainy day," he would say, with every coin that joined the rest.

"Bad out on the water, Da?" she asked, bringing him his plate and his glass, and settling herself in her seat on the other side of the fire with her own dinner. He was a handsome man, still, was Daffyd Prothero, and women still looked at him, though he hadn't eyes for any of them. Welsh to the core, as she was, dark of hair and eye, lean and fine-featured, and with a look about him of melancholy that women seemed to find irresistible.

"Only in the coming into port," he said. "That was when the black waves hunched up their backs like so many angry bulls and foamed at me." He was warming now, and he gave her his lopsided grin. "But you know your da. I never ran from bull nor wave, and never shall." Then he told her of his day, and she listened, loving the music of his voice. She knew folk who said that the Welsh were either mad poets or poetically mad, and she reckoned whoever had said such a thing was mostly right.

"Then I got into Criccieth, and I was the only one who'd got out on the water," he said, after telling her of the shaft of light that had broken through the clouds "like God's own finger," and the great shoal of herring it had pointed out to him. He chuckled. "Ah, if it weren't for the difficulty of it, I'd wish every day was a storm day. I think every woman in our little village was waiting for me on the docks. Oh, and they filled my ears full of the news." He took a sip of his beer as he finished the last of his bit of pie. "Such a fluttering and cackling and crowing in the henhouse as you never heard in your life. There's to be a constable stationed here."

She blinked at him. "A—what?" she asked, incredulously. "And for why, Da? Clogwyn's never had a constable before!"

"Now, what d'ye think?" he countered, his expression darkening. "The strikes, of course. Up at the mines." He smiled a bit bitterly. "Our English overlords have never heard of the word of God not to bind the mouths of the kine that tread out the corn. Begrudge a man a fair day's wage for dirty and dangerous work, and wonder why the men won't take it anymore. I would reckon there's being constables placed in every village bigger than two houses, just in case someone might be offering aid and comfort to miners who want a decent wage for their work and a bit less chance of dying under the earth." He handed her the empty glass and his plate; she took both, and while he stretched out to warm himself, she did the tidying up.

"You really think that's it, Da?" she asked, tilting hot water into the stone sink, and starting in on the plates.

"What else would it be, I'm asking?" he replied with a derisive sniff. "Worst thing we've ever had happen in Clogwyn was when Mrs. Bevan's dog stole them sausages—well, there's the usual dust-up at the pub every now and again, but I wouldn't call that enough for to station a constable here."

"Well then, where will they be putting him? Violet Cottage?" Violet Cottage had been the home to Mrs. Ithell the elder before she'd got pneumonia and died in the winter. Now it was empty. It was one of the smallest cottages in the village and one of the meanest. Mrs. Ithell had been a penny-pincher, and had not put a shilling into the repair of her place that she didn't absolutely have to, and never mind improvements. Like many of the cottages in the village, it wasn't freehold, it was rented, and belonged to the Manor. Nevertheless, with the rent being so cheap, the cottage had been hotly contested over. Now perhaps the mystery of why there had been no tenant found was solved.

"Likely," Daffyd replied, and sniggered. "Short of finding someone willing to rent him a room, or having him stay up at Criccieth or thereabouts, it's the only choice he'll have. And bad luck to him already. Roof's leaking, I hear tell, and chimney needs cleaning so bad the fireplace sends most of the smoke into the room, and if there's one mouse in there, there's likely to be a hundred. If he's some city man, used to laid-on gas and piped-in water, he'll be wishing he was back at home before he's there an hour."

Probably less than that, Mari thought. She considered the villagers. Would there be anyone there willing to help him? Fix his leaks, clean his chimney, tell him who had the best rat-catching ferrets?

Well . . . yes. Some would. For the money, if naught else. And some to prove that they were in no way in sympathy with the striking miners. But this was likely to divide the village soon enough, unless the fellow somehow managed to alienate everyone.

Which was possible, if he came in demanding things and acting as if he suspected everyone. Then everyone would be up in arms, giving him no welcome at all. He'd have to hire everything done from Criccieth.

Or if he's helpful and pleasant, they might all decide he's a good sort and warm up to him . . . "Da, there's no telling. He might be a good enough fellow," she ventured. "This might be a good thing."

Once again her father sniffed. "And I might be able to fly if I jump off the roof. One's as likely as the other."

She just didn't have a response for that. "Well ... tomorrow's market day. I'll be finding all about it then. And twice as much that's made up of whole cloth." She put the dishes in their places, covered the pie and the bread, and made all straight, then returned to the fire. "Was there anything you'd be wanting?"

He shook his head. The windows were rapidly darkening, the only way that you could tell the sun was going down in this storm. "Nothing worth spending money on."

He picked up the net she'd been mending, and took up where she'd left off. She took up her knitting; he always needed socks. They busied themselves, talking of commonplaces, until the fire grew too low to see by. Then they took themselves to bed; she climbing up the ladder to the loft and he to the bedroom. She stripped to her shift, and climbed under the blankets and nestled into the featherbed. The bed soon warmed to her body, and she relaxed. She listened drowsily to the wind slowly die away, and tried not to listen to the other voices she heard ... and finally slept.

Morning dawned clear and bright, and they both breakfasted heartily on the rest of the pie and toasted bread and tea. He hurried down to his boat, while she put things to rights, then took the path to Clogwyn.

Their little cottage stood far off by itself, within sight of the village (or at least of the church steeple), but it was a good brisk half-hour walk to the village itself. The cottage was an oddity; the only other dwellings that stood this far away from a village or town were those that belonged to great landowners, for the use of their tenants, or farmhouses. But the Prothero cottage, which had been in the family for many years, had no land to speak of, just enough of a garden to supply most of what she and her da needed and a henhouse that was empty now. No use trying to keep chickens without a dog; foxes and stoats would have them in no time, and until they found a dog that fancied fish instead of meat, a dog would just be another mouth to feed. It was easier just to trade for eggs. They had a cat, so to speak. It was an aloof beast, kept to itself, slunk in and hunted the cottage and slunk back out again. The only time it stayed inside was in the worst of weather, hiding under a chair or in the corner of the hearth, and running off as soon as the door was opened. It would come if she offered it fish, but ate with one suspicious eye on her, bolting the food as fast as it could. She wondered what had made it so wary, because neither she nor her father had ever so much as shied a stone at it. It was as if they were some terrible predators, and the cat was waiting for them to pounce on it and eat it.

The morning was as bright and beautiful and mild as if the sea had never dreamed of throwing a tantrum yesterday. Her way was clear enough, with the village visible along the curve of the coast, on their hill up ahead. The church tower rose up above the other gray-slate roofs like a hen above her brood, beneath a cloudless sky. The air was lovely, almost intoxicating.

And as for the sea, it was so calm that the little wavelets washing the shore barely made a sound. Only the debris of the storm told the whole truth; she'd be harvesting all those mounds of seaweed this afternoon and for several to come. She would pick out the laver to make God's own gift to the poor Welshman, laver-bread, and samphire for eating like salad. "Sea lettuce," her da called it. Kelp would be dried and burned and turned into the garden soil. There was driftwood too, and there might be sea-coal, the coal that washed out of the cliff rocks and got tumbled in to shore after such storms. Sometimes there were wrecks close to this part of the shore; the Lifeboat Service down the coast at Criccieth was there for a good reason. But tragic though a wreck might be, sometimes salvage came out of it. There'd been a wreck when her da was a lad that the village still talked about, when so many yards of red flannel came in to shore that every woman in the village had a half dozen red petticoats made of it and the men had as many shirts and nightshirts.

The path to the village was just off the shingle, beaten into the grass. There was a road proper to the village, further inland, but she saw no sense in traipsing across fields and over hedges and stiles just to get to it when there was a perfectly good path right here. The sheep to her right looked none the worse for the storm, with their lambs bumbling about and occasionally breaking into the incomprehensible skips and frisking that lambs were prone to do. On a winter morning, the trek was misery, and she was generally frozen clear through by the time she reached the village, but on a morning like today, she almost wished it took longer.

She swung her basket and sang as she walked, feeling a little like frisking herself. Was there anything better than a spring morning, with the air washed clean, and the sea just lapping at the shore?

She had most of the string of herring with her, and the household money under the napkin in her basket, which would go for things she could not get with barter. Clogwyn hadn't anything more than three places you could get things regular—a little bit of a store that also held the post office, the pub, and the village baker. So the weekly market was important to everyone hereabouts. A few enterprising souls even sent a clerk with a cart of goods over from Criccieth once a month to add to the stalls in the market—and now that it was spring, there were traveling peddlers known to turn up unexpectedly, and tinkers and even gypsies. The thought made her move a little faster. Not that she'd buy anything, but oh, how she loved to look!

But once she reached the marketplace, she sensed the change in peoples' moods in the tone of the talk; from a distance, the village sounded like a disturbed hive. The closer she got, the more apparent it became that there was one topic of conversation uppermost, and no one was happy about it.

In fact, as soon as she put herself close enough to talk to, she was drawn into it. The entire village was abuzz with gossip over the coming of this constable. That wasn't entirely surprising, considering it was the biggest bit of news to affect the whole village in a long while, but she was a little taken aback by the amount of resentment most people were showing. It was as if they and her da were all of the same mind about it.

"And what need have we of a constable, I'm asking you?" complained stout Mrs. Awbrey in her milk-and-egg stall, as she examined herring to trade for a dozen eggs. "Treating us like we was criminals! Shame to them as thinks we can't take care of our own!"

"I don't understand it either," Mari agreed. "I mean, except when it was tramping people, nobody's ever stole a thing. Well, leave aside apples and maybe a pie . . ."

"Yes, and I caught that young limb of Satan Aled Hulme red-handed, and believe me, he'd have wished I *was* a constable before I was done with him," Mrs. Aw-

brey said heatedly, and took as long over the tale of how
she had chased the lad and given him a right tanning as
she had in choosing her fish. Mari had heard it all before,
of course, since Mrs. Awbrey was likely to bring it up at
least once a month or so—but this time the round-faced
farming wife ended it differently. "But what if there'd
been a constable here?" she demanded. "The boy could
have been locked up—or worse! I've heard of boys
transported to Australia for taking a handkerchief, let
alone for stealing an apple pie!"

"That was a long time ago, Mrs. Awbrey," Mari reminded her. "They don't do that now." But as she moved
on to her next purchase, she wondered what the penalty
would have been.

"Pa says he'll be here to spy on us," whispered Braith
Wyn, the village beauty, as the two girls both looked over
every bit of frippery on a ribbon-dealer's little cart, and
Braith, predictably, selected red ribbons and a bunch of
artificial cherries for a new hat. Braith was always making new hats. "Pa says the landlords don't trust any of us,
and think we're all anarchists." Braith might have been
so pretty that every boy in the village and more married
men than admitted it cast longing looks after her when
she passed, but she had not let that go to her head except
in the matter of a little vanity. She loved hats. She had
even learned how to braid straw so she could make
more. And she was so pretty that no one was likely to tell
her how silly and overdone they were because she always looked so happy when she wore one.

Since that echoed what Mari's da had said, she nodded. "Well . . ." she replied. "They never have. But that's
ridiculous."

"Of course it is!" Braith agreed, with a sniff. "Who'd
want to be an anarchist? Anarchists have no money."

Braith was a practical girl; penniless anarchists might be romantic, but romance bought no ribbons.

"I don't think the landlords care . . ." Mari replied, doubtfully. "I don't believe they even think about it, they just say 'The Welsh are all together,' and have done. Honestly, I don't know where they think we'd have *time* to be anarchists. Who'd do the milking and the fishing if everyone was running about being anarchists?" She really wasn't at all sure what an anarchist was. The few times she had seen a newspaper and they had printed anything about anarchists, they all seemed to be bearded and throwing bombs. There were plenty of fellows with beards about here, but she hadn't the faintest idea where any of them would find a bomb.

Braith agreed, and they returned to the choosing of ribbons. Well, Mari advised; Braith was the one that did the buying.

Acquiring a quart of lamp-oil at the tiny store brought yet another complaint about the new constable. "Getting Violet Cottage, and rent free!" sniffed the postmaster, Andres Bythell, holding forth not just to Mari, but to a willing audience here to buy his goods or pick up mail. "Well, they'll not be getting free labor for the fixing of it, I can tell you that. And he'll not be putting a jail cell in *my* post office! I've barely enough room here to move as it is!"

Which last was true enough; Bythell's little store was crammed full of the sorts of things that people might need in a little village, when they couldn't make the journey downcoast to the town, and it was only one small room. The rest of the building was the house where he and his family lived.

"And I wouldn't be having someone who had to be locked up anywhere next or nigh the girls, either!" the postmaster continued, indignantly, his chest puffing out at the mere thought. "I won't have a drunk keeping us up at night, I won't have a gypsy getting a look at what he can steal, and I won't have some wandering laborer putting his eyes all over my wife and daughters. He can put a cell in Violet Cottage, that's what he can do, and that damned squire of a landlord up the hill can complain about the alterations to whoever had the daft notion of sending him here."

One thing was certain. This man was not going to find a warm welcome in Clogwyn.

By the time she finished her purchases and bartering, it looked to Mari as if there wasn't a single person in the entire village that wanted the man there. A great deal of this was the enormous resentment people had that he was going to get the vacant cottage rent-free. This was no small thing; there were no empty cottages in the village proper, which meant if a young couple got married, they'd have to move in with one or the other set of parents, see if there was a cottage farther away for rent, or somehow come up with the enormous amount of money it would take to build a new home themselves. There were at least three such courting couples that she knew of, who had been looking forward—with guilt, perhaps, but looking forward anyway—to the day when Violet Cottage would be empty. To have it snatched out from under them—for free!—was enough to engender plenty of anger. And not just in the couples themselves, but in their parents and in their friends.

She wondered, as she picked her way along the trace of a path in the grass just above the shore, how badly the Protheros were going to stand out from the rest of the village. Unlike most people hereabouts—or at least the ones who were not actually landholding farmers—she and her da owned their cottage rather than renting it from the owners of Gower Manor.

She had never actually seen the family nor the Manor; having no reason to pay rent, there was never any reason to go there. They were always referred to as the "English landlords," although as far as Mari knew, the family had been there for at least five or six generations. Still, the divide between cottagers and landlord was enormous, and not getting any narrower. *I wonder if that's who is behind bringing the constable,* she thought. It was logical. The monied folk at the Manor were also the targets of village resentment, for raising the rents, for not doing repairs. Were they taking an alarm from the mine-owners and reading resentment as the prelude to rebellion?

The Prothero cottage had been in the family since time out of mind. Yet it wasn't a farm. And it was set far apart from the village. They were different. The village was used to the Protheros being different, but they'd been different for generations. Would the constable see that as suspicious? Would he think, because their house was set apart, that they were holding anarchist meetings there? Would he start enquiring about how they got their money, why they were so prosperous, and think they were thieves or worse?

"And what are you all a-pother about, Mari Prothero?" a voice called to her from just behind her on the path.

Mari didn't freeze, quite—but she didn't turn to look at the speaker, either. The female voice was melodious, too melodious, really. Just like the little she-thing yesterday.

She hadn't seen anyone until the voice spoke to her. And it was coming from the verge of a little pond beside the path.

This wasn't one of the villagers, nor one of the farmer's daughters, nor anyone human at all. It was one of those creatures. And she didn't want to turn to see what kind, though she had a guess it was one of the Gwragedd Annwn. Two uncanny things in two days! It had been months since the last vision, but now two in two days! *If I ignore it, it will go away,* she told herself fiercely. *I am not going mad. I am* not *going mad!*

Behind her, she heard a peal of laughter.

"Pretending I'm not here won't make me go away," the voice called after her. "Just wait. You'll be learning the truth soon. Soon enough."

She shivered and hurried her steps, fixing her gaze on the cottage and its promise of safety; the beautiful, bright, sunny day no longer seemed so welcoming. Had that been a promise?

Or a threat?

It was a beautiful spring afternoon in London, with enough of a breeze to carry away the stink of the city and the warring smells of the harbor. The ship from France had docked, and it had been a crowded passage. The dock was full of people coming to welcome those just off it, complicated by porters and passengers disembarking.

Two young ladies coming down the gangplank were just enough different from the crush of similar young ladies before them that more than one eye fastened on them. It was not that they were pretty—although they were, or rather, the smaller of the two was definitely pretty in the conventional sense, though the taller was what might be described as "handsome." It might have been their outfits; both wore gowns of brown and gray that were rugged, travel-worthy Rational Dress rather than the constricting, colorful, and rather impractical gowns of the girls who had clearly traveled across the Channel in the luxurious salons. Both had sensible little hats rather than Ascot-worthy confections. But it was probably their laughter that attracted the eye once the ear had been caught; it rang out above the babble of the crowd, honest, clear, and happy. Not stifled little titters, gasping giggles, or wheezy little sounds that had a hint of sadness about them. People turned at the sound, looked, and smiled involuntarily. Both of them beamed answering smiles as if they considered anyone and everyone a potential friend.

Both of them cradled hatboxes, which was also unusual. Not that it was entirely unheard of for a young lady to be unwilling to entrust her precious new Parisian confection to the hands of a porter—but neither of these two looked at all likely to have purchased such a thing, and even if they had, they did not look likely to have it in such high esteem that they'd hold to it with both arms and such good-natured determination. Most young ladies dangled their boxes by the strings—for after all, a hat doesn't weigh very much, and such a pose was often part of the illustrations in the fashionable journals. No, these two held their hatboxes as if something inside them was made of glass, and the hatboxes themselves were not festively decorated cardboard, but the same sturdy, boiled and riveted leather as luggage that was expected to go around the world.

As they made their way down the plank, they scanned the waiting crowd and quickly spotted the woman waving a handkerchief at them. The taller freed a hand long enough to wave back, then resumed her grip on her hatbox.

The taller of the two, who might or might not have been a year or two older, was a dark brunette; the smaller had hair of golden brown, blue eyes, and the sort of face that might have been made into a Professional Beauty. Both had healthy, tanned complexions at odds with the fashionably pale faces around them. And as the gang-plank cleared in front of them, they hastened their steps toward the one who had signaled to them in a way that suggested they were used to a great deal of walking, and none of it in cities.

Which, in fact, they were—having walked over a great deal of Africa in the last year or so.

The woman who had clearly come to meet them continued to wave her handkerchief. She was not a beauty either, but like them, she caught the attention of more than one man. There was something about her that signaled a great deal of experience without bitterness—in fact, it was clear that it was not just the joy of seeing her companions that made her glow with happiness. One fellow in common laborer's clothing, but who had uncommonly fine hands, even stopped dead to stare at her.

"By heaven!" he said to his companion, who also stopped for a moment to admire. "There's someone who's had a life! I'd give my eye to paint her!"

"Ask, and you'll likely *get* a black eye," his friend said with a laugh, and pulled him on.

"Memsa'b!" cried the smaller young woman in a happy voice, as the two neared their goal, oblivious of the attention they were all getting. "I'm so glad to see you at last!"

All three of them finally converged, and the small one looked a little confused for a moment, as if she wasn't certain what to do next—it was clearly impossible to give a proper embrace to the woman she'd addressed, what with her arms full of hatbox, but she looked equally reluctant to put it down.

The woman addressed as Memsa'b laughed and put an end to her confusion. "Come along, you two. Sahib is seeing to your things; he brought the cart from the warehouse. Lord A lent me his carriage to get you. We can have a proper hug and greetings when you can put the rascals down."

One of the boxes uttered an indignant *quork*; the other whistled, as if to say "We're no rascals!" All three women laughed, and the two young ones followed in the capable footsteps of the elder. Even though the dock was crowded, people seemed to clear away from their path with willingness rather than resentment—perhaps because of the repeated smiles and thanks the three graced everyone with.

There was, in fact, a fine city carriage of the old sort, deep black with brass trim, waiting for them, pulled up alongside a few hansoms and more of the automotive cabs. It boasted a dignified coachman and a crest on the doors. The discerning and knowledgeable would have identified it as that of Lord Alderscroft, Member of the House of Lords, and reputably a confidant of the Prime Minister on certain mysterious affairs.

The coachman hopped down promptly, there being no footman, and handed in Memsa'b first. He then took the taller girl's hatbox with great care.

"'Allo Neville," he said to the box. "'Ow are you, old son? Africar agree with you?"

"*Quork!*" the box said with enthusiasm. Then, in a jovial and exceptionally human voice, "*I'm hooooooome!*"

The coachman laughed with delight. "Blimey! Neville, you're talkin' at last!"

"*I can talk; can you fly?*" said the other box, in a

higher, female voice. Both boxes gave credible imitations of the young ladies' laughs.

"He started chattering away as soon as we reached Sarah's parents' station," said the taller girl, after seating herself, taking her talking hatbox from the coachman. "It was as if he'd been saving it up until then. I don't know why it took him so long."

"If 'e's anything like my youngest, Miss Nan," the coachman replied, taking the second box and helping the shorter girl up into the carriage, "It's 'cause he was able to make hisself understood to you just fine without chatterin', but couldn't t'anyone else. That was fine when you was at the school, but Africar is when 'e needed other folks t'understand 'im. So that's when 'e started talkin'."

"Clever Sam!" said the second box, eliciting more laughter. The box went to its owner, as Sam grinned his approval.

The coachman closed the door, making sure no hems were hanging out inside, and hopped back up on the box. He chirruped to the horses, and they were off.

Once inside the plush interior of the coach, the lids came off the boxes, and out popped a handsome raven and an equally handsome African Grey parrot. Both jumped to the knees of their respective owners and shook their feathers out vigorously, as the boxes went down to the floorboards. The raven cocked a bright black eye at Memsa'b.

"Give us a kiss," he demanded.

"You outrageous flirt, Neville," Memsa'b replied with a chuckle. "I believe I shall." She held out her arm, fearlessly. The raven hopped up onto it; she kissed the top of his head, then began scratching the back of his neck. He closed his eyes in bliss and laid his chin along her shoulder, the better to enjoy the caresses.

"Cold," complained the Grey parrot, and Sarah obligingly held her coat open for the bird, who dove inside and wiggled around so her head was sticking out. Nan just grinned as hard as she could, watching Memsa'b renew her acquaintance with the raven.

"Well, obviously the trip was a success, no one was eaten by lions, and I'm sure you have many more stories than you were able to write," Memsa'b said. "I expect to hear them all. But what I am most concerned about is Sarah's parents—things do not seem to be altogether well in Africa. The London papers have been full of some most alarming affairs."

"If you mean that there seem to be a lot of justified uprisings, Memsa'b, you're right," Nan replied bluntly. "That was what we didn't want to write about. You never know who is going to open your letters between here and there, and we didn't want some officious oaf to come looking for us as insurrectionists. But Sarah's mum and papa are just fine, quite safe and . . . well . . . amazing." She shook her head. "Really, the relationship between them and the natives is remarkable."

"Beloved, is how I would put it," Sarah said, petting Grey. "Of course, you know they have never preached; no matter what the well-meaning people who sent them *think* they are doing, they've never paid the least bit of attention to anything but medicine. They have always worked with the tribes and their ways and there is mutual respect for what both sides know. They still may be the only 'missionaries' I know of who've been adopted by village chiefs."

"That's all very well," Memsa'b said doubtfully, "But . . ."

"I know. One village can't keep them safe if they are not prepared." Sarah nodded. "They *are* prepared. I've been assured by everyone in the village where the medical station is, and especially by shaman M'dela, that if bad things happen, they'll hide my parents and they have worked several escape routes out in advance. M'dela asked Grey to follow sick elephants while we were there, and the tribe harvested the tusks from the ones that died, so they have a stock of ivory to pay to the Arab traders to get Papa and Mum out. They have disguises, even. Papa knows Arabic and makes a credible Arab trader, and with Mum wreathed in veils there's no way to tell what she is under all the fabric. They found her the sort of burqa where you can't even see her eyes."

"And lest you think the traders would betray them— well, Sarah and I investigated them quite thoroughly, and they're as safe as may be," Nan added. "Mind, if Sarah's mum was the pretty little thing that came to Africa years ago, I would not trust Abdullah Haj' Aleph any further than I could pick him up and throw him, but he considers the lady to be in the same category as withered old hags, so she's safe from being carried off to his *harem.*"

Memsa'b sighed with open relief. "That takes a great deal of worry off my mind. But Nan—you said *justifiable—*"

"And so they are," Nan replied stoutly. "Terrible things have been done in the name of civilization to good, decent, honorable people, and now they have decided they shan't stand for it any more, and good for them, I say. Which I would not say around Lord A, so rest your mind on that subject. The bad part is that it's come to such a pass that some of them want their pound of flesh and an eye or three as well. But that's what happens when you back people into a corner and send them into a frenzy."

"Sow the wind, reap the whirlwind," Memsa'b said, and nodded. "A great deal of injustice has been done in the name of Empire." She paused. "I am saddened, but I am glad in a way that your eyes are open and you can see it for what it is. So many terrible things have been done in the name of God and profit . . . mostly profit."

They spent the rest of the journey with the girls relating more of their adventures—the ones they hadn't been able to write to their mentor about. Most of those had not taken place in Africa, but in Egypt, where they had been forced to wait for transport, as there had been a rush of Europeans fleeing the dangers of some of those "justified uprisings."

"And I don't know what we would have done if those archeologists hadn't come to our rescue," Sarah said, after describing the difficulty of finding any room at all, and the dangers of the rather dubious hotel they'd been forced into. It was funny now, the story of how Nan had fended off a man who'd tried to come in their window, using a basin as a shield and her big knife as a sword. But it had been hair-raising at the time, and more so when they'd found the cloth soaked in chloroform and realized he'd intended to make off with them both. Fortunately he'd been a coward and fled at the first sign of trouble.

"I do," Nan said bluntly. "After Yadakpa showed me how to use that big knife, I'd have sat up at night, every night, and God help anyone who'd put a finger inside our room." She looked fierce at the moment, and Memsa'b had no doubt she meant every word she'd said.

"Bite!" Neville agreed, and clacked his beak to show he would have been prepared to fight as well.

"Well I'm glad it didn't come to that," said Sarah. She turned back to Memsa'b. "We were having tea at Shepheard's when this amazing woman with a parasol marched right up to us and introduced herself. Neville and Grey were in the trees, and they immediately came down to examine her and she refused to allow the waiters to shoo them off. In fact, she ordered water and biscuits for Grey and water and goat-cheese for Neville."

Neville made a sound like lips smacking. "Hurrrrr tasty!" he said.

"Amazing woman," Nan repeated. "She said she'd noticed our Rational Dress and approved. Next thing I knew, she had coaxed our story out of us, and lo and behold, she invites us to come and stay with her, her husband, and their little son, and what turned out to be a menagerie not unlike our school, Memsa'b. They lived on a boat, and must have had half a tribe of Arabs with them who treated them like chiefs rather than masters. I confess, I was relieved. We were very comfortable, Neville managed to not kill their cat, the cat managed to leave Grey alone, and we even got to help a little with an excavation. All the natives treat her with great respect, and call her *Sitt Hakim,* which I think means something like Memsa'b, so we were quite at home. And I want a parasol like hers, when I can afford it. She showed it to me, how it worked. The ferrule is as stout as a sword, the tip is plenty sharp, and it has a cunning little kit of useful stuff in the handle. It's as good for defending yourself as a big knife, and causes less stir if a lady is carrying it about."

Memsa'b managed not to choke at that statement.

"I believe I would like to correspond with this lady," Memsa'b said instead. "She sounds worth knowing, and I would like to give her my thanks."

Isabelle Harton—Memsa'b to the many Indian servants of mixed races and creeds that tended to the Harton

School for Expatriate Children—was very happy to have two of her best (former) pupils back, but also a little worried. Happy, because the Harton School was a very special place indeed. It was not merely a school for the children of those who were serving the Empire abroad—it was also a school for those who had psychical gifts to be trained in the use of them. As such, it had a powerful reputation among a select circle of those who were more concerned that their offspring learn ethical use of their abilities—and not go mad—than they were that the children make the "right" friends from the "right" set. Isabelle would never have to worry that the school turn a profit, for ever since shortly after Nan and Sarah had joined them, the school had gotten a formidable protector and patron in the form of Lord Alderscroft, who was probably the most powerful Elemental Master and magician in all of England, if not all of the Empire. He was certainly the most powerful in and around London, and was often spoken of as "The Wizard of London."

Sarah was a skilled and fearless medium; Nan was something in between a psychic and a magician. She could, and did, channel another aspect of herself—or perhaps a former incarnation—that was a Celtic fighter, and a psychical warrior, but that warrior was armed with magical weapons, and one of those weapons was Neville. She also—at least as a child—had interacted with magical beings, Elemental Spirits, even the Elders like Robin Goodfellow. The children had been instrumental in freeing Lord Alderscroft from a malignant creature of Air that had nearly destroyed him; he was profoundly grateful, and that gratitude had translated into the Harton School having his particular patronage and being installed in his own stately home just outside London, while he had a new home of his own built on the grounds for his use. So Memsa'b was happy to have her girls back; it had felt as if family members had gone when, after graduation, they had gone to spend some time with Sarah's parents in Africa.

But on the other hand, she was worried, because she hadn't the least idea what to do with them. And they would need something to *do,* they were not the sort to want to go to parties and hunt for husbands, marry, and settle into a complacent and narrow life. Of course it was possible that they would turn out to be good teachers, in which case they could easily join the school in that capacity. But she was very much afraid that, no matter how well-intentioned they were, teaching was not something they were suited for.

So as she saw them settled back in their old suite of two rooms, a bedroom and a parlor, which still had feeding perches for Neville and Grey beside the fireplace and sleeping perches for them over the heads of the beds, she was very conscious of those mixed feelings.

"Oh," Sarah sighed, as she set down her portmanteau at the foot of her bed. "It's good to be back. Africa might be home to Mum and Papa, but . . . I've been away too long. I don't like the insects or the snakes. Grey didn't either, really. She liked the heat, and the lovely damp air, but she didn't much care for the rest of it. The spiders! Ugh! They are as big as cricket balls! And the snakes!"

Grey and Neville flew to their perches and examined the water cups with critical, beady eyes to make sure that the water in them wasn't stale. Grey bobbed her head, agreeing with Sarah; Neville made a comforting mutter.

"Lord A is coming to dinner, if that is all right with you," Memsa'b said, "If you are not horribly exhausted after—"

"Great Harry's ghost, Memsa'b," Nan interrupted.

"After traipsing around excavation sites in the heat from dawn to dusk, the trip back was restful! I just hope we've got a gown somewhere in our kit that won't totally revolt his lordship's sense of aesthetics."

"I was hoping we'd be able to see him soon," Sarah added, happily. "I was looking forward to it."

Memsa'b relaxed. Alderscroft had asked after the girls regularly while they were gone, and had specifically requested he be invited to dine as soon as they were back. She was hoping that perhaps *he* had some notion of something they could do.

"I'll leave you two to settle back in and tidy up then," she said with a smile. "It's so *good* to have you back!"

"Not as good as it is to be back, Memsa'b," Nan replied for all of them, as Sarah and the birds nodded. "Not by half!"

2

THE constable lost no time in making his appearance. Three days after market day, Mari saw a strange cart coming up the road from Criccieth, loaded with household goods. When she reported as much to her father, Daffyd mulled the news over for a moment, then nodded as if he had made up his mind about something.

"I expect that's the constable. Don't go to the village till market day," he decreed, and she agreed, even though she was somewhat disappointed. "If you go too soon, all you'll hear is likely worthless. If you wait till market day, he'll have shown his true colors, and you'll get a better notion of what the man is. Never fear; anything I hear, I'll sing back to you."

So that was what she did, heading off no earlier than usual, with her father's admonition to get a few pigeons for a pie rather than a hare or the salmon she'd fancied. "You won't know if the salmon or hare you're sold has been poached," Daffyd pointed out as he headed out to fish. "I'll go on the river myself today to get one, and better believe I'll be minding the boundaries."

She didn't ask him how he could be sure of getting a salmon without straying into the landlord's waters; he would, and that was that. She was also quite certain he would fish only where there were witnesses to exactly where he was. Her da was the clever one.

The first thing that she noticed as she neared the village was that it was *quieter* than usual. There was still the murmur of talk from the market, but it sounded subdued. She tensed, without really thinking about it. The murmuring sounded like the talk of people who are afraid of being overheard.

Once she got there, it was obvious why. There was the constable, in the glory of his dark blue uniform with its brass buttons and buckles, truncheon at his belt, helmet on his head, surveying all of them from a slightly elevated spot on the church steps. He stood out like a red apple in white snow. He didn't belong, he looked it, and he looked as if he knew that.

He might have been a pleasant man; there was no way of telling, for his expression was stony. And the glances being cast at him were heated and full of resentment. People weren't talking around him, and their conversations over goods in the stalls were in low murmurs meant to be kept from his ears.

What in heaven's name did he think he was accomplishing, standing up there like some sort of sentry? Did he think that he was preventing theft or trouble? Or was he trying to cow everyone?

She went first to the post office, ostensibly to get some flannel to patch her petticoat, for the cloth-merchant from Criccieth wasn't in evidence today. As she had expected, it was packed full, and away from the ears of the constable, the talk was as heated as the glances had been.

". . . and he orders me, *orders* me, mind you, that I'm to clean his cottage!" sputtered Mrs. Fychan, who lived next door to Violet Cottage. "I asked him what right he had to order me about, and he says, all high and mighty, 'By order of the Crown.' I gave him a right piece of my mind, let me tell you." She was actually red-faced with indignation, as the others gave her every bit of their attention. Her heavy eyebrows were going up and down, up and down with agitation. "I told him, 'The Crown got no right to order a good woman to let her childern starve and be left alone just so you can be waited on. You got some sort of paper saying you can order me about?' Well, of course he hadn't. So I said to him, I said, 'You go find yourself a charwoman and you hire her at a decent wage, and we'll be having no more of this nonsense. I won't be your char and I won't be treated like your sarvant.'" She snorted, and heads bobbed in agreement. "Then I marched back into *my* house and let him see I had better things to do than tend to His High and Holy self."

"Well, I expect you heard what Sawyl Cale was told he was to do: fix that chimbley for no pay," said someone in the crush. It sounded like one of the little boys.

"Aye but I heard he fixed it good!" said the postmaster, with a titter. "Heard it from Sawyl himself, I did!"

"So, what happened?" asked Bythell's wife, from behind him. "You never did tell me the tale."

The postmaster was only too happy to be prompted. "He waited till the place had been cleaned up, then came up with his old shotgun and shot it up the chimney with no warning and no covers laid. Soot and clinkers and soot dust, and bits of swallow's nest and a skellington of a rook, everywhere! A waterfall of soot! Sawyl was black as black, and grinning because he recked it was worth it!"

There was a gale of laughter. "I was there. He had t'hire my ald woman to char all over again. It looked like a coal mine in there!" exclaimed old Bran Codd, wheezing with laughter. "Oh, he was madder than a washed cat! He had to pay her handsome to get it cleaned up again!"

"And he had the nerve to ask Sawyl what he was doing, having a shotgun!" said Mrs. Fychan. "And Sawyl says, with a straight face, ' 'Tis for fishing. 'Tis how we get bream hereabouts.' "

The tightly packed crowd roared with laughter again, as Mari wiggled in to the counter to make her purchase. "Half a yard of red flannel, sir, please," she said. Mr. Bythell measured it out and sold it to her, then said, "Now, imagine this, if you please. The snoop has even been making inquiries about the Protheros!"

Mari blanched, as the others growled or muttered in indignation.

"Oh he has!" Mrs. Awbrey confirmed. "All manner of questions. Who's got the cottage? Why've they got a cottage where there ain't a farm? Who's their landlord? Why ain't they got one? Have there been unusual comings and goings? On and on . . . and not just to me!"

"Asked the very same of me, he did," Mr. Bythell confirmed. "Probably to half the village. Has a nasty mind, does that one."

"Well, and I told him as much. 'You've a nasty mind, Constable Ewynnog,' I told him straight to his face," said Mrs. Awbrey. " 'Daffyd Prothero is the hard-workingest, honestest fisherman on the water, like his father, and his father before him, and his fore-fathers back to Owen ap

Tudor. Out on the water in every weather, supporting that little bit of a girl all on his own, and evil to him that evil thinks, I say.' Sent *him* away with a bee in his ear."

"Well done, Mrs. Awbrey," Mr. Bythell said, and Mari sighed with relief, seeing that if the village was closing ranks, it was closing the Protheros inside those ranks. The postmaster patted her on the head as if she was a child. "Don't you worry, Mari. We'll abide no nastiness about your da."

She thanked them, and wiggled her way out of the crowd and down to the pub to see about getting her da's beer keg refilled. And there, in the other site where village news could be gleaned, she heard more stories.

If the man had wanted to put every man's hand against him, he could not have gone about it more thoroughly. To begin with, he was clearly a city man, and expected things that simply didn't exist out here. The cottage had clearly unsettled him. He'd asked about gas, about water lines, and with increasing desperation, about other cottages he might get, only to be looked at blankly.

Then he had done the most foolish thing he could have. Constable Ewynnog had begun his tenancy in Clogwyn by putting on airs of importance and ordering people about as soon as he entered the village and discovered the state of the cottage he was being given.

First, on being told there were no other vacant cottages, he had gone up to the "English landlords" at the Manor and tried to evict others from *their* rightful homes. That had gotten him short shrift up at Gower Manor, where—so Mari heard—he was told in no uncertain terms that no one was being displaced, that he wasn't wanted nor needed and hadn't been asked for, and that he could act like a man, hire what needed to be done, and get his own affairs in order. And if he didn't like it, he could appeal to his superiors for help, for he'd be getting none from the Manor.

Which was interesting, since it meant that the Manor hadn't been the ones that sent him or sent for him. From the approval with which that tale was told, it looked as if the village had decided that if the Manor was "the English landlords," the Manor was *their* English landlords and not such bad sorts after all.

He then came marching down to the village and began issuing his orders. But word of gossip had already come flying ahead of him down from the Manor, and he either got snubbed or ignored until he parted with money—and then he got as little help as people could reasonably get by with giving him. He'd wanted those with building experience to come and put a jail cell on the back of the cottage free of charge, since there was little enough room for one inside; those with building experience had told him bluntly that they had families to feed, and were not taking time off their work, and that he could hire it done in Criccieth if he wanted it. Same for the roof repairs. And it appeared that the man—in the midst of the bounty of the sea, the rivers, and the farms—was going to be eating out of tins, tinned food heated over the fire and tea boiled in a kettle, because not a single woman in the village would cook for him, and he seemed to lack all domestic skills. He'd bought all the tinned food that Mr. Bythell had, and had left orders for more.

Small wonder, Mari thought, he looked so sour.

It made her feel warm to know that the villagers included her and her father in their company. She really had not expected that. She and her da were off by themselves so much . . .

And unlike the tenants of the half dozen farms

around the village that belonged to the Manor, she and her da didn't have the protection of the Manor.

But for now, at least, it looked like they had the protection of the village.

Something told her not to let her guard down, however, and she made sure to keep at least two people between her and the eyes of the constable while she finished her shopping. And when she left the market, she did so by going the long way, so that when she took the path back home, she was out of his sight. Eventually, she knew, she was going to have to talk to the man. From the sound of it he was asking everything about everybody. But she was going to put off that day as long as possible.

To her relief, there were no uncanny things about today, no whispers in her ear, no odd creatures showing themselves. She couldn't run, carrying the heavy basket as she was, but she certainly kept her steps as brisk as she could without running, and whisked inside the cottage with a heavy sigh of relief. She made the pie, tidied up, put the rest of the shopping away, and did the washing. Last of all, she washed her newly purchased flannel to get the stiffness out of it—red flannel always bled out its dye, so she took advantage of that by washing one of her faded petticoats with the new flannel to freshen the color up a bit.

By now, there was a brisk wind blowing, holding her skirts against her legs as she pinned up the laundry. She was glad that the wash line was on the side of the cottage away from the village. A line of washing would have told the constable there was someone home, if he looked. He *might* be too busy making a show of watching the market to look, but then again, he might not. Would he actually walk all the way out here?

Possibly. From the little she knew of constables, they

were supposed to walk a great deal. "Making the rounds," it was called. So he might not consider the long walk a hardship.

But the wind was lovely, and it finally smelled like spring, all green and growing. The sun warmed her head and arms, and even the smell of seaweed—

Wait...

"And why are you so afraid of the new man, Mari Prothero?" asked a voice behind her. *"He is only one man. You are an entire village. You should not be so afraid of one man no matter who he is."*

She gritted her teeth. She was *not* going to turn around. She was *not* going to talk to this ... whatever it was.

But it didn't speak again, and when she was finished pinning the wash to the line, and turned, it was to see that there was nothing there but a damp spot and a strand of weed on the cat's favorite sunning rock. She marched back inside, her fear now slowly turning to annoyance.

Just as she was taking the dried clothing in, she saw Daffyd's river-coracle out at sea. Although the boats could actually be carried on the back, he often took the little thing out in the surf, trusting to his skills to get it home. She waited while he pulled in to shore, and pulled the round, single-masted boat up on the shingle above the high-water mark beside the bigger sea-going vessel.

She saw he had a salmon over his back, just as he had promised. He looked up to the cottage and spotted her, and waved.

"Took the long way home," he said by way of explanation, once he reached the bit of grass that extended out to the shingle. "Stopped in the village, sold the rest of my catch, made sure I had witnesses to my fishing to say I was in the proper waters. And did a fair lot of talking with the others." He shook his head. "Never heard of a man making himself enemies faster than Constable Ewynnog."

She nodded, and as he stood at the cleaning table outside and expertly dealt with the salmon, she told him what she had heard.

He pursed his lips. "Not sure what to be making of this, no, I am not. It might be that he is a pitiful stupid man, and this is all his stupidity. It might be that constables are being sent out everywhere, on account of the striking. It might be that he's *so* stupid, so *very* stupid, that he got himself in trouble, and this is his punishment — to be sent to our little village that's got no need of him, to live in contempt and discomfort. It might be he was sent here to be rid of him, put him where the only harm he can do is to himself. And if there just happened to be mischief here, well one pair of stupid eyes is better than no eyes at all, in the way of the thinking of our lords and masters."

Mari thought about that as she gathered the innards of the salmon for the cat. She put it all down on the stone the cat preferred to use as his dish, and brought her da water to wash with and a platter for the newly cleaned fish.

She began to feel that — whether or not the thing that had spoken to her had been real or some disturbance of her mind, it had made sense. Constable Ewynnog was only one man. Why was she afraid of him? Neither she nor her father had ever done anything wrong. The village thought well of them. Unconsciously, she stood a little straighter, as resentment overcame her fretting.

"If he's so stupid," she said slowly, "what would he do, given how things are in Clogwyn? Will he let well enough alone and just try to lord it over everyone? Wouldn't he try and make trouble, if there's none to be found?" She could imagine him doing so, actually, and more resentment built within her.

"He might. So that leads me to other thoughts. It might be he was sent here, knowing he'd make trouble, so there would be an excuse to meddle. Maybe send more constables. Maybe more meddling than that." Daffyd's eyes narrowed in thought as they both walked back into the cottage. "See now, I don't rightly know, and I expect no one rightly knows, but there is a lot of anger about the striking. The high and mighties have got their hackles up; there's talk even of having the army in." He shook his head. "Before this is over, there'll be blood on the rocks and blood on the coal. Probably killings."

Mari shivered. Something about his words ... they felt prophetic. They stood like a cold shadow between her and the bright day. But it wasn't fear that made her shiver, it was that shadow. Resentment began to blossom into defiance. If that was how they wanted it ...

"Here now ..." He patted her shoulder, making her jump a little. "It won't be coming here. Mostly, if the worst comes, there will be some baddish times. People being harassed, more laws to follow. We just need to be as clever as the stoat; we stay out of sight and out of trouble, keep out of the constable's eye. Don't try and make ourselves agreeable and don't be disagreeable. That's all."

She nodded, but he wasn't quite through. "See now, this is your da, and his story-telling, and this might be a story or it might not. I just try to think things through, like you do when you tell a story. So here is the third thing. It might be Constable Ewynnog isn't stupid at all. It might be he's clever. It might be he's clever enough to act in stupid ways to see what he can stir up."

Mari bit her lip, and looked up into her father's far-seeing eyes. He was clever, was her da. He'd thought not only of the obvious, but the not-so-obvious, and the not-at-all-obvious. "So. . . . we do the same as we would regardless?" she hazarded. She wasn't sure she liked that. She wasn't at all sure she liked being passive. If trouble was going to come, she preferred to meet and fight it.

"Aye. That we do." He smiled faintly down at her. "And for right now, lovey, we have some pie."

Nan sighed over her best friend and shook her head. Sarah sat quietly at her dressing table while her friend tried to make some sense of her hair. "If you had your way, you'd wear the same two plain linen dresses for summer and the same two plain woolen dresses for winter. Your hair would always be in an untidy bird's nest of a knot on the top of your head. And you would never wear a hat."

Nan had come a very long way from the wild little cockney street-waif who could barely make herself understood. Two things had stood her in good stead in her transformation from mudlark to respectable young lady: a gift for mimicry and the dawning realization that if she sounded like a guttersnipe, she'd be treated like one, no matter what she looked like. After that, it had been an uncanny sense of what she and Sarah looked good in that had guided her. They might be unconventional in dress, but no one could say they weren't attractive.

"I don't like hats," Sarah protested, as Nan finished combing out her hair, and with deft fingers began to roll it into a fashionable pompadour.

Nan could not for the life of her understand how someone who was so pretty could be so careless of how she looked. Literally care-less; she simply did not care. So knowing that Lord Alderscroft was coming to dinner, it was Nan who dug into their trunks, Nan who extracted two dresses she rather fancied for the occasion, Nan who ran them down to the laundry and with the help of one of the Indian servants, got them presentable.

Then it was Nan that turned her attention to the bird's nest; with a little work, she had wound it into a nice, soft chignon, and when she was done, Sarah looked quite lovely. A bit like one of those artist-women, since they both favored artistic gowns when they got dressed up, but altogether lovely.

"No lady is without a hat," Nan said, severely.

"Are you saying my mum isn't a lady?" Sarah countered.

"Oh honestly . . ." Nan threw up her hands. "You know very well your mum wears hats when she comes to England. Now hurry up and get dressed. I want Lord Alderscroft to see us and realize we aren't a couple of hoyden girls any more."

"Why?" teased Sarah, as she slipped into a flowing gown that completely obscured the fact that she wasn't wearing any corset. "Have you set your cap for him?"

In answer, Nan snorted. Neville laughed.

Sarah's gown was made of tussah silk and linen, with bands of heavy lace, in warm creams and golds. Nan's was brocade and damask, with bands of more brocade, in more somber browns. Sometimes Nan wished she could coax her friend into something even frillier, but that would be like trying to put Neville into a christening gown. No one would be happy about the process or the outcome.

"All right then, how do I look?" Sarah turned in place. Nan smiled.

"It's a good thing Lord A isn't bringing any handsome young men with him or they'd be smitten," Nan replied, and held out her arm. Neville pushed off his perch, flapped once, and landed lightly on it. Grey flew to Sarah's shoulder.

"Peases?" Grey said hopefully. She'd missed English garden peas in Africa.

"Memsa'b promised," Sarah reminded her. Grey whistled happily.

Neville just chortled. He hadn't met a food that humans ate that he didn't like, but Nan could tell that he was looking forward to some real English cheese again. And maybe a nice bit of rare meat.

The four of them went down the stairs to the parlor set aside for Memsa'b, which was where the adults of the school ate when they were not dining with the children—the original dining room of the house having been taken over for school use. Nan preferred it for small gatherings, and she suspected Memsa'b did too; she couldn't imagine how a small family could manage to dine comfortably in such a big room.

Maybe people who've grown up in houses like this are just used to it, she thought, as Gupta, on duty at the door, opened it and announced them. The others were already seated and having an animated discussion; Memsa'b wasn't one to enforce formal manners of waiting and going in to dine when the gathering was among friends.

Lord Alderscroft did have someone with him, but he wasn't a susceptible young man; he was one of his older cronies from his esoteric circle. Everyone looked up at Gupta's announcement, and the gentlemen rose. Nan flushed a little. She'd forgotten that gentlemen did that. Even . . . or perhaps especially . . . in that odd archeological household, that wasn't the norm. *I'm going to have to get used to English manners again.*

"Miss Sarah, and Miss Nan," Lord Alderscroft greeted them genially. "Your year away has done you good."

Sarah took Grey from her shoulder and set her on her perch next to Sarah's chair. Nan did the same on her side with Neville. Sarah laughed. "If you mean we are both absurdly robust looking and burned as brown as gypsies, you are right, my lord. I was glad to have gone, but gladder to be home. I hadn't realized how much England had become my home until I left it."

Grey turned her head sideways and looked at Alderscroft with one yellow eye. "No peas," she complained. Then she looked pointedly down at her empty feeding cup.

"Well, we certainly should not deprive the gracious lady of her peas any longer," Alderscroft declared, which the servants took as the signal to begin the meal.

Alderscroft asked both the girls any number of questions about their experiences in Africa, while his colleague spoke quietly to Sahib and Memsa'b. Some of them were political; they couldn't answer all of them. "That's quite all right," he assured them. "If you happened to hear—or sense—something, that would be useful, but if you didn't, you didn't. I am merely casting out my line at random, and waiting to see if the salmon of knowledge bites it."

"I really didn't have much in the way of psychical experiences at all in Africa, my lord," Nan confessed. "Only in Egypt, and then . . ." She paused for a moment. ". . . then, the experiences I had were related to the far, far past, rather than the present. Truth be told, while I didn't feel unwelcome at all, I got that sense that both in Africa and in Egypt, the local spirits were not particularly interested in *me*."

She looked to Sarah, who nodded. "I had the same impression, sir. I suppose if there had been the ghost of a European with an urgent message about, I would have been sought out, but in Africa, our local shamans were clearly the . . ." She sought for a word.

"Authorities?" Lord Alderscroft offered.

"That's as good a word as any," Sarah replied. "Like goes to like, I suppose. If we were Elemental Mages, it might well have been different, but I'm not at all, and the only time Nan uses magic is when she calls on that ancient warrior she once was."

"The only dangers we faced were disease or accident; not much call for a warrior," Nan admitted. "There were always two native guards with us to deal with the wildlife, and hostilities were so far off we didn't get word of them for weeks."

"I cannot possibly say I regret that," his lordship said gravely. "As useful as information would be on that subject, I could not welcome anything that put my friends in danger. So now that you are back, what do you intend to do with yourselves?"

Nan shrugged. "I supposed we'd become teachers here," she replied. "I would make a wretched secretary, a worse shopgirl, and even though I would enjoy it a very great deal, Memsa'b would faint if I went on the stage."

Memsa'b rolled her eyes, but said nothing.

Neville made a derisive chortle. "Show us your legs, ducky!" he barked, and Nan reddened. Lord Alderscroft put a hand over his mouth to hide the fact that he was trying not to laugh.

"Besides," Sarah interjected hastily. "Memsa'b is probably going to need us in *her* work, so we should stay near at hand."

"In that case . . . the White Lodge occasionally comes

across situations where someone of psychical talents is required, rather than magical. Would you consider working on my behalf from time to time?" his lordship asked, when he had gotten control of himself.

"If it's all right with Memsa'b," Nan replied, when a glance at Memsa'b elicited a little nod from her mentor. "We certainly owe you a great deal, sir, and I would like to discharge that debt."

"I have no objections, my lord," Memsa'b said, as her husband also nodded. "I have every confidence that Nan and Sarah can handle themselves in virtually any situation." The mentor smiled slightly. "In fact, I am given to understand that Nan has become quite proficient with an African knife not unlike the Gurka kukri."

As Lord Alderscroft's eyebrows rose, Nan could not resist adding, "Two, actually. The other is more like the Khanjar dagger. Curved blades and straight blades require two sorts of handling. My ability to wield that mystical sword that affects otherworldly creatures seems to have translated rather neatly into the ability to use very physical weapons made of steel."

"I see," Lord Alderscroft said, after a long pause. "Well. In that case, I shall not hesitate to rely on you. Cold iron is often extremely efficacious against the blacker evils, and I can supply some very special weapons that are even more efficacious."

Sahib frowned, and coughed a little.

"Of course," Lord Alderscroft continued hastily, "I would not send you into a situation I knew was dangerous without being part of a larger group. Ideally with Gupta or another of your martial friends. Or mine. Probably both."

"Naturally," Memsa'b said, smoothly. "But this is very nebulous, and we have quite a lovely fruit tart to finish our meal, and I would rather hear what your plans are for the summer, my lord. Can we expect you here for part of it, at least?"

"You would have difficulty getting rid of me," Alderscroft chuckled. "The heat in London is likely to be unbearable. The only thing good about summer in London is that at least the wretched pea-soup fogs are gone. And since you'll have two more sets of hands about, I wondered if you would let me take the school to the seaside for a treat? Only a week or so; Blackpool, perhaps."

"Oh really, Alderscroft, that is *far* too generous of you—" Memsa'b began to protest. Alderscroft appealed to Sahib, as the girls listened. Eventually Memsa'b gave in, only because he promised to make it an educational visit as well. "Even though I know very well that you'll somehow turn an 'educational' experience into one that involves taking them all to some cake-strewn tea, or handing out candy-floss and bull's-eyes," she grumbled.

Alderscroft did not even bother to try to protest his innocence. Nan recalled quite vividly the delightful time he'd provided on the last "educational" excursion he'd led the school on. They'd taken an entire car on the train to Hampton Court Palace, had romped in the great maze until they were tired, got told horrific tales of the hauntings in the Tudor part of the palace by their guides, and took over a tea-shop where they were encouraged to order anything they liked. They'd come home stuffed with cream-buns and treacle-tarts, with no appetite whatsoever for dinner. Thankfully there hadn't been any all-night stomachaches from the overindulgence, or Memsa'b would never have agreed to a repeat performance.

Though it was a wonder some of the more sensitive children hadn't gotten nightmares from the stories of

Anne Boleyn strolling about with her head under her arm.

When the final course was cleared away, the usual turn of affairs in polite society was for the men to repair to a billiard or smoking room to indulge in port and cigars, but this was hardly the usual sort of household. The gentlemen sat downwind of the ladies—although only Alderscroft and his companion reached for cigars—in a parlor arranged so that a draft carried their smoke up the chimney. "We have a draft in this dratted room," Memsa'b had complained good-naturedly on discovering it, "We might as well make it useful." Port or lager were offered to the gentlemen, sherry or tea to the ladies. Alderscroft's companion finally introduced himself, shyly, to Nan and Sarah, who hadn't caught his name.

"Beg pardon, but I'm rather certain I was so busy interrogatin' poor Mrs. Harton that we never got around to exchangin' names," he said apologetically. "I'm Evan Dumbarton. Only a mister, I fear, if you were hopin' for more blue blood."

Nan chuckled, Sarah laughed aloud. "I assure you, we met more descendants of Nubian kings and pharaohs in Africa and Egypt than I care to think about. A mere lord doesn't impress us any more," Sarah said impudently. "You'd have to be a prince to do that."

To Nan's relief, Evan Dumbarton took that as the joke it was and laughed. "Good-oh. I was just rather eagerly consultin' Mrs. Harton as we seem to have spawned a bit of a mediumistic creature in one of my younger sisters, rather than a magician. Don't want her to come to any harm, and fortunately, the lady knows of another lady close by that'll likely be willing to . . ." He seemed to be searching for the appropriate phrase.

Nan offered him one. "Give private lessons?" she prompted.

"Exactly so." Dumbarton nodded. "Now . . . I'm given to understand you two are talented in that direction too?" Without waiting for a reply, he continued. "I'd take it—the family'd take it—as a kindness if we could bring Meg up to London now and again, and she could . . . well . . ." He ran a nervous finger around his collar. "Ah . . ."

"Oh please, call a spade a spade, and not a pointed digging implement," Sarah chided.

"Well, she seems to have gotten the notion that she should waft around the old barn in white draperies and trail through the fields like Ophelia, barefoot and mutterin' poetry," he replied, reddening. "She never used to be like that. I'm hopin' this old gel that Mrs. Harton knows will put her right, but if she don't . . . I'd like her to see that, well, *normal* gels like you, who put their hair up proper and wear dresses that ain't made from old sheets have got the same talents."

Birds and girls erupted into laughter, which very much relieved him, although he was still blushing furiously. Memsa'b glanced at them curiously, Nan mouthed the word "sister" at her, and Memsa'b raised her eyebrows in understanding and went back to the conversation with the other men.

"I'll wager she got all of that nonsense from reading bad novels. I swear, those horrid gothic romances drive me insane," Nan said. "The people who write them have not the faintest notion of what they're talking about, and make up the most absurd idiocy out of whole cloth. How many haunts do you have at your—'old barn'?"

"Don't know for certain, but at least a few," Evan admitted. "All harmless. We're a singularly inoffensive family. Never murdered any grooms because they got too friendly with the daughters of the house, never drove off gypsies with bloodthirsty dogs, never took advantage of peasant wenches, stayed polite to both sides of the Wars of the Roses *and* the Civil War." He shrugged. "Near as I can tell, none of the family shades holds a grudge."

"I suspect," Sarah said carefully, "That may be the problem. A young lady of romantic nature, stuck in the country, suddenly discovering herself to be mediumistic, rather expects to become the channel for spirits wanting revenge or redemption. To find they only want to share tea with her would be something of a letdown, and in her place, I suspect I might begin trailing about in white weeds, looking for something more interesting to talk to."

"Huh." Evan got a thoughtful look on his face. "Well, in that case . . . I should think persuadin' Mater and Pater to let her come up to London a season early and stay with me might be a good cure for that."

Memsa'b must have been listening with half an ear. "Only after Adriana McDrew gives her basic lessoning," she said, interjecting herself into the conversation. "London is no place for a wide open medium. But after that, yes, I believe an early London season in the company of her brother would do her a great deal of good." Her eyes twinkled. "Though you might have cause to regret that when young suitors come calling."

"That won't happen 'till she gives up the weedy wanderin'," he said with confidence. "None of my fellers are interested in someone that looks like she might take a notion to go drown herself. Once she starts wearing pretty gowns again—well, then I'll dig out an aunt. I've got hordes of 'em in London, an' they'll all jump at the notion of goin' out to balls again."

Memsa'b laughed, and beckoned a little, and all three

of them joined the other conversation. Alderscroft prompted Sahib to enlarge on what he and Memsa'b had been doing while the girls were gone. Evan listened in fascination; the business of Elemental Magicians was common conversation with him, but the business of psychics, mediums and other purely mental talents was all new. Nan and Sarah were pleased enough to catch up on the news.

Sahib waxed long and eloquent on the subject of the charlatans that were occupying Conan Doyle, the author, while Alderscroft shook his head. "Well, it's a pity to see such a first-class mind taken in by even children, but would we really *want* him to be aware of our business? I've done my level best to keep him cleared away from any hint of the Council and the White Lodge."

Sahib pursed his lips, and frowned. "Hmm. You have a point, my lord," he said reluctantly. "The danger being that he *is* a first class mind, and worse, he is a writer. Writers simply cannot leave things as secrets, I've found. One way or another, the secret works its way into their work, and disguise it as fiction though they may, you find people who shouldn't come near the stuff trying to dabble in either magic or the occult and failing, or worse, they succeed, and we're the ones to clean up when the mayhem breaks out."

"It was bad enough when Dickens got a whiff," Alderscroft agreed. "Thank God Kipling saw sense in India. But that poor soul in the colonies? What was his name?"

"Poe, I believe you are referring to," Memsa'b offered.

"Yes, that was it. Poe. Poor fellow went quite off his head eventually."

"Oh," said Evan, looking wise. "It can always be much worse than that."

MONTROSE REGIONAL LIBRARY
320 SO. 2ND ST.
MONTROSE, CO 81401

"Eh?" Alderscroft gave him a curious look.

"When someone with one or another marginal talent tries to be an *author*." Evan shuddered. "Oh, the horrors! I read one, and tried to gouge my eyes out with a pen. Never saw such spelling and grammar in my life. The King's English wasn't murdered, it was drawn, quartered, hung, disemboweled, and burnt, only to be resurrected and done in again in the next chapter!"

Nan thought she had never laughed so hard in her life.

3

THE wretched constable was *snooping.*

It had been another perfect day, until he intruded into it. Mari was putting up washing, enjoying the fresh wind off the sea, when she saw him stalking toward the cottage from the distant road. He looked very uncomfortable and awkward; she guessed shrewdly that he was more used to tramping about on city streets than trying to make his way across a sheep-field.

This annoyed her no end. It had been a *lovely* day up until that moment, with a salt-tinged wind with just a hint of bite to it making the clothing flap like flags. She loved days like this, with the contrast of a cold wind at her back and the warm sun on her face, with the wind sending her skirts billowing out like the sails on a coracle. The only thing better was a hot day and low tide, and wading out in the shallows collecting shellfish. And here he was, ruining it, just by his unwelcome presence.

She watched him without watching him, feeling a nasty satisfaction in how labored his steps were. He took long enough about it that she had plenty of time to think about how she was going to deal with him, and the first thing that came into her mind was that she was *not* going to give him an excuse to go into the cottage. If he'd been in any of the other fishermen's homes in Clogwyn, and she had no doubt that he had with his snooping ways, he would immediately notice how much nicer it was inside their place. He would certainly notice how much nicer it was than Violet Cottage. Then there would be questions about the improvements, and where they'd gotten the money . . . or worse, no questions at all, and assumptions about smuggling or worse.

Which meant that she'd better be prepared to spend the rest of the afternoon outside, because he was going to have to force down the door before she would let him in. At least the weather was good, and it would be no hardship to be outside. She had no doubt whatsoever that she could outlast him. He would not want to walk back to the village in the dark.

Easy done.

She got everything that might possibly need a wash, and the basket of new peas, and brought both outside, along with some empty baskets. She closed the door behind her firmly and tightly so there was no chance it might blow open.

She put the clothing into the tub for a good soak. And she took her time hanging things up to dry. By the time he arrived, she hadn't filled a quarter of the line. He stood awkwardly, waiting for her to acknowledge him.

She didn't. She just glanced at him sideways, and hunched her shoulders a little.

"Good afternoon, miss," he said, when she didn't greet him.

She'd decided on a particular tactic to avoid saying anything more than she had to. She'd play shy. That way the more he tried to bully her, the quieter she could get without arousing suspicions. "Afternoon, sir," she whispered, ducking her head and avoiding his eyes.

He waited. She said nothing. She sensed his bafflement, and his annoyance. "You'd be Mari Prothero, then?"

She waited a long, long time before making an awkward little bob and replying. "Aye, sir," she whispered.

"And your father . . ." he consulted a notebook. "Daffyd Prothero? Where is he?"

She favored him this time with a brief, blank look, then averted her gaze. "Fishing, sir." She waved a hand vaguely in the direction of the sea, and went right back to hanging up the wash, moving away from him as she moved up the line. He had to follow her in order to hear her whispers.

"Where is he fishing?" Constable Ewynnog demanded. Now that . . . that had to be the most daft question anyone could ask. How would *she* know where he was fishing? He could be anywhere.

"Sea, sir," she murmured, again waving her hand at the ocean.

He muttered under his breath, then said aloud *"Where* on the sea?" he persisted.

This time she gave him an incredulous look, and swiftly looked away. "Don't know, sir," she replied. "Where there be fish," she added.

What kind of a fool did they send here?

Unless he expected her to give him the name of something nearby. But how could she possibly know where the fish would be running today? Only Daffyd would, and only after looking for the signs, and possibly a deal of sailing.

"And where is your mother?" he asked. She glanced at him under the cover of her hair. Now he was writing things in that little book of his. She went to the washtub without answering, and started scrubbing.

Although she was positive that he already knew the answer, she gave it to him, but only after a very long wait. "Dead, sir." She kept her head down and her hands busy, scrubbing in the first tub, rinsing in the second, then wringing out the rinsed garments and putting them in the basket to be hung up. She took great pains *not* to look grief-stricken. He surely must know she didn't remember her mother, not at all.

"Ah. My condolences." He didn't sound at all sympathetic. Then he revealed himself, possibly without realizing it. "I didn't find a grave at the churchyard . . . could you tell me where she is buried?"

It was a good thing that she had her head down, or she was sure she would have given herself away with her fury. Of course he knew; if he knew her father's name, then he knew how her mother had died. It was in the parish records and everyone in the village knew. He had looked for a grave anyway—perhaps assuming her mother's body had washed in to shore and been properly buried. She took several deep breaths before answering, and reminded herself to be calm. He was trying to trip her up. She must not let him. She truly must not.

"Drownded, sir," she told him, and fought with herself to keep from growling it out. Her voice did sound indifferent in her ears; good, it would be stupid to sound grief-stricken.

She risked another glance at him from behind her hanging hair as she took up the basket of wet clothing and went to the line again. He frowned as he scribbled in his notebook. "Isn't that unusual? For a *woman* to drown?"

Aha. Suspicious limb of Satan that he was. Oh, how she wanted to slap his smug face! How *dared* he? What kind of a terrible person would say that to someone who had lost her mother?

But she got control of herself, and averted her face, and doled out her words in short sentences with long, long pauses between the words. "Rogue wave, sir." *Take good long breaths, and try and stay ahead of him.* "Ask in village, sir." She took some more steadying breaths, and kept her voice barely above a whisper. "She was kelpin'."

He didn't ask what kelping was, though she was in doubt that he actually knew what it was. "Where?" he asked.

With both hands full, she nodded up the beach. "In sight of village," she told him, pitching her voice so low he had to lean in to hear her. "They say."

"And was she alone? Were there others with her?"

He was either a monster or unbelievably dim.

She paused for a good long time. "Just me brother." Another few breaths. "And me." She held pins in her mouth to avoid saying anything for a moment.

"And you saw all this?" *Angels and saints. He asks that?*

"I was in cradle," she corrected him. "Up on shore, sir." Which he would know, since the record of her birth was at the parish as well, he would know she was only a month or two old at the time.

"So you didn't see it?" Persistent as well as a monster.

"Been told," she said. She pinned up an apron, then a

dishtowel. "Rogue wave." One of her da's shirts. "It came an' took 'em both." A pair of her da's drawers. "Half village saw it."

He blinked at that; as if it had surprised him. Well. Interesting. Clearly he had *not* asked in the village after all, and perhaps had relied only on the parish records. Perhaps no one in the village had been willing to tell him anything. Well, too bad for whatever theory he had, because there were too many witnesses.

A moment later, an expression of disappointment and irritation passed over his face. "I am sorry for your loss," he said, though it was almost a growl. Then, to spoil the half-apology completely, he added "I'll ask in the village when I return to corroborate your story."

Oh, now she wanted to slap him *and* kick him. Why would she lie about such a thing? Yet he clearly thought she might, and more than that, he clearly thought there had been dirty work afoot.

She knew now what it was he had been trying to trip her up over. *He thought my father did away with her! His own wife! The mother of his children!* Well, of course he would. He was a stranger, and looking for trouble to boot. She hadn't much liked him before, but now, she hated him so badly that if a wave came up and pulled *him* out to sea she would stand there and applaud.

But she shrugged, and concentrated on her wash. Let him think her stolid and stupid as well as shy. "Don't remember."

There was only so long she could keep hanging up clothing, however. Fortunately, she had brought the peas out to shell. She put the empty clothes basket next to the house, sat down on the handy bit of driftwood she kept beside the door, and picked up the bowl of peas. She still would not look at him, nor speak unless she was spoken to. She would make him do every bit of the work. Not one word would he get from her without dragging it out.

He picked his way across the yard to loom over her. "Has your family owned this house long?" he finally asked.

"Great-great-great-great granther, sir," she said. "Maybe longer. Dunno."

Let *him* trace it back in the parish records. And good luck to him at it.

"Do you farm?" he prompted.

"Nay. Fishermen." Ignorant git.

"Then what is that?" He pointed at the dormant vegetable garden.

"Bit of garden, no more," she informed him. "Tisn't farming."

"Then who owns all that behind your house?" he demanded.

"Emir Jennyd." He had to know that.

"All of it?" he persisted.

"Dunno. Ask at farm." No more *sir*s for him. She was getting mighty tired of his presence.

He looked about himself as if he would like to sit down, and injudiciously attempted to move the cat from her rock. Outraged at this affront, the cat objected. Strenuously. She growled at him and laid her ears back, her eyes glowing with a dangerous light.

He was either too stupid or too sure of himself to heed the warning. He reached down to grab her by the scruff of the neck. He managed to get hold of her, but she was not the sort of cat to put up with *that* insult.

In fact, she somehow writhed around and got teeth and hind-claws into him; she mauled his hand, then sprang away before he could hit her. He let out a rather girlish shriek of pain and let her go. She fled, growling as she ran off into the fields behind the house. He swore and shook his bleeding hand, then cradled it against his chest.

Then he whirled to face her. "Your cat just savaged me!" he exclaimed angrily, with a face full of accusation, as if he blamed *her* for his own stupidity of putting his hand on an animal whose temper he didn't know.

"Not my cat," she said shortly, and went on with her work, not offering him so much as a rag to wrap his hand in.

Finally, after waiting in vain for her to offer to help him, he trudged down to the shore to wash his lacerated hand in the surf. He came back, face even more sour than before, wrapping his hand in a handkerchief.

She was finished with the peas by then. An idea had occurred to her, so she got up and set the bowl of peas on her seat. Restraining her expression with difficulty, she picked up another basket from the side of the house, this one very old and battered, taking the least battered from her selection of three. Then she got two net bags. Without saying a word, she trudged down to the shore. He could follow if he liked; she wondered if he would.

He did. "Where are you going?" he shouted, a little breathless, his tone angry. "I am not finished speaking with you yet!"

She looked back. "I got work," she said shortly, only a little above a whisper. "It needs doing."

"I demand that you answer my questions!" he shouted, red-faced, stumbling a little over the uneven surface. She doubted he'd even heard what she'd said.

She shook her head. "Then I reckon," she said, hunching her chin down and looking servile, "you'd best follow."

She plodded a good half mile down the shore to where the best kelp generally washed up. It was in the opposite direction to the site where her mother had been taken, but really, even *he* could not be so daft as to think she would go to that same spot! As she'd thought, the last storm had brought in plenty. It was almost dry now, perfect for her purpose. She began picking it up, shaking the sand out, and packing it into her basket, as he finally caught up with her.

"What in God's name are you doing, girl?" he asked, still sounding angry. She glanced at him again. He was angry—with an incredulous look on his face as if he thought she was playing some sort of trick on him. So she had been right. He had *never* heard of kelping. Did he think that the seaweeds washed up on the beach were worthless? Or had he been so spoiled all his life that he'd never had to find a use for everything that came into his hand?

City man. Pff.

"Kelpin'," she said shortly.

"Oh, he's a rude one," said a bright voice beside her.

The voice chilled her anger and made her swallow hard. She looked out of the corner of her eye, and spotted one of the seaweed-girls, like the one she had seen the other day, the ones that would lead her to good places for mussels and cockles. These were tiny little things, no higher than your knee, who were dressed all in green drapery, like seaweed, with hair as green as the seaweed. She glanced at the constable. Clearly *he* did not see her.

This was the first time one of *them* had turned up when she was with another person. And that other person didn't see the creature. So was this a confirmation? Was she really going mad?

Before she could get any farther in her thoughts than that, the tiny thing spoke up again.

"No fear; the likes of him can't see the likes of me. And I'm minded to do him a mischief," the little thing continued. And before Mari could blink, the girl was gone.

Do him a mischief? What on earth— Oh, she knew what that meant in the stories. The Tylwyth Teg folk didn't like rudeness, and they punished it in a number of ways. But if this creature was some symptom of madness... how could it do something against someone else?

Automatically, her hands had carried out the work while her mind had been watching and listening to the seaweed-girl. Where she saw fresh laver or samphire she added it to her net bags. And now the constable had caught his breath and was back to his questions. "Your father fishes every day?"

Good heavens, the man was persistent.

"Aye," she said, moving away from him, carefully picking up kelp and shaking it out. "E'cept Sunday."

"Why not Sunday?" He was writing again.

"We go to chapel." This time she allowed incredulity to creep into her voice. Didn't *he* go to chapel? Or church?

Oh. Wait. Anarchists were supposed to not believe in God. "Ask parson," she added.

"He goes out fishing every day but Sunday? Even when it storms?" He was making more notes. How could that possibly be of interest to him?

"Aye." She contemplated mischief herself, and sternly reminded herself that she was not to arouse suspicion. "Don't fish, don't eat."

Out of the corner of her eye, she saw, to her astonishment, a bit of rope snaking towards his left foot. It slipped around his ankle. He didn't notice, he was so intent on her. Or maybe the pain of his hand kept him from feeling the slithering rope at his ankle.

"Does anyone else go out when it storms?" What was he trying to get at? That her father was doing something nefarious under the cover of storms? How daft was that? "The other fishermen in the village. Do they fish in the storms too?"

Again, she shrugged. "Course." She moved off again, towards another patch of kelp. "Don't fish, don't eat." He started to follow. "Village bain't rich." Surely he had seen that for himself. Surely he had seen the number of deaths by drowning in the parish records.

The rope suddenly tightened around his ankle as he started after her; taken completely by surprise, he went sprawling on his face. And before he could notice what had tripped him, the rope whipped itself away and sped up the sand, to lie, all harmless-looking, too far to have been what caught him.

He came up with a face and fancy uniform full of sand, sputtering, and looking around for what had caught him. He glared at her, but she was too far away to have done anything to him, and what could he accuse her of? Say she was a witch and had bespelled him to trip? A right fool he'd look. Claim she'd planted some sort of trap in the sand that had managed to disappear as soon as he'd fallen? A greater fool he'd look then!

She resisted the urge to say something—although she could hear giggling from where the rope was.

His notebook lay a yard away, pages fluttering in the wind. She made no move to pick it up or give him any other kind of help.

Her basket was full, so she decided this was a good time to make him follow her again. She hiked it up on her shoulder and headed for the house. She didn't look back—but she did hear him fall twice more.

That delayed him enough that she was able to get the

fire started beside the bare garden and throw the kelp on it, then hang the kettle over it to start the laver boiling to make the fuel do double-duty. Kelp smoke was . . . fairly noisome. And as delicious as the laver was after boiling for a day, when it was boiling it was just as noxious. To her gratification, somehow, no matter where he stood, he found himself downwind of it. He waved at it ineffectually, coughing.

He probably wants to ask me why I'm burning kelp and boiling seaweed, and he can't get a breath long enough to get the words out. Does the wretched fool think laver grows in a garden? He's a Welshman; he has to have eaten laver-bread. Now she was highly amused, and some of her temper cooled. Clearly, clearly a city man, and one who'd never had to make what he could buy. The kelp ash was invaluable in the garden, and for making soap, and for scrubbing pots and the hearthstones. She'd have to wash the ash to get rid of the salt before she put it on the garden, but it would keep down the weeds between the rows just a treat, besides nourishing the plants. But he wouldn't know that. And she was not going to tell him. Let him ask in the village.

And clearly he had no idea where laver came from, nor how it was prepared. He probably didn't even know that the thin brown sheets she'd picked off the rocks *were* laver. As for the samphire, well, from the look of it, he'd think of eating grass before he'd think of eating samphire.

She'd told him that her mother had died going kelping, she'd shown him what kelping was, now let him try and figure out *why* anyone would go kelping, then burn or boil the kelp.

The smoke almost seemed to be chasing him. Before long, his eyes were red and weeping, and he kept trying to wipe them with the handkerchief around his wounded hand. The sea-water in those deep scratches and bites must have burned like fire. She was not in the least sorry for him. After all, he'd brought every bit of his suffering on himself. *Evil to him that evil thinks* had never, in her experience, been so immediate.

After opening and closing his mouth several times and getting a lung full of smoke for his troubles each time, sending him into a coughing fit, he gave up. Without so much as a "Good day"—although he probably would not have been able to choke even that out for the smoke—he stalked off, heading for the road. She watched him leave, carefully. His tormentor tripped him twice more before leaving him alone—or perhaps at this point, between the coughing and the watering eyes, he simply couldn't see where he was going very clearly. She sincerely hoped he'd been tripped into something nasty at least once.

When she was sure he wasn't coming back, and his figure was a stiff, distant little sketch nearing the road, she left the fire to tend to itself and took in her peas.

Clearly he had been trying to get *some* sort of information out of her—presumably to use against her da. That was troubling, but no more than her da had expected. *He came out here, figuring I would tell him something that would give him a reason to call up da for killing mother. Or at least something that would let him link da to smuggling or maybe the anarchists.* Why? Maybe he figured since they lived so far from the village that the village wouldn't care if he went after them. But why would he do so in the first place? Just because he was sour-natured? That didn't seem right.

She worried at that and worried at it as she put the peas to cook, and got a nice bit of salmon ready for frying. She still couldn't untangle the puzzle. Why was he coming after the Protheros? Or was he doing the same in the whole village?

Finally she just gave it up as being something she couldn't puzzle out. That was when the memory of the seaweed-girl practically leapt up out of the back of her mind. The seaweed girl, who Constable Ewynnog had not been able to see . . . but . . .

Who had been able to make the constable's afternoon a misery.

Which meant only one thing. That the creatures that only she could see, were, nevertheless, able to *do things*. Real things. Torment real people . . . and if they could do that . . .

Here was her proof. They were not fever-dreams or the phantoms of a mind going mad. They were real.

The revelation thrilled and terrified her. Thrilled, because who *wouldn't* be thrilled to know that they were not going to end up tied to a bedpost, mad-eyed and raving. But terrified . . .

Tylwyth Teg folk. They were not safe, no matter that they had been helpful to her all this time. They were not tame. They operated by their own rules, which often seemed to be as much whim as rules. If they liked you, as they seemed to like her, they could do you great favors. But you could not count on that liking to last, and when they were angry with you, they could do a great deal more than trip you up.

These were dangerous waters. And she was going to have to try and recall every tale that old woman had told her, just to have an inkling of how to navigate them.

She debated telling her da this, but given his reactions to her talking about her odd "friends" when she was a child . . . she finally decided, no. No, probably not a good idea. So instead, when her da came home, she laid out dinner and gave a faithful rendition of everything that had happened, including the constable's mishaps, but *not* saying what had caused them.

Her da was grinning as she spoke of the man getting savaged by the cat, and grinned wider at his clumsiness. "Must have been them city boots," he said, with mock-gravity. "I imagine he was fair put out."

"I imagine so," she said, and grinned a little herself. But then she lost the smile, thinking that it was bad enough to have the attention of the Tylwyth Teg, but having the attention of the constable was no better. "Da," she said, clasping her hands on the table in front of her, and ignoring the rest of her meal, "Da, I think he was trying to get something nasty he could use to put you in jail! But *why?* Why would he do that? Why is he trying to hurt us?"

The lantern-light from the lamp he'd hung above their heads cast shadows on his face as he looked up. "I believe you're right. But—oh now, that's several questions in one, my heart," her father said, gravely, and set his own fork aside. "Look now, first, I think *he* thinks that we are some sort of village outcasts for living out here. So he thinks we're the weakest out of all of the village—that no one will spring to our defense if he comes up with some daft charge or other."

She nodded; that made sense.

"He's a bully; bullies always pick on the weakest." He grinned at her. "But we're not weak, we're like the seals, strong and slippery and fast, and any rope he tries to cast around us, we'll just slip right through and be gone."

She sighed, feeling a little more comfortable. It sounded as if her da had spent a goodly long time thinking about all this, and was already planning things.

"Now as to why he would do this in the first place . . ." her da frowned. "I think we talked of this before. I'm going to say he's been sent to *find* trouble. Sent to hunt out lawbreakers. Whoever sent him just assumed that no matter where you looked hereabouts, you'd find anarchists and unionists, and sympathizers, and I'm thinking it must go further than the Manor folk, since they seem no happier to have him than we. I'm thinking it goes all the way back to the *big* landowners and the mine owners who hold the leashes of the constables. Money talks, my love. Money is what tells power what to do. Money is always there, any time you see power moving. Only there's no one here doing what he's been sent to look for, so now he has to twist and bend and even make things up for the ones that sent him, so that he won't find himself in trouble." Dafydd Prothero shook his head, sadly, but also angrily. "If he was a good, honest man, he'd tell his bosses that there's naught to be found here, and all their prodding him won't give them what they want. But he's not. He's a little, petty man, with large ideas of his own importance, and he's a bully, and those two things together are going to make trouble for *someone.*"

"Then we need to make certain it isn't us!" she exclaimed, with indignation.

"Aye, true, but we also need to make certain we come to the help of whoever it does end up being," he cautioned her. "Do as you would be done by. Or you'll be done by as you did."

And with that, he picked his fork back up and finished his dinner thoughtfully.

As usual, they worked for a bit, and sang together a bit, but the darkness seemed thicker tonight, and they soon went off to bed.

She thought about all that he had said as she went up

to bed. It was true that the folks in Clogwyn had come to her defense, but that was when none of them were in any danger of anything other than irritation. Would they still feel that way if it was one of their own with his neck being measured for a noose? After all, she and her da *were* something of outsiders. As far as she knew, no one was aware of Daffyd Prothero's truly extraordinary good luck in fishing, and the daily sails to Criccieth before he came home, but they did know he was always able to bring in enough to sell, and for some, that was enough for jealousy.

People had always been reticent to talk to her about her mother and her lost older brother too. Was that just because they felt it wasn't right to, or was there something more, something to make them wonder why her mother had taken them both out kelping on that particular day? She'd never thought twice about it until today.

Well, now she knew. She knew that the Tylwyth Teg folk were not some visions of madness, but just as real as she had supposed they were as a child. She knew that they could affect things in the real world—even do mischief to those who couldn't see them! So . . . what if *they* had something to do with her mother's drowning? It would explain why her father didn't want to hear about them. It would explain why the villagers didn't want to talk about it—because if *she* could see them, well certainly there must be others who could, or where would all those stories come from?

Or maybe they had seen something truly uncanny. Maybe they had just seen the wave coming for her mother as if it was alive—or some of them had actually seen her and the child dragged into it. There were plenty of the Tylwyth Teg that would kill a mortal if they could.

And if that was true, did it mean the Tylwyth Teg were coming for her next? Would they lure or push her into the sea? They'd never been anything but playful before . . . but who could tell for sure? They might do anything. There were plenty of stories about the malicious ones, the murderous ones. Even the prettiest . . . well, they were said to lure men to drown, too.

She shivered in her bed. This did not make for comfortable thinking. Bad enough that she was going to have to worry about Constable Ewynnog and his spying ways, but if the Tylwyth Teg were a danger as well . . . the Tylwyth Teg were more dangerous than the constable. Him, she could see coming. They could be invisible if they chose, or hide in the shadows, or creep in at night when she and her da were asleep.

But they never have before, she reminded herself. *Nothing other than a bit of theft or hiding something. Even the Pwca, he never offered me harm.*

And there was another thing to worry about. Was that why her da didn't want to hear about them? Not that he didn't believe in them, but because he *did,* and he, too, was afraid that his wife had been their victim? Was he afraid they were coming for his daughter as well?

What to think? Her mind went round and around in little circles, trying to reason it out, and she came to no conclusion at all before she was worn out and fell asleep despite her fretting.

The morning was another clear, clean day, and it seemed a day to ask the questions she had never asked before. Maybe not about the Tylwyth Teg, not yet but . . .

"Da," she asked, as her father stoked himself with hot food to keep him on the water, "Why do you always sell half the catch in Criccieth? You could sell it here. Especially on those days when no one else brings in much."

He stopped with his fork halfway to his mouth. "The long and the short of it is that in Criccieth I'm only one fisherman that only fishermen know, and not well, and only by 'Daffyd' and half of Wales is named that. No one cares who brings in fish, nor how many fish I bring in. In Clogwyn I'm Daffyd Prothero that everyone knows."

"Well yes," she admitted, "but—"

"It's to keep you safe." He practically bit off the words, as if he was afraid that to say more would be dangerous. This, from her da, who never let one word do when he could string out a sort of poem from many!

"Safe from what?" she asked. The next question she had never asked before. "Whoever would harm me?"

There were shadows on his darkly handsome face, and his brows knitted with unhappiness. "And why are you asking me this now?" he countered.

"Because it can't be to keep us safe from Constable Ewynnog; you've been doing this all my life." She twisted her fingers together, anxiously. "Da, if there's something that is a danger, aren't I old enough to know about it now?"

His mouth turned down in an unhappy grimace. "I—I can't talk about it yet," he said, finally.

Yet? What does that mean?

"Is it about my mother?" she asked. Still another question she had never asked. "Is there more about my mother you've not told me?"

This only increased his distress, and she was suddenly reminded again of the tales, the tales not only of the Tylwyth Teg and fanciful things, but of princes and frogs and fishermen, and how it was always best never to ask questions, for the mere asking of them brought trouble upon the asker. She had, as a child, thought it silly that the princesses and brides and other girls would persist in asking the questions they *knew* were forbidden—but now she knew first-hand just how impossible it was *not* to ask them. They burned in your mind, and ate at you, until you had to blurt them out or die from them eating at you.

She could feel all those questions, all those words, seething in her mind, as they had since she had awakened this morning, and she knew she could no more refrain from asking than she could refrain from breathing.

As for her Da, he looked startled as well as unhappy, as if he had not expected her to make that intuitive leap. And that, in a way, told her something; it told her that yes, this all did have to do with her mother.

"I can't tell you yet," he repeated, with an edge of desperation in his voice. "I will, I promise, but I cannot tell you yet."

"Is there anything I can do to help you?" she asked, softly now. She put one hand on the hand that still held the fork. "Da, there's nothing I wouldn't do for you, you know that. Is there—"

He was sweating now. "That's—part of it—" he got out with difficulty. "There will be something. But I can't tell you what. Not yet. Just . . . just forget the questions for now. There's troubles enough without us looking for more. Aye?"

"All right," she agreed, and he finished eating in a rush and was out the door as if he could not wait to be out on the water.

She watched after him—and at least he had not forgotten his kiss at the door, nor his wave as he pushed out to sea, but his leave-taking left her feeling uneasy inside. As if she had somehow broken another of those Tylwyth Teg-tale rules.

"Oh, oh, oh, silly girl that you are," said a voice full of merriment from somewhere near her left knee. She looked down. It was the seaweed girl again. She bit her lip, then, screwing up her courage, addressed the creature as she had not in years.

"And why am I a silly girl?" she asked.

The little thing tossed her hair, the movement making her seaweed-gown move as well, and revealing enough to make Mari blush. There was a fully formed woman under that weed, regardless that she was only two feet tall. *"There you go; you know, and you know that you know, that words are power and words can bind, but you go and tell your father 'I'll do anything to help you.' It's a good thing he is your father, or you could find yourself bound to serve him until white horses come out of the sea."*

She bit her lip harder. The creature was right. And then it struck her: if anyone was to know what the bottom to all of this mystery was, it would be the Tylwyth Teg folk!

"And what do *you* know about my mother?" she demanded.

The tiny green eyes twinkled, and was there a touch of . . . well, not malice but something with more darkness to it than mere mischief. *"And what will you give me for what I could tell?"*

Oh dear. She had forgotten that. The Tylwyth Teg, at least in the tales, had no generosity of spirit. Nothing was ever freely given. A gift enraged them; it put obligation on them that they had not agreed to. They'd steal what they fancied, but not food. The old woman had said it was because there was salt in most food, and salt was holy, so they could not steal it. You could leave food for them, though, and their rules let them have as much of it as they could eat in a sitting. If you put out bread and milk, say, they would take it, but would perform tasks to "pay" for it. Food was allowed. Put out more than that, without bargaining beforehand, and it enraged them.

So, what would a sea-creature want? Something it couldn't get in the sea, of course.

"Bread and honey?" she offered, tentatively.

The little creature scoffed. *"That's not enough for what I know,"* she said. *"You must do better than that."* She grinned, and Mari noticed that all her teeth were pointed, like a shark's. *"Secrets, secrets, oh, I do know them. Offer again."*

But though she pummeled her mind for something to offer, she couldn't come up with anything. She shrugged. "We bain't rich," she said. "I've not got much, and most of what we have, I won't offer without I talk to my da."

The little thing wagged her head back and forth. *"You've more than you think, Mari Prothero. Pledge me a service!"*

Oh no, she wasn't going to be caught in that trap. You didn't offer the Tylwyth Teg a "service" unless you were entirely certain of what that service would be, and even then you had to be careful lest you discover you'd bound yourself to them for years and years. "I'm not free to pledge a service," she temporized.

"Well then, you won't be hearing what I know." The Tylwyth Teg creature laughed. *"And if only you knew what I know you'd never need to bargain again, never fear some bumbling landsman lording it over his lessers, and never know want."* She laughed again, mockingly. *"But ask your da. If you dare. If he'll dare answer you. Oh, he'll be telling you one day, but the day he does, it will be too late for you to be bargaining!"*

And with that, she twirled around and vanished from

sight—but her laughter rang out over the pebbly shore, growing fainter as she sped for the water.

Mari frowned, much put out. It was very vexing to have finally acknowledged that these creatures were real only to have them turn about and act like this. She restrained herself from shouting after the creature. What would she say? "All right, just see if I don't!" Oh that would accomplish absolutely nothing.

So very irritating. The vexation was enough to make her feel less afraid of them, because this one certainly wasn't acting like a powerful and dangerous creature, but like a tormenting little brat.

She combed her hair back out of her eyes with her fingers, and went into the house. Uncanny creatures or not, mysteries could wait. She had chores to do. Just to begin with, that kelp-ash would need washing to get the salt out, and now was as good a time as any to get her buckets and go.

But when she went to the stream in the sheep-meadow to fetch fresh water, there were other surprises waiting for her. Two of them.

Again, these were tiny creatures, transparent as glass, and again, female. Instead of being clothed in seaweed, they were clothed only in their own hair, although they managed to be more modest that way than the little rude thing. They were clearly waiting for her, half-in, half-out of the stream, side by side, with their arms braced on the bank.

She looked around, nervously, to make sure there was no one about to see her talking with nothing. But there was not a soul to be seen, only the sheep. She looked down at the two—whatever they were. They didn't correspond to any Tylwyth Teg that she recognized. They smiled winsomely at her.

"We are very glad you are willing to see us now, Mari," said one, in a voice that sounded oddly like the burbling of water over stones. *"It made us sad when you stopped wanting to."*

Wait ... now ... she *did* remember creatures like these, though she still had no name for them. These were some of her childhood playmates; these, or something very like these, had taught her to swim at an age when most children were barely toddling. She'd never told her father that; he'd probably have gone quite mad if she had.

"I didn't know you were real," she said, shamefacedly. "Da—"

"Oh, we know," said the second. *"And Mari, he wasn't unhappy because he thought we weren't real. He was unhappy because he knows we are."*

She stared at them, speechless, as they toyed with the grasses at the verge of the stream. "But—"

"It means something very important," said the first. *"Some—we can't tell you, until your father does. But some we can say, and he should have. You have magic, Mari. Magic like the old Druids and older. You will be able to command the creatures of the water when you are taught. He should have told you. He should have seen you were taught. But he was afraid."*

Afraid? She felt a cold chill of fear herself. She didn't blame him for being afraid! Magic? What had she to do with magic? What would she *want* with magic?

As if the little creatures had read the thoughts in her mind, the second answered her. *"Magic is a power like any other, Mari. Master it, and it becomes a tool in your hand, and when you have tools, you also have weapons."* The water-girl looked about furtively, as if making sure *she* was not going to be overheard, and lowered her voice further. *"Listen and remember. This is important. Because you have this gift of magic, even though you are untaught, you are valuable to us of the Water. And that alone gives you power. Remember. It is power to bargain. There will come a time, soon, when you are presented with something that appears to be no choice. But you can bargain within that. So think well on that day, demand your choice, and make your bargain."*

She shook her head. "I haven't the least notion of what you're talking about," she said, bewildered. "Bargain? What would I bargain over?" The only bargain she could think likely was in the market at Clogwyn.

"It makes no sense now, but it will then. Trust us, and remember!" said the first, and the two of them suddenly dove down into the water and were gone.

She filled her pails and trudged back through the calf-high grass, beginning to regret that she'd accepted these Tylwyth Teg-things after all. At least when she'd thought they were bits of fever-dream, that was the *only* part of her life that didn't make any sense.

Now . . . there didn't seem to be much of her life that did, any more.

4

NAN held to her temper with both hands, and refrained from strangling that young ape Clive Waterleed. Clive, in his turn, glanced slyly up at her from beneath a fat comma of blond hair.

"What did I tell you, young sir?" she asked, severely.

"You told me not to put the ends of Jenny's braids in the ink again," he said. "And I didn't."

Of course he hadn't. "You put the ends of Jenny's braids in the paint," she pointed out.

"You didn't tell me not to do *that!*" he said, with an air of triumph.

Indeed he had. And indeed, she had not, specifically, told him not to put the child's hair in paint. The *ayah* was even now scrubbing the blue out of one braid, and the red out of the other, while Jenny cried because her favorite dress was spoiled.

Nan wanted to pick him up and shake him until his

teeth rattled. She didn't remember *any* of the children she'd been in the school with who'd been as full of the devil as Clive was. Nor did she remember any of them being so persistently *nasty* to one particular child.

She gritted her teeth and grabbed both his shoulders. "Why do you torment Jenny?" she asked, punctuating each word with a single hard shake—not enough to hurt him but enough to emphasize that she was very, very angry.

She had shaken the hair out of his eyes, and he stared into her angry face, blue eyes blank and guileless. "*I* don't know!" he said, as if he was shocked that she would say such a thing.

She took a deep breath, and forced herself to be calm. "You listen very carefully to me, Clive. You are not to touch Jenny. You are not to make her cry. You are not to touch her things. You are not to say things to her that upset her. You are not to spoil her lessons. You are not to pretend that she does not exist. You are to be as polite to her as you would be to Memsa'b at all times. Do you understand?"

She could practically *see* his mind working, trying to figure out a way around her prohibitions. "But what if—" he began.

"You will be as polite to her as you would be to Memsa'b," Nan reiterated, giving him another little shake. "If you make Jenny unhappy again..." she thought furiously. "I will not only tell Memsa'b and Sahib that you are to get *no* treats at all, no matter how many school prizes you win or how many treats the others get—I will tell Neville that for every time Jenny cries, *he* will be allowed to steal something from you. And *keep* it."

Finally she had gotten through to him. His eyes widened with shock. Everyone knew the raven's propensity to take shiny things, things children valued, like marbles and toy soldiers, and try to cache them in his hoard in Nan's room. Nan always made him give them back, because the children knew better than to try and dare that razor-edge beak to get their possessions back themselves.

But if Neville was going to be *allowed* to keep what he stole from Clive . . . there would be no holding the raven back. And the raven was faster than a mongoose and as clever as a monkey when it came to getting hold of what he wanted.

After all, what Neville couldn't open—Grey could. There wasn't a treasure-box made that could protect against bird-theft if both of them went to work.

But as Clive trudged out to join the rest of his schoolmates in their arithmetic class, Nan shook her head. This wasn't the answer. What was wrong with the little wretch? Why couldn't she get through to him except by use of dreadful threat and force?

And why, oh why, did he seem to spend every waking moment trying to figure out a way around the letter of the law that she had laid down to him?

She was just grateful that it was nearly tea-time. At least when he was eating, he wasn't tormenting Jenny. Though he wasn't going to be happy about tea-time; she had left orders that he was to get nothing sweet, no jam, no cakes. He wouldn't starve, not by any stretch of the imagination, but he wasn't going to get a treat either.

As she went in to her own tea with the adults, Memsa'b divined what she was thinking by her expression, and poured a cup for her immediately. Nan collapsed inelegantly in her chair, and took her cup with both hands.

"Clive?" Memsa'b said sympathetically.

Nan nodded, wearily. "I want to strangle him," she said.

"I can't say as I blame you," Memsa'b replied dryly. "I have some suspicions about him. I believe he is powerfully empathic—"

Nan didn't usually interrupt Memsa'b, but she did this time. "Surely you are jesting!" she exclaimed incredulously. "He spends every waking minute trying to torture the most sensitive child in the school!"

But Memsa'b nodded. "That is why I think he is powerfully empathic. He's an orphan; when he was barely old enough to toddle, his mother and father died when a rabid dog attacked them."

Nan covered her mouth in horror. "No—"

Again Memsa'b nodded. "They didn't die of the wounds, they died of the disease. Clive was kept away from them of course, but was still in the same house, which for an empath is close enough. Their suffering was terrible, and I believe that out of self-defense he tried to shut himself off. But being an empath, he instinctively understands that he *should* be feeling things, and now he can't unless they are very strong. So he has gone straight to the most sensitive child here and torments her so at least he can feel *something*." She tapped her index finger on the side of her cup as she thought. "It's possible because he shut himself off, he is now unable to relate to others except as objects of passing interest. From being empathic, he has become the opposite."

Nan frowned. "That sounds . . . dangerous."

"It isn't yet. But it could be. I believe Sahib and I will take over his education for a while. What did you do about his latest prank?"

Nan described the rather one-sided conversation

she'd had with the child, while Memsa'b listened intently. Then she sighed. "Well, you haven't made things worse, but now he is not only going to devote himself to finding ways around what you told him, but to making it impossible for you to catch him. He'll probably recruit a crony to help." Her lips twitched a little in a smile. "You know that there are at least three of them who take great pleasure in outwitting you."

Nan groaned. "Only too well. There are days when I want to take some of those boys and dump them out on the street and let them live the life I used to, just so they will appreciate the one they have." She grimaced. "Except that they would probably like it."

Memsa'b just sipped her tea. Nan gloomily reflected that she wasn't much good at this teaching business. How did Memsa'b and the others manage?

Her only comfort was that Sarah looked just as forlorn as she felt, when her friend came in. "Am I cursed with the thickest heads in the school?" she demanded, as she took her seat and reached for the cup Nan poured and handed to her.

"No," Memsa'b replied, her lips twitching again. "The cleverest."

Sarah stared at her. "But—we have gone over the same lessons every day for the past week and they *still* haven't mastered it!"

"Because, my love, you are too soft with them. Why should they have to tax their little minds with anything new if they can play at stupidity and convince you to go over what they already know?" Memsa'b asked.

Sarah's jaw dropped. She closed it with an expression of dismay. "I—I must be the worst teacher in the school!" she said bitterly.

"No," Nan contradicted her. "I am."

Memsa'b sighed. "Neither of you are very good," she said reluctantly. "I am very sorry to say this, but . . . if you were not who you are, I should ask you to pack your bags and find another position elsewhere."

Nan reached recklessly for the jam and spread it thickly on her toast, eating it glumly. "I'd have to agree with you," she said between bites. "Curse it all. I'm going on the stage."

Memsa'b only raised an eyebrow. They both knew it was a hollow threat. Although Nan would probably enjoy the stage very much, she was no beauty, and would probably not get very far—which would make it a far from pleasant career.

Not to mention that being on the stage would make it very difficult to pursue occult studies.

"I thought we had everything planned out so well," Sarah lamented. "We'd be teachers here, we'd settle down to a quiet life like you—"

"And when have you—or I, for that matter—had a quiet life?" Memsa'b demanded. "Did you think that life was going to go on in the same way forever? Did you really want it to?"

Nan made a face. "Memsa'b, Sarah and I saved all of England before we were out of leading strings, practically," she pointed out. "It's rather difficult to—"

This time it was Memsa'b who interrupted her. "Sahib and I have spent the better parts of our lives together saving England, or parts of it at least, over and over again. You can't rest on your laurels when you have the sort of gifts that we have."

Nan grimaced. "When you put it in those terms . . ." She stared glumly down into her tea. "But that isn't all the time. It isn't even most of the time. What are we to do with ourselves otherwise?"

"Well, you tried teaching. What else is there?" Memsa'b replied patiently.

"Nursing?" Nan and Sarah looked at each other and shook their heads. They'd already had a taste of that in Africa and it hadn't suited them. "Being a nanny or a governess . . . well I don't imagine that would go any better than teaching. What else is there?"

"What else do you want there to be?" Memsa'b countered. "Don't accept the walls that other people want to place you behind. In the meantime . . . Nan, Jenny *is* too soft and cry-babyish. Why don't you take her on? Help her grow a little more backbone. Sarah, help ayah Gulzar with the babies. They're too young to wrap you around their fingers, and Gulzar could use the help."

Nan and Sarah exchanged another pained look. This was make-work, and both of them knew it. But what else was there to do? Well, other than figure out just what they *might* be able to do with themselves . . .

Don't accept the walls that other people want to place you behind? Nan thought, as she took herself off to find Jenny. *That's all very well, but that means having to keep them from doing it in the first place, doesn't it?* And really, how many options did she have? She had no talent at writing or art. Clearly she had no talent for teaching. Nursing made her ill. She wasn't any kind of a scholar. Working in an office or a factory or a shop would give her even less freedom than the stage for doing what she really felt she *must* do, the sort of occult work that Memsa'b and Sahib did. And she couldn't, she wouldn't, sit idle.

"*Bother,*" she said aloud, crossly. Why did things have to be so complicated? It had all seemed so simple when they were children! They had it all planned; everything would be safe, they would know what to expect, and everything would go on much as it always had, except that instead of being the students, they would be the teachers. There would be no surprises.

Wasn't that how things were supposed to go?

"So what *do* we do with ourselves?" Sarah asked that night, as both of them were brushing their hair before bed. She sighed. "Memsa'b suggested we should work with the women's suffrage movement...."

Nan frowned. "I think that would be a very bad idea. You know what my temper is like. The first policeman who tries to bully or hurt someone is very likely to discover five inches of umbrella point in his belly or find his head broken by the shaft." She gazed fondly at her new acquisition, funded—with some trepidation—by Sahib. It was an umbrella made to the same specifications as their patroness's in Egypt. It had a backbone of stout steel as strong as a crowbar, the tip was sharp enough to pierce flesh, and the handle housed a small kit containing many useful objects.

"Surely you wouldn't . . ." Sarah trailed off as Neville gave a derisive *quork,* and Grey snickered.

"See? Even they know I would." Nan sighed. "You can take the girl out of Whitechapel, but you can't take Whitechapel out of the girl."

"I wouldn't say that," Sarah said weakly.

"You don't have to; I already did." Nan brushed her hair the last of the mandated one hundred strokes. "And there's another thing. You know we'll be thrown in jail. Have you any notion how haunted every jail in London is?"

Sarah paled. "You're right."

"And I can just see myself telling our jailor, 'Please sir,

let my friend out. She has thirty ghosts trying to talk to her; half are insane, and the other half are murderous.' I'm sure that would do us and the cause a world of good." She began braiding her hair deftly. "Neither of us are any good at public speaking, and we don't have secretarial skills, so there we are again. The most use we could be is as slogan shouters. Not very useful. Curse it all, I want to be *useful,* not ornamental or idle."

"I wonder ..." Sarah began, then shook her head. "No, that probably wouldn't work."

"What?" Nan asked, a little more sharply than she had intended. "Come out with it! You never know unless you bring it out in the open."

"Well ... I wonder if Lord Alderscroft could find something for us to do. He certainly hinted at it." Sarah sounded hesitant, and Nan wasn't entirely certain this was a viable idea either.

"Doing what?" she asked.

"Looking into things, I suppose," Sarah replied vaguely. "I'm not sure how we would do that, though."

"Hmm. Looking into things ... like Sherlock Holmes?" Nan hazarded. "Only looking for magic and the occult?"

"I think that was more or less what he was hinting at." Sarah toyed with the end of her braid. "I should think we'd need some skills or something, to blend in, though."

Nan sucked on her lower lip, thoughtfully. "Maybe not as much as you think. After all, it's unlikely he'd ask us to investigate ... oh ... a haunted office. We wouldn't need to be secretaries. We can easily fit in with Memsa'b's class, we could pass as governesses for a little while, I think I can probably get back my street ways—though it would probably be safer to disguise myself as a young man—and neither of us are afraid of working with our hands, so we could slip in below-stairs among servants at need. . . ."

Sarah clasped both her hands on her knees and looked intrigued. "When you put it that way—"

"About the only thing we can't pass as is country folk. But if it is possible to be . . . oh . . . romantical lady poets or something, we could probably tramp about the countryside with impunity long enough to find out what Lord A wants found out." Nan found herself warming to this idea the more she talked about it.

"But do you think he'd have enough work for us?" Sarah asked, doubtfully.

"There's only one way to find out," Nan countered, and grinned when Neville quorked and flapped his wings.

"Ask! Ask!" the raven said, with great enthusiasm.

"There, you see?" Nan spread her hands wide. "Even the birds like it."

Mari went to bed anxious. Tomorrow would be her birthday, and not just any birthday, but her eighteenth. As if that wasn't enough, she had learned from experience that as her birthday went, so the rest of the year seemed to go. The year it had stormed on her birthday was the year there were so many storms that Daffyd Prothero had been almost the only fisherman to reliably bring in catches. That year had been good from a financial point of view, and that had been the year that many silver pennies went into the jar under the hearthstone, but it had been a nerve-wracking one for Mari, and more somberly, they'd attended three funerals of drowned fishermen that year. There had also been several wrecks, and bodies had even washed up in front of the cottage.

On the other hand, the year that the day had not only been bright and clear but as warm as summer had been an unseasonably mild one, with just enough gentle rain for the garden.

She had another reason to be uneasy as she went to bed. As the day had neared, her father had been acting strangely. She caught him staring at her with an odd, apprehensive expression on his face, many times. But whenever she tried to ask him anything that wasn't a commonplace, he swiftly changed the subject. Maddening.

And somewhat alarming.

And there was the third thing. What would the coming year be like, if the day was marked by one or more of the Tylwyth Teg folk turning up? She shuddered to think.

When she rose at dawn, at least one fear was assuaged. The morning was bright and clear, with no signs of storm. Daffyd had somehow managed to smuggle a posy of violets into the house and it was sitting in a teacup at her place at table when she came down from the loft to make breakfast. He managed to do this every year, and every year it made her smile. Her presents were laid out there too; extravagant ones that made her eyes go round—a tortoise-shell brush and comb and a matching hand-mirror so she wouldn't have to use a bit of broken mirror propped against the wall. Two tortoise-shell hair-combs to put her hair up like a lady. And a string of beautiful blue glass beads, not the round cast ones, but the polished, faceted beads that sparkled like gemstones in the light.

Her da was nowhere to be seen—but she knew where he was. On her birthday, *he* did the work of bringing the water from the stream, and a moment after she picked up the lovely beads to admire them, she heard his boot knock at the door to push it open.

"Oh *Da!*" she exclaimed, as he put the pails down beside the door. "This is too much! I don't deserve all this!"

"Eh, well," he replied awkwardly. "You're a lady now, and a lady deserves some pretty fripperies that are all hers, and not passed down to her . . ." Then he sat down heavily, as if he had a tremendous weight on his shoulders. "And . . . I have something to be telling you, my girl. I don't want to, but I'm bound to. 'Tis about the Prothero luck, and how we come to it, and and what we must do to keep it."

She sat down, beads forgotten, though she clutched her hand around them. "I don't understand what you mean, Da," she said, slowly. Was *this* what the little Tylwyth Teg had been hinting at?

"You know how you used to see things, when you were small?" he asked, slowly and carefully, as if each word cost him dearly. "Creatures, I'd call them. Maybe . . . small people that came to play with you?"

Shocked, she took a deep breath. "I still see them, Da. I never stopped. And they talk to me and show me things. Like where to find things, like that lump of ambergris. I still see the Ellyllon — I saw three just the other day. One of them was the one that tripped up the constable. I just didn't tell you, because you were so upset when I spoke of them."

He passed his hand over his face.

"Da?" she said, hesitantly. "What's it mean, Da?"

"It means they never lost interest in you," he said, and shook his head. "More than that, I dun know." He furrowed his brow. "I have to begin at th' beginning. It was back, far back, afore Owen Glendower, maybe all the way back to Arthur and the Merlin and Gwenhwyfar. My da didn't know how far back, nor did his. But this is the way of it. There's Tylwyth Teg, and then there's Tylwyth Teg. There's all manner of the Verry Volk. What you're seein', you're seein' the People of the Water. Don't matter what kind, fresh, salt, still or running. Now, back in the days before even Arthur, Math ap Mathonwy was the brother of Don, and he was King in Gwynedd. That's here, that's the name of the old kingdom. When he needed a hand-maiden, his magician Gwydion advised him to seek out his niece, Arianrhod. Now she was supposed to be a virgin, you see, Math needed that power in bein' virgin because he was almost as much magician as Gwydion. When she arrived at the great hall, she stepped up to the throne and Math asked, 'Are you a maiden?' Not wanting to be shamed before the court, she replied that she was. Then Math took out his magic wand, bent it and said, 'Step over this.' As she did so she gave birth to two boys, right there on the spot. And that was Gwydion's doing, because he wanted her. In her shock and shame she fled the Castle of Math and has no more to do with this tale.

"One of the boys was taken up immediately by Gwydion and he became the hero of another legend. The one that was left was beautiful like no other child that's ever been seen, like the sun and the moon together, and there wasn't a woman that didn't dote on him as a boy, and lust for him as a man. On the day of his naming he was taken down to the sea. Upon seeing the ocean for the first time he leapt out of his nurse's arms and jumped into the sea. He became a god and Math named him 'Dylan'—that means 'wave.' Dylan Eil Ton was the first and father of the shape-shifters of the sea, the Selch. And he sired children on many women, and some of those women and children chose to live in the sea with him, in halls and villages they built beneath the waves. You know of the Selch, aye? The seal-folk?"

She nodded, because of course, those were some of the tales that old woman had told the children in her care.

"Well . . . they're real. And it happened that back in the day, when Arthur was just a boy, maybe, there was a fisherman who found a seal caught in his net. And since he had some of the magic in him, and could see it was something special, instead of killing it, he spoke to it kind-like, and said 'Now don't you move, for you'll tear my net. I'll free you and you can be about your business.' And so he did, and instead of swimming off, that seal followed him, and drove fish into his net so he had a catch the like of which he'd never seen. And when he beached his coracle, it came ashore, and before he could turn around, a man stood where the seal had been. 'You've done me a kindness unasked,' said the man. 'So I'll offer you a bargain.' This was the bargain. It seems that the blood of the Selch was growing thin and un-thrifty, and they were getting fewer. So they said to the Prothero of that time, 'You take one of our girls to wife. She'll have two children, one for you and one for us, and then she'll come back to us. In return, your fishing will never fail, and your boat will never founder, and you'll never drown. And that will be the bargain that you'll make for all your kin from now until when the sun fails. A Selch bride or a Selch groom, two children, and your nets will always be full of fish.' "

Mari listened to him wide-eyed, mouth agape. It sounded mad. But she had *seen* the Tylwyth Teg for her-self. She'd seen them trick the constable. And it certainly explained why her father felt confident on the water in any weather, how he never failed to come home with a catch and—

"Blessed saints!" Her hand went to her mouth. "My mother—"

He nodded, then gestured towards the sea. "Out there somewhere. And your brother with her. Now you know why we live away from the village and within the sound of the sea. Trust me, with Selch blood in you, away from the sea you'd run mad with longing. As it happened, when the time came for your mother to leave me, we both knew that times were different. A man's wife and one of his children missing—that'd be noticed. And people would talk about how my da's wife run off with a gypsy, and how *his* wife went out fishing and drowned ... in the old days we could keep ourselves to ourselves and never mind. But can't do that now, not with the village so near. So she went out kelping where the village could see, and your brother Ronan with her, and her folk made a great rogue wave to come up to shore, and away they swam."

"Constable Ewynnog doesn't like that story," Mari said, meditatively.

Daffyd shrugged. "Like enough there'd have been a constable here to see what was what if your ma had just gone off and no good explanation for it." He sighed. "But here's the long and the short of it. A bargain's a bargain, and you and I have had eighteen years of Prothero's Luck and were bound into the pledge as sure as in a net. You're eighteen, and the time has come for you."

For a moment she couldn't fathom what he meant. And then it came clear in a flash, and she brought up her head sharply. "You mean—*I* have to take some ... Tylwyth Teg man I don't even *know* to husband? It was all well and good for you, da, you only had the fathering! I'll be the one doing *work* with two babes, and for some stranger?"

Her father flushed. "Mari ... it's a magic made in the long-ago, and I don't know what will happen if—"

There was a snicker, and both their heads whipped around. It was the wicked-eyed seaweed-girl sitting on the water barrel. "*I can tell you that you won't like it. If you break the bargain, then you'd best find yourself a place far, far, far away from the sea, and then find a magician stronger than the sea. The magic grows stronger with each mating, and now it will tear you apart if you break it. If you run, the sea will call you, and you'll either run mad, or you'll answer it and go to it and never come out no more.*"

She tittered again, leapt up off the barrel, and vanished.

Mari felt her whole body go cold with fear.

Her father gulped audibly. "Well," he said, into the deathly silence. "There it is. You keep the bargain or . . ."

She looked up at him, fear turning to fury. "Or else?" she said, angrily. "That simple? Oh—oh I *hate* magic!"

And she burst into tears.

At first, her father was guilty and tried to comfort her. But then, as she alternately wailed and railed, he grew impatient, then angry.

And finally he shouted. "And just what did you think you would be doing with your life, you young limb? How is this different than if I'd said, 'Mari, I've found you a husband, you'll have him'?" His tone turned mocking. "Did you think you'd meet a prince riding on the sand and be whisked off to some castle? Or maybe you thought one day your Tylwyth Teg would show you a heap of gold and you could live like a duchess? Well, this is the wide, real world, my girl, and most of us do things we'd rather not for longer than we want, and you might as well get used to it!"

Such blatant unfairness shut off her tears and made her splutter. "Oh!" was all she could manage. *"Oh!"* because what she wanted to say was something so vile she wouldn't ever say it to her own father, however much she *felt* it right now.

Instead, before he could stop her, she shoved the table right into him, pinning him in his chair. "I know that no *good* father would barter away his only child like— like—beads from a peddler!" And she threw the beads still in her hand at his face, and ran out the door.

But not seawards. Oh no. Right now, the sea was the last place she wanted to be. And not to the village; what comfort was there for her in the village? No, she ran across the sheep-meadow, across the road, and into the hills. She thought she heard her father calling her name, but she shut her ears to it, and ran and ran and ran until she ran out of breath, and fell sobbing to the turf.

She heard the bubbling of water as she wept into the moss. And she heard a soft little voice nearby.

Please don't cry.

With difficulty, she raised her head. It was another of the Tylwyth Teg, one of the little water-girls dressed only in her hair. "And why shouldn't I?" she asked bitterly. "And why should you care?"

The little thing looked distressed. *Don't you remember what we told you? Didn't you hear what your father said? Why do you think the Selch wanted the first of the Protheros?*

It was hard to think through the fog of emotion, but think she did. Had her father said something about . . . that first man having power?

"The—magic?" she said, hesitantly.

The tiny thing nodded. *It's strong in you, Mari. Strong, strong, strong. You can't escape the net, but you can make conditions. Bargain, Mari, bargain. Don't be tame, like a sheep. Be strong, like a master!* The little thing looked about her quickly. *I have said all that I dare. Remember! Remember!*

And with that, she flipped over and vanished beneath the water of the stream.

5

WHEN Mari returned to the cottage, her father was gone. The beads he had bought her were laid on the table, and the kitchen had been straightened. She clenched her jaw. If he thought that was going to mollify her. . . .

She was thinking hard about what she had learned as she set things to rights. It was hard to think, she was so very angry, but doing things that required a good bit of main strength helped her wear some of that temper away. Although she was minded to give herself a holiday, she did the usual chores—all except for the cooking. He could just make do with cold rabbit from last night. The words of that helpful Tylwyth Teg kept going around in her head. *Bargain. Well, and what can I bargain with? And what would I bargain for?* She couldn't bargain away the business of being handed off; not without her da paying a price she really didn't want him to pay—no matter how angry she was with him. So where, in this trap, was there something that would give her some sort of relief and freedom? And what could she offer to get it?

All the stories she knew that involved bargains with the folk cautioned that you had to be very careful . . . and why would they bargain with her, anyway, when they already had a bargain and a pledge?

Unless . . .

The water-creature had implied that she was different from all those other Prothero girls. Very different. *Well, and I am speaking up for myself, and not being a silly ewe-lamb about this!* But that couldn't be all of it. There'd been that talk of magic, as if she herself had it.

Wait . . . she didn't actually know that much about her family, come to think of it.

She sat herself down with a cup of tea as a treat and pondered that. There might not have been that many Prothero *girls,* come to think of it, since the Prothero name had come down from the old times intact. Which meant that most, maybe all, of these bargains had involved a Prothero lad and a Selch lass, rather than the other way around. *I rather doubt there's many men in the world that would balk at taking a random girl into his bed provided she's comely enough.* She had no illusions on that score about her father—who *had* been known to tumble the odd girl in a haystack during harvest or the occasional Traveler wench that seemed willing. She had always assumed that his reticence in talking about her mother was due to grief but now . . . now she began to wonder if it was because he simply didn't know that much about her, hadn't really cared that much about her, and really didn't miss her. It wasn't as if she was actually dead, after all. She'd simply paired up with him, done her duty, and off she was back to her own people. So he wouldn't even really have guilt over her loss. Presumably, she was happier where she was now than she had been with him.

I wonder why she took my brother and not me?

It certainly would have been easier all the way around if she had.

Maybe he was more Selch than me? Or maybe she'd been told to bring the boy with her.

Or maybe—maybe this magic that had been hinted at made her dangerous to take to the sea.

She shook her head. No point in speculating; she was wasting her time doing that when what she needed was to figure out what the Tylwyth Teg had meant.

It was more than just that she had magic in her. That trait was possibly very desirable to the Selch, but hardly of any use to *her* if all it meant was that she could see the Tylwyth Teg.

Ah, but if she could learn to use it, that might well be a different story altogether.

How did you go about learning the magic, anyway? There were no Druids anymore, nor Bards, who also were supposed to know the ways of magic. She couldn't exactly march up to some university, even if she could *get* to one, and demand to be educated in it.

The more she thought about it, though, she realized it would be very, very useful if she had the knowledge of it. Just seeing what the Tylwyth Teg had done convinced her of that. *I could use it to make that cursed constable leave us be, for one,* she thought sourly. She didn't entertain any notion of jewels and princes and castles; even in the tales that sort of thinking generally bought you more trouble than it was worth. But little things, like making Constable Ewynnog take his bothering self elsewhere, or calming the storms so that the Clogwyn fisherman came home safe. . . . now that would be magic worth having.

Bargain, bargain, bargain. The Tylwyth Teg, both the good one and the naughty one, had implied the Selch were interested in her magic. And obviously they had some sort of magic of their own, or else how could they become seals and all? Could the Selch have teachers of such things?

It seemed possible. So . . . could she bargain for such a teacher? How would they take to that?

She drummed her fingers on the table-top, contemplating that notion for a good long while. Was that what the good Tylwyth Teg had meant for her to do? Possibly, but that was not all that it was; she felt that deep in her bones. There was another bargain she could make, or at least, another that the Tylwyth Teg had seen.

Then something new occurred to her. The vow was that she was bound to take a Selch to husband, but unless her father misremembered, it wasn't that *the Selch* could force *their* choice of man on her . . . it was she had to take the Selch husband. But the choice of who that would be. . . .

Now that was an interesting thought.

Hmm. The old tales all say that if a man mistreats his Selch-wife, her bond is free and she can go back to the sea. Does something like that work for us, I wonder? Not that her father was the sort to mistreat any woman. And the prospect of irritating an unknown man until he raised his hand to her did not appeal.

But this might mean she could make them give her the choice of husbands, especially if they wanted the magic in her blood that much . . .

I see it now, aye. I do believe I can make them give me the choice.

She actually got a little thrill out of that notion. She'd never had the illusion that she was a great beauty; certainly the lads of Clogwyn didn't go trailing about after her the way they did after Braith. Somewhere, vaguely in the back of her mind, she had always supposed that she would marry some fisher lad or other, probably as much because he had his eye on the Prothero cottage as because he wanted her, but as long as he was a good lad and gave her da help on the water, that would have been all right. But to *force* the Selch to send her their comeliest lads, and to have them vying with each other, each courting her harder than the last, well . . . that would give any girl a bit of a thrill. And it would ensure she'd get herself a temporary husband who would be pleasing and wouldn't try to force himself on her.

Even as those thoughts crossed her mind, movement at the beach caught her eye; she turned to look out the window and she saw her da laboring up the shore with a burden, and it didn't look like fish.

As he neared, she saw that it was his nets, all of them. *Now why would he bring them up here, wet, instead of spreading them to dry?*

Soon enough she had the answer to that question, as he bumped the door open. His face was weary, and for the first time, ever, she saw fear in his eyes. When he cast the nets down on the floor, she saw that every one of them had been cut up.

"Not a fish," he said, heavily. "Not so much as a minnow. And every net in ribbons. They know. And they're punishing us, just as they threatened. They have the whip-hand, Mari. They can ruin us without thinking twice about it."

He didn't have to say anything more. They had that money put by under the stone, of course, but when that was gone, they'd starve. Fishing was all Daffyd Prothero knew. Could they even go shellfishing in the tidal pools? Would they even dare, knowing they could be slashed by something they couldn't see? And what about winter? You couldn't wade in the freezing winter water without losing your feet.

Now she was in a rage all over again, but not at her father, but at the Selch. Cruel, nasty things they must be, to start on this before she'd even had time to get used to the idea!

Well, two can play the nasty game, she thought angrily. Before her father could say another word, she pushed past him and out the door, and if she hadn't been stepping on sand, for certain her footsteps would have been less "steps" and more "stomps" as she made her way down to the sea.

She had no idea how to make herself known, magically, so she settled for working up her anger into a mighty storm inside her. She waded ankle-deep into the surf, ignoring the chill that bit into her feet, and flung furious words out over the water.

"Oh, so you want me so badly that you'll cut up my da's nets and threaten to starve us, will you?" she shouted. "And what if I say I'll be selling myself in the streets of Cardiff before I let you force me to do anything that's not to my liking, eh? What then? What'll that be doing to my magic that you want so badly?"

She really had not expected an answer, but to her shock, before the last echo of her voice ebbed, a great grey bulk heaved itself up out of the surf in front of her.

She took a few alarmed steps back, as the bulk resolved itself into an enormous bull-seal, which snorted and bellowed at her. For a moment she felt a chill of fear, but her anger took it away again.

"Oh, so you don't like that, do you?" she spat, standing her ground. "Well, too bad for you! Tisn't Merlin's world no more; I'll make it known to you! I can be taking Da to Cardiff. I can be getting him a job in the shipyard, aye, I can!" A memory flitted through her mind about the Tylwyth Teg being unable to come near iron or blessed things. "I can be getting him a job on a great iron ship, and then you can froth and fume all you like and you'll not be able to touch him! I can be making myself Roman and taking myself to a convent, that I can! Then where will you be? Hmm?"

The bull-seal bellowed again, heaved itself taller, and then it wasn't a seal there in the surf, but a gray-haired, gray-bearded man standing up with a sealskin cloak about his shoulders. There was an angry fire in his eyes and a sour twist to his mouth. "Oh, you will do that then, will you, Mari Prothero? You think that will be the saving of you?"

"I'd like to see you be arguing with God over who's to have me, Selch," she challenged him. "If you want me, if you want the magic in my blood, 'twill be on *my* terms, and you'll be bargaining with *me* and not my da."

The Selch went cold as the sea in winter and as still as a glassy calm. There was still anger in him, but he had leashed it and brought it to heel. "Someone's been talking out of turn," he mumbled.

So the Tylwyth Teg had been right!

"What, I call it a friendly word," she countered, hands on her hips, and chin stuck out belligerently. "And so it is. For once, you won't be the one making all the rules, Selch. If you want me, you'll be bargaining with me."

"And for what?" the Selch scoffed, pulling himself up and staring her down. "Treasures? Ah, you mortal wenches, so greedy for gold and gauds! This isn't Merlin's day, as you said yourself, and the Selch can't be pulling great treasures out of the sea just on your say-so."

"Not treasures. Choices," she replied firmly. "This isn't the day of Merlin, that's true as true, and a maid doesn't go meekly to whatever man she's thrown to."

His eyes widened with surprise, then narrowed with speculation. "I'm thinking your father might have something to say about this."

"I'm thinking Daffyd Prothero has *nothing* to say about this, so long as the letter of the bond is kept. This is between me and thee. You'll be giving me two things, Selch. You'll be giving me a teacher for this magic, and you'll be sending a pod of your young men to proper *court* me." She tossed her head, and looked him in the eye. "I'm not a slave for your taking. On land, I have a choice of who I'll go with and who I won't, and I'll be having that self-same right on the here and now. I won't be bred like a sheep. I'll be proper courted and won. Or it's Cardiff and the iron ship and the convent, and an end to your nonsense. Forever. The bond and the bargain will end with me."

His face turned red, he shouted at her, he called her all manner of names, the half of which she didn't even understand, but she saw the fear in his eyes when she said the words "an end to your nonsense," and she stood her ground.

He was stubborn, but she was more stubborn than he, and she sensed that he had a great deal more to lose than she did. *Why,* she didn't know, but she was sure that he did.

Finally, as the sun set behind him, wreathing him in fire that made her squint, he gave in. Not with a good grace, but he did.

"Pah!" He spat in the water. "Mortal troublemaking

cow that you are! I should send for the sharks to cut you down where you stand! My grandsire ordered your mother to take the boy and not you, and he must have been a prophet, to see what sort of a virago you'd become! I've more than half a mind to make you shark-food."

"So do so, and be done with it," she countered, and with that, she knew she had won. His words confirmed it.

"Your teacher you will have, and I wish you joy of him," he snarled. "And your courting you will have, nor will I stint you, for Great Llyr knows why but you've plenty of our young bulls already bellowing and fighting over you."

Oh, so?

"But don't flatter yourself, nor think it's for your face," he added nastily. "'Tis the magic, as you said. And here will be *my* demand in this bargain—the better to be done with you, you'll be birthing twins, not singletons, and we'll be having ours once we've got a wetnurse. And they'll be boys, so there will be no more of this again! A man will not have this missish folderol about *choices* and *courting.* A man will take a comely wench to his bed and no foolishness. My father was a fool twice over for letting Afanyn choose what babies she'd bear." He snorted. "Sons it will be for the Protheros from this day on."

"Done," she said instantly, though the idea that he could somehow *make* her have twins, or boys, was laughable.

"Done!" he snarled, and then he was a seal again, and huffing and heaving himself back into the surf, and the deep water, and he vanished beneath the waves at the same time as the last of the sun.

🐚

Arguing with the Selch-chief had worn out her temper, so it was with a fairer face she talked with her da over the net-mending, explaining to him what the Tylwyth Teg had told her and how she had bartered.

He brooded over that a bit. "Your mother would tell me tales," he said slowly. "Not the old stories, but just what life was like with her people. She was fair sick for the sea, though we live right at the edge of it, and sicker for her own kin. I did my best to make her comfortable, not so lonely, until her part of the bargain was done. She had to wait until your brother was old enough to swim, you see. Seems seal-pups don't swim till they're at eight weeks old. For one born to human shape, it's twice that." He sighed. "She'd planned to slip her shape and birth him as a seal, but she got caught a little early, and once the birthing started, it was too late to shift. We were going to say she'd miscarried, and then when the pup was old enough, she'd have a row with me and storm off in public and I was to say she'd gone back to her people."

"Which would have been true," Mari pointed out, her head bent over the net.

"Aye . . . aye. I thought it was a daft plan. No dafter than having the Chief call a wave to take her and your brother, though." She looked up, and he shook his head, dolefully. "But I was sayin'—she told me tales. Seems usually they're short of boys, so the Prothero bargain has always made sons, but when the time came for my bargain, they were short of girls. Your mother told me that the Chief-that-was told her that 'the girl wouldn't do,' after you were born, and ordered her to take the clan the boy after all. So she did, and that's why you were left instead of your brother."

She thought that over, her hands moving swiftly with cord and shuttle among the cut strands. "Was the Tylwyth Teg right, I wonder? Is it that I have truly strong magic in me, and they wouldn't trust that among them?"

"Your mother never said and I never asked," he replied. "It didn't seem my place. What I know is this: they have a clan-hall of the old sort, everyone under one roof, on an island that no one can find. She said it wasn't really 'in the world,' whatever that means. Probably like the fae mounds the Tylwyth Teg live in—you can dig into the mound all you like and you'll never find the way into their halls unless they take you."

She pursed her lips, and nodded. And wished she was some great scholar who knew the ancient ways. All she knew were scraps of tales and bits of song and the stories the old woman had told her.

"The Chief rules all the clan. In the old days, she said, before Christians came, there was a deal of Selch-maids coming ashore and taking mortal lovers for the siring of children, but something about the Christians put a stop to that. I don't begin to understand it." He bound off the tail of his cord and rewound his shuttle. "That was why the bargain was made with the Protheros in the first place."

"But what about all the tales from land-side?" she asked. "About the fishermen catching Selch-maids and making wives of them? About Selch-lads coming to women who called for them?" She had remembered that story when she'd stormed down to the sea, how you could call a Selch to you by shedding seven tears into the ocean.

"I suppose that calling a Selch to be your lover counters being Christian?" he hazarded. "And as for the fishermen catching Selch-maids, in all the tales I ever heard, I never once heard of them as churchly sorts."

Well that made sense. Fishermen, especially ones like

her da, who worked alone, were generally either extremely devout Christians or a good bit pagan in their
relationship with the sea. The devout Christians would
obviously *not* be looking for Selch; if they ran across a
seal in their nets, well, they might be kind enough to set
it free, but most likely would kill it, and if being around
a Christian negated the magic that let the captured one
shift from seal to human, well . . . those fishermen would
never know the truth. The others would not be the least
bit surprised to find the seal turning to a girl, and if she
was pretty enough, would quite readily steal her sealskin
to keep her with them.

They worked on in silence for a while. And while they
worked, she felt something sour working its way to the
surface of her mind, making her stomach churn and putting a cold lump in it at the same time.

Because she had not forgotten her father's deception
in all this. And she loved him, but he had lied to her. She,
being herself, just couldn't leave that sitting.

But this time, no more tantrum, no raging. Just have it
out with him.

"Why did you lie to me?" she asked, bitterly. "All
these years . . . knowing what was going to happen. Why
did you lie to me?"

"I . . ." he began, then stopped.

"You had better not tell me you thought it was for my
own good," she snapped.

He sighed. "Well, how was I to explain it to a child?"
he countered. "I admit it, I was a coward. I didn't want to
talk about it. It's not the sort of thing a man feels comfortable about talking to a girl-child."

Her mind flashed back to the day he had unceremoni-
ously announced that they were going to Clogwyn, for
no reason that she could see, and she found herself left

alone with the postmaster's wife, who had cheerfully and without any hesitation spent the afternoon educating her on "the business of being a woman" while the two of them worked over the laundry tubs for her enormous brood. On reflection, now, it had been a logical choice. Mrs. Bythell clearly enjoyed the company of Mr. Bythell in every sense; she had a hearty, earthy, practical, no-nonsense attitude toward it all, and was no bad person for a young girl to come to for instruction in such things. But at the time, Mari had been greatly confused as to why it wasn't her da telling her all this, and why he'd left something so personal and intimate to someone who was almost a stranger.

"But—" she objected.

"Mari, I'm not a brave man when it comes to women," he said, desperately. "I knew there'd be crying. I knew there'd be temper. I knew there'd be all manner of carry-ing on. And I didn't want any of that! So I put it off, and I put it off, and finally I couldn't put it off any longer, so I bought you those beads, and—" He dropped the net out of one hand and ran it through his hair in frustration. "—and you know, fool that I am, I reckoned if I gave you something pretty, you wouldn't be as angry."

She didn't quite know how to answer that. "You were going to barter me away like a sheep, and you thought *beads* would keep me from being angry about it?"

"So I'm a fool!" he burst out. "If I were a cleverer man, don't you think I'd have got me a wife by now?"

She just stared at him, torn by so many emotions that she didn't know which one was uppermost. She just let them spin around her until they exhausted themselves and ran out of her, like water out of a cracked jar. And only then did she speak.

"You're not a fool, Da," she said. "You're the village idiot."

"I can't argue with that," he said mournfully. "The only fit wife for me was the one that was bound to me, will-she, nill-she."

Mari snorted. Then went back to her net-mending. "I can't say I forgive you, for that would be a lie," she told him crossly. "But I can see why you did what you did. Or—why you didn't do what you should have."

"That'll do," he sighed.

When at last she went back up to her bed and laid herself down in it, her disordered thoughts finally fell into a pattern. An epiphany of sorts. She realized at that moment that her da, much as she loved him, and she *did* still love him, was exactly what he had said.

He was not a brave man. Not just about women. He was not brave about anything. Going out in the teeth of the storm? That wasn't brave. Not when he *knew* the Selch and the Selch magic protected him. Fishing in all weathers? The same. Dealing with *anything* that made him uncomfortable? He fled or left it to others. Facing down the Selch? Not only would he not face them down and confront them on their bargain, he hadn't even had the courage to try and think of a way out of it, as she had.

No, her da was not a brave man.

But he loved her. He cared for her. And yes, maybe there was *some* self-interest in that, for after all, he would need to have a child to barter to the Selch eventually, but even though she might be deluding herself about it, she truly thought that had never entered his mind.

And despite being powerfully angry with him, she still loved him. Just now, she could see him for what he was.

A bit feckless. A bit careless. A bit of a coward. But he really had done the best that he could for her, and given the Prothero luck, that hoard of coins he had for her under the hearthstone could just as easily have been drunk away. There were plenty of men who'd have done just that.

She sighed. It was a hard thing to have to see her father for what he was. A hard thing and a sad thing. Maybe, though, this was what growing up was about.

Part of it, anyway.

Now I know why that bad Tylwyth Teg was laughing at me, she thought, frowning into the dark. *She knew my da for what he is. And there I was, binding myself with my words to whatever would save him. She must have thought me a right goose.*

But then again, according to the tales, the Tylwyth Teg knew nothing of love; could not feel it, could not give it. And, St. Mary help her, she still did love her da, her feckless da.

So let the fae laugh.

She would be the one laughing last.

She felt her mouth curving up in a little smile. Oh yes, she would be laughing. Tomorrow there would be handsome Selch here. And they would be courting her. And she could hold out for as long as she pleased, until one pleased her. Really, that was not so bad now, was it? Not so bad a prospect at all.

Better than the prospect you had before, now, be honest, she told herself. And it was true.

And there was the promise of a teacher in magic as well . . .

A pleasant thrill ran up her backbone. Now *that* . . . The Tylwyth Teg might well be singing a different tune if Mari mastered this magic. The Tylwyth Teg might well find herself in just a bit of a pother, facing off someone who could best her at her own game. This magic business . . . it meant that for once, she wasn't going to be thought of as Daffyd Prothero's daughter, nor the Selch's unwilling bargain piece. She would have something that was her very own, hers, and no one else's. Hers to do what she wished with. Her . . . power.

Oh yes. Oh, yes.

Now that was something to smile about.

Mari woke early, and the first thing on her mind was to wonder just when—and how—the Selch would put in their appearance. She didn't have to wait long.

It was a good thing she had gotten up before dawn and made herself tidy, for as the first rays of sun lanced into the eastern sky, they came out of the sea.

She saw them from the window—for what else could it be but the Selch—six great grey shapes rising up out of the surf, then rising taller, then approaching the Prothero cottage across the shore, striding solemnly up from the waterline. She came out to meet them, the wind off the sea pushing her skirts into her legs.

One she recognized: the grey-haired man she had confronted and bargained with yesterday, still frowning, not at all pleased. Beside him was another fellow, perhaps a little younger than her father. Not handsome, not unhandsome, but with an interesting face, an intelligent face, and eyes that seemed to see more than most. And just a hint of a smirk. She reckoned that he was secretly pleased about his chieftain's comeuppance.

The other four, though . . . her age or just a year or two older, and they ranged from handsome to so breathtaking that Braith would have fainted to see them. She felt a little faint and had the odd experience of feeling her cheeks and ears flush, just looking at them. All four of them were dark-haired. All four of them wore the same sort of clothing as her da, somewhat to her surprise. The one who had come to argue with her last night had, and still was, dressed in a sort of woolen tunic and loose trousers and a sealskin cloak. But these four, and the one she supposed to be a teacher, were all in the sort of thing that would not be out of place in the streets of Clogwyn: plain trousers, linen shirt, waistcoat, and jacket. Like her da, they all had waterproof boots. But the hems of their trousers were all dark and damp, and they, too, wore sealskin cloaks. She remembered the tales; you could always tell that someone was Selch, even if they had hidden their sealskins, because the lower hems of their garments never would dry.

First was one who was merely handsome. His hair was a bit longer than the others and he had mischievous blue eyes. He had one thumb tucked in his waistband and his other hand held his sealskin over his shoulder almost negligently.

The second was taller, more muscular, with solemn dark eyes between grey and storm-cloud blue. He stood straight, with his hands clasped in front of him. He looked like the sort of fellow who would call her father "sir" no matter how often da told him "Call me Daffyd."

The third . . . well, just to look at him, most girls would have come all over giggles. Black hair, not just "dark," crowned his head in fleecy curls. His intense blue eyes seemed meant to smile, and everything about him was perfect. A face and body that seemed created to be carved into statues and painted into paintings. Not too tall, not too short, not too muscular, and certainly not weak.

The fourth was shy and wouldn't look directly at her, but to her mind had the look of a poet or a musician. He was thinner than the others, though by no means *skinny*. His face and dark, dark eyes had a sort of innocence about them. There certainly could not have been four young men more unalike than these.

"Trefor," said the oldest Selch, gesturing abruptly at the first. He followed it with "Siarl. Rhodri. Mabon. And this would be Idwal, the teacher."

The last Selch gravely nodded his head, slightly.

"So. Courted you demanded to be. Courted you shall be. I leave you to it." Oh, he still sounded angry. Good. "Contrary wench that you are, don't take too long about this."

She raised her chin and looked the chief Selch in the eyes. "I'll take as long as I take, sir," she said coolly. "With or without your leave."

The merry one—Trefor—hid his mouth with his hand, covering what was probably a laugh that had tried to burst out. Rhodri looked mildly amused; Siarl looked shocked. Mabon looked like he didn't know how to react.

Idwal just raised an eyebrow at her and gave her a long and measuring gaze.

The chief reddened a little, but didn't lose his temper this time. "Women and cats," he said, in tones of dismissal. "I've business. You tend to yours."

And with that, he stalked down to the sea, leaving her with the four young suitors and her new teacher.

"Well then," she said, looking them over, trying to appear cool and confident, just as her father emerged, yawning and surprised, from the cottage behind her. "I suppose it's best to begin at the beginning. I'm Mari."

6

To date, Sarah and Nan's efforts at finding something useful to do had been no more successful than their attempts at teaching. This left both of them feeling more than a bit frustrated, so Memsa'b finally elected to fill their idle hours with transcribing certain old, rare books she had on loan to her into typewritten manuscripts. Neither of them particularly enjoyed the work—you couldn't type and actually *read* at the same time—but at least it felt like they were accomplishing something, and certainly the work was improving their typing skills.

It was with great relief, therefore, that they got a summons from Lord Alderscroft. Or not a summons precisely, more a carefully worded request, that if Memsa'b could spare them, he might have something he needed their observational abilities for.

Nan had scarcely finished reading the invitation aloud

when Sarah had her hat and was looking for someone to hitch the pony to the little two-person trap for them.

It was now summer, and anyone with any means at all tried to be out of London in summer. The buildings and pavement trapped heat, and the heat generated, and trapped, some of the most appalling odors ... rendering the city something of a misery. Alderscroft, who in winter preferred to reside in his club, was no exception to this habit of escape. He had built an expensive and very Indian summer bungalow on the edge of the estate, right on the river. That made it easy for his friends and associates to come to him without disturbing or disrupting anything at the school. It was far enough away from the school—for the lands that had come with the manor were quite extensive—that all but the oldest and most adventuresome of the children found it too wearying to venture there. But the proximity and the means of a pony-cart made it possible for him to pay congenial visits to the school at will and vice versa. With the birds clinging to the back of the seat, the girls sent the pony at a brisk trot toward their goal.

The place was closed and locked up as soon as London became livable again, for most of the work of the Wizard of London was by necessity *in* London. Constructed as it was to the Indian model, the place would have been a frozen nightmare to live in during the winter, but in the summer it was heaven.

When the girls pulled up to the front of the house and beneath the airy shade of the portico, one of the servants was at the pony's head so quickly it almost seemed that he had apported there. Sarah, who was driving, tossed him the reins, and the two girls were handed out of the trap by a second servant, and as the birds landed on their shoulders, they were conducted into the cool, breezy depths of the building.

As they knew, it was constructed like the capital letter H, with the center bar being very fat, the better to catch every breeze. In India, such a house would have been thatched. Here, it was roofed with clay tiles, whose red color contrasted pleasingly with the white walls. As much wall-space as possible was devoted to windows, overhung by the roof to keep the direct sun out. A wide, roof-shaded, slat-floored veranda encircled the house, with rattan furnishings, softened with cushions, arranged on it. It was always possible to find some part of the veranda that was out of the sun, no matter what time of day it was. All the windows were wide open, with netting and gauze curtains keeping the insects out. Lord Alderscroft was not on the veranda in the front of the house, but as Nan had expected, the servant escorted them through the foyer, the sitting room, and the dining room that comprised the bar of the H, and out to the part of the veranda at the rear of the house, facing the river. There was Alderscroft, enjoying the cool breeze off the water, with a gin and tonic at one hand.

He rose to meet them. "Thank you for coming so quickly, my dear ladies," he said, as the servant pulled out cushioned rattan seats for both of them and arranging a perch for each bird. "I would like to believe that your haste indicates your esteem for me—" he laughed a little, "but I fear it indicates the depth of your boredom."

"My lord, I would never say that," Sarah replied with a grin. "But we are certainly anxious to hear what it is you believe we can do for you."

He waited until they were seated, with lemonades in their hands, before taking his own seat again. "I trust you ladies are familiar with the exploits of Conan Doyle's famous detective?"

The manservant busied himself with filling the cups on the birds' perches with water and cut fruit.

It was Nan's turn to grin. "It would be more difficult to find someone at the Harton School who is not," she pointed out. "Memsa'b's investigations rely quite heavily on his methods, and she has drilled us in them extensively."

Lord Alderscroft relaxed visibly. "Ah, well then, there is much that I will not need to explain. Good! Here is my difficulty. The Elementals have been telling us that there is a new, and potentially quite powerful, Water Master out in the hinterlands on the west coast of Wales. Normally this would not be a problem; I would simply send a Water Master out there, he would introduce himself, we would make sure that the new Master was getting appropriate training, explain matters insofar as how we do things these days, let him know that if he were to run into difficulties he only had to call on us, then leave him alone until he decided to join the White Lodge."

Nan nodded; that was sensible. There was no point in exerting pressure on someone who was already feeling the pressure of learning his magic. It made more sense to—well, to introduce the Lodge as "good neighbors," then tactfully withdraw. A bit like leaving a calling card. "I take it that there are unforeseen complications this time?"

Alderscroft sipped his gin and tonic, and frowned. "I *believe,* although I do not know for certain, that there are other . . . interests . . . involved. Elemental Elder spirits, perhaps, like your 'little' friend from when you were children."

Nan blinked at that. She knew who Alderscroft was referring to, of course. The Puck. Robin Goodfellow; identified, rightly or wrongly, as a "fairy." Whatever a "fairy" might be. Some Elemental creatures were just that, and some "fairies" were definitely Elemental creatures. But some defied that label, or, indeed, any label at all. The Puck was one of them. God? An echo of Sylvan Pan? Perhaps. He claimed to be the "oldest old thing in all of Britain." For certain, though, he was extremely powerful, and if he was not a god, he certainly had god-like powers.

"I didn't know there was more than one like him," she said carefully, for she had learned from the Puck himself that it wasn't wise to name something unless you were willing to call it to you, and it wasn't wise to call it unless you really needed to.

"Oh, there are. There could be many; even I don't know how many. They simply tend not to interest themselves in mere mortals very often. The only reason we know as much about the Wild Boy as we do is because he *does* favor mortals, and is inclined to mix himself up in their business." Alderscroft finished his drink, and waved away the servant who made to refill it. "No, thank you, Dalton, that is enough for now. In matters like the one we are discussing, it is a good idea to keep a very clear head."

"A lemonade instead, my lord?" the servant suggested. Nan recognized him now; one of Alderscroft's very personal servants from his entourage at the club. Of course, they knew him for what he was—they themselves were Elemental Mages, albeit minor ones. Just as most of Memsa'b's servants and teachers were themselves gifted psychically. "Or a lager and lime?"

"Excellent suggestion. Lemonade, with a little less sugar than the ladies are taking." As the manservant nodded and took the empty glass, Alderscroft turned his attention back to the girls.

"So since there seems to be a greater power involved here, the Water Elementals are outright refusing to tell us *who* this new Master or potential Master is. This isn't unprecedented. But normally it takes place somewhere that we already have a Master in place or nearby. We have nothing and no one in Wales." He coughed a little with embarrassment. "Political situation, of course. Not as cursed difficult as Ireland, but . . ."

Both Nan and Sarah nodded. It was Sarah who ventured the next question. "I can see that, my lord, but I don't quite understand how we figure into this."

"Well, to begin with, you're women. You're sharp, you're clever, you're observant—and you're women." He cocked his head at them. "D'you see where I'm going?"

"People expect a girl to be negligible, unthreatening, curious as two cats, gossipy, and poking her nose into everything," Nan said bluntly, with a feral smile on her face. "But still, we aren't Elemental Magicians. We can't actually see the sorts of things they can, or even see the Elementals—"

"Well, I'm counting on your history with the Wild Boy," Alderscroft said carefully. "He made himself known to you; there's something about you two that attracted him. I am gambling that the same will happen in Wales."

Neville interrupted the conversation with a guttural laugh. Alderscroft turned to look at the raven. "I assume you have something to add, Neville?" he said.

"Sure bet," the Raven croaked, and laughed again, as Nan blushed.

"But what do you expect us to do, my lord?" Sarah asked.

"Identify the new Master. Let me know who and where he is. Observe him, if possible, get close enough

for an introduction, and pass on the greetings of the
Lodge." Alderscroft accepted a lemonade from the manservant. "There is nothing so far to indicate that you
would be at any hazard."

"That's comforting," Nan said dryly.

Alderscroft raised another eyebrow at her. "After
that rather hair-raising description you tendered me of
knife-wielding? I would be more concerned for the wel-
fare of this unknown than for yours, my dear."

Neville laughed raucously as she and Sarah both
flushed. Even Grey joined the laughter.

"You can consider this something of a test, if you
will," he continued. "You see, things are changing in this
world. Once, a good, God-fearing Christian who didn't
already *know* about magic or psychical powers would as
soon have spit on the Cross and declare himself a Sa-
tanist than meddle with such things. But now—" He
shrugged. "Now there is a burgeoning interest in such
matters and powers. Some of it is healthy, but not all.
There are all manner of occult societies and groups
springing up. Some are harmless. Some are idiots. But
some will get themselves, or others, into trouble. As the
Master of the White Lodge it is my duty to ensure the
safety of the people of the realm against the ghastlies
and ghoulies. I need agents, agents who can penetrate
these groups, determine if there is any threat, and advise
me if I need to continue to keep an eye on them."

Nan nodded; she was aware that Memsa'b was doing
something like that in a small way, investigating alleged
mediums and some of the occult circles and determining
if they were harmless, if they were frauds, and whether
or not something needed to be done about them. She
and Sarah had joined in her investigations at a very
young age and fully expected to continue to be a part of

them. The fact that they were *not* engaged in such an investigation at this moment, was, she suspected, largely due to the fact that even the greediest fraud tended to taper off his or her activity in the heat of a London summer—and Memsa'b did not tend to venture far from London out of necessity. Sahib's business was there, which meant he could not travel much, and of course, there was the school, which Memsa'b simply could not leave for any length of time.

But . . .

"Did you actually intend . . ." she ventured, and wasn't sure how to go about asking the embarrassing question of *payment.*

"Oh, this would be a very real job in every sense," he assured them both. "But I am being cautious for both our sakes. Memsa'b thinks you two would make admirable investigators, and I could certainly use someone in that capacity, but I would like to give this a proper trial. For the job of looking into the Welsh affair, I will merely cover all your expenses. Should this prove successful, I will be prepared to offer you a proper salary as well as expenses." He gave them both a very sober and penetrating look. "While the Club and the Lodge are closed to the fair sex, that has more to do with the prejudices of our members than mine. It will take some time to convince a great many of them that women are capable of vigorous action and rational thought."

Nan considered being resentful, then remembered the one time she and Sarah and Memsa'b had been admitted to the Ladies' Reception and Dining Room, and smothered a giggle. Yes, she could well believe that some of the old fossils that comprised the White Lodge had their brains firmly ossified in the last century.

"I find the two of you, my young friends, to be thoroughly unnerving," he admitted ruefully. "I suspect that Master Kipling's poem about the female of the species may well hold true in your cases, and I mean that in the most respectful way possible."

Nan impertinently stuck a finger under her chin and bobbed a mock, seated curtsey. "Why, thank you, my lord," she replied saucily. Then she sobered. "I do have a very real and pressing question, however. What is your estimation of the likelihood of us getting into difficulties? Given that the Elementals themselves have indicated that there is an interest in this person by a Power?"

"I can't estimate it," Alderscroft told her, and shrugged. "This is something outside of my experience. Normally Elemental magicians come from families who have produced many generations of Elemental magicians. But you will be able to telegraph me directly if there seems to be a problem . . . and I hope that old Power who was interested in *you* may be of service as well."

Nan and Sarah exchanged a speaking look. Neville cocked his head, and Grey bobbed hers. Nan thought she knew what they were thinking as clearly as if they were sharing the thoughts. Right now, the two girls could live on Memsa'b's charity, idle and useless except for the instances where Memsa'b was investigating some occult problem or other. This was distasteful to both of them.

Or they could take some risks, accept this trial offer, and potentially find themselves not just with a rewarding sort of job, but one which would definitely send them all over the British Isles. She and Nan had discovered they both liked traveling. They already knew they both liked *doing*.

Sarah nodded. Nan spoke for them both. "We'll do it, sir."

Lord Alderscroft beamed. "Splendid! Now what do you think your first steps should be? Remember, I am trying your paces, as it were. So I want to hear what your thoughts are."

"Before we actually go anywhere, we need to establish *personas,* as it were," Sarah said. "We'll need to have an excuse to be where we are going, to be together, and to be unchaperoned."

Nan snorted a little at that. "All I have to do is dress a bit more severely, and I could look as old as thirty," she pointed out. "So I can easily be the chaperone myself."

Alderscroft nodded. "Good, good. Go on."

"Have you a good idea of *where* in Wales this is?" Sarah asked.

"Somewhere around about a little seaside town called Criccieth," Alderscroft told them.

"In that case, I think I will be recovering from something unspecified, and sent to someplace cheap, on the sea, for my health, and Nan can be my older sister. We can be the daughters of a clergyman. That's genteel enough to mix with the gentry if we need to, but egalitarian enough to mix with everyone else." Sarah had gotten a little pink in her cheeks, showing her excitement. Nan just let her go—she was the one with the better imagination. "And if anyone asks that might be inclined to ask questions elsewhere, I can tell the truth, that my—our— parents are serving at a mission in Africa. Our family has your patronage, so you are kindly taking care of my illness."

Alderscroft rubbed his hands together with satisfaction. "Excellent. I'll—ah no. I was going to say that *I* would take care of the details, but I have a better idea. I'll have you work directly with my secretary. You can learn how to do this sort of thing yourself that way."

Now it was Nan's turn to feel excited. They'd done a certain amount of planning for their travel out to Africa and back, but the bulk of it had been handled by the Thomas Cook agency. Mostly things had gone well, but there had been that problem in Egypt ... if she and Sarah knew how to deal with bookings and the like themselves, they wouldn't find themselves in difficulties again.

Besides, she liked having the reins firmly in her own hands.

"Right then! We're all agreed." Alderscroft looked extremely satisfied. "You two put together the Sherlockian guises and work out what you will need for them. When you have your lists, come out here again, and you, and I and Whitely will go over them, then I'll leave you with Whitely to make the actual arrangements. He'll give you a list of Elemental mages that are nearest, and he'll make you out letters of introduction to the local gentry in case you'll need those as well."

"That sounds excellent, my lord," Nan agreed. "Better to have those in hand and not need them than need them and have to wait for them." She paused. "I've just got one question, my lord. Why us and not some lesser Elemental Magicians?"

"Because neither of you seem to have any gift for magic yourselves," he said frankly. "That makes you— well, not *immune,* but certainly *resistant* to its effects. I feel much safer sending someone like you than I would a lesser mage. Furthermore, if the person we are trying to find is of a competitive nature, both by virtue of your sex and the fact that you are not mages yourselves, you will not be seen as a challenge."

Nan and Sarah both nodded. "Smart bird!" Grey said approvingly.

"Ah! And that is the third reason, thank you for reminding me, Grey. You have protectors." He nodded at the birds. "I very much doubt that this magician, no matter how powerful he is, will have seen anything like them—nor will he be inclined to test them, if he is reasonably sane and cautious."

Neville shook his head and body vigorously, and snapped his beak, as a reminder that he was not just "armed" with occult weapons, he was armed with a very physical one.

"That makes me even more pleased to hear, if that were possible," Nan said with satisfaction.

"Well then, my dear lady-Sherlocks! The game's afoot!" If Nan had had any lingering doubts as to whether this was some sort of make-work urged on the Wizard of London by Memsa'b, his enthusiasm and obvious relief told her the opposite. She and Sarah were going to provide the Elemental Master with a much-needed service. "Now, since the hour has stretched well into the afternoon, would you care to join me for tea?" His eyes gleamed. "And perhaps a rubber or two of bridge with Whitely?"

Nan chuckled. "Still smarting from your defeat last week, my lord?"

"Bah! Unlucky hands is all!" he proclaimed. "I am sure that Sarah and I can best you and Whitely and give you the trouncing you so richly deserve."

"In that case, my lord, I shall take that as a challenge," Nan proclaimed, and Lord Alderscroft chortled in triumph and rang for tea.

Whitely and Nan defeated Sarah and Lord Alderscroft, but only by a hair this time. Alderscroft sent them back to the school in the soft twilight expressing himself very well satisfied with the results of the day. Memsa'b, too, expressed her satisfaction, so there was nothing more for the two of them to do than to work out the *who, what,* and *why* of the characters they planned to play.

Nan began to realize that this was a little like acting in a play—except, of course, that they would never be off-stage—which she had enjoyed very much while she had been a student. She had been excited about this whole project from the beginning, but this realization just added another whole layer to her pleasure.

Her first taste of acting had come during her very first year as a real student at the school, when a kind gentleman had offered Memsa'b the use of his country manor for the school for a summer holiday. Memsa'b had conceived of the notion of having the whole school involved in acting *A Midsummer Night's Dream* as a way of keeping some of them out of mischief—and as a way of making their lessons into something less than onerous. Nan and Sarah were Helena and Hermia, natural roles for both of them. Nan had originally hoped to be Hippolyta, the Amazon Queen, more for the sake of the armor than anything else, but after she came to read through the text, she realized that Hippolyta's role was rather flat and uninteresting next to that of Helena. Even if she *was* going to have to act as if she was all in a pash over a boy!

All the roles had been settled but that of Puck, which was proving difficult to cast, given their limited number of potential players and the limited abilities of all of them. Memsa'b, Nan and Sarah had gone out to a half-deserted part of the garden to rehearse their parts, and Memsa'b had used a pause in their rehearsals (in which she was playing Puck) to lament that very fact. That was when it happened.

"Ah, dear lady, and tender maidens," said a bright voice from the doorway, making them all turn. "Perhaps I can solve this problem for you."

There was a boy there, perhaps a little older and a trifle taller than Nan. He had a merry face, sun-browned, with reddish brown hair and green eyes, and wore very curious clothing.

At first glance, it looked perfectly ordinary, if the local farmers hereabouts were inclined to wear a close-fitting brown tunic and knee-breeches rather than sensible un-dyed linen smocks and buff trousers, but at second glance there was something subtly wrong about the cut and fit of the garments. First, they looked like something out of a painting, something antique, and secondly, they looked as if they were made of leather. Now, the blacksmith wore leather trousers and the village cobbler, but no one else did around here.

And there was something else about this boy, a bright-ness, a spirit of vitality, that was not ordinary at all.

And that was the moment when Neville made a sur-prised croak, and jumped down off the marble seat where he had been pecking with great interest at a hole in the stone, to be joined on the floor by Grey. Both of them stalked over to the boy's feet, looked up at him—

—and bowed.

There was no other name for what they did, and Nan's mouth fell agape.

But this was not the only shock she got, for Memsa'b had risen from her seat, and sunk again into a curtsey. Not a head-bowed curtsey though; this was one where she kept her eyes firmly on the newcomer.

" 'Hail to thee, blithe spirit!' " she said as she rose.

The boy's eyes sparkled with mischief and delight.

"Correct author, but wrong play and character, for

never could I be compared to Ariel," he replied and swiftly stooped down to offer Neville and Grey each a hand. Each accepted the perch as Nan stared, her mouth still open. "How now, Bane of Rooks!" he said to Neville. "I think you should return to your partner, before bees see her open mouth and think to build a hive therein!"

With another bow, and a croak, Neville lofted from the boy's outstretched hand and landed on Nan's shoulder. Nan took the hint and shut her mouth.

Wordlessly he handed Grey back to Sarah, who took her bird with round eyes, as if she saw even more than Nan did to surprise her. "So ho, fair dame, did you think to plan to play my play on Midsummer's Day and not have me notice?" he said to Memsa'b, fists planted on his hips.

"I had not thought to have the honor of your attention, good sirrah," Memsa'b replied, her eyes very bright and eager. "Indeed, I had not known that such as you would deign to notice such as we."

He laughed. "Well spoke, well spoke! And properly too! Well then, shall I solve your conundrum with my humble self and let your restless Tommy play the ass?"

Nan blinked hard, as a furtive glimmer of light that could not have actually been there circled the boy, and then her brain shook itself like a waking dog, everything that wasn't quite "right" shifted itself into a configuration she could hardly believe, and she burst out with, "You're him! *You're* Puck!"

Oh she would never, ever forget that moment. It was the moment when something truly magical entered her life. The occult was one thing; by that point she had encountered ghosts, mediums, psychical manifestations, a distinct mental bond with Neville . . . but these were all things that had, if not an entirely rational explanation, surely they were something that was not *magical.* But

Puck—Elves, the Fair Folk—they *were*. Magic was *real*. And it came in the form of an altogether enchanting playmate.

Puck had agreed to play himself for their production, and he had shown up, just as he promised, on the night.

She remembered what Memsa'b had said about him, when he had left them after that first encounter.

"Ah, now. . .I hesitate to pin down someone like him to any sort of limited description," Memsa'b temporized. *"And the Puck of Shakespeare's play is far more limited than the reality. Let's just say he is—old. One of the oldest Old Ones in England. As a living creature, he probably saw the first of the flint-workers here, and I suspect that he will see the last of us mortals out as well, unless he chooses to follow some of the other Old Ones wherever they have gone, sealing the doors of their barrows behind them. If he does, it will be a sad day for England, for a great deal of the magic of this island will go with him. He is linked to us in ways that some of those who were once worshipped as gods are not."*

"Will we see 'im again afore the day?" she asked.

"Now that I cannot tell you." Memsa'b pursed her lips. *"If you do, be polite, respectful, but don't fear him. He is the very spirit of mischief, but there is no harm in him and a great deal of good. You might learn a good deal from him, and I never heard it said that any of his sort would stand by and let a child come to harm. His knowledge is broad and deep and he has never been averse to sharing it with mortals."*

"But would he steal us away?" Sarah asked, suddenly growing pale. *"Don't they take children, and leave behind changelings?"*

Here Nan was baffled; she had no idea what Sarah was talking about. But Memsa'b did.

"I don't—think he'd be likely to," she replied after a long moment of thought. *"Firstly, I don't think he would have revealed himself to us if he was going to do that. Secondly, what I know of such things is that his sort never take children who are cared for and wanted, only the ones abused and neglected."* She held out a hand and Sarah went straight to her to be hugged reassuringly. *"No one can say that about any of you, I do hope!"*

No indeed. No one could. No one could have loved Nan better than Memsa'b.

As if her thinking about Puck had communicated itself to Sarah, her friend looked up at her from across the table where they were both making lists and notes. "Do you think we should try and call him?" she asked, without needing to specify what *him* she was talking about. "I expect he'd come here if we did; it's lovely land and the back grounds are half wild."

Nan shook her head. "I have . . . a feeling about that," she said, after a moment. "It was all very well to call on him whenever we wanted to see him when we were children; children are allowed to be playful and a little thoughtless. But we're adults now. I think that we should only try and call him if we run into difficulties in this task that we just can't work out answers to ourselves. I think he—rightly!—expects a great deal more of an adult than of a child. Self-sufficiency, for one thing."

Sarah nodded agreement, but sighed. "Well, perhaps he'll come to us without us trying to call him. I'd like to see him again. Sometimes . . . sometimes I find myself thinking that everything about him was just a dream."

Nan couldn't help sharing those sentiments. She remembered the night of the play, for instance.

At the moment when they were all milling about back-stage, waiting for Memsa'b to announce the play, Nan felt a tug on her tunic and turned to find herself staring into those strange, merry green eyes again. This time the boy was wearing a fantastic garment that was a match for those Titania and Oberon were wearing: a rough sleeveless tunic of green stuff and goat-skin trousers, with a trail of vine-leaves wound carelessly through his tousled red hair.

"How now, pretty maiden, did you doubt me?" he said, slyly. "Nay, answer me not, I can scarce blame you. All's well! Now, mind your cue!"

With a little shove, he sent her in the direction of her entrance-mark, and as she stepped out into the mellow light of lanterns and candles, she forgot everything except her lines and how she wanted to say them.

Now, Nan was not exactly an expert when it came to plays. The most she had ever seen was a few snatches of this or that—a Punch and Judy show, a bit of something as she snuck into a music-hall, and the one Shakespeare play Memsa'b had taken them all to in London.

But the moment they all got onstage, it was clear there was real magic involved. All of them seemed, and sounded, older and a great deal more practiced. Not so much so that it would have been alarming but—certainly as if they were all well into their teens, rather than being children still. Everything looked convincing, even the papier-mâché donkey's head. Lines were spoken clearly, with conviction, and the right inflection. Nan and Sarah even made people laugh in all the right places.

And as for Puck—well, he quite stole the show. From the moment he set foot on stage it was clear that the play was, in the end, about him.

Yet no one seemed to be in the least put out that he took the play over. Not even Tommy. And perhaps that was the most magical thing of all.

There had been no sign of him after that—until the hour that the two of them ventured to investigate a bridge just off the property that had given them bad feelings, and discovered that what haunted it was very dangerous indeed. They had, in fact, come under attack, and it had been Puck who rescued them.

It had been a hungry, evil spirit that had ensnared another, the ghost of a little girl, and was sucking the life out of her. Nan and Sarah had immediately come to the ghost-girl's defense, and had been attacked in their turn. They had been very young, of course, and not strong, and certainly not as practiced as they became even a few months later, and the horrid thing had come very close to taking them too.

But then their savior had appeared.

"Not so fast, my unfriend, my shadow-wraith!" cried a fierce young voice that brought with it sun and a rush of flower-scented summer wind—and blessedly, the release of whatever it was that had hold of Nan's throat.

She dropped to her knees, gasping for breath at the same time that she looked to her right. There, standing between her and Sarah, was Robin Goodfellow. He wore the same outlandish costume he'd worn for the play, only on him, it didn't look so outlandish. He had one hand on Sarah's shoulder, and Nan could actually see the strength flowing from him to her as she fed the ghost-girl with that light, which now was bright as strong sunlight.

The ghost-girl thrashed wildly, and broke free of the shadow-woman's hold, and that was when Robin made a casting motion of his own and threw something at the shadow-form. It looked like a spider-web, mostly insubstantial and sparkling with dew-drops, but it expanded as it flew toward the shadow-woman, and when it struck her, it enveloped her altogether. She crumpled as it hit, as if it had been spun out of lead, not spider-silk, and collapsed into a pool of shadow beneath its sparkling strands.

The ghost-girl stood where she was, trembling, staring at them.

"She's stuck," Sarah said, her voice shaky, but sounding otherwise normal.

Grey waddled over to the ghost-girl, looked up at her, and shook herself all over. Neville returned to Nan's shoulder, feathers bristling, as he stared at the shadow-woman trapped in Puck's net.

"She doesn't know where to go, or how to get there, or even why she should go," Sarah continued, pity now creeping into her voice.

"Oh so?" *Puck took a step or two toward the ghost-girl, peering at her as if he could read something on her terrified young face.* "Welladay, and this is one who can see further into a millstone than most . . . no wonder she don't know where to go. Hell can't take her and Heaven won't have her, but there's a place for you, my mortal child."

His voice had turned pitying and welcoming all at the same time, and so kindly that even Nan felt herself melting a little inside just to hear it. He held out his hand to the ghost-girl. "Come away, human child, or what's left of you. Come! Take a step to me, just one, to show you trust your dreams and want to find them—"

Shaking so much her vague outlines blurred, the ghost-girl drifted the equivalent of a step toward Robin.

He laughed. Nan had never heard a sound quite like it before. Most people she'd ever heard, when they laughed, had something else in their laughter. Pity, scorn, irony, self-deprecation, ruefulness—most adults anyway, always had something besides amusement in their voices when they laughed.

This was just a laugh with nothing in it but pure joy. Even the ghost-girl brightened at the sound of it, and drifted forward again—and Robin made a little circle gesture with his free hand.

Something glowing opened up between him and the ghost-girl. Nan couldn't see what it was, other than a kind of glowing doorway, but the ghost-girl's face was transformed, all in an instant. She lost that pinched, despairing look. Her eyes shone with joyful surprise, and her mouth turned up in a silent smile of bliss.

"There you be, my little lady," Robin said softly. "What you've dreamed all your life and death about, what you saw only dimly before. Summerland, my wee little dear. Summerland, waiting for you. Go on through, honey-sweetling, go on through."

The ghost-girl darted forward like a kingfisher diving for a minnow, a flash, and she was into the glow—and gone. And the glow went with her.

But that was by no means the end of it, for the horrid, hungry ghost was still there.

Puck, however, had an answer for her, too.

He turned to Nan and Sarah. "Close your eyes, young mortals," he said, with such an inflection that Nan could not have disobeyed him if she'd wanted to. "These things are not for the gaze of so young as you."

She kept her eyes open just long enough to see him take a cow-horn bound in silver with a silver mouthpiece from his belt, the sort of thing she saw in books about Robin Hood, and put it to his lips. Her eyes closed and glued themselves shut as three mellow notes sounded in the sultry air.

Suddenly, that sultry air grew cold and dank; she shivered, and Neville pressed himself into her neck, reassuringly, his warm body radiating the confidence that the air was sapping away from her. All the birds stopped singing, and even the sound of the river nearby faded away, as if she had been taken a mile away from it.

She heard hoofbeats in the distance and hounds baying.

She'd never heard nor seen a foxhunt, though she'd read about them since coming to the school, and it was one of those things even a street-urchin knew about vaguely.

This did not sound like a foxhunt. The hounds had deep, deep voices that made her shiver, and made her feel even less inclined to open her eyes, if that was possible. There were a lot of hounds—and a lot of horses too—and they were coming nearer by the moment.

She reached out blindly and caught Sarah's hand, and they clung to each other as the hounds and horses thundered down practically on top of them—as the riders neared, she heard them laughing, and if Puck's laugh was all joy, this laughter was more sorrowful than weeping. It made her want to huddle on the ground and hope that no one noticed her.

The shadow-woman shrieked.

Then dogs and riders were all around them—except that, other than the sounds, there was nothing physically there.

Feelings, though—Nan was so struck through with fear that she couldn't have moved if her life depended on it. Only Sarah's hand in hers and Neville's warm presence on her shoulder kept her from screaming in terror. And it was cold, it was colder than the coldest night on the streets of London, so cold that Nan couldn't even shiver.

Hoofbeats milling around them, the dogs howling mournfully, the riders laughing—then the shadow-woman stopped shrieking and somehow her silence was worst of all.

One of the riders shouted something in a language that

Nan didn't recognize. Robin answered him, and the rider laughed, this time not a laugh full of pain, but full of eager gloating. She felt Neville spread his wings over her, and there was a terrible cry of despair—

And then, it all was gone. The birds sang again, warmth returned to the day, the scent of new-mown grass and flowers and the river filled her nostrils, and Neville shook himself and quorked.

"You can open your eyes now, children," said Robin.

Nan did; Neville hopped down off her shoulder and stood on the ground, looking up at Robin. There was nothing out of the ordinary now in the scene before them, no matter how hard Nan looked. No shadow-woman, no ghost-girl, no dark emotions haunting the bridge. Just a normal stone bridge over a pretty little English river in the countryside. Even Robin was ordinary again; his fantastical garb was gone, and he could have been any other country boy except for the single strand of tiny vine leaves wound through his curly red hair.

"What—" Sarah began, looking at Puck with a peculiarly stern expression.

"That was the Wild Hunt, and you'd do well to stay clear of it and what it Hunts, little Seeker," Robin said, without a smile. "It answers to me because I am Oldest, but there isn't much it will answer to, not much it will stop for, not too many ways to escape it when it has your scent, and there's no pity in the Huntsman. He decides what they'll Hunt, and no other."

"What *does* it hunt?" Nan asked, at the same time that Sarah asked, "What *is* it?"

Robin shrugged. "Run and find out for yourself what it is, young Sarah. And go and look to see what it hunts on your own, young Nan. There's mortal libraries full of books that can tell you—in part. The rest you can only *feel, and if your head don't know, your heart already can tell you."*

"Well," Nan replied, stubbornly determined to get some *sort of answer out of him,* "What was that thing at the bridge, then?"

"And I need to tell you what you already know?" Robin shook his head. "You work it out between you. She's not been here long, I will tell you, and I should have dealt with her when she first appeared, but—" he scratched his head, and grinned one of those day-brightening grins "—but there was birds to gossip with, and calves to tease, and goats to ride, and I just forgot."

Now, of course, she knew better. Puck didn't "just forget" anything. The truth of the matter was that to a creature like him, mortal time was something of a blur. It wasn't that he forgot—it was that *when* he got around to something was a matter of indifference to him, unless he found that the thing he had not done suddenly loomed important in the lives of the mortals he chose to keep an eye on.

He had certainly chosen to keep an eye on them. He had turned up again to warn them about Lord Alderscroft, who at that juncture had been under the deathly sway of a very nasty creature indeed. It had been Sarah, at that point, who had sworn there was good in the man, while Puck had made veiled warnings that if things got out of hand . . . he would take matters into *his*.

They hadn't known at the time that Puck had actually delivered a warning of his own to Lord Alderscroft as well.

The very last time they had seen Puck, it had been as the Guardian at the Gate, the Prince of Logres, prepared to do battle to save his Isle, even though that battle would mean his own banishment.

But thanks to Nan and Sarah, that hadn't happened. Lord Alderscroft had been saved, saved by the offer of simple, unasked-for, friendship.

"You know, we all owe each other," Sarah said, matter-of-factly. "Even Robin owes us. So I expect if we really, truly need him, he'll come."

Neville nodded vigorously at that.

"Still," Nan felt urged to point out, "it's better if we show that we are doing the best we can. I don't think he likes the shirking sort of lazy, much."

"Probably not." Sarah stared down at her list, and sighed. "Do you suppose it will be possible to get the sort of dresses that good little vicars' daughters wear that *don't* require we be corseted within an inch of our lives?"

"Great Harry's ghost, how would *I* know?" Nan asked, with surprise.

And Neville and Grey both broke into laughter.

7

IT seemed that Mari was something called an *Elemental Master.* Or at least, she would be when she had properly learned how to handle the magic that was her birthright.

But first there were history lessons. Not dry things, but the history of her own family and the history of the Selch clan that had attached themselves to the Protheros.

These lessons were far more agreeable than the ones she had taken in that stuffy little parlor. The Selch didn't care for being indoors when the weather was fine, and all of the fellows assigned to court her lent their hands to the outside chores with a will, so by midmorning there was nothing much left for her to do. In fact, they rather overdid in some areas, not that she was going to complain. The stacks of driftwood and sea-coal against the side of the cottage had never been so high, and she wouldn't need to go kelping for weeks, if not months. There was plenty of laver boiled and put by now, and all she had to do was mention that she needed more, and more appeared. One of them had mended the rain-barrels that Daffyd never had gotten around to fixing, so there would be a steady source of fresh water that didn't require trudging to the spring in the sheep-meadow. She didn't even need to go shellfishing, not with them about.

So, by luncheon, there was nothing *to* do but lessons. And mending, but that was easily done with the lessons.

"So, if the magic is in the Prothero blood," she said, her hands industriously at work mending a stocking, "Why is it that none of them were these—Master-things before this?"

She no longer expected Idwal to be offended at questions; he took them at face value, being something she wanted to know the answer to, not something she was trying to plague him with. He continued his carving on the little whalebone knife he was making while he answered her.

"The shortest answer is that none of them had that much power," he replied. "The longer answer is, according to all I know of the history, a good bit more complicated than that. The bargain we made with the first of the Prothero fisherman wasn't just about fish and husbands. It included the magic and our use of it."

She looked up from her stocking. "*Your* use of it?" she said in surprise. "Is magic a thing you can be lending, then?"

He nodded. "Something like. 'Tis in part like your rain-barrel, if you had no need of the water. We say 'lad, you store up that water, and we'll come and take it away at intervals before it overflows.' With every new Prothero brought into the bargain, we would say 'Do you want the magic now?' and they would say 'No, have it.'"

Rhodri, who had been lying at ease nearest her, mak-

ing her a very pretty little necklace of shells and shell
fragments hardly bigger than a baby's fingernail, laughed
at that. "You forget the part about telling them first that
it wouldn't bring them wealth or ease."

Idwal nodded. "And that is true. When you take up
the cloak of the Elemental Magician, it binds you to
serving the Element, even as the Element serves you.
Take Water—you're a keeper of waters, and it's your
task to see they stay clean, your task to help or heal the
Elemental creatures that do your will, and your task to
help against dark magics, greater or lesser. So the Prothero men, when it was put that way to them, said, 'I'd
rather fish; you have the magic.'"

"So I could say that now?" she asked. It was a logical
question.

Idwal furrowed his brows at her. "Nay. The power in
you is too great. You're like a great, strong man. Everyone about you sees you're strong, and you'll have no
choice but to use that strength, or there will be those
who'll take you as a threat to be dealt with."

Idwal looked as if he expected her to object to that, to
say "But that's not fair!" or something of the sort. But
his analogy had been a keen one, and she could see the
logic, and logic didn't care about fairness. Sometimes
things just *were,* and no point in whinging and wailing
about it. You might as well wail that the storm was unfair, for that made about as much sense. Fair, unfair, the
storm just *was,* and you might as well accept it and deal
with it.

"All right," she nodded, and Idwal's face cleared and
his frown turned to a look of approval.

Mabon was whittling at a bone too, but he was making a little whistle or flute of some sort. "'Tis said," he
began, in a voice so quiet you really had to listen to hear

it, "That the North Star Clan knew the magic was strongest on the female side of your kin, and they did some magicking of their own, all this time, to make sure the Protheros sired only boys."

"As Gethin promised to do?" That was Trefor, who was weaving a net to replace one of the ones his kin had cut up.

"Many things are *said* that may not be true," Idwal warned. "And even if 'tis true, that would be the doings of the women. No matter what Gethin threatened, he can't do it without women's magic, and there's an end to it."

"Women's magic is that different?" she said in surprise.

"Among us . . . aye. Older. Deeper. Tied with the roots of the sea." Idwal nodded. "We are the Selch, and we are half-and-half. The creatures you've been spying till now have been all Elemental, and mostly dwell in their own realm that lies alongside your world like two pages in a book. But we are the Selch, and we are half-mortal and can live in either world. Our women have their own magics that are older than anyone remembers."

For some reason, his words put a little shiver up her back. She was hesitating about asking another question, when Trefor chuckled.

"You say 'mortal' to the lass as if we lived forever, elder," he chided.

Idwal frowned a little, but then nodded as if he had conceded. "You speak truth, boy," he said, a little grudgingly, and turned back to Mari. "We're no longer-lived than you. We are the creatures of land that returned to the sea, but we share the years of those who live on land still."

She blinked a little at that; she had simply taken it for

granted that, regardless of Gethin's gray hairs, all the Selch must be like the other Tylwyth Teg, and live forever unless something destroyed them. "Oh . . . and that's why . . ."

Idwal nodded. "Aye. The other reason for the bargain. To keep up our numbers. But that is neither here nor there. This is the last of the history you should know. Now it is time for learning the ways of the Water Master. Now tell me, what is water to you?"

She chose her words slowly, and with great care. "Water is life. Water is nothing you can confine, for it will always find a way out. Water takes the shape of whatever you put it in, for it has no shape of its own. Water can wear away the hardest stones. Water is patient. Water cleanses."

Idwal nodded with all of these. "The opposite—the enemy—of water is fire, for fire can turn water to vapor and water can extinguish fire. The allies are earth and air. The closer ally is air, for there is little water and air can do to harm one another, and much they can do together. This holds for all of the Elemental Creatures of those Elements. Water's true power is in its persistence, as Earth's is in its patience, Air's is in its ability to be everywhere, and Fire's is in its volatility. We will not be studying the others much, but it does pay to know about them, for there will come a time when you will work with a Master of another Element to confront something dark and powerful."

Again, a shiver ran up her spine; he must have seen that in her expression, for he laughed.

"I am not soothsaying, but remember what I said. There are those who will see what you are, and if their power is dark, they will, because they must, seek to remove you. It is in their nature, as it is in the nature of the shark to hunt." He shrugged. "So I am merely speaking of the inevitable. It may not be for years, but it will come."

"Oh, perhaps not," Trefor said lazily. "We are at the end of nowhere here. How likely is it that there would be a Black Magician here? What would he want, anyway? Sheep and fish?"

Idwal didn't admonish him, though it looked to Mari as if he thought Trefor was being a fool. Or, at least, overly optimistic. "Well," said Idwal. "Let us now speak of magic. In particulars, not generalities."

Her interest now sharpened abruptly; this was what she had asked for, bargained for. Needed, if it came to that.

"Magic," said Idwal, "Is neither good nor bad, dark nor light. It is like the sea, like a fire, like a knife. A tool. It is the hand that wields it for good or evil, it is not good nor evil in itself."

It was her turn to furrow her brow, because it had seemed to her that this was not entirely true. At least, not if some things she had vaguely sensed were accurate. "But —"

"It can be corrupted, tainted," Idwal replied, before she could finish her objection. "And so it will seem evil. But what has been corrupted can be purified. The hand behind it, however, cannot. It is also everywhere, though it runs stronger in some places than others, and each Elemental Magician will sense his own magic more strongly than the others, though he can sense all of them."

She considered that. "How?" she finally asked.

One corner of his mouth quirked a little. "Why don't you tell *me?*" he replied.

She was about to say something injudicious, when suddenly she remembered something — how, when she had been a child, all the world had been wreathed in transparent colors . . . and how, over time, when she discovered other people didn't see these colors, these auras and bursts and flows of tinted light, she forgot to look for them.

But if she thought about it, and turned her thoughts just the right way . . . then maybe . . .

And there it was.

All of the Selch were haloed in greens and turquoise, and more green swirled around Idwal as if he had a little whirlwind around him laden with motes of light. There were other colors too, but they were subtle, dim, compared to the brilliance of the Selch colors. "Oh!" she said in surprise, her eyes widening as she gazed at them all. "It's—green!"

"So it is," Idwal replied genially. He sounded pleased. "It is Water; the idea, the essence, the soul of Water. And now that you can see it again, I wish for you to study it before we use it in any way. It has currents and deeps and shallows. It is not just of one kind. Learn how it looks and tastes and smells and feels. Learn where it is and is not. For this day, I wish you merely to wander as you will, and learn about the power hereabouts, until you grow weary and your Sight fades. Then come and tell me of what you have learned."

With a feeling of cautious delight, she nodded to him, but did not immediately move away. Though her four suitors soon grew bored and went off on their own business, Idwal remained serenely where he was, carefully and slowly carving his bit of bone, while she studied the currents that flowed around him.

They were, she soon saw, not uniform. First, there was a sort of shell around him, like a bubble, except it had many layers, each a different, subtle shade of green. And every layer moved, so that fleeting patterns rippled across the surface of the whole.

She stared at it for a long time, and saw that it was not just that the nested bubbles of magic existed; it was that there were little wisps and eddies of more green light feeding into them. She longed, suddenly, to touch one of them—but he hadn't said to do that. He'd said to just look. So look was all that she did.

Idwal watched her, without any expression that she could see, as she prowled around him, observing him as narrowly as the cat would watch something she couldn't identify. How was he doing this? That he *was* the one controlling it was a certainty. This had to be some of the magic that he intended to teach her, and she suspected it must be elementary in nature. Probably one of the very first things that a magician was taught.

All right, *why* would someone construct such a thing?

She pondered that question. These bubbles looked so fragile . . . and yet, was it possible that they represented protection? Like a kind of wall? A wall made of magic?

No, not a wall, *walls,* in plurality. She didn't know why you would do things that way, but there must be a reason.

"Have you guessed what I am doing?" he asked, breaking the silence.

"Made a shell to protect yourself?" she replied, as she stopped prowling and faced him. "I can't see how it would, though . . ."

"Oh it wouldn't protect me from a rock or a rainstorm—not the way it is constructed at the moment—but it would defend me against a direct magical attack," he said, with a pleased little smile. "It would also keep any purely Elemental creature from attacking me."

"Like the little nasty Tylwyth Teg I saw here the other

day?" she asked in surprise, and described the ill-tempered little creature.

He nodded. "That is a creature of pure magic, and there are many names for them. Tylwyth Teg will do. It's more the sort of thing to create malicious mischief than actual harm, and if you don't fly into a rage over what it's doing, it generally gets bored and goes away. Unlike some, it isn't feeding from your anger; it just likes seeing you losing your temper. It finds that amusing. Mostly harmless."

She nodded, and got back to the original subject, doggedly. "I can't see how you're making that shell." She thought a moment. "Is it like the circles that witches make to do their work in?"

He smiled just a little more. "Very good. Yes it is. As it happens, the circle a witch draws is just the boundary line for a sphere of protection exactly like this. She puts the line on the ground to remind her of where she wants the boundary to be, and to fix that boundary in place so her protection doesn't grow and become thinner, or shrink and leave part of her sticking out of it."

Mari blinked a little, and tried not to laugh at the sudden mental image of a woman with her arms, legs and head sticking out of a big translucent bubble. "But why would she need a line?"

"Because you don't need to be able to *see* power to be a witch." She was glad that her questions were pleasing him, rather than making him impatient. She felt like a dunce. "It does help tremendously, of course, but to work with the lower levels of magic, you only need to be aware it exists, to have the concentration to perform certain actions without being distracted, and to have the power of will to impose on it."

"Is that what they call a spell then?" Certain things were falling into a pattern in her head.

Now he was delighted. "Exactly!" he applauded. "A spell is a process, not a thing. That is why you are said to *cast* them. Not in the sense of casting a net, but in the sense of performing an operation, or even, in a sense, of giving shape to something. As you would *cast* lead into fishing weights, giving it shape with the mold you have, so you *cast* a spell, giving shape to the magic with your will. And when the magic has the right shape, your will maintains it. That shape can be, well, almost anything." He actually smiled broadly at her. "I see that you not only have the power to be a Master, you have the mind to be one as well. I fully intended to keep you merely observing for the next day or two, but ... go ahead. Touch some of the power. You can either touch my shields or the power feeding into them."

"With my—hand?" she asked, hesitating.

He nodded. "In time you won't need to use your physical hand, but for now, yes, use your hand."

She didn't really like to touch that bubble—fragile as it looked, she had the feeling it was not fragile at all, and she didn't want a rude surprise—so instead, she reached out to one of the wisps of sparkling nothingness and tried to gather it up on her fingers, as if it were a spider-web.

And it *did* gather, tangling in her fingers at first, and then, to her surprise and delight, flowing around them. That was when, in addition to seeing the power, she got sensations of touch and taste ... it was soft on her skin, like rainwater, and had the same clean, pure taste as rainwater, drunk fresh as it came out of the sky: cool, pure, and just a little sweet, yet a little metallic at the same time. How she could taste it when it was getting nowhere near her mouth, she hadn't a clue, but there it was.

"Well?" he asked.

"I can feel it. And taste it, though that makes no sense at all." She moved it over to her other hand, then amused herself by passing it from hand to hand.

"That's just how your mind interprets the sensations," he told her. "That's fine. Every mage experiences his or her magic a little differently. Now, *want* it to form a little ball in your right hand."

He'd barely given her the instruction, and she had barely *begun* to think about it, when the magic flowed politely into her palm and obligingly became a whirling, sparkling little ball of blue-green motes.

"Well . . ." His voice was surprised and pleased. "If I had known you would be this apt a pupil, I would have turned up here long ago. I wish my blockheaded kin were this adept."

She felt irrationally pleased at having pleased him. "I'm glad I'm not a disappointment."

"The exact opposite. Are you feeling tired?"

Until he asked, she hadn't been aware of it . . . but once he did, she realized that she felt very much as if she had run all the way to Clogwyn or as if she had filled the rain barrel from the spring. Not exhausted, but definitely as if she had been doing work. And there was beginning to be a kind of ache in her head and inside her chest, the kind of ache you would have if you were using muscles you'd never exercised before.

"A bit," she said, then admitted, "More than a bit."

"I'm not surprised. The use of magic isn't—well, *magic.* It doesn't come out of nothing, and the strength you use to work with it comes from inside you. Time to stop. You've made a good start, Mari." And with that, he made a tiny gesture with one of his fingers, and the sphere in her hands spun out into a skein of threads and whirled into his bubble.

"But—" she felt a little deflated. They'd hardly done anything!

"Another lesson just before your father comes back," he promised. "And more tomorrow. We must build up the strength of your will as well as your understanding and your knowledge of the processes." The smile he gave her made her feel good again.

"I suppose baby has to crawl before she can walk," she admitted, and was rewarded by another smile.

"If only all my students were that sensible!" He laughed. "Come and sit down, and I will reward your patience with a tale."

This was going to be quite the journey, Nan had decided, looking at all the train-changes and tickets. In time, as long a journey as some they'd made in Africa, though the actual distance was a fraction of what those had been. *The problem is, of course, that there's no way to get there directly . . .*

First, they'd get up before dawn and take a train into London to Victoria Station, and a hired vehicle would be waiting to take them to Paddington. From there, it would be the long journey on the Great Western Railway to Shrewsbury, which would take them through Birmingham and Wolverhampton.

From Shrewsbury, they would be taking a new train line into Wales. This would occasion another train change at a city called Maclynnleth. Once there, they would transfer to the Cambrian Line that would finally drop them in the seaside town of Criccieth, where for the short term they had rooms at what was purportedly the best hotel in the town. Well, that didn't much concern Nan; she and Sarah had stayed in places that would likely have turned the hair of most British women pure white—even the ones that counted themselves lucky to get a bed at night at all. But this was going to be just a bit grueling. Lots of changes at stations, since there were very few "expresses" in that direction. This was where she thanked her lucky stars for Lord Alderscroft's name; they would be in private, first class compartments most, if not all of the way (she wasn't entirely sure on that, and the tickets didn't spell it out), and their baggage would be seen to without either of them lifting a finger.

She was very glad that she and Sarah and the birds were all seasoned travelers. And even gladder for the new carriers that Lord Alderscroft had had made for the birds. Not only were they vastly superior and easier to carry than a hatbox, they were beautifully appointed. Made of hard leather, and fashioned after the manner of a little dog kennel, each had leather flaps over openings screened with linen mesh that could be buckled up or down, water and food dishes, and a sturdy perch made of a natural branch with the bark left on for the birds to grip. Each had a food container and a water bottle attached to the side, though the food was more in the nature of "emergency rations," since the birds preferred to share what the girls ate. The arched tops had a good, padded handle just like a fine portmanteau. Both were waterproof, and should the air in Birmingham be so bad that even buckling the leather flaps down would not help, there were cotton gauze pads that could be placed over the openings to further filter the air.

The birds would never have to leave their sides, and would be protected from just about everything. And as for two-footed problems, Lord Alderscroft had seen to that too.

The first had been that he had *insisted* that they each

have a traveling outfit that was appropriate for . . . well,
to put it bluntly, *his* class. Since they were going to be
traveling in first class compartments the entire way, and
didn't want to look out of place, even Sarah had sighed
and agreed. Several fittings later, they had their traveling
gear, a pair of sober traveling suits of impeccable tailor-
ing, and to Sarah's relief, were fashioned after the sort of
things that ladies wore to hunt, so they had to be comfortable.

Not only had he supplied *both* of them with the sort
of umbrella that *Sitt Hakim* had wielded, he had provided them with a stout escort in the form of a young
fellow with the burly shoulders of a footballer and the
watchful eye of a suspicious older brother. He was associated in some way with Lord Alderscroft's club and
was a member of the White Lodge; he'd meet them at
Victoria and see them as far as the change to the Cambrian Railway, where he would go on to Torquay where
he had some business. Nan didn't particularly think they
would need an escort, but his presence seemed to make
Sahib feel more at ease, so she hadn't objected.

The trip into London was one they had made many
times, so there was nothing particularly stressful about it.
The sun was just high enough to see when they arrived.
Victoria Station, with its glass-and-iron roof that seemed
to stretch on for half a mile, was its usual confusing self,
but with the two porters assigned *just* to get their baggage out to the waiting vehicle, Nan and Sarah, hats
firmly on their heads, umbrellas firmly in right hands,
and bird-carriers in the left, threaded their way to the
front of the station and the ranks of waiting cabs, both
horse-cabs and a few rare automobile-cabs. There the
young man—Andrew Talbot—met them and guided
them to the hired vehicle, which to Nan's relief was not

one of the automobiles. It was not that she distrusted the things so much as she didn't want the birds subjected to the noise and smoke they seemed to produce.

The porters followed and loaded on the baggage, and they were off.

"Well, this is much more convenient than what we usually do," Nan remarked to Andrew.

"Omnibus?" he hazarded. She nodded. "Well, I had to reject the first one that turned up," he said, with a grimace. "I didn't like the look of the horses. Mistreated." He shuddered a little. "Be glad to get out of the city. Hate this place. Makes me sick, and if the Old Lion hadn't called me in for a spot of business, I wouldn't have come."

"Ah, Earth Master then?" Sarah said, sympathetically.

"Not Master, but adept. Need to gather up an apprentice the Old Lion wants me to teach, then it's back to the 'varsity. Old Lion's sponsoring us both through Cambridge." He smiled a little at that.

"What, not Oxford?" Sarah said in surprise. He laughed.

"I'd have gone, but father wouldn't hear of it. A Cambridge man he is, and the idea of a son of his going up to Oxford made him turn puce." He and Sarah had a good laugh at that; Nan just mentally shrugged. Since neither she nor Sarah were ever likely to see the inside of *either* university, it didn't matter to her.

The timing of their arrival seemed to coincide with slightly lighter traffic on the streets; their vehicle arrived at Paddington well before their train was due to depart. And already, Nan sensed a difference. Victoria was in the heart of London; Paddington, where the Northern and Western lines began, was very near to the country. Their escort felt it, too; his shoulders, which had been a little hunched, as if he felt the need of self-defense, relaxed—and his expression eased.

If Victoria's glass-and-iron roof had been impressive, Paddington's was more so. And with plenty of time to get to their train, with unspoken consent, they took their time looking about. "I don't much like buildings," Andrew said, finally, "but this is like a cathedral of steam."

That, Nan thought, was a very good way of putting things. The roof was more open here, and there was plenty of light. The great engines sighed and hissed and huffed at their places, like enormous living things, their carriages arrayed behind them, gleaming with brass and polish. Paddington was large enough that despite having all the trains here, it didn't seem crowded.

Their train was waiting at its appointed place, and Lord Alderscroft's cachet worked the usual magic of convenience. Although most people wouldn't be allowed to board this early, those in the private compartments were. Andrew left them briefly to make sure their luggage got stowed safely, then returned to them.

They had plenty of leisure to get settled before the majority of the passengers descended, in a great hurry to get themselves aboard. There were four compartments in the first class carriages, each with its own private entrance. It was certainly a far cry from the coaches Nan and Sarah had traveled in until now. It had been fitted up as nicely as a little parlor, with lovely soft armchairs, a round wooden table, curtains at the windows, oil lamps and even a stove—cold now, of course, but it would certainly make things more pleasant in the winter. On the side opposite to the exterior entrance was one into a corridor, which would give the stewards and the conductor access to them, and which they could use to get to the rest of the train.

Sarah and Nan put their cases down at their feet and got comfortable in the plush-covered armchairs.

"Out?" Grey called—definitely a question.

"Not until we're well on the way," Sarah told her. Andrew had started a little at the sound of a human-sounding voice from the leather case.

Neville made a rude noise. "I know you don't like it," Nan told him. "But you have to admit it is much superior to a hatbox."

"Can't see," he croaked.

"And you couldn't in a hatbox, either," she pointed out. But she did lean over and pull open the flaps on the side, buckling them on the top of the case like the earflaps on a deerstalker hat. Sarah did the same for Grey.

"What's more," she continued, "If we'd been traveling by third-class carriage, you wouldn't be let out at all."

Andrew grinned sheepishly. "And I was under the impression that you traveled like this for the Old Lion all the time." He ran his finger under his collar in what seemed to be a nervous gesture. "This is several cuts above how I am used to traveling."

"You mean to say that you aren't to the manor born?" Nan teased. "What a disappointment! I was getting ready to set my cap at you." She switched to her lowest gutter-Cockney. "Oi! An' 'ere oi was, all ready t' nobble a dook!"

Andrew looked startled again. "My word! Miss Nan, you should be an actress!"

"So I've been told. But Memsa'b would have palpitations if I even suggested it." Nan did not tell him that Cockney was, more or less, her "native tongue."

"Those are remarkable birds. Lord Alderscroft told me that they were as intelligent as people, but I must confess that I thought he was exaggerating." Andrew didn't bend down to peer at the carriers, which would scarcely be polite, but he did crane his neck a bit to try and see Neville and Grey behind the mesh.

"I can talk; can you fly?" Grey asked, which seemed to be the birds' favorite phrase for greeting doubters of late.

"Not as yet," Andrew told her. She laughed.

"And how on earth did you manage to get a raven?" he asked Nan.

"It would be far more accurate to say he got me," she replied, and described to him the childhood visit to the Tower of London where Neville decided that Nan was going to be *his*, regardless of what anyone else might say, and the machinations of the Master of Ravens to accommodate that desire.

Andrew shook his head. "I hope he didn't get into any trouble over it."

"Sahib made certain he didn't," Nan replied, as people began to stream toward their train, and the sound of carriage doors opening and banging closed was added to the sound of the engine gradually building up steam. She shrugged. "But after all, he is the Master of Ravens; he doesn't really have to answer to anyone if one of them chooses to fly off. He only has to keep them from being teased or hurt or stolen at the Tower."

"I suppose that's true enough." He turned to Sarah. "And how—"

The conductor interrupted them at that point—politely tapping on their door before opening it, and waiting deferentially for them to produce their tickets. This was certainly different treatment than Nan had gotten in the third-class carriage. The conductor appeared a bit startled when Nan and Sarah produced their own instead of Andrew giving all three sets, but he clearly wasn't going to say anything.

It was clear now that the train was about to pull out of the station. Conductors were calling "All aboard," and people were running past their window, hoping to get on before the train left.

Finally the last of the doors slammed, the last whistles sounded, the train blew its own whistle, and they were off.

Paddington Station really was on the edge of London. Within moments, they were traveling through real countryside, slowly gathering speed.

"Out!" shouted Grey, followed by an equally insistent *"Now!"* from Neville.

Not wanting to risk a show of temper, the two girls unfastened the doors of the carriers. Lurching a little with the movement of the train, the birds stalked out to be lifted up by their respective partners. Andrew eyed Neville with a faint air of alarm.

"I've never seen a raven this close," he admitted uneasily. "That is a very . . . formidable . . . beak."

Neville cocked his head and gave Andrew a wicked look. "The better to bite you, my dear," said Grey sweetly.

Both girls laughed. Nan took a newspaper out of her portmanteau and spread it on the carpet, holding Neville over it. The result that plummeted to the paper made Andrew's eyes widen. Grey's deposit was a little daintier. "That was probably why they wanted out," Nan explained, as Sarah put Grey briefly on the back of her chair and folded up the paper around its contents.

Neville gave *her* a look, this time of affronted dignity. "Want to see," he croaked in complaint. And to underscore his statement, he jumped to the back of the chair and turned his back on them, pointedly looking out the window.

"What would you have done in third class?" Andrew could not help asking.

"Take him with me to the ladies' WC and let him deal with it there," Nan said, without a blush. That was all right, Andrew blushed for her, as she had pretty much expected he would.

The poor fellow really didn't quite know how to react to them. But in Nan's estimation, that was all to the good. It meant he was less likely to try and stop them if they did something unladylike.

Since she had no intention of changing her behavior, that was entirely likely. She and Sarah were going to have to watch what they did quite carefully once they were on their own—at least, insofar as when they were likely to be observed—so she was going to make the most of this freedom.

The countryside sped by. This was not an express, which meant that they stopped at virtually every station. At least the level of comfort made this a great deal less onerous than it could have been. A steward appeared, bearing tea, and did not even blink at the birds. "If you would care for a late breakfast, the dining car is available to you or I can bring you a repast. I also have been informed as to the nature of your pets, miss," he told Sarah with great dignity. "The Great Western Railway is prepared to offer them the same care as our human passengers." And to prove it, he next produced a stack of yesterday's newspapers, and asked if, in lieu of birdseed, the birds would prefer curried rice with chicken or vegetables.

"*Chicken!*" shouted Grey, spreading her wings with delight, while Neville bobbed with excitement and clucked. *Now* the steward looked startled.

Sarah shrugged, and chuckled. "I think you have your answer," she said. "I think vegetables along with the chicken would be wise, if that is possible."

The steward blinked. "Pardon, miss, but that does seem a bit like . . . cannibalism."

"Hawks eat chicken," Grey retorted.

The steward looked a little discomfited at talking to a bird, but bravely made the attempt. "So they do . . . ah . . . miss. Chicken with vegetable curried rice for two."

"They like digestive biscuits too." Sarah turned to give the birds a stern look. "But *only* if you eat them over the newspaper. I won't have crumbs all over this compartment. And no playing with the food. Eat it neatly and nicely." She turned back to the steward. "Thank you; we will take our breakfast in the dining car. If you would be so kind, spread the papers on the floor, put the carriers on the papers, and put the food and water in bowls on the floor in front of the carriers. That will be the most secure. They'll manage from there. When they are finished, they'll return to the chairs."

Now, Nan had been planning on doing all that herself, but evidently, this was the sort of request that the steward was expecting, as he nodded, said "Certainly, miss," and retired. As he did, she heard him muttering to himself "Blimey. Them birds behave better than some peoples' brats."

Nan looked askance at Sarah. "We could have done all that," she pointed out.

Sarah nodded. "We could, but we shouldn't. We are expected to demand a certain level of service, and if we don't ask for things like that, we won't fit. Memsa'b explained this all to me. I don't really like it myself, but she promised me that this would ultimately make less trouble for us. A couple of wealthy girls with odd pets is eccentric. A couple of girls who *clearly* aren't accustomed to first class travel, with odd pets, is suspicious."

"Yes, true," Andrew put in, "But what could they *do* about it?"

"For one thing, as soon as we changed trains, our first class compartment could mysteriously become unavailable," Sarah told him. "For another, the authorities could be notified. We could find ourselves held up for hours, answering questions over and over. Worst case, we could find ourselves locked up as potential ticket thieves, ticket forgers, or mentally unstable." She sighed. "Memsa'b has had to deal with this sort of thing before—I am more than willing to take her word for it. And I am willing to go along with it as long as all it takes is pretending to a little arrogance. Besides, Lord A gave us spending money, plenty to tip generously for his services when we leave this train."

Nan had to chuckle at that. "You might not have heard him as he left, but I did. He said the birds had better manners than some peoples' children."

Soon as he had promised, the steward arrived with dishes of curried rice, water, and biscuits on a tray. "If you'd care to step along to the car, miss, sir, I'll take care of your pets," he said—quite cheerfully. His face grew even more cheerful when, after he had put down the tray and opened the door for them, Sarah pressed something into his hand and with a sweet smile, murmured "Thank you."

The dining car was the equal of any restaurant that Lord Alderscroft had ever taken them to, and so was the menu. Nan was in heaven. She did enjoy her food, and she and Sarah had endured many an absolutely horrid meal to and from Sarah's parents' mission in Africa. Andrew came more to life over the table, and at Sarah's prompting, told them stories of how things were at Cambridge for a second year student. Nan was quite content just to listen.

Finally Sarah sighed. "I would love to go to university," she said wistfully.

"Why not go, then?" Andrew asked. "There are colleges for women."

"Because neither Oxford nor Cambridge will allow us degrees, so what's the point?" Sarah retorted sharply, at odds with her usual good humor.

That occasioned some silence. "What would you do with a degree if you had one?" he asked, finally.

"The same thing that a man would." Sarah looked him in the eyes and dared him to contradict her. He looked suitably cowed. "There are plenty of men out there who do absolutely nothing with their degrees other than to reminisce about their days at university and impress people who don't have one," she continued crossly. "At least I would make some use of it."

He quickly changed the subject.

She was in better humor over the tea, and they returned to their compartment with Nan, at least, feeling entirely pleased with the world. They were greeted enthusiastically by the birds, which were perched politely on either side of a sturdy wooden smoking stand set in front of the window, with papers underneath them, and saucers of water and biscuits in front of them. The contraption had a pair of protrusions that were exactly like perches, perfect for the birds. It also had heavy wrought-iron feet, so unless the train came to a *very* abrupt stop, the birds were unlikely to get thrown off it.

"Great Harry's ghost!" Nan exclaimed. "What a clever fellow that steward is!"

"Nice man," Grey said complacently.

8

BIRMINGHAM was horrid.

The smoke from thousands of factory chimneys hung low in the air and could be seen from well outside the city. Not only did the birds go into their carriers, but Andrew suggested, and carried out, the precaution of wetting the gauze they layered over the netting "windows" before they fastened the flaps down over them. Nan was glad that they had, for the gauze was grey when she took it out.

The trip until then had been lovely; the train had gone through Reading, Didcot, Oxford, Banbury, and Leamington Spa, stopping at each station, but not for terribly long. By unspoken consent, they took the opportunity to plumb Andrew's brain for ideas on how to go about their appointed task.

"What would you do in order to locate an unknown new Elemental Master if the Elementals refused to tell you who it was or where he was?" Nan asked bluntly. The birds turned their attention from the landscape rolling past to the occupants of their room.

Andrew blinked. "Is that what Lord A wants you to do?" He rubbed the back of his neck, looking puzzled. "I suppose if the Elementals are holding mum on the subject and they aren't afraid, he reckons that you've got as good a chance as anyone else he knows of. And you can't exactly hire an investigator and tell him you're looking for a magician."

"True, true. So? Where would you start?"

Andrew drummed his fingers absently on the arm of his chair, brows furrowed, thinking hard. "Well . . . a lone Master, just beginning . . . and up there on the coast . . . he can't really know anyone, since if he did, it would be one of us, and Lord Alderscroft would have gotten word by now."

"It might be a she," Sarah pointed out. "That alone might be why the Elementals won't tell him. Lord A is a dear, but . . ." she made a face, "he hasn't got a high opinion of women in general. I think he thinks that Memsa'b and Nan and I are the exceptions that prove the rule."

Andrew nodded earnestly. "That might be. Or could still be *he,* but someone very common. Actually, all alone on the coastline, that's a near certainty. *And* Welsh. So there're more problems. Does he even know what Element?"

"Water," said Nan immediately.

"So, he's Fire, that's Water's antagonist . . . there's another reason why the Elementals might stay dumb. Working man —"

"Or woman," Sarah insisted.

"Or woman, Water, Welsh, and without a regular Master to teach him. Plenty of reasons for Water Elementals not to talk about him to a great Fire Master. For all *they'd* know, Lord A would be looking for him to crush him."

"So who would be teaching him or her?" Nan wanted to know.

"Could be the Elementals themselves. If the mage is powerful enough? Could do them damage without even knowing, and certainly without intending it, so it would be in the Elementals' interest to teach him." Andrew nodded, to emphasize his own statement. "It's not unknown. And after all, someone had to teach the first Elemental Masters, aye? Likely it was the Elementals then, too."

Or Puck, Nan mouthed at Sarah, who nodded slightly. Yet another reason why the Elementals would have remained quiet. Lord Alderscroft himself had hinted that the Great Powers might be involved. If not Puck, well, there could be a sea-born equivalent to the Oldest Old One.

"So . . . how would I go about looking for him . . ." Andrew thought some more. "I expect I'd go looking for where Elementals were thick. You get a Master, even untaught, you get a lot of Elementals about. But they probably won't show themselves to you, and you wouldn't see them unless they did, since you haven't the Sight for it. So that won't help."

"Bother." Nan would have said something a lot stronger, but she didn't want to shock Andrew more than he already was.

"Now . . . someone coming into their magic alone, at least amongst Earth Masters, tends to keep himself to himself," Andrew continued. "At first, you aren't sure what's going on. Then sometimes you think you're going mad. Sometimes you actually do," he added darkly. "But

I guess Lord A doesn't think that's going to be the case here. So . . . I'm thinking what you might be able to find is someone who lives well away from other folks, with one or two other people at most. He'll be on the shore or on a river or a lake. He won't want to be far from water. And there'll be things about him that look like uncommon luck, because the Elementals will be helping him." He shrugged. "That's the best I can offer. At least you've got a general idea of where he is."

"An uncommonly lucky hermit by the sea . . ." Nan made a face. "I'm glad it's summer. If we're going to have to promenade up and down deserted shores, it's a lovely time of year for it."

The entire trip from Paddington to Shrewsbury was roughly five hours, and they put into Shrewsbury around noon.

There was just time to make the transfer to another lovely first-class carriage for the trip by express to Machynlleth.

By now they were all starving again, not wanting to chance the food stalls at the station. When Sarah asked their new steward if it would be possible to have a late luncheon, the steward actually looked offended. "This is the Cambrian Railway, miss. Everything is possible," he said with great dignity. "I shall bring you a cold collation, if that is acceptable."

When luncheon arrived, the "cold collation" was happily shared by the birds. There were some truly lovely cheeses, cold beef and ham, pickles of many sorts, lots of fresh fruit, and some of the best bread Nan had ever tasted. She decided that if Lord Alderscroft was going to send them careering about the countryside in the future, this sort of treatment was more than going to make up for any other hardship or difficulties.

They whiled away the time until arriving at their final transfer by interrogating poor Andrew with every question they could think to ask about Elemental Magic and Masters. The poor fellow must have felt as if he was up before the Inquisition before they were through with him, but despite being associated with Lord Alderscroft, they really had never had too much to do with his *magic,* and he wasn't the sort of man you plagued with questions. So poor Andrew had to stand substitute teacher. He did put up with it very well, and Nan, at least, got a good basic grounding in it all. Normally Nan and Sarah would have kept their hands busy with mending, but that sort of thing simply wasn't done by girls of the class to which they supposedly belonged. They wanted to look busy so that the steward, good fellow that he was, wouldn't interrupt them, thinking they needed something, and perhaps overhear something he shouldn't. So they took out the sketch-books they hadn't used since they were in school-lessons, and worked at drawings of the birds and their surroundings. The birds were perfectly fine with this; it allowed them to doze off their meal.

This train sped along without stopping at all, and had them in the station for the last transfer before five.

Here they parted from Andrew. By this point he expressed no misgiving at all as to their ability to fend for themselves, which was just as well, because they really had not wanted him to spoil the impression of a clergyman's daughters that they needed to establish. Only the eye of a very knowledgeable person (such as the steward on a first-class carriage) would distinguish their sober suits from the same sort of thing that their personas would wear—but Andrew's rig-out screamed "gentry."

This last train took a good two hours to go the relatively short distance to Criccieth, not because it stopped at every station, but because this was a smaller line, and the rail right-of-way twisted and turned the entire time. The Welsh countryside was lovely, but Nan was very glad neither she nor Sarah was inclined to sea-sickness, for all the twists and bends did make for a lot of rolling of the car. This was fitted out with two beautifully upholstered bench seats, firmly attached to the floor, with a table bolted to the floor between them. Even the little oil stove was bolted down. They were both glad they had prevailed upon their steward for that late luncheon be-tween Shewsbury and the last station.

So it was that around seven in the evening, the girls stood side-by-side in the last light on the platform at Criccieth, watching their baggage being taken off with a critical eye. Both of them were beginning to feel the journey, which at this point was well past twelve hours, and they were looking forward to its end.

A gentleman with truly formidable mutton-chop whiskers approached them diffidently. "Miss Sarah Lyon-White? Miss Annabelle Lyon-White?" he asked, peering at them. He had a definite—and rather musical to Nan's ears—accent.

"So we are, sir." This time Nan took charge, for Sarah was now supposed to be something of an invalid, and as fatigued as she was, she looked it. "Are you from the Lion Hotel?"

His face lit up with a smile, and he tipped his hat. "In-deed I am, indeed I am, and I am most particularly charged to see to your comfort. Are those your trunks?" He indicated the porters, who had hand-carts loaded with their luggage. Without waiting for an answer, he made little shooing motions, as if they were sheep he wanted to move along. "Come along, my dear young ladies, come along. I have the hotel conveyance waiting for you."

It was an ancient carriage of uncertain vintage, but looking in good repair, with a crest and the words "The Lion Hotel" inscribed on the side of it. Now it was Nan's turn to tip the porters and act like the one in charge. Now it wouldn't matter if she made any little mistakes; from here on, they were to be the daughters of a country clergyman, and Sarah was recovering from some unspecified shock. An extended holiday at the seaside had been prescribed, introductions to local society were in their portmanteaus as well as having been sent on ahead via Lord Alderscroft's extended network of "mutual acquaintances," and because Sarah was supposed to be recovering her strength, no one would be the least surprised that she and Nan took long walks, excursions in a pony car, or horseback rides. On that note, Nan was now very grateful indeed that in her youth Lord Alderscroft's groom had persuaded her onto the back of a horse, much against her own better judgment. Riding was a skill that was likely to prove useful.

The carriage was indeed old, and much in need of new springs, but it got them to the hotel without being shaken to bits, and they arrived just at dusk to see the welcome sight of warm light coming from the many windows of the four-storied hotel. The hotel had been forewarned about the birds, though it appeared from the opulently dressed lady taking a late promenade with a little monkey on a leash that they were by no means the only guests with odd pets.

By the time they were installed in their room they were both so weary that Nan rang for a maid and ordered dinner brought to their room. This was not a luxurious room, but it was in keeping with a pair of young

ladies who were well bred, in modest circumstances, but
had a generous family friend. But in comparison with
lodgings in Africa, this comfortable lodging might just as
well have been luxury. Everything was seen to; there
were even perches for the birds, created by putting pretty
china pots with food and water in them on another
smoking-stand. The floor had a slightly worn Turkey carpet, cabbage-rose wallpaper with matching curtains,
lovely oak furniture, and twin brass beds. There were
flowers on the dressers, oil lamps on bedside tables, and
a beautiful toilet set on the washstand. No electricity out
here, of course, but the oil lamps were good ones. There
was a third lamp, unlit at the moment, at a little desk, and
an easy chair beside the window.

The birds were just as tired as they were at this point.
Neville, who ordinarily would have been clamoring to be
let out the window for fresh air, just gulped down the
dinner presented to him, perched himself on the foot of
Nan's bed, and tucked his head under his wing. Grey was
almost as tired, ate slowly, and took her own perch on
Sarah's bed. Nan spread newspapers for both of them.

"I thought I wanted a bath more than anything,"
Sarah said, with one look at them. "But I think . . . they
have the right idea."

Nan was already pulling out their nightgowns from
the trunk. "I don't think there is anything that can't wait
until tomorrow," she said firmly. "I'm nearly cross-eyed
wanting to lie flat."

"Be quiet," Grey ordered, crossly, as Neville murmured under his wing. "Go to bed."

"Yes ma'am," Nan chuckled, and obeyed.

In the morning, despite the day dawning overcast, everyone was more alert and in a much more cheerful
frame of mind. Nan pulled out the maps she had pro-

cured, and when the breakfast tray came up, she and
Sarah looked them over while munching toast and mar-
malade.

"Lord A has our mysterious person somewhere along
here," Nan said, tracing a stretch of coastline with her
finger northwards from Criccieth. "We have introductions to the family that holds Gower Manor, here, which
seems right in the middle of this, but inland. He thought
once we got oriented, we might see if they have a cottage
they let to visitors. According to what I've been told,
many people here accommodate summer visitors."

Sarah nodded. "That would give us more privacy."

Neville quorked. Nan looked up. He hopped from the
floor where he had been eating onto the windowsill and
pecked at the window.

That gave Nan an idea. "Neville, do you think you
might be able to winkle out magic if you looked for it?"
She still didn't know everything the raven could do. He
kept surprising her. She'd had a rather lively correspon-
dence with the caretaker of Neville's father, a former
Master of the Ravens of the Tower, who had told her
that rather than the twenty-five to thirty-year lifespan
most well-cared-for ravens had, this equally remarkable
bird was already forty, and looked to reach fifty or more.
Not only that, but the wise old fellow had a vocabulary
that would put many humans to shame. Not unlike his
son Neville, in fact.

Neville cocked his head to one side, considering her
question. "Can try," he croaked.

She got up and opened the window, standing well
back. Neville had quite a wingspan, and a buffet from
one of his wings was no joking matter. He launched himself heavily from the window, and flapped off, heading
northwards. Grey watched with interest, but clearly had

no intentions of following. That was probably wise; seagulls didn't much care for parrots, and she was nothing like the acrobatic flyer that Neville was. Nor could she defend herself as readily. There wasn't much that a raven was afraid of, short of an eagle.

"Well," Nan said, as they watched Neville flap away. "Now it's time for us to get to know the town, I suppose."

They quickly came to the conclusion that the Welsh were the most gregarious creatures ever created. It seemed that all of Criccieth—or at least, everyone close to the hotel—knew about the "young invalid lady," and any dislike for them being English was overcome by sympathy for Sarah's having been ill, and further overcome by their background. The Welsh were, for the most part, chapel, not church, and that they made their first contact with the minister of *Capel Mawr,* or rather, his wife, to find out when services were, apparently won everyone.

They were invited in for tea, which was presented in a shabby-genteel parlor, painfully clean, with the windows left open to let in the scent of the rosebushes under them. "We're mostly Nonconformists here in Wales," the little, dark woman said cheerfully. "The English gentry go to St. Catherine's of course, but almost none of us do. If you must have services in English, and don't mind church—" She paused, and the doubtful look on her face made it plain that she, at least, would rather be seen in sailor's den of sin than a service in the Church of England, "then that would be where you would go. There's St. Deiniol's for our church folk, with services in Welsh. There's our chapel, and the new *Capel Seion,* who of course we don't speak to now that we've split—" her eyes twinkled merrily at that, making Nan quite certain that was *not* the case. "And the Congregationalists have their chapel, and the Scotch Baptists have *Capel Uchef,* but *they* split years ago, so the Particular Baptists have their own chapel as well. And there's even Papists. And we all of us have a hymn-sing down on the green at *Abermarchnad* every Sunday night. You really must come."

That occasioned some passionate praise of Welsh part-singing, which convinced Nan that the stereotype of the Welsh being able to sing was a truism. And she did love music . . . it might be nice to go.

They discussed — or, Sarah discussed; Nan kept quiet on subjects she knew nothing about — Ladies' Beneficent Society, sewing circles, altar guilds. Nan wondered when and where Sarah had learned all of this, because at the Harton School, though they did have a chapel and did have services, said services were decidedly not of the sort that a parish church or chapel would conduct.

Maybe she got all this from letters from her mum.

"And you have birds, then?" the minister's diminutive wife said, pouring out more of the tea that was a requirement of any formal visit, excepting only one in the evening . . . and since she was a Methodist, probably even then. "How did that come about?"

"My parrot came with my parents from Africa after their mission duties, and she decided that I was the person she wanted," Sarah explained. "Parrots are rather like cats; *they* tend to choose the person, not the person choose the parrot."

The minister's wife brightened. "Oh! African missions! We support a little mission in Liberia . . . well, by 'we' I mean most of the chapels hereabouts together. It's not much we can send, but we do our best?"

Nan had noticed that many sentences spoken in Wales, even though they were declarative, ended sound-

ing like a question, as if the speaker was asking for your
permission to say it . . . or, perhaps, for your agreement.

"Our mission was in the Congo, but believe me, every
little bit that comes out to the missions is truly, truly, appreciated," Sarah lied gracefully, as Nan kept her face as
straight as possible but dared not say anything. She remembered all too well the hilarity over the "charity
boxes" that would come to the clinic, full of completely
unsuitable, unusable things like frilly petticoats and
woolen waistcoats and thick, heavy shoes. Somehow
Sarah's parents made use of it all, though the petticoats
got disassembled into the component parts, the plain
part turned into bandages, and the frills went off to glad-
den the hearts of certain Muslim ladies in the families of
the traders, who yearned to wear lace under their *burqas*.
As for anything of wool, that often ended up being re-
duced to threads, and threads turned into wound-wool
bangles and anklets. Not what the good-hearted ladies
that had sent the boxes pictured when they packed their
bounty up.

But that, of course, was exactly what the dear lady
wanted to hear, and by the time the visit was over, Nan
was fairly certain that there would be nowhere in this
part of Wales where they would not have a good reputation.

Then it was back to the hotel for luncheon, and to let
Neville back into the room. He hadn't found anything
overtly magical, but he *did* bring back a sprig of oak, a
twig of ash, and a leaf from a thornbush.

"Oak, ash and thorn, hmm?" Nan looked at her bird
askance. "You think I ought to try calling him, then?"

Neville shook his head.

"Ah, so this is more in case he wants to find us?" As
Neville agreed, Nan reflected that made sense. If Puck

decided to help them out, it would be easier for him to get to them across any barriers to magic, such as iron or salt or churchly ground, if she had his tokens about her. She tied the bits of foliage together with a bit of red thread, and tucked them inside her watch-case.

"Since you're an invalid, do you mind horribly if I leave you here to laze about while I look into hiring horses or a pony cart?" Nan asked.

Sarah rolled her eyes. "At least I have some books."

"I'll look for a bookshop," Nan promised, and put on her hat and went out again.

Finding a bookshop proved to be the least difficult thing of all. The Welsh, it seemed, loved books. Nan took a quick inventory of what was on offer, was assured by the proprietor that "anything you can find advertised in *The Times*, I can have here in a week," then hiked up to the ruins of the castle that overlooked the town. It gave her a fine view of Cardigan Bay, and she reckoned that if she was going to spot anything that looked like a stable, she would see it from up there.

She was a little sad that they actually were *not* going to be able to do much real sightseeing. After Egypt, she'd gotten a taste for poking around in ruins, and it looked as if there were a fair number of them scattered about, not including the castle.

She had thought the air at Lord Aldercroft's manor, which housed the school, was wonderful. It was not to be compared with the air here, which was in turns gusts off pristine, hilly meadows dotted with sheep, and straight off the sea, salty and alive. As for the view, it was green and glorious on land for as far as the eye could see: hills practically vibrating with greens and the yellow of gorse-blossom to the west, and to the east, the Bay spread out barely rippling with tiny waves. The presence of a lifeboat station, however, was mute warning that the Bay was not always so tranquil.

Nan could not for the life of her spot anything like a livery stable, and walking the streets of the town proved no more fruitful. In fact, all that she did actually learn—beyond that the Castle Bakery produced the most delicious smells—was that she really wished she could learn Welsh instantly. Being able to speak only English was going to be a distinct handicap, especially if their quarry was one of the folk that had no more words in English than she had in Welsh.

So when she returned to the hotel, she sought help there. An inquiry at the desk swiftly brought out the manager. Evidently Lord Alderscroft's man had been most particular in his instructions when the reservations had been made.

"My sister has been told to get easy exercise and go about in the country and on the shore as much as possible," she explained, "And we can both ride, so I wondered if there were any horses for hire?"

"Hmm. Horses, not so many, and not at this season," the manager said. "But a pony cart could be managed, if you can drive? Several beaches are hard enough to drive on. I'll make the arrangements for you."

"That would be exceedingly helpful, thank you," Nan replied with gratitude, for after an afternoon in town, she had become less and less certain that even if she *could* find a stable, she would be able to negotiate for the use of horses.

She came back upstairs to find Sarah at ease, the remains of what looked to have been a lovely tea on the table, feeding bits of toast to the birds. Her friend looked up and saw her dismay, and laughed.

"Don't look so stricken; your tea is intact on that tray,

under the cover." She nodded at a covered tray on a side table. "Though it was a battle to keep the starving peasants here off it."

Grey made a rude noise. Nan was famished, and fell on the meal like a starving peasant herself, making her report between bites.

"Well," Sarah said at last. "I've got a notion that what we should do is combine looking for our magician with looking for a cottage to rent."

Nan nodded. "I really do not think that we'll find him anywhere near Criccieth. The two of us can take care of a little cottage easily enough, and we can both cook." She sighed. "Much as I would *rather* have someone else do it for me. . . ."

"Oh, listen to milady! *Now* who's to the manor born?" Sarah teased.

"It is the life to which I would very much like to become accustomed, thank you," Nan replied. "But I *believe,* if what I was told about having holidays in Wales is correct, I can have a standing order put in at the grocer, the butcher, and the bakery, and have one of their boys bring it all out to us once a week. So . . . Gower Manor should be my next goal, once we have the pony cart, and we can see about the cottage."

"That sounds like the best plan," Sarah agreed. "Now, the important part. *Did* you find a bookshop?"

Something of the thrill of being courted had rapidly worn off for Mari.

She had, now and then, heard girls—Braith in particular—complaining about how "tiresome" it was to have several young men at their heels, and had thought they were engaging in a sort of showing off. Now she was not so sure. Compliments were lovely . . . but after you heard them several times, you began to wonder how sincere they were. The young Selch seemed to be a great deal like most other young men, who wanted to get the courting part over with as quickly as possible, and on to the bedding part.

These young men were thoroughgoing young pagans, too, which meant they had even less patience with courting than the boys up in Clogwyn.

Although she did her very best not to show her partiality, because she was using the "courting" to put off making a decision for as long as she could, Mari had rejected Mabon within days of the Selch turning up. He was a nice enough lad, but it was hard to have a conversation with the top of a head. "Shy" didn't even begin to describe him. He was the only one of the lot who seemed to have no idea why he had been selected to woo and win her.

Well, she had no idea either, unless it was someone's idea that if she didn't respond to the beauteous and ever-so-pleased with himself Rhodri, she might respond to someone who was the opposite. And although it was *tempting* to decide on someone she probably could treat like a pet or a rug, she would be living with whatever man she chose for months, and she really didn't want a lapdog.

They were all nice enough lads, for a lot of heathen magic creatures with no notion of what the world was like nowadays and quaint ideas that were probably considered old-fashioned when Owen Tudor walked the hills, but while all this was amusing in its way, it was not something she wanted to live with and cope with for however long it would take to produce a couple of babies. *She* was the one who was going to have to deal with a curious village, an even more curious and hostile constable (who was certainly going to want to know just where the new husband had materialized from) and the repercussions when husband and one of the babies vanished.

And none of them seemed to grasp the difficulties, or be willing to accept that things on land were not as they always had been.

None of them, that is, except Idwal.

She had discovered this when she was trying to convince Rhodri that no one truly believed in the Selch anymore except children and a few old people.

"That's nonsense," he said, waving his hand as if that would make it all go away. "Completely daft. It isn't a matter of *believing,* as if we were gods no one can see. We're quite real and solid when we choose to be. How can anyone not believe in us?"

Idwal came up behind him where he was sitting on the sand, making net-weights out of stones and cord, and cuffed him on the back of the head. "Ow!" he exclaimed indignantly. "What's that for?"

"For being a great goose," Idwal said in disgust. "Idiot. The gods walked the hills once, real and solid, too. Tis an easy thing to learn to not believe, particularly when your liege and your neighbors and your priest are all telling you to believe in something else entirely, and making it worth your while to do as they say." He made himself comfortable next to Mari. "Look at you! You're doing it this moment! You're *not believing* Mari as hard as you can, because believing her will mean you'll be put to some trouble."

"Are you saying I'm lazy or a fool?" demanded Rhodri.

"Both."

Rhodri stared at him, blue eyes burning a hole in the older man, plainly seething. "Your status as Master, Druid, and teacher has gone to your head."

"My experience as Master, Druid, and teacher has taught me how to recognize a fool when I see one, and my experience with *you* tells me that you'll avoid being forced to think about consequences at every possible occasion." Idwal raised an eyebrow.

Rhodri made a great show of tying off the last net-weight, and got to his feet. "I think I can tell when my company is a burden," he declared. "Enjoy your puttering about with magic, Mari. And mind, I'm going to walk with you in the moonlight on the shingle tonight."

"So I promised," she agreed, and the handsome Selch—well, he didn't exactly *flounce* off, but there was pent irritation in every step.

Idwal sighed. "It seems," he said, carefully, "At least from what I overheard, that mortal life is more complex and fraught these days. I do not know that I can help with any solutions, but would you begin at the beginning and just explain what this *constable* person is all about, and why he should be troubling you?"

Mari began by explaining what a constable was, then why she and her da surmised that he was here in the first place, then what would likely happen when he got wind of not one, but five strange men turning up daily here at the cottage.

The Selch's brow furrowed. "I believe I see. The others look at you, and see someone who lives away from the town, and think this distance protects you, as if you were a hermit. Perhaps in the old days, it did. But now it does not protect you, and the overlord may send his sheriff at any time to enforce whatever decree he has made." He shook his head. "Perhaps this is one reason why we returned to the sea in the long ago, because men were creating overlords who answered to no will but their own and professed to be master and owner of not only the land but the people thereon."

She sighed with relief at having finally gotten through to one of the Selch, at least. "It wasn't like this in grandfather's time. Being out here in our cottage did keep people from nosing about. I don't really think that anyone actually knew, in the town, that Grandfather even *had* a wife until he turned up with Da, and told everyone that the gypsy he'd spent a season with had come by and left the baby with him saying it was his."

Idwal nodded. "And . . . if I understand correctly . . . the tale that your grandfather had pleasured himself with a gypsy without the bonds of marriage was seen as something admirable?"

She had to shrug. "Maybe not that. Well, the women would have said things. But the men would have pretended to be shocked, but secretly thought he was quite the sly, clever fellow."

"But for you . . . having congress without a marriage is a deep disgrace." Idwal frowned deeper. "We do not think in this way. We do not think congress is a bad thing, with or without marriage. And we welcome every birth. Inheritance among us comes through the mother—as does lineage. After all, no man can be absolutely sure of who his father is, but there is no doubt who is his mother."

She giggled at that, a little embarrassed by his frankness, then sobered. "But we don't think that way, and I could even be in trouble from the—the sheriff. I'm not sure, but it is possible. There might be laws about it, town laws, not just church or chapel laws. Without a marriage and banns and all that, we could be in real difficulty.

People might refuse to buy or trade for da's fish, or to sell us things."

"Well then, there must be a marriage," Idwal said firmly. "Would it be possible to take a journey in the coracle to the greater town, and find there someone who would make a marriage? Then you would have your paper, and all would be well."

She blinked at that; it was something she hadn't even thought of for herself. And certainly there were enough Nonconformist sects in Criccieth that *one* of them would surely be willing to marry a couple that just turned up out of nowhere. Oh . . . but then there were the banns to be posted and those had to be posted in the chapel where you lived. Or you had to get a special license, and how did you do that?

"Also," he continued thoughtfully, "I have heard it said that the captain of a ship may conduct a marriage. Ship captains are always in need of money. We could bring up some gold and pay one to do this, and we would not be concerned with propriety *or* silence, for who would ask him?"

Her mouth fell open. Now that was a *very* good idea! Not only that, but this idea gave birth to another. "And if we said my husband was a sailor—sailors are *always* dying at sea! So when he goes back—I can say he's joined his ship. Then maybe da goes into Criccieth, and sends a telegraph about him dying to me here, and I go into mourning and—but how do I explain a missing baby?"

"You will have twins, as our chieftain said," Idwal replied, as if it was as certain as the sun rising. "And you will merely hide one. This should be of no matter and no great difficulty."

"If you say so . . ." But she could not help but admire

how Idwal, instead of arguing about how she was certainly wrong, or mistaken, or just being foolish, had asked for explanations, bent his mind to help her, and done so.

And that was when it struck her.

She wasn't attracted to any of the "boys." In fact, that was how she thought of them. But Idwal . . .

Saints. I could be happy with Idwal . . . I think. And he wouldn't need to leave when I'd chosen; he could keep teaching me about magic. He'd be good company. Da never grumbles about him.

In fact, the notion of being with Idwal gave her a little thrill in her stomach. Whereas the notion of being with the boys gave her a feeling of resignation.

This was worth exploring. But in the meantime—

"You were going to show me how to summon Water creatures," she said, deliberately choosing the word "summon," although that was not what he had said.

"No, my student," he corrected with a smile. "And I know that you are testing me. I did not say that word. I am going to show you how to *invite* them. While it is true that a Water Master can always compel an Elemental to come with his will, I shall not teach you that. To summon is to exert the will of the master over the slave. To invite is to ask, politely, for the assistance of an ally. Which would *you* prefer, if you were the one being called for?"

She chuckled. "The latter, of course. If you please?"

"I knew you would say that." He smiled broadly. "Let us go to the spring."

9

GOWER Manor had a cottage, a newish building, not a traditional "cottage," built and kept especially to lend to friends of the squire who chose to holiday here rather than in some more fashionable watering spot. This much Nan had learned with careful inquiry around Criccieth. Then, her letters of introduction in hand, she paid a visit to the squire.

That the cottage was vacant, she already knew. That much was common knowledge in the town. What wasn't known was whether or not someone was likely to take up tenancy there in the next two or three weeks. The squire, despite the fact that his family had lived here for four generations, still considered himself English, not Welsh; the residents of Criccieth felt exactly the same. By this point there wasn't much (if any) animosity, but there also wasn't much communication, either.

So Nan and Sarah took the hired pony-cart off for an

investigative visit, which had turned up the satisfying information that there were no friends who wished to avail themselves of the cottage this year. And a little more conversation about how Sarah preferred more privacy than they got at the Lion Hotel, and a bit of name-dropping, induced the information that the squire would be perfectly happy to let it to two such delightful—and well-connected—young ladies.

Nan had a pretty good notion of what he was thinking. He might be able to find a tenant in the form of some "sporting fellows," who would make a great deal of work for the maid, who would drink when they were not fishing, and might well make more than work for the maid. Whereas, clearly the daughters of a clergyman would be up to no mischief in such a spot, remote from the temptations of a city.

Even if he briefly entertained the idea that they might want privacy so that some illicit liaison could take place, the only way to reach the cottage required that anyone who cared to visit them would have to first drive or ride up to the Manor itself.

And Nan looked like quite the stern fire-breathing old spinster; hardly the sort to allow her prettier sibling to do anything other than what she was *supposed* to do: recover her strength.

And they were so *very* well-connected!

It was quite clear to Nan that the squire had weighed all this quickly in his mind before agreeing to lease the cottage to two unchaperoned women, which was why she had covertly studied the dress and behavior of some of the more puritanical ladies of Criccieth in order to imitate them. She hadn't gone too far—she wasn't sure she'd have been able to keep a straight face—but she'd managed to make herself look years older and sufficiently unattractive to satisfy the conscience of both the squire and his even-more-suspicious spouse.

Gower Cottage was *not* a cottage of the sort that one of the local people would live in; it was the gentry's idea of a cottage. This meant it had been built to modern lines, copying local architecture. It had thick stone walls, three hearths, with nice iron stoves instead of fireplaces, stone floors with carpets instead of pounded earth, and a girl coming over from the Manor twice a week to do for them and bring them whatever they needed in the way of food-stuffs. It was actually more comfortable than the hotel for a lot of reasons, not the least of which was you could throw open the windows and have a cool sea breeze flowing right through the place. One of the first letters Nan wrote to Lord Alderscroft recommended the place to any of the White Lodge who felt the need to escape for a rest.

That had been the very day they moved in. The little maid had come over to see what the "English ladies" needed doing, and Nan had sent her back with letters to be posted with the family mail. She'd done so deliberately, so that the squire was aware that her name-dropping had the backing of truth. She knew very well that the addresses would be examined minutely, and that Lord A's address would cause no end of high excitement.

It was probably the first time anyone in that lofty a set of circles had been written to from Gower Manor—though what with David Lloyd George being the MP from this area, the Criccieth post office would be seeing missives going off to those with even loftier titles. Criccieth was very proud of its native son, and Nan must have heard a hundred predictions that "He'll be the Prime Minister one day, never doubt it." Still, the squire was not included in those circles, as he was not "political." That was yet another bit of Criccieth gossip.

Their first night had been restful; there had been no singing from the bar to wake them, and the beds had been soft and scented with lavender. Breakfast had been just as tasty, if plainer, than the fare at the hotel. Cooking on the pretty little stove was like playing at keeping house. It felt as if they were really here to enjoy themselves.

Unfortunately, as Nan was all too well aware, they were not. Nan turned away from the kitchen window that gave a view of a lovely little garden. "Well . . ." Nan began, only to be interrupted by Sarah.

"I wish we really were on holiday," her friend sighed. "This is lovely."

Ordinarily Grey might have chimed in with an agreement, but Grey was stuffing herself with new peas, fresh from the garden, with a gluttonous abandon that could only be matched by a toddler with a jar of jam and no adults in sight.

"Well we're not. Neville was off like a shot when I let him loose, I think he might actually have a—scent, or whatever it is that you can trace magic by." Neville had been so eager to get out, he'd practically been dancing on his perch, and he hadn't been at all coherent in his speech. He and Nan had other ways of communicating though, and she had gotten the distinct impression that as the cart carrying them and their belongings had neared Gower Manor, he'd picked up something promising.

Lord A had expressed no disappointment that they had as yet found nothing—but Nan didn't like to keep him dangling like this. She wanted to be able to write "We've found the party you are looking for, and we are watching him for trouble" sooner rather than later.

"Well I hope this business lasts a good long time,"

Sarah replied as she put their clothing away in the com-
modious wardrobe. "If I were to pick one spot in Britain
where I would like to spend the whole summer, it would
be here."

Nan had to agree with her. For one thing, the weather
around here was nothing like she'd been warned they'd
get in Wales—rain, fog, and more rain. Instead, they got
beautiful, sunny days, temperate nights, heavenly sea-
breezes. For another, the cottage was just nice enough
that it felt special, and not so luxurious that she felt uneasy, as if she was somewhere she had no right to be. It
had three nice, cozy rooms below—a bedroom, a sort of
sitting room, and a little kitchen—and a loft with a bed
in it above. Sarah had claimed the loft immediately. The
kitchen even had its own pump. Baths might be done the
old-fashioned way, heating water in a kettle and bathing
in a tin tub in the kitchen in front of the fire, but at least
they wouldn't be doing so on a riverbank, with a crowd
of curious native children around them, waiting to see if
their pale color was something that would wash off, like
a layer of white mud. Or with other native children on
guard for them, watching for crocodiles or hippos or
snakes.

The former had been amusing; the latter, not so much.

The furnishing of this place had obviously been done
out of the attics of the Manor, which was not to say that
the furnishings were shabby or uncomfortable, merely
old-fashioned, perhaps a trifle countrified, which suited
both of them.

Grey looked up from her peas. "Neville's coming," she
remarked, and put her head back down in her bowl.

A moment later Neville landed in the doorway,
stalked into the cottage, then used a chair seat and the
back of the chair to get to his perch. He shook his head

and quorked, querulously, his way of saying that his vocabulary didn't extend to what he wanted to say.

Nan came over to him and put her hands around his head, staring into his eyes, letting impressions come to her.

As often happened, she got a raven's-eye view of things. By now she no longer felt dizzy when experiencing memories of flying. Finally she let him go, and got him a bowl full of bits of bread soaked with milk and some curds and currants for good measure.

"He's frustrated. There is definitely magic down on the coast, but he can't make out exactly where it is. It's like a fog over a certain area. He has the sense that whatever is doing the magic is making that fog deliberately, in order to confuse," she told Sarah.

"That sounds difficult . . ." Sarah replied thoughtfully. "I should think that would denote a high level of skill."

Nan could only shrug. "All right. I think we have done as much as we can by ourselves. I'm going to see if you-know-who answers when we try calling. If he doesn't, we're no worse off, and if he does, he'll save us a great deal of trouble."

"I have the Shakespeare." Sarah produced two little brown volumes immediately. "I had the feeling we were going to need them."

"And I found a fairy ring when I was exploring the garden." Nan raised an eyebrow. "Which makes me wonder if we've been expected . . ."

"You never know . . . hmm . . . you know, I think we should not be empty-handed this time. We should bring tea." Sarah began cutting slices of bread. She wrapped them in a napkin, then got a pot of strawberry jam, another of butter, some hard-boiled eggs and a bit of paper with salt in it, and put them all in a basket with knives and more napkins. Nan looked at her curiously, then shrugged and filled a jug with water from the pump. Sarah added some pottery mugs to the basket and put the books on top. "That should do," she said. She took the basket, Nan carried the jug, and led the way to the fairy circle she had found, a ring of mushrooms growing as neatly as if they had been planted there.

They put the jug and the basket down carefully outside the circle, stepped into the ring with great care not to disturb any mushrooms, and took the books, opening them to the familiar pages.

Nan took out her sprigs of oak, ash and thorn, put them on the grass between her and Sarah, and pitched her voice low. "How now, spirit! whither wander you?"

That was Puck's part. As the fairy queen Titania's handmaiden, Sarah replied. "Over hill, over dale / Thorough bush, thorough brier / Over park, over pale / Thorough flood, thorough fire / I do wander everywhere / Swifter than the moon's sphere; / And I serve the fairy queen / To dew her orbs upon the green. / The cowslips tall her pensioners be: / In their gold coats spots you see; / Those be rubies, fairy favors / In those freckles live their savors: / I must go seek some dewdrops here / And hang a pearl in every cowslip's ear. / Farewell, thou lob of spirits; I'll be gone. / Our queen and all our elves come here anon."

Nan continued, still taking Puck's part, shading her voice with warning. "The king doth keep his revels here to-night: / Take heed the queen come not within his sight; / For Oberon is passing fell and wrath / Because that she as her attendant hath / A lovely boy, stolen from an Indian king; / She never had so sweet a changeling; / And jealous Oberon would have the child / Knight of his train, to trace the forests wild; / But she perforce withholds the loved boy / Crowns him with flowers and makes him all her joy: / And now they never meet in grove or green / By fountain clear, or spangled starlight sheen / But, they do square / that all their elves for fear / Creep into acorn-cups and hide them there."

Now Sarah narrowed her eyes and pointed her finger at Nan, her voice full of suspicion. "Either I mistake your shape and making quite / Or else you are that shrewd and knavish sprite / Call'd Robin Goodfellow: / are not you he / That frights the maidens of the villagery; / Skim milk, and sometimes labor in the quern / And bootless make the breathless housewife churn; / And sometime make the drink to bear no barm; / Mislead night-wanderers, laughing at their harm? / Those that Hobgoblin call you and sweet Puck / You do their work, and they shall have good luck: / Are not you he?"

Before Nan could answer, the sound of slow applause stopped her. They both turned.

A very handsome young man stood there, clapping his hands with approval, wearing the sort of clothing that would not have been unusual on any of the young farmers hereabouts: linen shirt, open at the throat, heavier smock over it, loose brown trousers, barefoot. He had a shock of reddish, curly hair, a very merry round face — and there was no mistaking the green eyes that danced amusement at them. He confirmed Nan's guess by clearing his throat and taking the next lines. "Thou speak'st aright; / I am that merry wanderer of the night. / I jest to Oberon and make him smile / When I a fat and bean-fed horse beguile, / Neighing in likeness of a filly foal: / And sometime lurk I in a gossip's bowl, / In very likeness of a roasted crab, / And when she drinks, against her lips I bob / And on her wither'd dewlap pour the ale. / The wisest aunt, telling the saddest tale, / Sometime for three-foot stool mistaketh me; / Then slip I from her bum, down topples she, / And 'tailor' cries, and falls into a cough; / And then the whole quire hold their hips and laugh, / And waxen in their mirth and neeze and swear / A merrier hour was never wasted there."

Then he grinned, and held out his arms. "And merry met again, my pretty girls! Your Robin has missed you!"

"Puck!" squealed Sarah. Nan just grinned, and without any sense of embarrassment whatsoever, the two of them skipped out of the circle to embrace him like the old friend he was.

He kissed the tops of their heads, being more than a head taller than either of them. "Eh, now, you've grown, you two."

"And so have you!" Sarah retorted. "Thou naughty sprite! We know *now* you can take whatever shape you want to. You're just humoring us!"

"Welladay, welladay, would you rather I was your beamish boy, all apple-cheeks and innocence?" He stepped back from them, and between one breath and the next, became the boy they had first met.

"We like you however you choose to be, boy or man or Prince of Logres," Sarah said firmly. "Or Pooka or Hob or sprite. You're still Puck and still our friend no matter what shape you take."

"Eh, well said, sweet Sarah." A blur and a blink and he was the young man again. "But I think I'll be wearing this suit o'skin for now." He sniffed. "Do I smell jam?"

"Very nice jam," Nan affirmed. "We brought you a tea—though we didn't actually bring tea, just water."

"Piff, I can remedy that." He waved a hand airily. "Well, spread your carpet on the green, and let's have tea whilst you tell me what brings you to the land of Daffyd and Deryn."

They had brought a cloth to save their skirts from staining, and Nan laid it down while Sarah spread out the food. On pouring out the water, it appeared that Puck had done something to it. "Cowslip wine," he said, around a mouthful of buttered, jam-spread bread. "Never fear, 'tisn't strong enough to get a child tipsy, I just fancy it."

"Well, it's a short tale," Nan said, carefully buttering her own slice of bread. "Lord Alderscroft got wind of a new Elemental Master somewhere hereabouts. A Water Master, he says, but the Elementals won't say who it is or exactly where the person is. He wants us to find this Master and . . . well, explain the Lodge and the Circle, and see what happens."

"Hmm-hmm, and spy in the meantime to see if the new Master is likely to fall into dark paths." Puck nodded. "Seeing as he trod that road himself, nearly to his own undoing. With pain comes wisdom, at least in his case." He finished his slice and started on another. "And I reckon you two have come to the conclusion that you aren't going to find out who it is."

Sarah sighed. "Yes. So . . . well, we thought we'd see if *you* would help. Since you're the Oldest Old Thing—"

"Ah, on land but *not* in the sea, my pretties, and this new Master has a Master, and that Master is Llyr." He nodded, though both of them looked at him, mystified. "Oh, yes, Llyr, wave-crowned, Oldest Old Thing in the Sea as I am on the Land. Sea-lord as I am Land-lord, and guardian of the Selch and the Pooka and all the other Fair Folk of the waters. He saw this one, and saw the power in her, and claimed her as his own, and no more ready to see power go to the bad than I am, he's seen she gets training."

Nan gaped at him. *She!* Well that would give Lord A a bit of a turn!

Puck grinned at them. "Aye, aye, a girl-child it is, and your lord never considered that, now, did he?"

"Not really," Sarah said, and smiled just a bit. "Well, then, can you help us?"

"Hmmm, now that is a question. I wouldn't want to tread on Llyr's toes, no I wouldn't. He's a bitter thing, and cold, and his thoughts are dark, on account of family troubles in the long-ago, and oh, but he is quick to anger." Puck finished his second slice of bread and leaned back, mug full of cowslip wine in hand. "Mind, he almost never shows his own self, leaving working his will up to his creatures. And he's like the sea, all smiles and sunny on the surface, but dark and deep and sometimes deadly beneath. Welladay. I shall tell you what I can do. I'll show you where she is, and I'll give you the means to see through Llyr's magic, and what you do then is up to you. Bearing in mind that you won't want to anger Llyr."

Nan let out her breath in a long sigh. "That's more than I'd have dared ask for," she said. "I don't want to presume on our friendship."

"Which is why you are my friends still, oh pretty goose." He passed his hand over the top of the jug, which was still half-full, and gravely poured out mugs full of something golden as honey for each of them. "And now that I think of it, I want you to be keeping an eye on this maiden for me, as well. Dark things are watching her and will try and use her. It is so with all who are strong and ignorant."

He handed them each the mugs. "This will give the power of seeing the Fair Folk and the Elementals, and the means of seeing through Llyr's sea-fog. Drink!"

Nan did so without hesitation; it was sweet and sharp, like wine, but with the taste of honey. It seemed oddly familiar to her.

"That's mead, the old, old drink of gods and kings and warriors." He winked. "Don't drink too deep, now, 'tis treacherous. And here." He passed two slices of bread over, each holding a slice of red-fleshed salmon on it, though where it had come from neither could have said. "Now eat of this. 'Tis the Salmon of Knowledge, and it will give you the tongue of the locals, and the knowledge of here and inland, so you can pass as something other than English—there's still little love here wasted on the English in general, though pretty maids may be given better shrift."

Now this was *just* what Nan had been wishing for, when they first arrived at Criccieth! Eagerly she bit into her share, just as Grey and Neville winged over from the cottage.

Neville bowed to Puck, who laughed and fed a scrap of salmon to him and to Grey. "You two might as well speak the speech of Daffyd too," he chuckled. "Oh my wisest of birds!"

Neville bolted his scrap down, shook all his feathers and posed with obvious pride at Puck's praise, while Grey daintily held her bit in her foot and ate it morsel by morsel.

"Will it last?" Nan wanted to know.

"Oh, aye, it's a useful gift and one worth having." Puck nodded. "Your girl is living in a bit of a stone cottage, all alone, just outside of a little village called Clogwyn, up the coast from here. You're in a good brisk walk south and landward of where she is, high enough above the sea not to be in danger, close enough for her father to heave his coracles on the beach. Her name is Mari Prothero, and her father is Daffyd. Creatures of Llyr are teaching her the ways of her magic. Now, when you've anything for my ears, just look for the fairy ring in your garden and put my token in the center and I'll come. And I'll likely come without a summons when I fancy tea." He leapt to his feet. "Merry meet, merry part, and merry meet again, my pretties!"

There was a shimmer, and a brightness, and then he was gone.

Mari was just a little vexed at the way things were progressing—or rather, were not progressing. Here she was, trying to get Idwal's interest, and he was absolutely oblivious to her hints. And she just couldn't seem to get rid of the others, except for Mabon, who had stood up one night after Idwal finished telling a tale, announced that he simply could not offer anything that the others couldn't do better, and that he was going back to the sea.

Poor Mabon. It didn't help that it was true. He couldn't teach her magic, he couldn't tell a tale, was not any sort of musician, wasn't as handsome as Rhodri, wasn't as amusing as Trefor, and wasn't anything like the help with the fishing that Niarl was. She had felt terribly sorry for him—but not so sorry that she was going to run after him and beg him to come back.

After all, if she didn't eliminate *someone,* that unpleasant creature, the clan leader—she still didn't know his name—would begin to suspect what she was up to. She was supposed to be deciding among these suitors. He had clearly sent her good choices, so *some* delay was perfectly natural as she was spoiled for choice. Still, if she had gone much longer without one giving up, things would look suspicious indeed. Mabon did her a favor.

She couldn't stay vexed at Idwal for long, however, since what Idwal was teaching her was so very fascinating. It was all so exciting that as soon as a lesson began, she would completely forget she was supposed to be annoyed.

Already she could reliably invite the three Tylwyth Teg—Idwal said they were true Elementals, and not actually Fair Folk—that lived in the spring nearest the cottage. One would always come, often two, and reasonably often, all three. This, Idwal said, meant that her "calls" would work, and more to the point, if she needed an Elemental, one would likely turn up without her needing to call.

And she could *see* other creatures now, though she couldn't really communicate with them in a meaningful way—others being the creatures of the other three elements, Fire, Earth and Air. Air, she saw most often, the transparent winged girls that were the primary Air Elementals; Earth now and again in the form of little hobs and good-tempered creatures she couldn't put a name to in the meadow; and Fire, once, in the fire that heated the oven, a strange, lizard-like creature with glowing eyes.

Idwal had taught her how to protect herself, how to hide herself from the eyes of magicians, and promised to teach her how to defend and attack at need. She was looking forward to that. But today he had been quite mysterious, and told her only to come down to the shore at dawn, because he wished to surprise her.

So down to the shore she went, in the early morning before the boys came, for that was when he had specified. She crept out of the cottage without waking her da, who was going out with Niarl to fish for salmon today, and saw him waiting there for her, at a distance, standing so quietly he could have been the stump of an old mast sticking out of the sand. The sky was still dark to the west, so he was little more than a thrust of shadow against it. But as she walked toward him, carefully feel-

ing her way with bare feet, the sun was lightening the
horizon behind her, and by the time she was halfway to
him, she could make out the pale oval of his face against
his hair. It struck her then, what was so different about
these Selch men: they all had hair longer than most men
hereabouts wore it, yet they were also curiously clean-
shaven. All but the clan-leader, that is, who had sported
a great beard and moustache of grizzled brown.

As she neared him, she saw there was something dark
pooled at his feet, as if he had thrown something down
there. Soon she realized what it was: a sealskin cloak, the
means by which they transformed from man to seal. She
felt a twinge of disappointment; she already had seen
them transform, this was nothing new. She was hoping
that since he had urged her here at such an hour, he
might have something more interesting in mind than
teaching her—say—how to tell a Selch from a true seal.
She already knew that; she'd noted that to her newly
awakened eyes, the Selch all had a faint, greenish glow
about them when they were seals, and she guessed that
true seals probably did not have any such thing.

"You come in good time, my student," he said genially, and bent to pick up the cloak. That was when she
saw that there were two, not one, as he picked up the
other, and handed it to her. "You'll want to shake the
sand from that," he advised, doing the same with his.
"Make sure there's none on the inside, particularly."

It was very heavy, surprisingly soft, and moved in her
hands like fabric, not like the stiff hides she was used to.
"What's this for?" she asked, shaking it vigorously. Had
he meant to give it to her as a gift? If so, given that he
was a Selch ... it was a rather macabre gift.

"It's my surprise. I've gotten a Selch sealskin for you;
that's what that is," he replied. "That's a hard thing to do,

to get one for someone who hasn't one of her own; mostly we grow our own as youngsters, since rarely do any Selch live on land to man- or woman-hood. Once in a great while, someone keeps one about that came from a relative who died in human form. I had to go almost to Selkie-waters to find this one."

She felt a little queasy. "The Selch—wasn't killed— was he?" she asked, the sealskin suddenly feeling very heavy in her hands, and she wondered if it was tainted with blood. The skin from a dead Selch! Wasn't it rather like the skin of a dead man? Who would keep such a thing?

He chuckled. "She, and no. She went to land for love of a mortal man, lived with her faithful love all of her life, had many children, half came to the sea and half stayed with her, and she died at a very old age in his arms. A happy tale. She never missed the sea, for he told her to don her skin when she needed to be free on the waves. She helped him with the fishing until she grew too old for it, then one of her sea-children came in her place. And when she died, she left the skin, right and proper, to her children. One of her land-children brought it to the sea-kin, in case anyone should have need of it. He minded him of the stories of unhappy Selch and Selkie, kept from the sea when their lovers hid their skins. But it never was needed to be used for such a thing, and when word came around I was looking, it was brought to me."

She felt much better after that, and the sealskin went back to being a lovely object in her hands. She still couldn't imagine why he'd brought it, though. If he'd just wanted her to see what one looked like, he could have shown her his own skin.

"So, so, so, now put it on," Idwal commanded, swinging his own sealskin about his shoulders. "It's time you heeded the heritage of your blood. More than time, and if it had been me, you'd have been taught at a time when you could still have grown a skin of your own."

"Eh?" she replied, startled by his order. He couldn't possibly mean that *she* was to transform! "But—"

"But you've as much Selch blood as your brother, and though Clan Leader Gethin would not like me telling you this, 'tis your birthright to come to the sea as much as it is his." He gestured at her. "As I said, I'd have had you taught when you were but toddling unsteady on the shore. More than that, I'd have let you know what the binding was on your blood from the time you understood it, and came to the Clan to see all the likely bulls while they were still pups. Then there wouldn't have been the shock and the fuss and the carrying on, for you'd have known them, and they you, and there would have been friendly persuasion on both sides. Put it on, now. 'Tis time you saw your proper world, as much as you are Elemental Master as you are Selch."

She copied his motions, swinging the skin over her shoulders, so that the head hung down her back like a hood. It felt heavy and warm for a moment, then unaccountably got lighter . . . and warmer.

"Now," he said, "Put on the face. Like this."

He reached back and pulled the seal-face over his own, his eyes looking out through the empty holes in the skin.

She did. She got a strange, shivery feeling all over herself as the head came down over hers, and she looked out through the eyeholes. Already the world looked a little different; a little more gray, and a little clearer and sharper. Was that just her imagination?

Idwal nodded with approval. "The transformation is

nothing more nor less than will. No fancy casting of spells, no preparations. Just as natural as a babe learning to walk. Now. *Want* to be Selch. Long for the sea. Know the sea is our mother, and know she will welcome you when you come to her. Feel yourself being held and cradled by the water. *Be* Selch—"

This was easy. Her da had taken her out in the coracle many times, and she knew the seals in their very home. Idwal hardly needed to urge her; all of her life, she'd watched seals in the sea, how they seemed to fly through the water and dance on the waves, and even as a child she'd longed to be able to do the same. They had seemed so free, so happy—and how could they not be happy, since they didn't need cottages or clothing or nets or gear. They could go where they liked, and never went hungry, for fish hadn't a chance of escaping them. Oh, how she *wanted* to be one of—

With a surprised yip, she found herself falling forward, splashing down into the waves of the incoming tide as her suddenly stubby arms flailed, her legs no longer able to hold her upright—

Not legs.

She snorted water out of her nose and curled herself around and looked with shock at her hind-flippers, at her own sleek brown back, and then at her fore-flippers. And the sealskin was no longer a hood over her face. It *was* her face!

She was warm—the biggest surprise was that now her feet were warm, for they had been cold, bare as they were.

She heard a bark to one side that she recognized as laughter and swung her head in that direction. A handsome, slightly scarred bull looked down at her—bulls being twice or three times the size of a cow-seal. Idwal, she knew it already, and knew that she would have known it even if he hadn't been standing next to her when they transformed. Her seal-form recognized his, just as her human-form recognized the human shape of her teacher.

That was a fair transformation, my student, she heard in her head. The voice was recognizably Idwal's and it was full of warmth and amusement. *But next time, be ready for the change, and start to crouch as it comes. You're less like to fall upon your nose that way.* He snorted in amusement. *Now you see why I told you to shake the sand out. Even the littlest grain would be under your skin now, and an itch and a torment until you changed and got it out.*

She held up one fore-flipper, and the other, marveling at them, then marveled at the feel of the waves over her back. To her human-self, they'd have been cold as a loveless grave; to her Selch-self, they were cool and comfortable, like caresses.

Come along, Idwal ordered. *We've much to see before you go back.*

But—she thought at him. She didn't know how to swim! That is, she didn't know how to swim as a seal—*But I*—

Evidently thinking hard at someone was how you communicated in this form, for he answered. *All the knowledge you need is in the skin and our magic. Trust me. Come!* And he turned and plunged into the waves.

She tried to imitate him, and to her delight, her body responded as if she had done this every day of her life. As her head ducked under the water, she felt her ears close, and didn't even realize she was effortlessly holding her breath until she realized she had been swimming just under the surface for a good long time, and felt the need to come to the top for a breath.

She followed in his wake, plunging through the surf,

her body taking up the pattern of breathing, holding, breathing, holding as her head broke the water or she skimmed below the surface. Now the sun was well up, the water sparkled, and beneath the surface was an entire new world that held her entranced. An entire forest of kelp grew here, waving in the water, and the water itself was alive with shafts of golden light as the sun played on the surface and was reflected or let through.

Then she spotted a fat fish peering out of the kelp; her stomach growled, and without a single thought, she raced after it. It twisted and turned to evade her; she was just as fast, and this body was more clever than the fish was. Was this because the skin had come from a very old Selchwoman? That must have been it; to her, it felt as if everything she did came out of *decades* of practice and experience. She out-maneuvered the fish, and lunged, and *caught* it in her teeth. The thrashing body in her mouth, the taste of the scales on her tongue, awoke more seal-memory in her; she brought it to the surface, tossed it up, took a breath as it was in the air, caught it head-first in her mouth, and swallowed it down whole. All within the space of a moment. All without thinking about it at all.

She snorted with glee, and did a little leap out of the water to celebrate.

I told you, Idwal said, cheerfully. *The skin holds the knowledge. Are you still hungry?*

I came out without breakfast, she confessed. *I didn't know what you were going to ask of me and sometimes it has been better not to have a full stomach.* More than one of his lessons had left her feeling sick for half a day, though she never would complain. She hadn't wanted to annoy him, or give the clan-leader the excuse to order him to stop teaching her.

He snorted with broad amusement, as if he had

known very well what those unpleasant lessons had done. *Well then, let us hunt. Follow me. I know where tastier fish than that one are.*

He plunged through the water, his heavy body shoving it aside; she slipped through it without a thought except to enjoy how fast she was going, her sleeker, smaller body slipping along as if she had been oiled. Before long she could taste what he was leading her to in the water. Fish! Her body even told her what sort. Herring! Her mouth watered. As a human, she loved herring. As a seal . . . her seal-body *craved* herring. Herring was to a seal what a juicy, well-cooked piece of beef and batter-pudding and peas were to a human.

Soon they were on the school, which filled the water ahead with flashing silver forms. And for a moment she paused in her swimming, her eyes dazzled, her mind confused. How was she to catch a single fish when she couldn't even make out a single fish in all this chaos?

Don't think, came the advice. *Be hungry! Let your body, let the wisdom of your skin guide you!*

It wasn't hard to let her hunger take over, not with all that delicious scent in the water. And when she did, her body darted forward and she did her best to keep her mind blank and just—let it do what it wanted to do.

And in moments, her mouth was full of fat, delicious herring and she was swallowing and chasing another, and another, until she was finally stuffed so full she could not possibly have eaten another. Her body still wanted to chase, but now she let her mind take over, and just watched as Idwal plunged into the school with grace and speed totally at odds with his bulk, coming out again and again to swallow and plunge back in.

When he was sated, he came to hang in the water next to her, as a strange seal—one, as she suspected, with no green glow about him—dove into the school to hunt. *Salmon is even better,* he said, meditatively. *I shall take you to hunt them one day soon . . . but for now, I want you to look at this all with a magician's eyes, and tell me what you see.*

There is green light about you, she said immediately. *None about that seal there, and none about the fish.* She studied the water around her, went up for a breath, and came back down again to look some more. *There is . . . there is another glow. In the sea. It is faint . . . it looks like a path.*

So it is, he said with approval. *And if I were to let you follow it, it would take you to our home beneath the waters. But you must not do that, or at least, not yet. You can see it from the surface too. What else do you see?*

Off in the kelp now she could see things moving. Hiding, really, watching them furtively. They, too, had that glow, although in different colors of green. *Creatures in the kelp, like us, magic, I suppose?*

Even so. The darker the green, the less likely to be friendly. They hide because they do not know you, so they are cautious. Some are true Elemental Spirits, others are things like the Selch or your Tylwyth Teg. Come.

They both surfaced together, and took a breath. He cocked his head at the sky. *Now, that is enough for one day. These things should be approached by degrees. And I promise you, when you get your own form again, you will be very weary, as if you had done a full day's work.*

Reluctantly, but obediently, she followed him back to the shore below the cottage. She did not need his instruction this time; before he could give it, she *wanted* to be herself again, concentrating all of her thoughts on being human, and found herself on hands and knees in the surf, with the sealskin draped over her.

She hadn't even gotten to her feet when he pulled it off her, and she stifled an objection as he took it from her. When he did, just as he had said, she felt a heavy exhaustion fall on her, and she staggered a little.

"These things are dangerous to have about," he said of the skins in his arms. "I shall keep it safe for you." Then he smiled. "And you, I think, would not find a short rest to come amiss."

"I'll be all right," she said stoutly. "Besides, there's samphire to wash and bread to bake and a pie to make if I am to feed all of you tonight."

He chuckled. "Very well. I know better than to argue with a woman. I will be back in the afternoon for your next lesson."

And with that, he became a seal again, and plunged back into the sea, taking "her" skin with him . . . and she wondered if the feeling of faint loss she felt was for his absence, or the fact that he had taken it away.

10

IF anyone had looked very hard, they might have been able to see the two young ladies burrowed into the gorse on a dune above the beach, posed in a very unladylike fashion. They might also have noticed that both of them had spyglasses pointed at the vicinity of a cottage near the shore.

But of course, there was no one about to see this remarkable phenomena except sheep. Or—sheep and the one or two Elemental creatures who happened upon them. But there was—or so Nan had been told—something of an invisible sign on them, that suggested to said Elemental creatures that it was best to move briskly along and pretend that they had *not* seen anyone. That was Puck's doing, with the idea of preventing any of the Elementals from telling tales about the watchers to the ones being watched.

"Pass a mint, would you please," said Nan to her companion in a very low voice. "The worst part about all this is that we daren't drink anything, and my mouth is horribly dry."

Sarah reached into a canvas bag beside her and wordlessly passed Nan a peppermint rock in a twist of parchment paper. "I really do not think this is the best way of going about what we need to do," she replied. "There's only so much you can see through a spyglass."

"Well, we've gone to Clogwyn, we've wandered about, and we've asked about the cottage," Nan pointed out. "That got us absolutely nowhere. Well, other than that we know Mari and her father live there, that her father is very well liked, and Mari is considered a good girl who devotes herself to him."

"There's the constable . . ." Sarah said.

"Oh yes. We've learned that the constable is one of the nastiest pieces of work I've ever seen that wasn't roaming the worst parts of London looking for a chance to hurt someone." Nan made a sour face. "He's a complication we didn't need."

"We did find that lovely bakery," Sarah replied, impishly.

"Yes, but that doesn't signify." Nan sighed. "Well it does, I suppose, since Clogwyn is nearer us than Criccieth, and the butcher and grocer have errand boys, and the errand boys are willing to bring the baker's things too . . ."

"I know what you mean, though," Sarah agreed. "All we can see from here is that she is with several young men, and two slightly older ones. One of those looks to be her papa. The other . . . there is no way of telling what he is, but logically, he would be the teacher. We've reported all of this to Lord A, but we can't learn anything new from this distance."

"If this were just London, we could get as close as we liked," Nan fretted. "That's impossible here. As soon as we are on that beach, we are visible for . . . well, quite a long ways."

Sarah took the spyglass from her eye and turned to look at her friend. Her expression was thoughtful. "Well, what if we try the direct approach?"

"What? Go right up to her?" Nan could only blink at her.

"Why not? And we tell her we can see what we know she can see, and ask if she knows anything about these creatures." Sarah bit her lower lip. "I think it would be better than what we are doing now."

"And I think a bold move is a good move," said Puck, startling them both, as his head thrust through the gorse branches beside them. "I've been doing my own snooping, I have, my pretty girls, and while I have not seen any harm in her, there are dark thoughts moving about her that I cannot read. Not all the sea-things are fond of the maid, and as for me, well, earth and water are allies, and I like what I see of her. I do not wish to see harm come to her. So. I counsel the bold move, and what say you?"

"I say if you counsel it . . ." Nan hesitated. "You've never given us bad counsel."

"Then let us hope I have not now." He winked at them, and his head vanished.

The girls looked at each other, and Nan sighed.

"He makes it look so *easy*," she complained, and she and Sarah began the torturous process of wriggling out of the gorse, back to the shelter of some trees where they could stand up at last and make their way back to their cottage.

In the morning, they put on walking dresses that had *not* been subjected to the unkind embrace of the gorse, and took a well-worn path down to the shore, carrying a picnic basket between them, and accompanied with Grey on Sarah's shoulder and Neville flying above them.

Thanks to Robin, now they could actually see the other creatures around them, and there were quite a few, all of them intensely curious about *them*. Nan supposed it was all because of Puck's mark on them, the "Do not meddle with these mortals" sign he had placed on them. Without knowing the proper names for the creatures, there were some that Nan simply couldn't identify—but there were others that were familiar to her from her reading of fairy tales and myths. The little goat-legged faun, for instance, made her wonder (since it was supposed to be a creature native to Greece and Italy) whether there were also centaurs here. The translucent winged girls— were they fairies or sylphs? Or both? The fire-winged bird was probably a phoenix, and the green-haired women who seemed to peek *out* of the bark of trees were probably dryads, but what were the beautiful, nearly naked spirits that flocked to the verge of the pond they passed? Naiads? Or something Welsh? And what was the black horse that came rushing up out of the water, stomped a hoof in annoyance, and plunged back in? And what was the thing that blazed with an odd blueish flame that had another sort of winged creature at the heart of it? It was hovering above a bit of marsh they passed, and Nan would have called it a will o' the wisp if she had been back home.

Once, a band of three crows approached them, and there was something about the purposeful way they were moving that made Nan feel a moment of alarm. But then Neville swooped down to land between them and the girls. He puffed out his chest and uttered a harsh, warning *quork,* then, oddly, jerked his beak towards Nan. The crows all jumped, as if they had been startled, then fled away.

Neville flapped to Nan, and she held out her arm for him. "Thugs," he croaked scornfully.

"Well thank you," she replied. He beaked her hair, gently, and took off again. Clearly he was greatly enjoying his free-flying freedom in a place where, unlike Africa, he was the biggest, strongest bird around.

They were both used to walking for quite long distances in Africa—and besides, given that they weren't closely counterfeiting the good daughters of a clergyman, neither of them were wearing the corsets they'd been forced to don in Criccieth. So it was quite the enjoyable walk to the beach, despite all the creatures that would appear and disappear again, making Nan, at least, feel as if she was some sort of spectacle.

"Do you think they know we can see them?" she finally said aloud—and as soon as the words were out of her mouth, the ones currently trailing them gave various sounds of alarm, and vanished.

"I think that answers your question," Sarah said, dryly.

On reaching the shore, they continued their walk toward Clogwyn, and soon enough, the little cottage showed in the meadow above the beach ahead of them. As they neared it, however, someone got up from the ground beside it, and began to move. A moment later, it was obvious that the person was moving toward them, quite deliberately.

Soon enough, it was equally obvious who it was. Mari Prothero, who took a stance between them and the direction in which they were going, and stood there, waiting, arms crossed over her chest.

They glanced at each other over the basket. Nan shrugged. "Well, either she knows, or she's just seeing who it is that's about to march past her. In either case, I suppose we get what we want, which is a closer look at her."

Sarah bit her lip. "I just hope—if she knows, she isn't too annoyed."

"Oh, chances are, it was the Elementals that warned her that someone who could see them was coming, and that's what she's curious about," Nan said. "In any case, there's no point in retreating now."

That was fairly obvious, as the girl waited, unmoving, eyes fixed on them. Nan decided to take the initiative, and was very glad that Robin had given them command of the Welsh language, for otherwise she'd have been at a great disadvantage even if Mari knew English. "Good morning!" she called cheerfully. "My sister and I are visitors here; we're staying at Gower Cottage."

"Are you, then?" Mari said, coolly. "Then perhaps you can tell me why you've been overlooking me these past several days."

Ah, she knows. Well . . . tell part of the truth. And part of the story. "Well . . . that's a bit of a tale," Nan replied. "And tales go better over luncheon, if you'd like to share ours." She and Sarah together lifted the basket. "There's ham," she added temptingly. "And scones."

Mari weakened visibly at the mention of ham, and more at the mention of scones. "Well . . ." she said, hesitantly.

"And jam and clotted cream," Sarah added.

It was probably the clotted cream that did it. Wales was not far from Devon, and the making of that delicacy had managed to percolate over the border, but not too many people on the shore made it or made it well. Nan loved it so much she'd *learned* how, and had made a batch a couple days ago. Now she was rather glad she had, and even gladder she'd brought it.

"Very well," Mari replied. "But the tale had best be a good one."

It appeared that she was alone, but for an ill-tempered cat who scampered away, hissing, when Neville came down out of the sky and quorked challenge at her. Nan took the rug off the top of the basket, and spread it, and Sarah unpacked the contents. They each took a corner of the rug, with Mari eyeing them suspiciously. Nan quickly passed her a scone and the pots of cream and jam before beginning.

"I don't know if you've been over to Clogwyn since we came," she said. "I expect Clogwyn is like our village, and the moment that anyone arrives, everyone knows everything there is to know about him."

"Hmm," Mari confirmed, around a mouthful of smothered scone.

"Then you know our father's a clergyman and Sarah's here to get over a bit of a—shock," Nan continued. "Actually . . . *they* don't think it's a shock. They're hoping it was just being suntouched, because . . . well . . . she's been seeing things."

Mari swallowed. "Things?"

"Both of us, have, actually," Sarah put in, and made a face. "I was just unwary enough to say something about it, when one jumped up in my face and tried to frighten me."

"Little wretch," Nan grumbled. "Nasty little thing, like a wizened old man made out of a gorse-stump. Jumped right at her and then ran away laughing. Poor Sarah went over backwards and said something and then had to pretend that the sun had made her faint. And even so, that was enough for father to decide we needed to have some time at the seaside, and our friend Lord Alderscroft said he'd pay for it." She hesitated. "And truth to tell, since no one else ever saw them . . . we were rather beginning to doubt if we were in our right minds."

"People already thought we were a bit odd because of the birds, and my blurting out about that gnome just made it worse. But that's why we were watching you," Sarah continued. "Because we happened to see you out on one of our walks, and we saw some of the same sort of creatures with you."

"And since *you* were talking to them, obviously they weren't something we were seeing out of our own heads, and we weren't actually going mad." Nan let out a huge sigh of relief, although it was because Mari had suddenly relaxed, rather than a bit of acting. "So we've been watching you, just to be sure, you know, and when we were sure we decided to come down here and see if we could talk to you." She held out her hand. "I'm Nan Lyon-White," she said. "This is my sister Sarah."

Mari leaned over the cloth, and took it, shaking it firmly. "Mari Prothero," she replied. "But that's an English name, and you speak Welsh as good as anyone."

"We're from over near the border, as you can probably tell from our horrid accents," Sarah said, also shaking Mari's hand.

Mari looked from one to the other of them and back. The girl was, as Nan now knew, as typical a specimen of a Welsh female as could be; she was tiny, dark, with dark hair and eyes, and wearing the usual working-day outfit of scarlet flannel petticoat (just showing under her skirt), brown flannel gown, woolen skirt striped in black and brown, apron, woolen shawl, and a handkerchief folded and tucked into the top of her gown. She wasn't wearing the frilly cap or the stovepipe hat that you saw in prints and photographs of Welsh women, though, nor the jacket that would have matched the skirt, and her feet were bare. But Nan and Sarah had found that there were not too many of those odd hats to be seen on ordinary days, only on Sundays, and then most often by much older women. So they had decided that since they were supposed to be from near the border, their own simple walking gowns would pass muster without going out and drawing attention to themselves by trying to buy Welsh dress.

"Well then," Mari said, as Sarah passed her ham and bread and butter. "I can tell you that you're not mad, at least."

"But what *are* they?" Nan persisted. "We just started seeing them the last year or so, and there's no one to ask!"

Mari rolled her eyes. "There's as many names for them as there are kinds," she said. "Some are the Tylwyth Teg, and some are something called Elementals, and I haven't sorted them all out myself. Some are good and some are bad, and some just like to make as much trouble for a body as they can, like that gnome." She tilted her head to the side. "But for some reason, you've got a mark on you that says to leave you be, and it's the mark of one of the High Ones of the Tylwyth Teg, and perhaps you can be telling how you got that?"

Nan and Sarah exchanged a look, and Nan turned back to Mari to shrug. "It might be that boy we did a kindness for, right after we started seeing them," she said, with hesitation in her voice. "I can't think of any other reason."

"It was the strangest thing," Sarah continued. "We found him standing in the middle of a meadow, acting like he wanted to leave and couldn't. He didn't speak to us—I don't think he knew we could see him—but he was acting as if he was getting frantic. I thought—I thought I saw something like a line, a circle in the turf, all around him. Glowing. And I don't know why I did this, but I knew I had to break it, so I scuffed my shoes in it until I kicked up some sort of powder under the grass, and that did it."

"I told him, 'Try leaving now,'" Nan put in, "And that was when he realized we *could* see him, and he jumped over the break in the line as quick as quick. And then he said 'My mark on you as thanks, pretty maids,' and he just disappeared."

Mari's eyes were big and round at this point. "Well! You made the right choice!" she said. "They don't like to be beholden to anyone, and him wanting to discharge the debt right straight away probably made him give you that mark instead of something smaller, which he'd have bargained for if he hadn't been in such a hurry." She nodded. "Aye, I reckon that's the case. And I think you two had better start studying the tales so you can watch for the things that would harm you but for that mark—because one day, one of them might decide to try anyway."

They both shivered, and it wasn't feigned, because they knew very well that there were plenty of things out there that were deadly dangerous. They *still* didn't know what it was that had haunted that abandoned house in Berkeley Square; it might have been the most powerful ghost they had ever encountered, or an inimical Elemental, or something old as Puck but wicked beyond belief. All they knew for certain was that it had tried to kill them *and* Memsa'b, *and* Sahib and Karamjit and Selim, and it had very nearly managed. "Sarah sees and talks to ghosts," Nan said, after a moment. "She's always been able to do that, but they—the ghosts—warned her not to talk about it a long time ago. Sometimes I can see them too. We wondered if being able to see ghosts was making us go mad and see things, or that maybe the ghosts were doing it to us so no one would ever believe us."

"Really?" Mari looked impressed. "I can't do that." Her face darkened. "I wouldn't be surprised, though, if one of them decided to make you see the Elementals and all, just to get you out of the way. Idwal says that ghosts are rarely nice. Most of them want to hurt people."

Sarah nodded solemnly. "I haven't seen very many that wanted to stay because they needed to help someone or they need to do something. Most of them either stay because they don't know how to go on, or they are angry or bitter or vindictive. I don't mind the ones that don't know how to go on, because I can help with that. But the others . . ." She shuddered "The others are horrid."

"I'm glad I don't see them," Mari said decidedly. And suddenly, she smiled. "Thank you for the lunch. Would you like to stay? Idwal should be here soon, and he can probably help you more than I can."

"Oh *could* we?" Sarah said, gratefully. "That would be wonderful! We don't know anyone here, and I miss my friends."

Grey chose that moment to climb down off Sarah's shoulder and walk ponderously over to Mari. She looked Mari in the face, and said, imperiously, "Up!"

"She wants you to pick her up," Sarah explained, as Mari looked startled. With a wary look, Mari offered her hand.

Grey stepped up onto it. "Shoulder!" she ordered.

Hesitantly, and with a care for that beak, Mari let the bird transfer to her shoulder.

Grey leaned down and began whispering in Mari's ear. Mari's eyes grew big.

"Lord love you!" she exclaimed, looking at Grey. "I never!" She turned to look at Sarah. "You didn't teach this bird to say all that, did you?"

Sarah shook her head. "Grey is . . . special," she said, finally. "Whatever she told you is in her own head. She's helped protect me from ghosts, and other things, before. Neville is special too."

Mari turned again to look at the parrot. "Lord love you!" she said again.

Grey just laughed in Sarah's voice. "Down!" she ordered, and Mari transferred her to Sarah's outstretched hand.

Mari looked over at Neville, who was preening himself industriously. "I don't suppose you have any advice," she said, in tones that indicated she half expected that he did.

Neville looked at her and yawned. "Lovey stuff and nonsense is for girls," he said dismissively.

Mari stuck her tongue out at him. "Just wait till you decide you want a mate, boyo," she told him. "Then it won't all be *for girls.*"

Neville went back to preening. Clearly he had his own opinion on the subject.

When the four Water creatures arrived, Mari introduced them as Rhodri, Trefor, Niarl and Idwal, her teacher. All of them were surprised to see strangers with her, and shocked when she introduced them openly as Selch. Not that Nan and Sarah had any idea what a *Selch* was until Grey and Neville whispered the information in their ears.

Only Idwal was close enough to have heard that at the time, and it was clear immediately that this was precisely what had happened, because he gave both birds a shocked look — then peered at them closely and nodded.

After that, his attitude toward Nan and Sarah was not that different than his attitude toward his pupil.

The other three, however, huddled up together, and did a lot of whispering and arguing among themselves while Mari related to Idwal the story that they had told her. Nan held her breath, hoping he did not have some magical way of telling that they had not told the entire truth.

Evidently he didn't. He listened and nodded, gave them a sharpish look when Mari spoke about Puck, and then nodded some more.

"I can see the mark of the Land-Ward on you, truly," he said at last. "And though our lord is the Sea-Ward, and he is often more prone to rage than the Land-Ward, none of the Great Warders is evil, nor inclined to evil — nor are they inclined to war with the other Wardens. Therefore, I take that mark to be the sign that your intentions here are good."

Nan let out her breath in a sigh of relief.

"I also see no sign on you that you have the gift for magic," he continued. "It is unusual that you can see the Elemental creatures. But perhaps this is merely that your ability to see spirits is so broad that it extends to the Elementals."

"That might be," said Sarah, and shrugged a little. "It's enough to know we aren't going mad, actually."

He grinned a bit. "I can well understand this. Well, Mari has made you welcome. So, welcome you are. But if you will forgive us, it is time for her lessoning."

That wasn't a hint, it was almost an order, and they

hastily bid farewell to Mari and Idwal, while the other Selch continued to huddle and mutter—and as they walked back up the beach, stared after them. Nan could feel her neck prickle from the force of their stares.

They didn't talk freely until they were back in their cottage—and were sure there weren't any Elemental creatures about.

"That was a bit of a narrow escape," Nan said, feeling as if she had just had a lesson in knife-dueling with Selim, one of the school's guards.

"I felt sure he would know we were . . . stretching the truth," Sarah agreed, plopping gracelessly down into a chair and fanning herself.

"Stretching it? Great Harry's ghost, we deformed it so badly it hardly looked like its former shape!" Nan exclaimed. "Do you think maybe he actually knew that, and elected not to expose us to Mari? After all, we do have Puck's mark on us."

"You could ask Robin yourself," said Puck, poking his head in at an open window. "Especially if you still have some clotted cream about."

"Well," Mari said, when the lesson was over, since she and Idwal were alone. "Do you think those two girls were telling the truth?"

The other three Selch, who had gotten bored watching her learn to scry in a water bowl, had wandered off and not yet returned. It seemed a good time to ask such things.

"I think . . ." Idwal pondered the question for a moment. "I think that if they are not, it is not because they intend any harm. In fact, I think they intend only good, and the Land-Ward's mark upon them proves that." He pondered more. Mari kept silent, as she was used to him thinking long on a question before he finished answering it. "I think the Land-Ward knows the truth, whatever it is, and is satisfied by it. Earth and Water are allies; he would never anger Llyr."

Mari nodded. "All right then. *I* got the feeling that some of what they told us was made right up, but it didn't seem like they meant anything other than to have a reason to talk to us. And I *like* them, Idwal. I'd like to be friends." Then she added, wistfully, "I haven't got any friends but you and Da, not in the way that the girls in the village like Braith have friends. I *know* people, and they do think friendly toward us, but they aren't actually friends."

Idwal smiled sympathetically. "'Tis hard for the mage—more hard in these days, I think, since you dare not *be* a mage where anyone can see and you dare not speak of it. My teacher's teacher's teacher said it was easier on the landfolk in the days long ago, when the mage was honored and sought out for her wisdom. And of course, it was easier for the Protheros, in the days when everyone knew of the Selch, and thought no harm that Selch brides came to the Prothero cottage."

"I suppose you'd know all about that," she said, "Being immortal and all."

But to her surprise, Idwal threw back his head and howled with laughter. "Immortal? Don't you remember what I told you? Do you forget it and now you take us Selch for the Tylwyth Teg, who do not die unless they are slain?"

She blinked at him in confusion. "You aren't immortal?" Yes, he had told her . . . but now that she knew him, and knew the power in him, it seemed strange that he *wasn't* immortal.

He shook his head. "As mortal as you—and never mind that Gethin spits that word at you as if it were a curse. We number the same years as we did when our kind walked on the land, neither more nor less than you. It is only that we can change, and are as much at home in the Water-realm as we are here in the Middle Earth."

Well *that* certainly answered any number of questions! "That's why you need us? Land-people that is." she hazarded. "That's why you've been keeping the Bargain going even though it's getting harder." He nodded.

"The Selch are not as fertile as we need," he said. "We must replace our numbers, and that is easiest done with land-spouses. For we grow old and die, even as you do, and there are hazards in the sea as there are hazards on land. The orcas, the sharks . . . the great storms sometimes catch us unawares . . . and hunters, not knowing we are not seals." He pondered again. "It is said that if we withdrew to the Water-realm entirely, taking ourselves from this place where there is iron that interferes with our magic, and there are strange machines now that we do not understand, and you land-folk use the sea to dispose of poison . . . it is said we would become more fertile on our own again." He shrugged. "I do not know. It may be that one day it will no longer be an option, but a necessity. Many of the Tylwyth Teg began such a withdrawal centuries ago. It is why you no longer see the very Great Ones except for the Land-Ward; if you must see them, you must go to them."

"I—am not sure I understand you," she replied, a more than a little confused.

"I speak of those creatures that once walked among us," he elaborated. "The ones often taken for gods. Those who are said to dwell beneath the hills and the waves. They walk among us only rarely now."

She thought about that. "Like the Wild Hunt?"

He nodded. "When have you ever met anyone who has seen that fearful thing himself?"

"Never," she said firmly. Which was true. Nan and Sarah had *heard* it, when it came to take a thoroughly wicked and murderous ghost, but they hadn't seen it.

"Which is, perhaps, just as well," he told her, with a kind of resignation. "Many of the Great Ones were not gentle with mortals." He waved his hand, dismissively. "But these girls, you wish them to be your friends, then?"

"Shouldn't I?" she asked. "Is it wrong?"

"On the contrary; there is something about them, and it is not just the Mark of the Land-Ward, that makes me feel we can trust them. That is a good thing." He beamed at her. "One can never have too many allies."

"Good," she said, and looked to the sea to spot the dark shapes coming back to land. "Now all we have to do is convince your kin."

11

A KNOCK at the cottage door startled both girls as they were packing up a hamper to go down to the cottage.

Up until that moment it had been another beautiful and serene morning, full of flower-scent and lark-song, and things were going swimmingly. They had been daily visitors with Mari Prothero now for the better part of two weeks, and had been sending letters on their progress to Lord Alderscroft every other day. In the last week, they had been getting letters back—short ones, basically telling them he had read what they had written, gone over it carefully with one of his Water Masters, he was pleased with their progress, and they were to go on doing what they were doing. The latest letter, which had arrived yesterday, had added that since both they and Puck (Lord A had referred to him as the Wild Boy) felt Mari's teacher was a sound one, although it was unusual, and he was not aware of any other case of an Elemental creature schooling the Master who could potentially command it, he would not interfere. *After all,* he had written, *someone had to teach the first Masters. There is no reason why it was not the Elementals themselves.*

But he cautioned them to keep their guards up, and Nan entirely agreed with him. Mari had not been quite as forthcoming about her situation as Nan would have liked. She suspected there was more going on with the three young Selch who were courting Mari than just the tradition of Selch and the bargain they had with the Protheros. And at some point she was going to try and tease Idwal's motives for teaching Mari out of him.

One thing only they had not told Lord Alderscroft about, because they were both in agreement that he would probably not approve. That was, in fact, the presence of the other three Selch—and the reason for it. Mari had confided that to them only two days ago, and they both agreed that since "being courted" by preternatural creatures had nothing whatsoever to do with Mari's magical education, it was none of Lord Alderscroft's business. Nan was not entirely sure that *she* approved of Mari being the unwitting bargaining-piece in an agreement that her ancestors had made hundreds of years ago. But that wasn't *her* business, either.

Except that she did wonder—if Mari knew there was an option, such as the protection of the White Lodge, would she still go along with it? That had been on Nan's mind when she woke up this morning, and she decided to broach the subject to Sarah.

They had been discussing the matter while they packed up food for luncheon and tea, when they were startled by the knock on the door.

Nan was the one who went to open it, and blinked in

consternation to find the constable for Clogwyn on the front stoop. There was a bicycle leaning up against the front gate. "Morning, miss," he said, touching his fingers to his hat, stiffly. He said it in English, setting the tone immediately. His slightly pinched face (Sarah said he looked like a ferret) had a suspicious look to it. Nan immediately went on her guard. Though she couldn't imagine what had brought him here, it was clearly no social call.

And he'd used English, although he was ostensibly Welsh.

Well. Interesting.

"Good morning, Constable Ewynnog," she replied in the same language, the words feeling odd in her mouth after speaking so much Welsh. "Is there something I can help you with?" She stood very carefully so that she blocked the door (which was, thankfully, narrow).

"Might I come in?" he asked. "There are some things I believe I should discuss with you and your sister." He narrowed his eyes, and his face got even more pinched as he stepped forward a little, deliberately crowding her, and probably hoping to make her step back so that he could step inside.

Now, Nan hadn't much liked the constable the times she had seen him in the village, and she liked him even less now. "Actually, constable, we were just leaving for our walks," she said briskly, and planted both feet, crossing her arms over her chest, so that he would have to shove her to get in. "Being out in the fresh air is very important for my sister's recovery."

"Ah," he said, clearly taken aback by the fact that she was *not* going to behave like a good, obedient, hospitable female and invite him in. "Well then, perhaps you might answer a few questions here and now?" It was phrased as a question, but his tone made it quite clear that it was an order.

Oh, no one gives me *orders, lad,* Nan thought, her temper rising. *Not without earning the right.*

"Perhaps you might tell me by what right and for what reason you are asking them?" Nan countered sharply, drawing herself up and putting on her most prickly spinster-face. "So far as I am aware, there is nothing we have done that could cause you to be interested in our comings and goings, nor anything else about us, for that matter. You already know who we are, you already know why we're here, and that's quite enough for anyone. We keep ourselves to ourselves, and we thank others to do the same."

His mouth fell open in shock. It was obvious that he had never been addressed by a female like that in all of his life. Nan actually felt a little amusement, but it was heavily overlaid by her annoyance.

His face darkened a moment later with temper. "Well, miss, you and your sister are out here, alone, without a—"

"Unless the Gower property has suddenly acquired a horde of bandits, a plague of gypsies, or an anarchist army, I hardly think we are in any danger, sir, though I *thank* you for your kind *concern*," Nan interrupted him, her voice heavy with sarcasm. "The squire and the Manor are between us and the road, and the worst invaders we've had were the rabbits in the garden. We are quite all right alone, I assure you."

His face darkened further. He *really* did not like being talked back to. "Well-bred ladies—" he began.

She was not sure where he was going with that, because suddenly something large and black—Neville, of course—darted down off the roof and knocked the helmet right off his head. And Nan was sure that if the helmet had not been there, Neville would have given the head itself quite a disorienting rap with his extremely formidable beak.

Neville bounced up off the constable's head into a tree near the door, turned to face the man, and made hideous, threatening noises. Every feather on his body was standing out as he crouched down and half-spread his wings, looking quite ready to repeat his attack.

Constable Ewynnog was startled, and perhaps a bit frightened now. But there was worse to come for him.

For Neville was not alone. A moment later, a perfectly enormous fawn-colored bull mastiff with a black muzzle came bounding around the corner of the cottage, barking thunderously. The constable actually yelped and scuttled backwards, face white.

Nan immediately noticed the faint, green glow of magic all about the mastiff, and her quick mind put two and two together in an instant.

"Robin!" Nan shouted, *"Off!"*

The mastiff dropped to the ground at Nan's feet as if he'd been shot, and remained there, growling. The beast was nearly the size of a fainting-couch, and only that faint glow of magic about it had warned Nan that it was very probably Puck in the shape of a dog. But when he responded to the name "Robin," she knew she had guessed right.

"As you can see," she said, turning to the constable. "We are quite well-defended. My pet does not react well to the appearance of strangers that he believes are threatening me, and as you see, the Gowers have lent us one of their dogs, which seems to be very protective."

The constable remained frozen in place, mouth working, but no words came out.

"So now that you have ascertained with your own eyes that we are in no danger, thank you for your concern; my sister and I are going off for our walks." Sarah joined her at the door, hamper in hand and Grey on her shoulder, and Nan took half the weight of it from her.

The two of them stepped out of the door, and Nan closed it very firmly behind her. She had a notion that if it had been left ajar, he would have invaded the cottage on some pretense or other as soon as they were gone — but if she closed the door, he probably wouldn't dare to.

Not that it would do him any good. The most he would find if he searched were letters from Lord Alderscroft, which said precisely nothing, since he never used Mari's name, but only referred to her as "your friend." For the rest, their belongings looked exactly like the belongings of the girls they were supposed to be. Even their reading material was nothing out of the ordinary.

She eyed him with disfavor, as he stood there without moving. "I would stay where I am for now, if I were you," she continued. "Robin always comes with us, and I am afraid he doesn't seem to like you. Once we are out of sight, it will probably be all right to move." She smiled evilly. "I hope you enjoy your own journey back to Clogwyn. It is a lovely day for it. You might want to call on the Squire before you leave, seeing as this *is* his property and he *does* have a right to know who is on it."

She and Sarah set off down the path, the hamper swinging between them. Neville launched himself out of the tree, flying close enough to the constable to make him duck, and Robin got up and trotted along at their side. She didn't look back.

"What is he doing?" she whispered to the dog as they headed off to the beach.

"Standing there like a cream-faced loon," Robin replied, the human voice sounding very odd, coming from a dog. "Don't worry, I've put it into the squire's head that he really did lend you a dog. Welladay! Now I know what all the pother is about with him! What could have brought him out here, I wonder? Clogwyn never had a constable before."

"Nan might not have been so far off the mark when she spoke of anarchists," Sarah said quietly. "We're not that far from the mines, where the men are striking for better wages."

"They are?" Nan said, a little surprised. She generally didn't read the newspapers, but Sarah always did.

"I shouldn't be surprised if Parliament hasn't put new constables all over, looking for people who are helping the strikers," Sarah continued. "But what a pity they should have sent someone so unpleasant and so suspicious *here!* He's a complication we could well do without!"

Puck snorted, and shook his head. "Interfering busybody that he is, he'll probably go up to the Manor and try and bully his way around there as well."

"I wish him luck with *that,*" Sarah said tartly. "Squire is going to show him the door as soon as he starts trying to play that game. Squire Gower might be the local gentry, but that doesn't mean he'd consider a constable a friend or ally. And Squire is very particular about being treated with respect. He'd be much better off trying to toady up instead."

"Little worm like that," Nan muttered, "He'll probably toady. Or he will if he's the sort to bow and scrape to authority."

"Someone like him?" Sarah made a rude little noise. "Of course he is. He won't have gotten this position without being a toady. Not that he'll learn anything except how delighted Squire is to have two such respectably connected young ladies as his tenants for the summer. And how many letters we've gotten from the great Lord Alderscroft in the last week. And how we told him we have especially recommended Gower Cottage to Lord Alderscroft, should any of his friends feel in need of peace and quiet."

Robin snickered. "A cream-faced loon indeed. I'll have a talk with the rest of the squire's dogs. I think he should have a proper escort back up the road to Clogwyn—just to encourage him to make good speed."

"It would be nice if he had an escort of a swarm of bees as well," Nan said, vindictively.

Robin barked laughter. "I shan't promise anything, my pretty maid, but there are a few mischievous spirits that would enjoy plaguing him, I suspect."

By now they were well out of sight of the cottage, and Robin turned from a fawn-colored mastiff to a white and brown one. "I'll just double back and make sure he doesn't go snooping and prying in your belongings," the spirit said, turning on his heel and bounding back up the path.

"That made a good excuse—for him," Nan said, when he was gone.

"Oh?" Sarah turned to look at her, puzzled, one hand holding her hat on as a brisk breeze suddenly came up from the sea.

"You remember him saying he didn't want to meddle in anything that Llyr might be concerned in?" Nan reminded her. "I suspect he's keeping well away from Mari Prothero. If Llyr—or the Selch—knew he was still helping us, they would start to suspect we haven't exactly told the truth, and then they would want to *know* the truth, and that could put us in a very difficult situation. And Llyr might feel he needed to interfere."

"And that would not be good," Sarah replied, nodding thoughtfully.

"Exactly," Nan agreed.

They walked on for some time, until Nan finally broached another subject. "When do you think we should actually tell Mari the truth?"

Sarah groaned. "I wish I knew," she confessed. "But maybe we won't have to. After all, *all* Lord A asked us to do was find out who she was, if she was getting trained, and by whom. Sooner or later he is going to tell us that our work is done, and we can just go home. It isn't as if she isn't getting good training, and it isn't as if she is some kind of danger or *in* some kind of danger. The worst that is happening is that she is being asked to pick one of those young Selch as a sort of temporary husband."

"Pfaw," Nan replied, making a face. "That's bad enough. Maybe if she knew the White Lodge would protect her—"

"But *would* they?" Sarah demanded. "I mean, I know it would be different if Mari was a young man and really reluctant to deal with this bargain—Lord A would offer him the protection of the Masters immediately! But she's not a young man, she's a young woman, and I have the terrible feeling that what Lord A would say is something like, oh—"

"Young ladies enter into arranged marriages every day in this country," Nan said, imitating Lord Alderscroft at his stuffiest. "She is one of the more fortunate! She is going to be able to *choose* her husband, it won't last for more than two or three years, and then she will be free! Her husband is hardly likely to beat her, or indulge in drink, and the magic his kin provide will ensure prosperity for her and her father for the rest of their lives! I fail to see the problem."

Sarah sighed. "Exactly."

"But that doesn't make it *right,*" Nan persisted.

"No, it doesn't. But . . . well, she doesn't seem unhappy to me. She likes us, and thinks of us as friends now. If we *tell* her, we could spoil all that and make her very unhappy indeed!" Sarah chewed anxiously on her lower lip. "Is it fair to make her unhappy just because *we* think she shouldn't have to go through with this bargain?"

Nan sighed. This was giving her a terrible headache. "I don't know," she confessed. "Except I suppose we should just leave things as they are for now."

After a few more paces, Sarah cast Nan a sidelong glance. "I know something that might make you feel a little differently about all this."

Nan sniffed. "And what would that be?"

Sarah grinned. "That Selch Rhodri fancies you."

Now, of all the things that Sarah could have said, this was the least likely that Nan would ever have imagined. She almost dropped her side of the basket.

"He—*what?*" she sputtered.

Sarah giggled. "He fancies you. He doesn't fancy Mari at all, which is just as well, because she doesn't in the least fancy him. But he certainly fancies *you.* He can't take his eyes off you!"

"That's only because he's never seen a girl with a face that looks like a raven's," Nan muttered.

Above her, Neville quorked derisively.

"Stop that, you silly goose. You *don't* look like a raven, and he *does* fancy you. Try paying him some attention! You'll see!" Sarah giggled again. "I'll even bet you. I'll bet you . . . I'll bet you that pair of gloves I'm embroidering. The blue-gray ones."

Nan truly coveted those gloves. She loved the color, and she couldn't embroider to save her soul. "Done," she said, immediately. "The gloves are as good as mine, you silly wench!"

By that time they were down to the beach and walking along the shore. It looked like another beautiful day . . . and Nan had another idea.

"What do you think about sending for some bathing costumes and learning to swim?" she asked.

Sarah skipped at the very idea. "Oh I would *love* that! Proper swimming, not just paddling about in the surf! I've wanted to learn how to swim for ever so long!"

"Well, we've got Selch right here, and if they can't teach us to swim, there's no one who could," Nan pointed out. "If we're going to be gallivanting about the countryside for Lord A, you never know what sort of pickle we might find ourselves in. Knowing how to swim could be important."

"Then we should ask them as soon as they come up out of the sea today," Sarah agreed. "Besides, it will give them something to do while Mari gets her magic lesson from Idwal. They get horribly bored when they are not allowed to get her attention."

The young Selch were already there when the girls arrived, and as Nan had expected, they were in agreement over the idea of teaching the girls to swim.

"There's no telling what may hap," Rhodri said sagely. "And at least if someone throws you in a pond to test if you're a witch, you'd be able to swim away."

Nan blinked at him. "That's . . . you surely don't mean that?" she asked.

"Oh aye, he does." Siarl bobbed his head. "That's a common way to test for witches. If you're a witch, they say, the water rejects you. If you're innocent, it accepts you."

"Aye," Rhodri said cheerfully. "So you drown. But you drown innocent!"

All three of the Selch seemed to find that hilarious. Nan wasn't quite so amused.

"But look you," Rhodri continued, sobering. "If you really want to learn to swim proper, and not just paddle in the shallows like a pup, none of those rig-ups we've seen daft women in down the coast. All skirts and caps and wool—no!"

"Why not?" Nan demanded.

"Why not? Because you'll get soaked with water and drown, that's why!" He shook his head in disgust. "If you're not going to go proper naked—"

"Rhodri!" Mari interrupted him, affronted. "That's right pagan!"

Rhodri shrugged. "And so am I," he pointed out.

"Well, what should we wear?" Nan demanded.

"As little as possible," he said flatly, and at her outraged stare, he added, "And 'tis not so I can see your legs, girl, nor any other part of you. 'Tis so you don't become a corpse."

Nan and Sarah exchanged a long look. "I suppose . . ." Sarah said, hesitantly.

"It wouldn't be any worse than when we bathed in ponds in Africa," Nan pointed out, then turned to the Selch. "No taking liberties!" she said sharply.

Rhodri leaned back, hands up in the air. "I'd never dream of it!" he exclaimed.

"Oh you would so dream," Trefor accused. "Such a liar you are!"

"I never would even think—" Rhodri protested. And at Trefor's continued skeptical looks, he colored a little, and muttered, "—well, maybe a little. But only think!"

"You are all pagans," Mari said severely, but her dark eyes were sparkling with amusement.

"Well we certainly aren't Christians now, are we?"

Siarl pointed out, logically. "But aye, we'll be gentlemen. Our oaths on it."

"Well, whatever fancy city-woman things you plan to bring, bring a spare set," Mari said, all practical now. "You'll be swimming in salt water, you ken, you won't want that drying under your dress, and you surely won't want it all dry and itchy on the walk back to Gower Cottage."

"I hadn't thought of that," Nan admitted. "But then, I'd thought we would be wearing swimming dresses."

"If those are anything like the daft things I've seen in the papers, Rhodri is right," Mari said bluntly. "You'll drown. Skirts and trousers and jackets . . . the sea here isn't for paddling in. It looks calm and lovely, but once out of the shallows, it's tricky and it can turn traitor on you."

Well, that just made Nan the more determined to learn to swim. "Then we'll do what we did in Africa," she said firmly.

"Well, if you've done with the talk of teaching land-folk to swim, do you suppose something could be done about that hamper?" Trefor was always hungry—and all the Selch were eager for the foodstuffs Nan and Sarah brought down from Gower Cottage. Which, Nan supposed, only made sense. There were not a lot of chickens in the sea . . . nor bake-ovens (though Mari could, and did, make fine pies and bread). Nor were there strawberries, or cows, and fizzy lemonade was a complete unknown. Even Mari hadn't had fizzy lemonade before the girls brought down bottles to share, and now she looked forward to the luncheon as much as the Selch did.

Now, Mari could have fed the Selch too, just as well as the girls did if not better . . . but Mari was the keeper of the household money, and Nan had the shrewd notion that Mari didn't care to expend a single precious penny on her visitors, nor did she see any reason to feed four perpetually hungry young men who could very easily go jump in the sea and hunt their own dinners. But if Nan and Sarah wished to share, that was another thing altogether.

Not that Nan and Sarah came the worse out of it. The hamper always came back up with some sort of sea-delicacy in it.

And there's worse things than fresh kippered herring for breakfast, Nan thought to herself with a little smug content. *Or lovely salmon!*

She was keeping a careful eye on Rhodri, mindful of what Sarah had told her, and she wasn't at all sure Sarah was wrong. The handsome fellow *did* seem to pay her more attention than he did Mari. His eyes *did* seem to linger on her longer than was strictly necessary.

Then again, it was probably no more than curiosity. The women he knew were all country Welsh or his own kind. She must seem as exotic to him as a lioness.

And possibly just as dangerous!

"Today, you will learn to touch on, and use, Air and Earth magic," Idwal said, calmly, as if he was saying "Today we will bake bread."

Mari stared at him. "That's daft!" she exclaimed. "How can—"

"Because every Master can make use of the magic of her allied Elements," Idwal replied, interrupting her. "That is part of what makes her a Master. You will not be able to use them *well,* no better than a simple Elemental Magician at best, but you will be able to use them. And it is important that you learn."

By now, she knew that when Idwal made statements

like that, he was waiting for her to reason out the *why* for herself. So she thought about it.

"I might be some place someday where there are no Water Elementals about," she said, finally. "So I'd have to use what I've got."

He nodded. "Or an enemy who is a Dark Master of Water has cut you off. There is this: those who are Dark Masters almost never know the magic of more than their own Element."

Again, he waited for her to reason out the *why*.

"Because they work by coercion, and they've got their hands full dealing with the Elementals they can control from their own Element," she declared. That one was easy. "If they started mucking about with Elements they aren't strong in, they're likely to get themselves into trouble."

"And then?"

"And then . . ." she thought about this, hard, because he hadn't actually encouraged her even to *think* about Dark Masters until now. "Their own Elementals would revolt as soon as they sensed there was trouble?"

Idwal smiled. She felt warm all over. "And they would rend him in pieces. Another good reason why we do not coerce. It does tend to engender hard feelings." His eyes twinkled, and she giggled.

They had left Nan and Sarah and the Selch boys on the shore, where the boys were going to teach the girls to swim. Nan and Sarah had brought with them the prettiest underthings Mari had ever seen to use as swimming costumes. "Combinations," the girls called them, something like a chemise with legs to it, made of lovely snow-white, soft linen, thick enough not to do anything revealing when wetted down, but with such pretty embroidery and lace! Compared to her own plain chemise and drawers . . . Mari's heart had immediately yearned after the garments, and she'd had to quite wrench her mind back to where it should be, on her lessons.

Idwal had taken her quite a distance from the beach, and now they were sitting in a little sheltered grove in a pocket valley between two low hills—absolutely invisible from the road or the sea. Although he was as lean and dark as the other Selch, he had the most interesting eyes, eyes that changed color with his mood. Right now they were a blue-gray, but she had seen them go almost silver, and all the way to storm-cloud black.

"Now, the easiest way to learn to use the magic of other Elements is to layer the energies into your shielding," he was telling her. "It also makes your shields that much more effective. You must layer it, because you can never actually *mix* the magics. Put earth and water in a jar and shake them together; no matter how hard you shake, the earth separates from the water once you stop agitating the jar. Send water into the air as mist and eventually it will condense and turn back into water. So today you will learn how to make layers. On another day, I will teach you how to braid the magics together. Begin by making a simple Water shield of one layer."

At this point that was second nature. She enclosed them both in a bubble of green iridescence.

"Now . . . I brought you here because there is a good source of earth magic at this spot. Can you see it?" he asked.

She unfocused her eyes a moment, and tried to look for something other than the familiar green of water-magic. Was it—

—no—

—or—

—not that either—

Ah! When she finally saw it, she saw it all at once, a golden glow that was part of a broad band of energy, like a beam of sunlight laid on the ground, running north to south. They were sitting right on top of it.

"It's gold," she said. "And we're sitting on it!"

"So we are. It is what is called a ley-line, and this sort of power is quite strong. It should be relatively easy for you to use it, but take care. I do not want you to disturb the flow." He reached down to the earth and gently teased up a little strand of golden light. "Like this. And when you have some, make a second shield of it, inside your first one."

It seemed very heavy to her; reluctant to move out of its path—it felt like heavy grain, or a live fish in her hands. She tried holding on to it tightly, but that only made it slip away faster.

She knew better now than to let herself get frustrated. Instead, she sat and thought. *Well, if trying to hold onto it makes it wiggle away, then what I should do is try and pick it up gently.*

She tried again, and this time, the power came up, still a little reluctantly, to her hand.

Once she had it, she found she could treat it more or less like the energy of Water. She made a bubble of it, and expanded the bubble to fit just inside her bubble of Water. To her great relief, when she released it, it stayed where it was.

"Well done." Idwal smiled on her, and she warmed all over again. "Now make another of Water, then another of Earth, until you have three of Earth and four of Water. Always begin and end with Water; it is your strongest Element, and it will help shape the others."

She followed his orders; it was easier to build the

Earth shield the second and third time. When she was finished, she just had to stop and *look* at her creation for a while. It was prettier than anything she had ever made before. Prettier than anything she had ever *seen* before, except perhaps a rainbow.

"Do you think you could make a shield of only Earth energy?" he asked.

"Probably . . . but it wouldn't be as stable," she answered, as she studied her construction. "I'd have to keep correcting it. This way, the Water shields do that for me."

"Very well put." He put an approving hand over hers. Quick as a thought, she turned her hand over and held his.

Startled, he froze for a moment, then briefly tried to pull his hand away—

Then stopped.

"Mari," he said, slowly and carefully. "I should like to know what you mean by this."

Using everything she had learned from him, she hardened the shields, then made them so strong that nothing magical would be able to see or hear what went on inside them. "Mabon is gone," she told him, lifting her chin and staring into his eyes—which had gone dark—with a note of defiance. "Rhodri fancies the other girls more than me. Siarl never wanted a wife in the first place, but he's here out of loyalty to Gethin. Trefor—I don't know, he is trying, but it feels as if his heart isn't in the courting. Why are you still here, Idwal? You've fulfilled the letter of what I asked for. You could have gone a week, two weeks ago. Yet now you are teaching me more than Water Mastery. Why are you here?"

He looked down at her, gravely, but with just a hint of hope in his expression. "I am here, because I cannot bear

to be anywhere else," he said. "I thought ... perhaps ...
you might be inclined kindly towards me, for all that I
am an old man."

She snorted. "You, an old man? You are younger than
my da."

"Well ... I am older than the boys," he said, and
laughed weakly. "And I am not nearly so comely."

"My da is comely," she said, "And feckless. He is my
da, and I love him, but feckless he is, and if he'd not had
the Selch magic and the Prothero bargain helping him all
this time, we'd be eating crusts and he'd be working on
another man's boat." She tossed her head. "I'd rather a
kind and sensible *man* than a comely boy."

Idwal let out his breath in a long sigh. His expression
told her all that she needed to know. "Gethin will not
like this," he said, gravely. "The best thing to do will be
to wait for the others to do as Mabon did; give up and go
back to the clan or declare some other choice. Then
Gethin will come to complain to you that you are driving
away those who would court you."

She squeezed his hand, and grinned, a smile full of
mischief. "Well, and when that happens should *you* declare to him that to serve the clan, you will take me? Or
should *I* declare to him that since you are all that stayed,
I'll just be forced to take you?"

He laughed. "A bit of both, I think. I shall declare that
I'll sacrifice my freedom on the altar of the clan, and you
will grudgingly accept, on the grounds that I am at least
not some trollish old walrus."

And with that, he pulled her into his arms. Which was,
after all, what she had been hoping for, so she did not
even put up a token resistance.

"Ah, you entrancing little thing," he said, as he bent
his head down to give her a proper kiss—and the first

she had ever had from a man that was not her father. "Why do I have the feeling this was what you had planned all along?"

"Not *all* along," she murmured, and then there was no more time for talking.

12

BREAKFAST was almost ready. In the garden, the roses were almost spent, and the asters and pansies were in full bloom. Since they kept their time here by the sun and not the clock, they were rising a little later every day, and lighting the candles a little earlier. But it hadn't quite dawned on either of them how far the summer had progressed until this morning.

"It can't be September already!" Sarah exclaimed with dismay, as Nan turned the calendar on the wall to the new month. Or months, actually, it was a Pears Soap calendar that had two months to a page. That might have been why they had managed to ignore the fact that time was passing so quickly; so long as July and August reigned on the wall, they could delude themselves that the summer was endless.

But September it was, there was no doubt of that. And they were still here, in Wales. "I think," said Nan carefully, "we've been lulling ourselves into an illusion that any day now, Lord Alderscroft would order us back, and we would be saying goodbye to Mari with regret and popping ourselves onto a train." Nan poured herself a cup of tea, and another for Sarah, then set out the scones and double cream and jam. "It was all very well to spend the summer here, but I think we need Lord A to make some firm decisions," she said after a moment. "And I think we need to consult with—"

"Are those scones?" asked Robin, poking his head in the window. Despite the fact that it was the first day of September, the weather was still as warm and pleasant as it had been when they first arrived, and the windows were, as a consequence, wide open. They had gotten used to Robin showing up out of nowhere—usually when there was food about. Nan was glad of it; it was good to be able to discuss Mari with someone besides Sarah, and Puck was always good company, not to mention his occasional, timely intervention. Bearing in mind that the Fair Folk didn't like to be *thanked* for help—since thanks implied obligations—she just made sure to be extra generous with whatever of their treats took his fancy.

Nan shook her head as Grey bobbed and Neville quorked a welcome. "You have the most uncanny ability to be right where you are wanted, when you are wanted," she said.

He smirked. Today he was dressed all in moleskin and leather, like something out of a child's book about Old England. "That shouldn't surprise you, pretty maid," he said. "I am what I am. And are those scones?"

"Yes they are, and yes, I have clotted cream, and yes, you are invited in, but you must be serious, Robin," Sarah told him, her tone earnest. "We need some good advice. We just realized that we have been here much longer than we thought we would, very much longer than we had intended to stay, and now ... well, Lord Alderscroft has still not said that we should come back. It was all very well to play at holiday-making while it was summer, but ..."

Her voice trailed off.

"Practically speaking, for one thing, all we have are our summer clothes," put in Nan. "For another, we don't know what the winter will be like here—Neville will do well enough, but Grey needs to be warm! We don't even know how snug this cottage is against winter storms. Even I have heard about winter storms on the coast, and how terrible they are. For all we know, this place is a sieve for drafts. And—"

"Wait, wait, let me come in!" Puck did so by way of the window, not so much climbing in as leaping in. He took his place at the table, and reached for a scone as Nan got another cup and poured him tea as well. "Firstly, my pretties, the storms are bad here, but the winter itself is mild. And you know I would never let our Grey Girl suffer." He put out a finger to Grey, who nibbled it in thanks. "Now, I've been keeping my eye on things—you know, betwixt the Prothero girl and the Selch—"

"I thought you had," Nan said shrewdly. "I've got my guess, but honestly, she and they are being mightily secretive about—well—the courting and how it is going. And ordinarily I would say it is none of our business, but Lord Alderscroft has made it our business."

Puck nodded, spreading cream, then jam, on his scone. "This is what I think is the situation with the Prothero maid. When all this began, she was reckoning to stretch out her time before she made a decision as long as she possibly could." He shrugged. "Who could blame her? Out of nowhere she finds herself saddled and bridled with that bargain! She was going for a year, if she could get it; I doubt the Selch Clan Leader would have put up with more than that. And, of course, because she is a practical wee thing, she was making very sure she would not find herself burdened with a lad who'd bully her, or who she misliked." He wagged his head from side to side a little. "And I know all the arguments, how she *could* have found herself marrying some fellow she didn't know because of her father's say-so, and all that, but a maid has a right to think she has some *choice* in a lad, if you ask me." He heaved a great sigh. "But there, I've hobnobbed with you mortals for a long time now. We-ell as it happens, now things have got a bit more interesting. Because, and I *might* be wrong, but I *think* I'm not, she's gone and gotten all love-lorn over that teacher of hers. And he over her."

"I *told* you so!" Sarah exclaimed to Nan in glee. Then her face fell. "Oh, but that complicates things, doesn't it . . ."

"Not so much as you might think," Puck replied and ate half a scone in a single bite. Grey begged shamelessly at him, and he broke off a little piece and gave it to her. She held it in one foot and ate the cream and jam off first. "The Selch are as mortal as you daughters of Eve. Plenty of 'em have chosen to come home from the sea and live on shore. He's a clever fellow, and he knows this. Even better, he wouldn't be a captive, since she's not likely to hide his skin from him. So he *could* choose to stay with her, they could still let half their children go to the sea, and all would be well. Better than well, really; they could have an entire tribe of children and be able to feed them all handily, and that would certainly please the Selch. *But!*"

"But?" Nan asked, suspiciously. She didn't care for that word.

"Welladay, there's your Elemental Master of the White Lodge to be satisfied by all this. He might not take to having a Water Master bound permanent-like to a half-Elemental, magical creature, no matter how mortal he is. *And* there's all your mortal laws and what-all to be dealt with. A lass can't just up and say 'oh, I've got married,' and think things will go on smooth in these degenerate days when every man jack has his nose in your business. People will want to know from where he's jumped up from and all. There's churchly nonsense that must be done. And writings and recordings. And like as not that snoopy constable will think Idwal's another malcontent, some sort of organizer from the mines, hiding with them. That's a pother; it was better in the old days when a man and a maid could jump over a broomstick and hey presto! They were wed." He ate another scone while they thought about that.

Nan grimaced. "We talked about that a little. She said when she first told us about the bargain that she was going to say he was a sailor, and they'd been married on a ship, and he would come and go a great deal to make it look like he still was. Then she'd get word he'd drowned, so when he didn't come back, there'd be no trouble. But that was when she was planning on staying with her Selch for no more time than it took to have two children."

Robin nodded. "Well, unless things change, I don't believe she'll be staying with that plan now. And then, there's the Master of the White Lodge who, if he is approving of this mortal-fae alliance, will likely want to know that all goes well over the babies, which means, I think, he'll be wanting to keep you here over winter, to keep an eye on things and summon help if it's needed."

They exchanged a sober glance. "Do you really?" asked Nan.

"I won't be putting words in the Master's mouth, nor thoughts in his head, but I do believe that is where his plans are tending," Robin replied shrewdly.

"But—clothing—the birds—" faltered Sarah.

"Explaining our staying to the squire," Nan added glumly. "That could be ... difficult ... and I don't know that we'd be welcome here."

"Ah, now ... the explaining part? Not so hard as all that." Puck grinned. *"You* may have your morals and misgivings, but I'm Puck, and I do as I like. If you can't come up with a simple way to stay, I shall make all smooth. You just wait until you know whether you are to go or stay, and the next time the old man takes his hounds out for a stroll, there'll be a bit of a wind and a scattering of leaves, and it will be that you are welcome as welcome to stay, always were, for as long as you please, and Lord Alderscroft is ever so grateful that he's leasing the cottage to you. *And* he himself will be ever so pleased to have the rents in the winter."

"Which he will be," Nan said dryly. "Or rather, his wife will be. The other day, Delyth said over tea that she was going to miss the extra income. Not in so many words, because that would *hardly* be polite or correct, but ..."

"Well, *she* gets the rent of the cottage as pin-money, and the squire asks no questions of how it's spent," Sarah giggled. "But *oh,* the *hats!* I am not sure I want to be responsible for the creation of more of them!"

Squire's wife had a weakness for hats, and a lack of taste that was as strong as her weakness, and the two of them broke into a fit of the laughter they had not given vent to when the hats had been displayed for their admiration. Puck looked at them in bewilderment, then shrugged.

"Look you," he said finally. "You be getting an answer with some backing to it from yon Lodge-Master. *You'll* be giving the Selch an education in what must be done so that interfering man-milliner you lot call a constable don't make trouble for them."

His tone was so sour, Nan looked at him in surprise. He made a face. "That mortal meddler makes me so bitter I'll have to eat more jam to sweeten my temper," he said, and suited the deed to the word, spooning it onto his plate and eating it as if it was a bit of pudding. "I don't like him, my creatures don't like him, and my people don't like him."

"Village doesn't like him and Squire doesn't like him, either," Nan offered. "He wanted Squire to build him a jail, the cheek! Squire told him he could have a jail built out of his own pocket; jails were none of his business, nor did he intend them to be his business, even though he's the magistrate here. He told the man that Clogwyn had never needed a jail until now, and he still saw no good reason for there to be one. Then he told Squire he'd got the money from his chief, but it wasn't enough for a whole jail, so he wanted to put a cell at the back of the cottage! Squire told him no, but it seems he had to let it happen. Oh! He was hot!"

Squire had, in fact, taken most of a week to cool down again, for most of the cottages in the village actually belonged to him, and he leased them on long terms. The only thing that mollified him was his wife pointing out that once Constable Ewynnog had been sent packing, the room could be turned into something useful. That would make it a two-room cottage instead of a single room, and the fact that the police had been forced to pay for the new room eased his temper the rest of the way.

"Well, he's been tossing harmless old drunks in there

overnight," Puck said crossly. "Which *nobody* likes, not the drunks, not the wives of the drunks, and not the neighbors, who get to hear the drunk shouting until he falls asleep. If he was any good at being a constable, he'd simply see 'em to their own doorstep and no harm done. What he's about, I don't know. It's a sad day when a man can't walk home drunk from a pub without being molested and thrown into a bare cell."

"I think I know what he's doing—or thinks he's doing," Sarah said, surprising both Nan and Puck. "I think he's been sent here to find subversives and anarchists, and he thinks if he listens to drunks in their cups, he'll hear something useful. Why he should keep doing it after he doesn't, though ... I can only think it's because he's horribly stupid."

Puck snorted, and pointed his chin at the drawer in which they kept their letter-writing gear. "You go write to your Lodge Master, make sure he knows there could be some hardship here over-winter and you'll be needing some extra help if he wants you to stay, then borrow the squire's trap, take the letter to Criccieth and post it yourself. That'll be the fastest way. You make it sound urgent enough, you should get a quick answer. If he brings you home, well, you leave the Prothero maid to me; I'll keep her out of trouble. Unlike the Sea-Ward, *I* know a raven from a writing-desk, and I come and go and look and know in the mortal realm." He laid a finger alongside his nose. "There's always her sailor idea, or she might get accepted into the Selch clan, and then we can say they've gone to America."

"And if he bids us stay?" Nan asked, anxiously. "There are still so many problems—"

"Then it'll be on him to make it no hardship on you."

Puck nodded with authority. "If I don't misjudge, you twain are comfortable here? You're liking this place?"

Nan, child of the London streets, would never have dreamed this could be so, but she nodded. "It's peaceful. It's easy to get books and things, and really, I don't miss shopping. It's rather lovely to be playing house like this when there's a maid coming over to do all the rough work. It might get difficult when winter comes, if there are a lot of bad storms, but if we don't absolutely have to go out every day, and the cottage can keep warm, I think I'd like being all cozy and reading and sleeping late. I'm even learning how to cook things I had no notion of. I don't miss London. I thought I would, but I don't."

"I miss the music," Sarah said wistfully. "And the plays and museums and operas and things . . . but we didn't get to go out to plays or operas that often, and the Welsh *do* sing so beautifully!"

Puck laughed, reached out, and ruffled their hair as he used to do when they were children. Nan supposed that to him, they still *were* children . . . she hated to think how old he was. "Oh, ask yon Selch to be singing!" he exclaimed. "Or Daffyd Prothero. You'll not miss the fat geese in London with their caterwauling through their noses. Every Brunnhilde I've ever seen would have crushed her horse beneath her, I trow! Now let's put this in motion, while things can still be done."

Nan had not mentioned the Selch Rhodri as one of the things that kept her here, even though it had become quite obvious that, as Sarah had claimed, he fancied her. For one thing, while she did enjoy his attention, she was not at all certain he actually *meant* it, not in the way that Idwal meant his attentions to Mari. For another . . . she was not, absolutely not, going to give up the exciting and

fulfilling life that Lord Alderscroft offered. Especially
not for a half-human creature who, while he was handsome and exotic and had very charming ways, was not
much of a person you would think of as a husband. What
could he bring to such a union? That he could turn into
a seal and she would never lack for fish ... that would be
useful if she were like Mari, a fisherman's daughter and
content with that, but she had plans, and she didn't want
to change them. This life had been all very well for—oh,
say—a year. But for the rest of her life? No. Then she
would miss London, but more than that, she would go
mad without something to do—just as she and Sarah had
nearly gone mad trying to think of what they could do
with their lives before Lord A had made his offer.

Perhaps she was being too practical, but better that
than have her head in the clouds. An early life where she
was the one who found her own food, more often than
not, had made something of a hard shell inside her. She
never wanted to go hungry again, and she would do anything honest and decent to make sure she wasn't going
to. She wanted to know that she was doing more than
just existing. And if that meant sacrificing *romance* to
practicality, well, she'd shed a tear and do it.

And about being practical—she went to the drawer
and got the pen, the ink and the paper. Puck was right;
they had better start making arrangements while there
was still time to do things. "Here," she said, handing pen
and paper to Sarah. "You write what you think is important, I'll do the same; that way, we won't miss anything."

Sarah nodded, and they both bent their heads over
the table and got to work. One thing was certain; they
had to make sure that these were letters Lord Alderscroft could not in any way misinterpret or ignore.

"He's watching us again," said Mari, not looking up from her peas. She had a whole bushel of the dried pods, and was shelling them into a rough burlap bag. Not a pleasant task, even when done out of doors, but at least Idwal was giving her lessons while she did it. It was too bad; it was a lovely day, difficult to tell that autumn was coming on fast, with a strong breeze that picked up the bits of dried pea-pod and carried them away as she rubbed the peas briskly between her palms. When she finished these, there were beans to do next, the same way. She sat on that bit of wood; Idwal sat facing her, cross-legged on the earth. He made a pleasant thing to rest her eyes on.

Rhodri had taken to going out with her da, not only cutting his fishing time in half, but bringing up things from the sea-bed Daffyd would never have gotten himself. Mussels in plenty, which were usually hers to gather, and clams, but also oysters and whelks, which lived deeper. Spider crabs, which Daffyd had thought were pests until Rhodri showed him how to cook them and how good they were. Idwal's lessons bored him; he'd rather be out fishing. The shellfish weren't something you could sell, for anyone along the coast here could easily forage as much as he liked just by being willing to go out into wretched cold water at low tide, and Daffyd didn't want to compete with the lads who sold them in Criccieth, but they made a lovely addition to their normal fare. Mari usually had too much to do to go shellfishing on her own too often.

"Well, that constable won't be seeing me," Idwal said firmly, shaking his hair back. "Nor Rhodri, when he comes in with your father." The Selch used Water Elementals as messengers as casually as a Clogwyn housewife sent one of her children on an errand. A moment after he said that, a seabird flew down and landed on the sand next to them, *looked* at him in a penetrating way, then flew off. That was Rhodri sorted.

"What on earth can he be wanting?" Idwal asked, clearly bewildered. "Surely he's satisfied himself that you're not one of those—what did you call them? anti-christs?"

"Anarchists," she said. "Which I can't make head nor tail of." She had studied all of the old newspapers she could get her hands on—well, everyone in the village was doing the same, since Daffyd had gone about imparting his favorite theory about why the constable was here in the first place—and she couldn't, for the life of her, understand why he was looking for anarchists here. The miners inland weren't striking because they were anarchists; they just wanted more safety and a decent wage instead of working like slaveys and dying like rats in a hole. And there was no one striking here in Clogwyn, anyway! Furthermore, unless someone was hiding a rogue cousin somewhere in their family tree, no one in Clogwyn was even distantly related to the miners. Clogwyn and Criccieth had been towns that lived by the sea as long as they had existed. And rough and hard as a fisherman's work was, there wasn't one of them that would trade it for the sunless hell of a miner's life, no matter how much it paid. Never had the twain of mine and sea even met. The miners might go to Criccieth on holiday, if they could scrape the money together, but they wouldn't bother to go to Clogwyn; there was nothing for them to do there, unless all they wanted to do was forage for shellfish, laver, and samphire, cook on the beach, and stuff themselves. Which they *could* do, and she supposed there might be some that did, but then they would have to find somewhere to stay, for the only place there was to rent was Gower Cottage. And Gower Cottage was more than a miner could afford, even if the squire would let it to him, which, of course, he wouldn't.

Constable Ewynnog was up on the hill; the very same hill and the same patch of gorse that Nan and Sarah had hidden in to watch her and the Selch before they had finally come down openly. He had a spyglass, and thought he was concealed. And so he would have been, had the Water Elementals not taken it as their duty to warn her when he was there, just as they had when Nan and Sarah had watched her.

"He is a very foolish man," Idwal said severely, in tones that said *this man is a bloody fool, and I wouldn't trust him to know which end of a cow to milk.*

Idwal was teaching her one of the tricks of going invisible, which in the easiest case wasn't actually going invisible at all, as it turned out, but more a case of convincing someone's mind that you weren't there. That was simplicity itself for the Tylwyth Teg. *No one* expected to see them. For Mari, however, it could be a deal harder, especially when she was somewhere that she was supposed to be. There was no way, for instance, that she would ever convince the constable that she wasn't right here at the cottage. He expected to see her here, and so he would, no matter how hard she worked at trying to convince him otherwise.

Still, it would be very useful if she was somewhere else she didn't normally go . . . in the village, say. And once she had mastered this, Idwal said she could learn the trick of truly going invisible.

"I think he just wants to find someone he can put trouble on," she said, as she always did. It was an automatic answer by now. Her father had said so over and over, and she didn't see any reason to doubt his reasoning.

"But why? Why would he want to do such a thing? Isn't that counter to the law? And isn't he supposed to be the enforcer of the law? That is why he is supposed to be here, is it not?" Idwal didn't usually care about such things; like the other Selch, he was here for Mari, and dismissed other land-dwellers without a second thought. But it was clear that this behavior on the part of Constable Ewynnog bothered him. Idwal was genuinely puzzled, and that made her look a little more closely at her own answer. And at what she knew about the constable.

"Well . . . he's just a human, and a not very nice human at that," she said. "People aren't much different than Selch; when they take on a position, they don't always do as they're supposed to in it. If you ask me, and if you ask half the village I'd say, the answer would be that he went for the job of being a constable because he's a bully." She rubbed more pea-pods between her hands and the peas fell down into the bag while the flecks of pod blew away like odd-colored snow. "He isn't in it to represent the law; he's in it to be able to make people do things whether they want to or not. And he thinks he can especially bully me, because when he comes to talk to me I act like I'm feared of him." Had that been a mistake? She thought about how Nan had been with the man, for her friend had described their single encounter and the outcome. How she had stood up to him, how the squire's dog had protected her, and how she had made him back down and leave her and Sarah alone. Certainly the wretch had never bothered Nan a second time.

But Nan is not from here; she's from farther inland, closer to the border, closer to being English. And she's almost gentry. And the squire won't let the constable med-

dle with someone on his land, she reminded herself. *And besides all that, Nan has a lord who looks out for her and Sarah. I don't.* No, as much of a nuisance as it was, he never would have backed down if she had stood up for herself, and she likely would have just stirred up more trouble for herself and her father. What kind of trouble she didn't know—but then, she wasn't a constable, and she didn't know what mischief he could work if he was minded to.

"I don't think he's as able to bully people in the village," she continued. "Because they all stick together when he tries." She thought some more.

"I still cannot fathom why he would be looking for troublesome persons here, where they do not exist," Idwal objected. "Why doesn't he look elsewhere? Looking for these *anarchists* in the village and here is like looking for a rose on the seabed. You cannot find something that simply is not there, no matter how hard you look."

"I think he was sent here a-purpose, and so does Da," she reminded him. "The people that he has to take orders from don't know Clogwyn from Criccieth or Criccieth from Cardiff."

Idwal considered this. "But shouldn't he tell them?"

"Would they even listen?" she asked in return. "Would Gethin listen if you told him this bargain with the Protheros is more unfair to a girl than a boy-child?"

Idwal considered that. "Probably not. And Gethin is sometimes reasonable. He does listen when the clan speaks with one voice."

Mari truly hated to be so … objective. But Idwal had taught her, over the summer, that an Elemental Master must truly be able to see every side of a problem, because the answer might be hidden somewhere he might not otherwise think to look.

I wonder if all his questions now are a test?

"Oh! It grates on me like sand to say this! But though he's a bully, he could be getting bullied by the men who rule him," she said reluctantly. "And if they were hard enough about their orders, and threatened *him* with losing his place if he doesn't find troublemakers, it would make him want to find whatever he thinks might appease them. It might even be he has those *he* fears, who'll make things hard for him or even get him dismissed if he doesn't find someone." That left a bad taste in her mouth. She didn't like to think of the bully as also *being* bullied, but—

But there it was: Idwal had told her, and schooled her, that of all things, a magician must be honest. For if she was not, it would taint her magic, and the Elementals would not trust her. And if they did not trust her, they would not help her. And if they did not help her, she would find herself tempted to force them.

And the end of that path was darkness.

"Well, and that may be true," Idwal replied, weaving his magic about himself as he spoke, so that it looked as if he was sitting in the midst of a dome of lace. "And it would explain why he is being so desperate-stubborn. But he is a man of the law, and would it not be the better for him to be an honest man and say 'I can find nothing,' than to bear false witness? Is it not better to be honest, and stand up bravely against the consequences? Would his superiors respect him more? They certainly cannot respect him now, at all."

Ah, now ... that made her feel better again. "It would," she agreed. She looked to the sea. "Do you think Rhodri has been warned yet?" Rhodri was the only one of the four Selch left; Siarl had left at midsummer and Trefor a week ago. She expected Gethin to turn up any day now to demand that she wed the younger Selch, and she still didn't know what she was going to say. Idwal seemed content that she would think of something, or he would, or they both would.

"I do. Although he is always cautious, and has had his own watchers watching for those who should not be here." Idwal sketched in another section on his casting. "And I would not concern myself that Gethin will appear any time soon," he added soothingly, as if he had read her thoughts. "Siarl decided that he would go to visit our Scottish kin, and Trefor conceived of a notion to have a look about in Ireland to see if there was a Selch maid that suited him. Truth to tell, they volunteered out of a sense of duty to the clan, and not because they fell in a passion over you at first sight. I think how things fell out gave them relief rather than otherwise. They have not told Gethin that they left, since the less he knows, the less he can forbid."

"Well, I wish you had told me all this!" she exclaimed. "Here I was fretting that Gethin would be turning up at any moment!"

"I just did," he teased.

"I would throw something at your head, but the peas will not shuck themselves," she retorted. This was part of the business of preparing for winter. True, her father could go out fishing, but you could not live on fish alone, and there were times when the storms were bad enough that even he would not go out—nor could they get to the village for provisions. Dried peas made a good soup, tasty with a bit of bacon, but they did need to be hulled, and it was better to do it now rather than later. Being left in the hulls made them more prone to mold.

"We sound like a married couple already," he observed. "You, threatening to throw things at my head—"

"And so I will, if you don't reweave that last bit of your magic, so I can see how you did it," she replied serenely. *"Teacher."*

He laughed. "And if we are fortunate, yon snoop will perish of the boredom of counting every pea you shuck."

13

THE postal service could be astonishingly rapid ... especially when you took your letter directly to the depot so the postmaster could put it on the next train out. Both Nan and Sarah had written to Lord Alderscroft, each voicing similar, but not identical, concerns.

The reply came in three days, and it was not what Nan and Sarah had expected.

A messenger came in person from Criccieth to the cottage with a telegraph. *Brother arriving Criccieth tomorrow. Meet at Lion.* Naturally the messenger's arrival caused a stir at the Manor, but no one intruded to ask what the telegram was—yet. Nan expected to get an invitation up to the Manor from Squire's wife as soon as the messenger passed her door on his way back to the town.

"Brother?" Sarah's eyebrows arched. "We had better have an explanation for *that!* And for the telegraph, I suppose ..."

"That must be Andrew Talbot, of course." Nan laughed. "I must say of Lord A, he does think of good answers very quickly. Andrew speaks good Welsh, and he can easily pass as our brother. And since tomorrow is Saturday, he can meet us and be back at school without missing too many classes."

"And the Lion is the Lion Hotel." Sarah nodded. She noted that Lord Alderscroft had not signed the telegram, so it could easily have come from their supposed father.

"I'll go up to the manor and arrange for the trap and pony." Nan pursed her lips. "I had better look worried. Telegrams generally mean bad news. Be prepared for an invitation for tea and sympathy; I expect we'll be at the Manor until suppertime being reassured."

So that was what she did, and as a result, the next day they were sent off by an anxious squire, who urged on them that if there was *anything* he could do to help them, they must let him know, and if they needed to leave right away, they could trust him to pack up and send their things on.

The birds always enjoyed a ride in the trap, clinging to the back of the seat in Grey's case, or flying free in Neville's until he tired of it and joined Grey. The day was cool, and the pony eager to get to Criccieth where he knew he would find a comfortable stall and a bag of oats waiting at the Lion Hotel for him, so they made good time.

Andrew was waiting for them, doing a tolerable imitation of an anxious elder brother. He ushered them into a private dining room and closed the door. There was tea and cakes waiting, the universal British comfort in times of stress. Nan examined the cake-tray, for in her experience, the cakes one was presented with were an indication of what the staff assumed was going on. The cream cakes arranged there indicated that the staff had learned enough to think that Andrew's "news" was bad. Servants, as she had good reason to know, knew everything, often before their masters did.

Andrew relaxed, once the door was closed, dropped down into a chair, and helped himself to a cake. "Well! Lord Alderscroft suggested that our supposed family has come down with something contagious, and your siblings are getting it one by one. Have you any suggestions? I was vague when I got here, I was careful to imply it was not life-threatening, but I think I mentioned quarantine. I also mentioned the usual numerous siblings; it seems to be expected in the families of clerics. Well, other than Roman Catholic priests!" He chuckled at his own joke.

"Measles? Mumps?" said Sarah. "Scarlet fever or smallpox won't do; those are more likely to be fatal, and we would have to look tearful and anxious all the time, and whooping cough generally takes off babies rather than adults."

"You have a very good point," Andrew said after a moment. Nan nodded. "If it were something where someone might die, we'd have to have reassuring telegrams at regular intervals. Instead, we can have letters, and express that we are grateful to be here instead of there."

"Definitely measles, I think," Andrew decided. "I've known it to take an entire season to go through a family, and most folks get through it just with a great deal of annoyance. And then we can have the mumps if we need to."

Sarah nodded; Nan left this part up to her. Between Lord Alderscroft and Memsa'b, the School had rarely seen any serious illness, so she had nothing to offer for this part of the subterfuge.

Sarah and Andrew worked out all of the details while Nan waited for them to get to something she *could* contribute to, sipping her tea. The cakes were very good, and the staff was right about cream being soothing. Finally, Andrew got to what his real purpose was. "Obviously in light of what is going on with that girl and the Selch, Lord Alderscroft is most anxious for you to remain. Candidly, we've never known of a Master to be so ... intimately involved with an Elemental creature before. I mean, obviously the Selch are a different matter from most Elementals, because they're half mortal and quite physical, and certainly enjoy no longer lives than the rest of us. But ... still."

"Still," Nan agreed.

"Ordinarily, he'd have one of us here—but you are dealing with a young female with whom you have established a friendship." He shrugged. "Most of the White Lodge is made up of the upper classes, and all of them are male. To insert a strange man into this situation— probably a strange man with a title—well, that would just be asking for trouble."

Nan would have snorted, but Neville beat her to it by making the rudest noise imaginable. "Neville, you are absolutely right," she said, giving Andrew a look that made him shrink a little. "Asking for trouble? Oh, you would get trouble, all right. At the very least, you'd be attracting all sorts of unwanted, unasked-for attention to Mari. And Mari would probably show the lot of you the door, if not shy a rock or two at you as you left, and quite properly too, for meddling in her affairs."

"Ah," Andrew managed.

"Really, Andrew, how can you sit there and talk about Mari as if she was some sort of—interesting insect?" Sarah demanded.

Andrew withered beneath their gazes. "I really am sorry . . . I can see that was dreadfully rude . . ."

"All right then. You just make sure that his lordship is *well* aware that this girl is not some abstract thing he can move about on a game-board," sniffed Nan. "And since he's asked us to stay, and I presume you are about to tell us how he intends to support us in doing so, you can tell him that we will make sure to keep him well informed and to do our best for Mari."

"Ah. Yes." Andrew cleared his throat self-consciously. "Yes. Lord Alderscroft is going to make sure you have everything you need. Winter clothing, for instance. We've arranged for that already. Memsa'b will be sending it as she has your old winter stuff, and knows your sizes and can have more made up. And as for the cottage . . ." He grinned. "Lord Alderscroft is going to invite your good landlord and his lady to London out of gratitude for hosting you all winter. They'll even be presented to the queen. While they're gone, I'll come down again with a couple of helpers and we'll make sure the cottage is ready for winter. It probably won't take much but having one of the Air Masters out to find all the leaks and drafts, get them sealed up, and put in a stove or two. But whatever it takes, your feathered friends will be as cozy as if they were at home."

Grey bowed her head to him. "T'anks," Neville quorked.

"Now . . . here is where we need to put our heads together, for Sarah, you were entirely right. On the strength of your letter, Lord Alderscroft has done some discreet inquiries. That constable has been sent to find trouble, and if he can't find any, he is the sort that will make it."

"That's what I thought," Sarah replied, and frowned. "This is utterly vexing. Things would be so much simpler if he would just *go away.*"

But Andrew shook his head. "Not with the miner un-
rest. His superiors are the sort to see conspiracy everywhere. And we have an entirely unexplained man here,
with no known origin, who is going to take up very visibly
with Mari. We *must* make sure this marriage looks as regular as possible, and we *must* at all cost divert any suspicion from the Selch. So that means explaining the Selch,
somehow—then doing it all *right*. Posting the banns, a
proper wedding of some sort." He sighed and looked
mournful. "His lordship left all that up to me. And this is
where I come a-cropper. You two have been living here all
summer. Just how are we going to make this work?"

It seemed to Nan that military campaigns had been
planned with less precision. Fortunately, Sarah'd had the
forethought to bring one of her sketchbooks to take
notes in, for Nan was certain she would never remember
it all.

As they left the room, Sarah was lamenting just loud
enough to hear a combination of how unjust it was for
"poor, dear mother" to have to deal with a house full of
children who would all, surely, get the measles, and a
modicum of guilt that they would be "enjoying ourselves
in our own little hide-away," while their mother managed alone.

"Well, you're better off than I am," Andrew grumbled.
"I'm banished to university; I won't even be allowed
home for Christmas." Then he brightened. "But Lord Alderscroft said I can come down to London at least. That
should be jolly."

That was the signal for Sarah to urge him not to drink
too much, or stay up too late at card parties, or eat too
much fancy food. To which Andrew reacted as any older

brother would to such unsolicited advice, by looking put-upon and hustling them to their little cart and urging them to get back to their cottage before it got dark. It was a tolerably good acting job on all their parts.

Squire and his wife were waiting anxiously, and the stableboy that came to take the pony stopped them before they could go down to the cottage. "Squire and the mistress are waiting for you in the parlor, miss," he said sturdily, and in a tone that informed them that it would not be a good idea to beg off. So they went up to the door, and the head maidservant was waiting just inside to usher them up.

Nan privately thought it was the best job of acting they had ever done. She was ridiculously proud of it. In that slightly stuffy, old-fashioned parlor, she and Sarah and the birds (who thankfully remained silent) were given the best seats and urged, "Please, you can tell us everything."

She was the older sister who was not at all averse to being here where it was "so nice," and reminding Sarah over and over that "she was not to undo all the good the summer had done for her," and that "running after the little ones will only make you ill again." She even improvised two maiden aunts who "will be sure to come help Mother, so she won't be coping alone," because there was, after all, an empty bedroom in the house (theirs) and they could be put up splendidly. "They'll even manage Christmas; you know Aunt Beatrice does the goose better than Mother."

That was the cue for Sarah to lament Christmas away from the family, apologize that they were inflicting themselves on the squire over that time, and get reassurances that the squire couldn't be *happier* than to have them at his family festivities.

And *that* gave the opening for his good lady Delyth to

wax eloquent on her two sons and daughter, all married, who would be bringing their broods—and how all of them had safely weathered measles, mumps, croup, and a variety of plagues. "So all will be well, my dear, and we'll love to have you with us!"

Much pleasure was expressed over having "two such good girls in the cottage," much sympathy was tendered, and much assurance given that "we'll see everything is cozy and pleasant, and soon this illness will have run its course and you'll be back with your family."

By then it was suppertime, and their host would not hear of them going down to their cottage and fixing a sad and lonely meal. So they enjoyed a perfectly done saddle of mutton with the two good old people, and afterwards one of the servants lit their way down to the cottage with a lantern.

"That went well," Nan observed, as she went around lighting the lamps and seeing to the fire in the stove. It was definitely tending fall; no more leaving the windows open at night, and they were grateful for the stove. Soon enough they would be grateful to have three.

"You were wonderful!" Sarah said, grinning. "I never would have thought of the aunts."

"It was logical. It seems we come from a numerous family," Nan observed. "A couple of spare aunts wouldn't come amiss in a crisis like that."

"They'd be entirely handy." Sarah yawned hugely. "All right, I am in favor of a little reading in bed and then sleep. Tomorrow should be . . . even more interesting."

Nan snorted. "Tomorrow we find out if we're as persuasive with the stubbornest girl I ever saw who wasn't me." And her face clouded a little. "You know, we are going to have to tell her the truth."

Neville fluttered up onto Nan's shoulder and rubbed

his beak against her cheek. She reached up to scratch his neck.

"She'll be angry, but she has sense," Sarah pointed out. "As long as we can get her to listen to us, I think it will be all right."

"Yes, well." Nan got her book and dropped ungracefully into her now-favorite chair. "It's the getting her to listen part that I am worried about."

Mari could tell just from how Nan and Sarah walked that they had a lot to tell her. And she knew they had been gone off to Criccieth twice in the last week, the latest time being just yesterday. So she wasn't entirely sure what to expect . . .

Idwal watched them approach with his head tilted to the side, but said nothing.

Nan was the first to speak, taking a deep breath. "I think we need to be somewhere that we are all sitting down," she said, looking both determined and a little apprehensive. "Where we won't be watched."

Mari nodded towards the cottage. "We'll still be watched, probably, though he won't be able to *see* us," she said with undisguised contempt. "You know, 'tis the first time I ever regret that there's not more trouble in Clogwyn. If there was, at least yon fool would have something to do besides lie on his belly under a gorse bush and snoop."

Nan snorted, but was happy to follow Mari into the cottage. When they were all seated around the fireplace, Mari looked at her expectantly.

"We . . . haven't been entirely honest with you, Mari," Nan said, rubbing her thumb nervously over her forefinger. "You see, we were sent here. To find you."

It was a little difficult to grasp, even for herself, how Mari felt as Nan outlined the entire story. How the Master of this—White Lodge—had found out there was a new Water Master, and sent Nan and Sarah to look for him. How they'd found Mari, and Idwal, and been ordered to investigate further. How the Puck himself had gotten involved. How they'd worked out how to approach her. "And we really *are* your friends, truly!" Sarah said, pleadingly. "If we weren't, we'd have told Lord A we couldn't do this any more and gone home. We want to help you, and we think we've worked out how."

Truth to tell, at first she was so very angry she couldn't speak, which was why she'd let them rattle on rather than getting up and giving them more than just a piece of her mind. The idea that a lot of foreign rich men off in London could sit in judgment on her and her life when they didn't know *her*, didn't know *here*, and didn't know the first thing about the Selch or the Bargain or anything else—

But it was that very anger that turned on itself. Because, when you thought about it, a bunch of rich foreign men in London were *always* sitting in judgment on the Welsh. That was why the constable was here in the first place, and he was making a lot of people angry and unhappy with his meddling and prying. At least this particular lot of men had had the good sense to leave things up to Nan and Sarah, who were not at all meddling, who had treated her like she was a sister, almost, and who, if they had lied to her, had done so to protect her.

So by the time that Sarah got to the part about them wanting to stay over-winter and help, the anger had burned out. Because, really, there were only two things that *mattered*. She loved Idwal, and her da, and she needed a way to have both without causing more trouble. You couldn't rightly say that Nan and Sarah had used her in any way. Nor had they manipulated her. Nor had they entrapped her. And as soon as they possibly could be, they were honest with her. If that didn't mean they really were friends . . . well, then Mari didn't know what she *could* call a friend.

She also knew that if Nan and Sarah had the friendship of the Land-Ward, they were very special indeed. And they had pled her case with a very powerful lord, more powerful than just his title indicated, if he was the Master of the Masters. Why, who knew what he would have done if these two had not come here on his errand?

"I have heard of this Master in Londinium," Idwal mused. "Oh, not his name, but that he had organized many of the Masters of Logres, and drew them to work together. The Selkies have to do with some of his people. They say he is a good, if somewhat . . ." he tilted his head to the side. "Somewhat limited man."

Nan blinked. "What does that mean?" she asked.

"That he . . . he limits his thinking. That to his mind, the important and powerful must always be men of his sort." Idwal pointed a finger at Nan, who was staring at him. "And you, little maiden, know precisely what I mean by that."

Nan was surprised into a laugh. "Yes. Yes I do," she said, without an explanation.

Well, this Master in London didn't really concern Mari at the moment. What did concern her was the situation sitting here at her hearth. So she took a good, long, deep breath. She reminded herself to look at *all* sides of the thing, and it was no more than a moment's worth of thought to tell her that her friends were truly her friends, and they were not happy with having had to deceive her for so long.

"All right then," she said. "I believe you. So now what does this Lord of yours mean to do about me and Idwal?"

The relief Nan and Sarah felt was obvious in the sighs they heaved and the way the tension just ran out of their bodies. Even their birds reflected it, going from slicked-down and wary, to fluffed, with wings relaxed.

"I suspect he's not entirely *happy* about this, but since it's not something that anyone is going to change, he wants to make sure nothing interferes with you two," Sarah said earnestly. "He understands about the Bargain. I think he's wary about an Elemental creature being the teacher of an Elemental Master, and I think if he dared, he'd offer you another teacher—"

"Wait," Mari commanded, holding up a hand. She turned to Idwal. "Is that a good idea?"

He pondered the question. "Eventually, yes," he said, finally. "I know only the oldest of the teachings. There could very well be much that a teacher who is not from an isolated Selch clan living beyond the sea you know could teach you. But I should like to wait until I know you are firm in your understanding."

Nan nodded. "Fair enough."

"And," Idwal added, "Since there will be a wedding and a bedding, there will soon be wee ones to consider and work around about."

Mari felt herself blushing a little, and hoped it didn't show. "Well, and there's another problem," she said instead. "Here we have that constable looking for trouble. And here we have a strange man coming to live with the Protheros, and no one knows him, nor where he's from. I thought, before there was a constable and when I just wanted to get it all over with, we could make the man a sailor, but . . . well we still *could,* but where would I have met a sailor? And the constable will be wanting to make questions." She almost felt like crying now. "What should we do? Should we be running away? But where would we go?" She couldn't imagine, given his attitude, that Gethin would welcome her among the Selch even though now she had a skin of her own.

Ah but ... maybe this great lord would give us a little place of our own, away from constables and all, where we wouldn't have to explain ourselves to anyone ... For a moment, she lost herself in the dream. But then she brought herself down to earth again. Why should this man do anything of the sort for her? No—and besides, she'd be away from her da, never to see him again. No, that was not a good plan.

"About that ... we think we have a plan," Sarah said, and opened up the sketchbook she had brought with her. "How would you care to be as reluctant a bride as you were when your father told you of the bargain?"

Mari's brow furrowed. "I don't know what you mean," she said, cautiously.

"We think that old snoop is never going to believe in you being happy to marry someone who has just popped up out of nowhere, so far as he knows," Nan explained. "But what if you *aren't* happy and it was an arranged marriage? Say ... a distant cousin? Someone your father promised you to, and you're just now finding out?"

"We can pick somewhere remote enough for him to be from that the snoop won't be able to discover you don't have a cousin," Sarah elaborated. "You can be angry you're being forced into this." She looked at Nan. "We can steal a page from Jane Austen, and the cousin gets the cottage when her father dies," she pointed out.

Nan laughed. Mari frowned. "I don't know what you mean," she pointed out again.

"It's just that there is a book we both like, a book that has the situation of a young lady being urged to marry a rather odious cousin because he will inherit the house they are living in when their father dies," Nan said.

A distant cousin, and an arranged marriage. It wasn't unheard of. And since the Protheros had always kept themselves a bit apart from the rest of the village, no one would really know how out of character that would be for Daffyd to force his daughter into *anything* against her will. Everyone knew inheritance was a tricksy thing, and no one would be surprised to discover that some far-off fellow was claiming the Prothero cottage. Slowly, Mari nodded, then turned to Idwal. *"Can* you be odious?" she asked.

"I can imitate Gethin," he suggested, with a smile.

She grinned back at him. "That will certainly do!" she agreed. "I believe that is a very good idea!"

"You say that you know Selch clans in Scotland? Could you come from that part of the world?" Sarah prompted, as Mari got up to fill the kettle and make everyone some tea, since this discussion looked to go on for some time.

Idwal considered this. "Are the Orkney Islands remote enough that there would be no easy way to say I was *not* from there?" he asked, finally. "In the days of our bargain, there was much coming and going between the Orkneys and here. Enough so there was even some intermarrying, mostly among the clan-leaders and war-chiefs and Druids and the like. You may have heard of some of this—the war-chief called Lot of Orkney—"

Nan glanced at Sarah, who mouthed the words *King Arthur* at her. So Nan nodded, as Sarah did, though Mari looked a little puzzled. "I think the Orkneys are remote enough," Sarah agreed. "And isolated enough! Even if

Constable Ewynnog gets suspicious, first he'd have to get his superiors to enquire up in Scotland—"

"Which is *not* very likely, as they seem inclined to make him do everything on his own—" put in Nan.

"Then they'd have to find someone in the police service stationed *in* the Orkneys to ask about Idwal—"

"And if my experience of the Scots is anything to go on," Nan said with a twinkle, "They're not terribly likely to be willing to cooperate with some busy-body Englishman. And to them, a Welshman is the same as an Englishman."

"And then the information has to get back down here, and even if he can't find anyone who knows you, it doesn't prove anything." Sarah accepted the cup of tea from Mari with murmured thanks.

"Why the Orkneys?" Nan asked, accepting her cup in turn. "And thank you, that's lovely."

Idwal laughed, and smiled broadly. "Because my clan knows a Selkie clan there, I have actually lived there long enough to describe where I was accurately, I've studied with their Master, and I can fair well imitate the accent. 'Tis not unlike the Cymric." He cleared his throat, and what followed was in English, and a little slower, and a little more sing-song than the Welsh he had been speaking. "We doon speak Gaelic at hoom. Gaelic, ye ken, is mo-ore the west coast; people think because we be in the noorth we speak it as weel, boot up until James, ye ken, what we spook was Norn."

"*Brilliant!*" said Grey, and Neville flapped his wings in agreement. Idwal bowed to the birds.

"I can keep to that from sunup to sundown," he said, chuckling.

"You'll only have to do it when others are about," said Mari happily. "And, I suppose, pretend you don't speak

Cymric at all. I do understand English; I learned it in dame school, though not all that well. I didn't see any need for it, since it was just me and da most of the time."

"And knowing you, what you didn't see a need for, you stubbornly refused to learn," Idwal replied, gently chiding. Nan got the feeling this related to something that had occurred between them—probably having to do with Mari's magic studies—that she wasn't privy to. From the way Mari blushed, she was pretty sure she was right.

"But that's all to the good now," Sarah pointed out. "First, she has this unwelcome husband thrust on her, second, he doesn't even speak her language, and third, he's not a very nice person. Constable Ewynnog isn't going to question anything at that point, not the way he would if this beloved betrothed suddenly pops up out of nowhere." Then she snorted. "He probably *will* feel very superior, however, and hold forth about the barbarity of arranged marriages to anyone who will listen."

"Let him," Mari said dismissively, then beamed at all of them and all but clapped her hands with glee. "This gives you another reason to keep visiting me all winter, at least so far as the constable is concerned—if you are my friends, wouldn't you want to be sure that I am not left too much alone with this man I do not like?"

Nan blinked. "Great Harry's ghost, you're right! Good idea, Mari!"

Mari's eyes sparkled. "This is so much of a better solution than saying he is a sailor who Da knows!"

Sarah nodded. "I'm glad you think so. Nan and I really worked very hard to think of a solution that would make Constable Ewynnog leave you alone."

Idwal chuckled again. "Well," he said, "The weather will do that soon enough. I do not think even one so

deluded as he is likely to wish to spend his time in cold
rain, sleet, and snow, just to watch the cottage." He
turned to Mari. "I will be going out with Daffyd come
winter, do not fear. Nothing will happen to him while I
am with him, and as long as I—and possibly even some
of the others—are about, he will make his catch, and be
home and safe quickly. In fact, he may be out after
breakfast and back at luncheon."

Mari bit her lip. "Well, and while I love my da . . . I am
not *altogether* sure I wish to see that much of him . . ."

That got a laugh even from the birds.

Daffyd Prothero was enthusiastic about this new plan, as
was Rhodri. Daffyd, probably because it was going to
allow him to use his acting skills, which he always enjoyed, and because he would be tweaking the nose of the
constable, who he had come to despise. And Rhodri approved not so much because of the plan itself as the fact
it meant Nan would still be coming to the cottage on the
shore. Nan still had mixed feelings about *that* part, although she was getting fonder of Rhodri all the time.
Nevertheless, the main thing was to make sure that they
created their little plot as tightly as they could, the better
to foil the constable.

"So . . ." Daffyd rubbed his hands together. "The first
thing I must do is arrange the reading of the banns." He
counted on his fingers. "We've missed the first and second Sunday of September, so two readings of the banns
in September, and one in October, and we can be having
the wedding the second Sunday of October." It didn't
seem to concern him that Idwal hadn't actually *asked* if
he could be wed to Mari, but perhaps the main thing on
his mind, understandably enough, was the Bargain, and

the fact that Mari was willing to take *any* of the Selch before winter came. Then his brow creased with a sudden concern. "Idwal, you *can* cross over a church threshold . . . ?"

Idwal laughed. "Aye, no fear of that."

Daffyd relaxed. "Well then! And with these two kind misses, we have our two witnesses, though doubtless that pesky constable will be in attendance."

"Da, you don't think he'd object when the banns are read, do you?" Mari asked in sudden alarm.

"He has no grounds," Sarah reminded her. "And he won't have time to dig up any. And anyway . . . well, if we must, we'll appeal to Lord Alderscroft."

"That would be chancy," Daffyd brooded. "Then the blackguard would be all over questioning why his lordship got himself mired in such a little doing. No, if he decides to snoop even further, I think we'll have to depend on authorities seeing no reason to accommodate one little interfering constable in a tiny town in Wales."

"Daffyd, you are getting a bit ahead of yourself," Nan corrected him. "The very first thing that must happen is that Idwal must come openly into Clogwyn and come looking for you."

Daffyd snapped his fingers in annoyance. "True enough. And just how is that to happen? He can't walk up from the beach, nor swim in on the tide!"

"Ah now, you just leave that to us," Sarah said. "You'll see. We want you to be genuinely surprised. Just make sure you're in Clogwyn tomorrow afternoon."

The next afternoon, one of the bigger fishing boats, one with a full crew of four, came sailing into Clogwyn harbor. It put in at the shore, where a rough and surly fellow asked in oddly accented English where he could find Daffyd Prothero. Since Daffyd was selling part of his catch not thirty feet away, there were plenty of people who could point him in the right direction.

Daffyd appeared surprised to see this man, but oddly, also appeared to know him. Daffyd took the stranger into his little coracle—which could hold two, though only just—and they sailed down the coast toward the cottage.

This caused enough of a to-do that several of the locals felt the need to question the sailors before they put out again.

"We're from Criccieth," the sailors said, and when offered a drink before they left "to stave off the chill on the water," they proved to be willing to answer more questions. No, they didn't know who the fellow was; he'd turned up at the docks, looking for a passage to Clogwyn, and paid well for it. Who had he *said* he was? Oh, well that was different, he said he was kin to Daffyd Prothero, and had business with him. No, he hadn't said anything else, a close-mouthed fellow he was, but he couldn't speak a word of Welsh, nothing but that sing-song English, which was nothing like anything *they* had ever heard before.

And there was Constable Ewynnog, hard-eyed, frowning, taking notes in a little book.

There wasn't much more that the fishermen could add, and so they sailed out of the harbor leaving behind them mostly questions and a severely vexed constable.

Some of those got answered the next day, when the both of them, Daffyd and the stranger together, turned up at the minister's house. And when they left, it wasn't a minute before Fflur Morris, the minister's wife, came *flying* out of the house and down to the post office and store to spread the gossip.

"Oh, such a to-do!" she said, quite out of breath, as

every woman that was at the store and every woman that
had seen her run there gathered about her. "Can you
believe it! The banns are to be posted for Mari Prothero
and that stranger!"

The babble of "What?" and "Why!" filled the store
until Fflur got them all to hush so she could speak.

"Now, this is all that I know, but Daffyd was going on
about how Mari *would* be there and she *would* be wed
or she'd be the worse for it! The stranger—his name is
Idwal Drever, have you ever heard the like!—is from
Stromness in the Orkney Isles. He's Daffyd's cousin, and
he's to have the cottage when Daffyd dies. Mari won't get
it, and that's a shame and a disgrace, to turn the poor girl
out of her own home!"

There was a great deal of agreeing with that very
thing, that it was a hard thing for a girl to be sent out and
some stranger no one knew to get what she should inherit. When all that died away, Fflur went on.

"Now Daffyd wrote to this fellow, it seems, and offered to wed Mari to him, so that he'd have a civilized
wife and not some wild thing, and Mari would still be
able to stay in her own home. And the fellow agreed.
And so he's here to wed Mari!"

"And what's Mari to think of this, then?" someone
asked.

"From the bit that Daffyd said, and his grumbling
about serpent's teeth, I do think she's none too pleased,"
Fflur declared.

So excited were all the women that they never even
noticed that once again the constable was at the back of
the crowd, his frown deepening, still taking notes.

And so roused was the village by this unexpected excitement that no one paid any mind when he pedaled off
on his new bicycle, heading towards Criccieth.

14

IT was the first Sunday in October, and a sullen Mari Prothero stood beside her father and the stranger as the banns were read in church for the last time. It was a small, plain, stone building, with a small, plain altar covered only with a white cloth, a pair of candles, and the Bible. This was only proper for a Methodist chapel. Sunlight streamed in the small windows, but Mari's face looked like a storm about to break.

Constable Ewynnog sat at the back of the church, looking as sour as Mari. It was easy enough for the entire congregation to know why he was here—him, who never set foot in the chapel before, choosing to bicycle all the way to Criccieth to go to the squire's church of a Sunday. He was not a member of this congregation, although no one would have been so unchristian as to turn him out—

for there was always the chance that he would see the light. But everyone knew he was not there to worship; he was there to watch with suspicion and disapproval.

And it was common knowledge he'd done all he could to find out something about this Idwal fellow, preferably something *bad,* and had got nothing for his pains. He'd sent letters and even three telegrams from Criccieth, and got nothing back in return. He'd tried to find people inland who recognized Idwal—preferably as one of the agitating miners. He'd done everything short of journeying up to Stromness himself, and most people assumed he'd tried to get leave to do so but had been turned down by his superiors.

Not that public sentiment was all that much in Idwal's favor, for Idwal had remained silent and frowning every time he had gone into the village, waiting for Daffyd to do most of the talking. Most of the village was just glad that the wretched constable had found something to occupy him besides *them,* was sorry for Mari, and wondered if perhaps for once they ought to wish Constable Ewynnog luck, so that that ill-tempered stranger could get hauled away, leaving Mari to go back to her own life again.

But no one in the village was going to interfere. Quite honestly, with sharp eyes on their own daughters, every father in the village felt it was important that they be seen to favor Daffyd in this business. It was a father's right to tell his daughter what she would do with her life, up until the moment she got a husband. Then that right went to the husband. And with both father *and* husband-to-be hauling her to the altar, well, it was her Christian duty to go there and be content with it. Their own daughters could look on this and be properly grateful that *their* das were likely to approve their choice of a lad. Mari was serving as an example of what *could* happen if a father really exercised his rights. Too bad for Mari, but likely she'd soon resign herself and grow content. At least she wasn't going to be turned out of her own house now if Daffyd came to a bad end on the sea, and for that she ought to be properly grateful.

And for the third Sunday in a row, when the service was over, the surly man seized Mari's hand, led her out of the church without a word of farewell to anyone, and hauled her back towards the seaside and the cottage, and no one raised his voice to object. Daffyd lagged behind, so that they were well out of sight by the time he had left the chapel grounds.

Of course, they all would have been astonished if they could have heard what Mari was saying. They'd have been even more astonished to hear the laughter in her voice.

"Oh come on, you lazy dog-seal! Can't you pull me along any faster than *that?* No one is going to believe such a lackadaisical performance!" Mari shook her head and pretended to dig her heels in. Idwal gave a playful tug on her wrist.

"Perhaps," Idwal said, laughter brimming in his own voice, "If my darling betrothed would eat a little less of those fat herrings when we go a-swimming and lose a little weight, I *might . . .*"

He didn't get a chance to finish that sentence, as Mari interrupted him, first with a rude noise, and then with a mocking accusation of her own.

"And who is the one who has been lolling about the beach, tossing down those fat herrings by day and eating entire loaves of my bread by night? And all the laver-bread that has been consumed has nearly run me out of bacon, and who is it that has eaten most of it! Hmm? My adorable husband-to-be might consider a little more exercise would prove to him that it isn't *my* weight that is the problem here!" She was hard put to keep from laughing. "You are puffing like an old walrus, and here I am barely more weighty than a thistle!"

"Alas, not only will I be saddled with a fat wife, but one with a shrewish temper as well!" Idwal mock-lamented. "I thought that plump women were supposed to be jolly!"

It was a good thing that they were well out of the range of anyone from the village hearing them, because Mari burst out laughing, stopped resisting, and skipped up beside him. "Oh, you goose, I am never going to be able to have a serious moment around you! And I think you can stop pulling at me now, and I can stop digging my heels in. We're far enough away no one can tell what we're doing."

Idwal dropped back to a more normal walking pace, and shook his dark hair back out of his eyes. His broad smile made her feel warm inside. "That's as well. You are exceedingly good at resisting being dragged along like a sheep at the end of a halter, my love; I was like to strain something. And it isn't your weight, my heart. Haven't you noticed how much stronger you are now?"

"Actually, I had." Now the two of them were walking at a brisk, but normal pace, side by side, fingers interlaced, and she longed to lay her head on his shoulder. Well soon enough they would be at the cottage and she could do just that. "Is it all the swimming? I used to struggle lifting the big bags of peas, and now it's easy."

"Likely, it is," Idwal agreed. "You have become a lovely swimmer in your sealskin."

She blushed, this time with pleasure. There was almost nothing she liked better than swimming as a seal.

Though she would never want to give over being a human, either; there were plenty of good things about going on two legs. "I could not do that if it had not been for you being so clever," she reminded him. "All that cleverness is what made me wish you as a husband!"

He laughed happily. "Well, do you think you are ready for the wedding next Sunday?" He squeezed her hand, and she felt herself blushing, this time with . . . a little shyness as well as pleasure. Not that she and he hadn't already anticipated the wedding by several weeks . . . that was common enough hereabouts. No one ever bothered to keep too accurate a count of months between a wedding and a birth, unless the bride had managed to make herself disliked, so long as the bride wasn't about to give birth at the altar. But to put it all into words, well, it sounded both strange and lovely and made her feel things she had never anticipated feeling, ever.

Then a little chill cooled her ardor, for there was something that *could* set everything awry.

"Actually there is nothing saying we can't have it done sooner than that, and I'd rather," she replied, sobering. "Tomorrow, even. I'd rather *not* do it in front of the whole village, and we've satisfied the banns. The sooner we make the bond, the less opportunity for mischance."

"Well enough, I follow your lead," he replied, as the cottage came in view. "When the ladies arrive, we can consult with them, if you like."

No one around here would ever consider *not* going to church, and Nan and Sarah had taken to going on alternate Sundays to the squire's church. By now everyone in Clogwyn and half the people in Criccieth knew about the plague of measles that had allegedly lengthened their stay. Offers to make things "more comfortable" had poured in, and Lord Alderscroft had not needed to send

anyone at all—the squire had happily accepted both the
offers and his lordship's financial aid in making the cottage a fit place to winter-over. It now boasted one brand
new stove to replace an elderly one, a fine store of wood
and coal in a brand new coalshed, every chink and draft
had been found and stopped, and the Manor ransacked
for additional rugs, blankets, comforters and two feath-
erbeds. They had all needed airing and some had needed
recovering, but the girls were now well-equipped for the
worst winter. "Which Sunday is it now?" he asked, as
they reached the cottage at last, with Daffyd taking his
own much more leisurely time, and so lagging far behind
them. "Is it the near-Sunday or the far-Sunday?"

"The far one," Mari told him. "They'll not be down
here until well near tea-time. They'll be asked to dine
with the squire, and so it will take them longer."

Mari privately felt there was a great deal to be said for
the Selch way of doing things. The parson of *Capel Cym-
mer,* while not a bad man, had certainly made it exceedingly plain that so far as he was concerned, God and all
of his angels were firmly on the side of Idwal and Daffyd,
and that Mari should simply bow her head and accept
the husband her father had chosen with grace and resignation, and do all her wifely duties. This, of course, was
quite good for their plan, but Mari couldn't help but feel
a good deal put-upon and a bit angry with him, and when
Idwal compared him rather dryly to Gethin, she couldn't
help but agree. Mari thought about that story book that
Sarah had. *I would really like to hear that story some
time,* Mari thought. *I wonder if I could get one of them to
read it to me over-winter?* While she could stumble
through English, and read some, she despaired of making her way through a book meant for English adults.

Idwal gave a whistle as they neared the door, and a

pretty little head popped up out of the rain barrel. "Are we overlooked?" he asked the water-creature—which Mari recognized as the same mischievous one that had gloried in playing tricks on the constable.

"Nay," the water-girl said, pouting. "Yon fool has not come wandering this way in three days. It seems he got weary of ants in his trews and spiders in his hair." She sighed. "And I had all manner of gifties for him, too!"

Idwal chuckled. "Well, I am sorry you cannot work your tricks on him, but that's all to the good for me." He turned to Mari. "So, a swim? Soon it will be cold for you, and colder when coming out of the water and shedding your skin."

It was *almost* too cold now, but being able to fly through the water was so magical, she couldn't bear giving it up until she had to. "Just let me put my Sunday gown up."

She had taken to swimming as Nan and Sarah did, in her underthings, since she was going to get wet regardless once the sealskin was off, and it was just as well not to have to deal with a soaked dress. She popped into the house, slipped off most of her clothing, and quickly ran down to the surf in little more than her bedgown (which Nan and Sarah called a "chemise").

Idwal was waiting for her with her skin, and with the ease of someone putting on an old, well-worn and well-loved dressing gown, she slipped not only into it, but into the form of the seal, and fell into the embrace of the waves.

It was not only as humans that she and he had anticipated the wedding; it was in seal-form. In fact, it was rather more frequent in seal-form, since they had all of the wide sea to give them privacy, and the meeting of bodies was so effortless and so joyful in these shapes.

Not that being with Idwal in human shape was unpleasant—at least not after the first fumbling couplings. In fact, it was rather wonderful. But there was none of the sweating and bumping and *heaviness* of human mating. Not to mention that no one accidentally bumped his head on the headboard and fell to cursing . . .

It was clear from his frisking about and rubbing up against her that Idwal had that sort of fancy now, and so did Mari; what *was* it about being in chapel and pulling the wool over all those eyes that put them in such a mood? But they gave in to it, and then they went chasing the herring, and when they were both full and tired, and sated in all their senses, they hauled up on a bit of rock in the sun and basked, sometimes reaching over to nuzzle one another lazily.

It was good to be a seal.

When it looked, from the sun, to be near the time that the girls would come, Mari gave Idwal a good shove with her nose, and when he didn't respond, dove into the sea and came up with a mouthful of cold water that she fountained all over him. He woke up with an indignant snort, and she dove away, him pursuing, all the way to the home shore.

She came up out of the water and out of her skin with a laughing gasp—laughing because of the threats of retribution that had followed her, and a gasp for the cold of the surf. Without being asked, she handed him her skin; he carried both off to wherever it was he put them, and by the time he returned, already half dry by means of his own unconscious magic, she was dressed and had tea started, and one of his favorite things frying in a pan.

"Ah, laver-bread," he said, looking at the seaweed and oatmeal creation so beloved of all Welsh. "I forgive you for the dowsing." Her da was already tucking into his with an expression of bliss.

"You got none for breakfast, so it's only fair you get some for tea," she told him. The girls ate it as readily and happily as the Welsh did, though they had been skeptical at first. They often cooked it for themselves, though it was Mari who made the laver for them—making the stuff involved an all-day boiling that was best done out of doors. But since this was a church day, Nan and Sarah would have had breakfast with the squire, and nothing as low as laver-bread would be served at Squire's table. Laver-bread was the food of the poor. *Squire's loss,* Mari thought with amusement, as she fried more patties.

"Laver-bread!" Nan cried as she and Sarah came in the door, birds riding on their shoulders and basket between them. "Oh, Mari, does this horrible, unnatural seal-man know what a treasure he has?"

"This horrible, unnatural seal-man has asked Rhodri to bring back spider-crab especially for you, so you should mind your manners, witch," Idwal chided.

"I take it all back," Nan said promptly, although Mari knew very well that *all* of them were going to greatly enjoy the spider-crab feast when Rhodri came in.

Spider-crabs were terrifying creatures, some of them with an expanse of long (delicious!) legs as far as Daffyd could spread his arms. Most fishermen killed them and tossed them back in the sea when they caught them; partly because they cut up the nets, and partly because the horrible things were the only crabs that could reach to grab you *anywhere* you held them if you weren't quick. It was hard to imagine that anything that looked that ugly could be edible. But after seeing a dead one, Rhodri had brought in just to show them, and recognizing it as a huge variant on something she and Sarah had

eaten in Africa, Nan had suggested throwing it in with
the cockles and mussels to boil. They chopped the thing
up so it would fit in the cauldron, and they had discovered that the now-red legs were full of the sweetest meat
any of them had ever tasted. Rhodri was the better of
the two Selch at catching them; he'd never tell his secret,
but he could bring back the smaller coracle that Daffyd
usually used only for salmon fishing full of the things,
quite enough to stuff everyone, and all of them somehow
asleep. They stayed asleep just long enough for one of
the girls to tip them all into a kettle of boiling water, and
then after that, being caught with those claws was no
longer an issue.

"Idwal said he thought we should get wed sooner
than Sunday," Mari said, as she scooped laver-bread onto
plates, with bacon and cockles, and the girls set to. Even
Grey had her little piece of laver-bread, though Neville
had eyes only for cockles, and was very clever at win-
kling them out of their shells. There was soon a small pile
of shells under his perch.

"I think that is a fine plan," Daffyd said, setting his
knife and fork atop his empty plate with a contented
sigh. "I've no objections, none at all. I'd just as soon not
have the wedding under the long faces of the congregation, truth to tell. So long as the minister is not busy, I
expect I can go see him tonight and arrange for it tomorrow."

"Really?" Mari beamed at him. "I keep having nightmares of Gethin turning up and making me wed one of
the others." She did, too. She would wake up shivering,
and Idwal would have to soothe her back to sleep. Even
worse were the ones where Gethin made her marry *him*.

Daffyd chuckled. "I was lagging because the old fool
caught me by the elbow and advised me that now that

the banns were read, if I didn't want to have a runaway on my hands, I'd better get you wedded quick as possible. He'd even gone and gotten the license, if you can believe it." He snorted. "Saved me a trip, so I'm grateful. He'll be happy to get the two of you shackled up so long as we have the two witnesses."

"That will be us," Sarah said merrily; Nan's mouth was full, or she would have responded.

"Done, then." He shoved away from the table. "Now that my darling daughter has fed her old da proper, I'll just take the coracle back in and make the arrangements. Enjoy your last night of freedom, Idwal."

"Enjoy your sail, Daffyd Prothero," Idwal countered. Daffyd laughed, waved at them all, and went out the door. Mari went out long enough to hang the kettle, fill it with water, and get the fire going under it. When the spider-crabs arrived, she wanted to be ready. Then she returned, and found that Nan had made her the last of the laver-cakes in her absence and fried up a last batch of cockles, and Sarah had begun the washing up, so she could sit down and eat at leisure.

"Will Gethin know what we've done?" she asked, between bites. "Or will we have to tell him?"

"Oh, he'll know," Idwal predicted. "A real wedding is a spell of binding, and though he's no magician, he's a thing of magic and he's the clan chief. He'll feel the addition to the clan, and he'll feel the spell. He'll be at our door by sunset, if not before."

"But there's nothing he can do about it?" Mari asked, a question she had not dared before this.

Idwal shook his head. "The spell is set, with or without his blessing. There is naught he can do to set it aside. And he agreed; the choice of mate was yours and yours alone, and if you did not take your mate from the ones he set before you, you still took a mate from our clan. The Bargain will be fulfilled. In fact, with the banns read, it is largely a matter of form. What is said three times in public is also a spell, and possibly even more powerful than the actual wedding vows."

Hardly had the words left his mouth, when the door burst open, and the doorway was filled with an outraged clan chief.

Nan had never seen Gethin, but there was no question of who this could be. Idwal and Mari stood up together. Nan was scarcely a second behind them, and already she could feel the Celtic warrior rising in her, demanding to be unleashed. But she felt a restraining hand on her wrist, and reined in herself, glancing at Sarah.

Sarah shook her head, slightly. Nan knew why. Idwal and Mari had to deal with this themselves, or Gethin would do whatever he pleased with them. They *had* to assert themselves, and show him he could not bully them; they certainly couldn't live under this threat all their lives. Better to have it taken care of now.

Still . . . Nan readied herself. Because she wasn't going to allow people who were her friends get punished for doing *nothing* wrong without a fight.

"How dare—" Gethin roared, and Mari stepped right up to him and made an odd little gesture, as if she was gathering up something in one hand. Gethin's words were literally choked off, and he fell into a fit of shocked coughing. What had she done?

Some magic with water, I suppose. Made him choke on his own spit for a moment, maybe. Clever! Nan thought.

"Don't you come blathering to me about what I dare and dare not, Gethin Selch," she said, her eyes flashing. "The bargain was that you sent me men to court me and a teacher. You never said, not once, that the teacher was not to court me. You should be pleased I picked the teacher, since if I had not, I would be telling you this minute you had better send me more men." She sniffed with disdain. "It seems the ones you sent cannot hold their own with a woman who knows her own mind."

Gethin gaped at her, eyes wide, as if he could not believe what he was hearing, and then he spluttered, trying to get words out past his anger and shock.

"Fortunately, with the boys, you also sent a *man*," she continued, and reached for Idwal's hand. "So. With this good man, I've made my choice, the marriage is made, the Bargain is set."

Finally Gethin found his voice again. "I never told you that you could steal away my Druid!" he bellowed.

"You never told her she could not, either," Idwal pointed out, moving to stand beside Mari, and putting his arm around her shoulders. "Nor did you forbid me to do what the others were doing." His lips curved in the faintest suggestion of a smirk. "Perhaps you should have considered that when you sent me. It's not as if I were already mated, after all. I am also free to set my fancy where I will, and this is where I will."

"The Bargain is set," Mari said, stubbornly. "And the marriage is made and there is nothing you can do about it but accept what has come to pass with a good grace."

Gethin's face darkened with rage, but it was clear that he knew he was beaten. "The Bargain is set," he growled. "The marriage is made." He started to turn, then turned back. "And consider your own words in the Bargain, Mari Prothero," he added.

Then he stalked out of the door, heading for the sea.

The door slammed shut behind him, and there was silence but for the surf for a long, long moment.

Nan relaxed, as did Sarah. Neville gave a derisive quork, and Grey made a very rude noise.

Idwal laughed. "Well said, birds," he chuckled. "And thank you for being here, friends. Gethin is an intemperate man, and I think there might have been more consequence than confrontation if you had not been here, and willing to stand with us."

Nan didn't know how he had been aware she had been ready to launch herself right at the Selch clan-chief, since he'd had his back to her and Sarah, but it was clear that he had known, and that was all she needed.

"It was only fair," she pointed out. "We *are* your friends, and we are not going to stand and watch as you get put in a bad situation. Besides, he made the Bargain in the first place, and since he wasn't more careful of how he worded it, he has only himself to blame."

Sarah started laughing at that. They all turned to look at her curiously.

"Oh . . . you know, in all of the stories, it's the human that has to be careful of how he makes bargains with the Fair Folk," she pointed out. "I think half the reason he was so angry was because today it was the Selch that got hoodwinked by the human!"

Idwal gave Mari's shoulders a squeeze; Nan could see that she was shaking a bit, though whether it was because of repressed fear or relief, she couldn't tell. They both sat down again, but Mari didn't seem to have any more appetite. Nan hardly blamed her.

They spoke of trivialities for a while—of the preparations that Nan and Sarah were making for winter, some description from Idwal of the sorts of weather they could expect, and of the sorts of provisions that Idwal thought they ought to lay in, here at the cottage. "Lord Alder-scroft has given us a fairly generous allowance," Sarah mused. "You know, we hadn't actually gotten you a wedding present yet. Would you object to some provisioning? We could have the lion's share of it waiting for Daffyd to ferry over from Criccieth if you like, if you'd rather Constable Ewynnog didn't know about it."

Mari had recovered enough to answer normally now. "That . . . that would be just splendid!" she said. "And yes, I really would rather the constable knew nothing of what comes into this house. Anything he sees that he can't account for, he is going to assume came from wrong-doing."

"Then tell us what you need—and then tell us what you *want*—and what we get for you out of the wanting part will be the surprise," suggested Sarah. Nan nearly chuckled at that; knowing Sarah as she did, she also knew that Sarah was probably going to arrange for every bit of whatever Mari wanted to be purchased, counting on Daffyd to never look a gift horse in the mouth and overcome his daughter's objections.

So the two of them encouraged Mari to name off all manner of things, including some she clearly thought were the height of extravagance, and Sarah wrote them down on the back of one of her sketches, until they were interrupted by a tap on the door. Idwal opened it to find Rhodri standing there with creels full of spider-crabs.

"Is it safe?" Rhodri said nervously, peering into the depths of the cottage as if he expected Gethin to jump out at him at any moment. "Is he gone?"

"It's as safe as it is ever going to be when Gethin is involved," Idwal told him. "And yes, he's gone. I would keep clear of the clan-hall if I were you. At least for a time. He's going to blame the lot of you for this."

"Of course he is," Rhodri said, crossly. "When has

Gethin *ever* accepted blame for anything on himself. Not that there should be blame!" he added hastily, with a little bow in Mari's direction. "You made your choice as was your right! And you outwitted him."

"I didn't actually intend to, at least, not in that way," she replied ruefully. "It just came out that way."

"And now you sound as if you regret your part of the Bargain," Idwal teased, feigning hurt. "Am I suddenly turned troll because now you have me?"

"No!" Mari exclaimed, and flung herself at her husband to glue her lips to his in a most passionate and unmistakable manner—

"I believe I'll boil some crab," Rhodri said hastily, backing out of the door.

"We'll join you!" said Nan, and she and Sarah quickly edged past the two, and shut the door behind them.

15

THE wedding was almost an anti-climax, so small and simple it was, with just the girls standing as witnesses and signing the book. Somehow Daffyd and the parson managed to keep Constable Ewynnog from finding out about it, so they did not even have his unwelcome presence in the old chapel. Sarah had given Mari one of her artistic gowns for the wedding so that she looked like a splendid princess of the ancient times, with her hair streaming loose down her back. The preacher was quite startled when he saw her, and Idwal could not restrain his pleasure at seeing her. The minister also seemed surprised that Mari did not put up any sort of resistance to the marriage, and perhaps she and Idwal should have made more of an effort to keep up the façade, but without the constable present, neither of them wanted to be bothered. They did, however, slip quietly out of the chapel and out of Clogwyn without encountering anyone else, so it probably didn't matter what the minister thought.

Then it was the frantic spiral from autumn to winter. The girls found that autumn was the busiest season of a country year; everywhere there were crops to be brought in, hay to be cut and dried and brought to barns, animals to slaughter, food to preserve. The weather at harvest time was always chancy in Wales, and every good day had to be leapt upon and worked as long as anyone could stand. Everyone helped everyone else, and the helpers got the gift of a share of whatever was being harvested, thus ensuring everyone got some provisioning for over-winter in the form of trade-for-labor. Even the fishermen of Clogwyn participated, by bringing in huge catches of fish for pickling and salting, handing over part of the catch to those who came to help. Nan was amazed at how quickly people moved on the good days. She would not have believed that so great an expanse of land could be harvested in so short a time. Constable Ewynnog was beside himself; it was clear he found all of this helping and giving to be entirely suspicious and unnatural.

Squire's fields were left last, not out of meanness, but so that he could give a great feast to everyone around about. He had, for the most part, more than enough labor to bring the harvest in himself, since he not only had his own tenants and laborers but hired some of the itinerant harvest-workers that passed through every fall. But he preferred to leave his fields last unless the weather made it imperative that he rush the harvest, so that everyone around could come to his Harvest Home.

It was quite the celebration. Every hand was pressed into duty in the Manor kitchen and at ovens and pits and fires outside too. Nan and Sarah got to introduce the populace to the succulence of the spider-crab, and it was clear that there would be no more tossing away of the monsters when they were caught.

There were gallons of beer and ale and cider; a roasted pig and a young roasted bull, too old to be called a calf, but not considered, by the squire, as good enough to be allowed to grow up to breed nor strong enough to be gelded and raised as an ox. There was oat pottage and cream, oat bread and wheat bread, potatoes, and cheese, fish in plenty and no one was allowed to leave the least little bit hungry.

Nan and Sarah were quite amused at some of the curious customs, which until now they had only read about. The last sheaf of the year had been left standing in the middle of the field and the men threw their sickles at it until one of them cut it down. It was bound and braided and called "The Mare," and the men tried to smuggle it into the Manor without it getting wet, while the women threw water at them. This year, the men were successful, despite a couple of the handsomest almost being stripped to their smallclothes by women looking for the Mare, and the successful smuggler was given a shilling. The Mare was then hung in the rafters, and the Mare of the previous year taken down and burned; the seed from it had been thrashed out and mingled with the seed to be sown next spring "to teach it to grow," or so it was explained to Sarah. A couple of the young men of Clogwyn made very public presentations of beautifully carved wooden spoons to young ladies, which baffled both the girls until it was explained that these were Welsh love spoons and this was essentially asking for the girl's hand in marriage. Fortunately both of the young women had been prepared for such a presentation and both were willing, but Nan could easily imagine such a bold declaration backfiring on the hapless fellow.

There was a game played which Nan viewed with a little alarm, where six men with their arms linked in pairs would toss people who had been laid across the arms up in the air several times. She couldn't be persuaded to join, certain she'd end up dropped on her head.

Then they all sat down to eat again, and when the sun was down and everyone was full, the smaller bonfire that had devoured last year's Mare was built to a great size, the fiddler came out and the dancing began. Nan and Sarah didn't know the dances, so they had to watch, but they enjoyed it for all of that.

That marked the end of the hardest of the work. There was still canning and making of jelly, smoking and drying, thrashing and stowing, but it wasn't the frantic business of getting everything in before the weather turned.

Which it did, and the cold rains came, and after the rains, the snows.

But the cottage stayed dry and warm, and when the weather wasn't terrible, Nan and Sarah went down to the cottage by the sea to keep Mari company. Idwal and Rhodri went out with Daffyd now, making his work much lighter. Mari did the chores or sewed, a great deal of sewing as it happened, because shortly after Harvest Home it was pretty obvious the child-bearing part of the Bargain was going to be fulfilled by summer. So Sarah read *Pride and Prejudice* while Mari sewed and knitted baby things, and Nan worked on baby napkins and bedding. The cradle came down from the rafters, and Idwal nearly drove Mari half mad with trying to anticipate her every possible need or desire.

When the weather was terrible, Nan and Sarah stayed at home, feeling altogether lazy and luxurious as they

wrote reports for Lord Alderscroft or read, or did hand-
work, or Nan practiced her cookery. The week was only
broken by Sunday—services with the squire and dinner
afterwards, or services at the chapel and a brisk ride
back in the pony-cart. Only Neville ventured outside
now, and even he preferred to drowse with Grey beside
the warm stoves.

Then came Christmas, which had always been a great
deal of fun at the school, but which was something altogether different at the Manor. Suddenly the quiet old
place was alive with the squire's children, their spouses,
and *their* children. The nursery overflowed, and Nan and
Sarah were pressed into service to keep the smaller children occupied with games and stories. Not that they
minded at all; the children were all on best behavior,
mindful not only that being naughty would mean coal
instead of presents and candy but that there were worse
things that might befall them.

One of the "worse things" turned up the evening before Christmas.

There was a terrible pounding on the door and everyone ran to see. Managing to peek out a window, Nan saw
the most horrific apparition on the doorstep—what
looked like a horse's skull, swathed in a white sheet, be-
decked with draggled ribbons and snapping at the gathering of men around her. There was a fellow in a fine suit
and a top hat, what looked like two men dressed as
Punch and Judy who kept swatting each other with in-
flated bladders, and a crowd of others in their best outfits. The skull was led by the man in the top-hat, and as
soon as the whole family was gathered around the door,
the children shrieking with fear and excitement, the
group outside began to sing.

"Open your doors,
 Let us come and play,
 It's cold here in the snow.
 At Christmastide."

Squire cleared his throat, took a sip of the port he had in his hand, and bellowed his reply through the door.

"Go away you old monkeys
 Your breath stinks
 And stop blathering.
 It's Christmastide."

The besiegers were not deterred.

"Our mare is very pretty.
 Let her come and play,
 Her hair is full of ribbons
 At Christmastide."

"What is this?" Nan whispered to one of Squire's daughters.

The young woman whispered back. "'Tis the Mari Lwyd, the Grey Mare. She is brought 'round like this at Christmas and ... well, wait, and you'll see."

There was expectant waiting. The adults conferred among themselves. Finally the squire cleared his throat again and called through the door. "Mind! There's ladies present! Watch your language!" Then he sang.

"Instead of freezing,
 Take the Mari home,
 It's past your bedtime
 It's Christmastide."

The Mari Lwyd romped and snapped her teeth, and the group outside prepared to do battle. But it was a battle such as Nan had never seen before, a battle of wit and song, with rhymed verses crying insults on those on the other side of the door, sharp barbs that flew thick and fast amid a great deal of laughter. Nan got the feeling that if the ladies and children hadn't been there, a lot more indelicate things might have been said, for several of the rhymes hinted at some extreme salaciousness, terrible secrets that would be exposed if the squire did not let them in. It was clear both sets of singers knew each other—and their potential weaknesses—very well.

Finally the squire capitulated, and the entire party came in, with the Mari snapping at the children deemed "naughtiest" during the year, half-frightening and half-exciting them. There were cakes and ale all around, a shilling dropped in the cup of every one of the singers, and then the party went on to the next destination and that was more than enough excitement for the children, who gladly went to bed after it.

The children all made charms called *calenigg,* hard green apples with three twigs for legs and split almonds stuck into it so it looked all spiky. A small candle was stuck into the top, along with three tiny sprigs of evergreen, and the whole was brushed with bitter almond oil. These got put in every window; Nan was told that they brought good luck and the luck would last as long as the *calenigg* did.

Christmas Eve brought carols and taffy-making, but everyone went to bed early. The girls were warned that this was because Christmas Day began earlier than they might expect, and so when they were roused by the sleepy maid before the first hint of dawn, they were not surprised. Off the entire group went in a caravan of carts and the old coach that seldom got pulled out, Squire and family to church, Nan and Sarah parting with them to go to chapel, where dawn was ushered in with a service of all carols, quite unaccompanied, called *Plygain*. Nan found herself unexpectedly moved by the singing; everyone in the congregation seemed to be in perfect tune, and the Welsh reputation for beautiful part-singing was certainly upheld.

They rejoined Squire and his family and came back to the Manor for a great day of feasting and presents, more taffy-making, games, and more singing.

The next day, Boxing Day, Nan and Sarah took presents and two great baskets down to Mari, Idwal, Rhodri, and Daffyd, and got most welcome presents back—and how on earth they had managed to keep the things secret with Nan and Sarah in and out of the cottage, neither of the girls could imagine. Mari had covered two little boxes with an intricate mosaic of shells no bigger than a baby's fingernail; Daffyd had carved them intricate spoons—though *not* love-spoons—out of whalebone. And Idwal and Rhodri had gone diving for treasures.

Idwal had used his magical powers to clean the objects once they had been found . . . they weren't things of gold, or even much silver, and perhaps they would not have meant much to anyone but the recipients, but they were, well, perfect.

For Daffyd, the two had gotten two full sets of blown-glass floats for all of his nets and fish-traps. Only quite well-off fishermen could manage to get so many together. They were not as fragile as one might think, but they did break, and they were expensive for such a small fisherman as he to replace.

For Nan, Idwal had brought a knife and Rhodri the matching sword of fine Toledo steel. These were obviously old, and why they had not rusted away to nothing on the sea-floor, she could not tell, and decided not to ask. She was more than touched and thrilled by the gift, she was astonished that Rhodri had actually had the insight to choose something like this for her. "I tried to find a bodice dagger, but alas, there were none down there," he said, with a shrug and a grin.

For Sarah, there were a curious bronze ring, and an equally curious diadem. Idwal nodded as she unwrapped them and looked at them curiously. "Spirits will recognize them," was all he said. "If they are old enough. Some even if they are not old enough. These will give you some measure of protection, and in some cases, the spirits will follow your commands."

And for Mari, there were four packages, two for her and two for the baby that was coming. For the baby, there was a teething ring of ancient ivory, and a rattle made of narwhal tusk. For her ... Nan didn't recognize what the things were, but it was clear that she did. One was a mirror-like piece of black glass, the other a silver-mounted shell. She clasped both to her with an expression of amazement.

"Eh, a good workman deserves good tools," said Rhodri with a shrug.

Idwal just smiled, as if he was well aware he had found something special.

Nan and Sarah had brought more commonplace things, but since Rhodri and Idwal had never seen the like before, and Daffyd and Mari were not used to Christmas luxuries, there were many exclamations. Everyone got one of the peppermint pigs that the Welsh loved to give their children. Everyone got an orange. The

Selch had an incredible appetite for sweets, not too surprising, since sugar wouldn't survive long in the sea, so
besides the peppermint pigs, the two Selch got hoards of
bullseyes, cut rock, peppermint drops, lemon drops, and
a great amount of the taffy that had been made up at the
Manor, for the crowd there had made *far* more than was
good for the children to have. And the baskets they had
lugged down held the small goose they'd carefully
roasted in their little kitchen, along with all of the usual
Christmas dinner goodness.

"'Tis the first time we've had something other than
salmon for Christmas," Mari said in wonder. "Not that
there's aught wrong with salmon!"

So there was a second Christmas feast. And just to fill
out all the corners of the baskets, Nan and Sarah had
been knitting stockings of the softest possible lamb's
wool for Mari, Daffyd and the baby-to-come for months.
None for the Selch, of course, who always went barefoot
and seemed not to feel the cold, but Mari and Daffyd
immediately put on a pair and reveled in the warmth.

The Welsh, it seemed—at least when they were of
families who had sufficient means and leisure to do so—
celebrated Christmas all the way to Twelfth Night. New
Year's Eve was the occasion for another feast, rather
than a ball or a dance as were held in London—and Idwal had asked privately that the girls *not* come down to
the cottage for it. "It is something of an . . . uncanny
night," he warned. "We'll be locking and warding Daffyd's cottage. The Land-Ward's mark will likely mean
you will never know what's about, but it would be best if
you take no chances traveling any farther than between
your dwelling and the Manor."

So the two took up the squire on his hospitality again,
especially since New Year's was more of an occasion for

adults than children. It snowed, hard and thick, which made both of them glad they were not going down to the sea and made attending the dances in Criccieth quite impossible, and the children romped in it until they were utterly exhausted and it was easy to put them to bed. The party for the adults then began. One of the squire's daughters played the piano, so there was dancing, and a great deal of hilarity as Squire and one of his sons undertook to teach Nan and Sarah the local dances.

But just before midnight, there was a tremendous pounding on the door, and the music ended with a discordant chord from the startled piano player.

"Oh no," said Squire's wife in dismay. "I'd hoped the snow would keep them away—"

"That lot?" The son teaching Nan to dance snorted. "Not unless it was a blizzard. I'll get the tribute, Pater, you answer the door. The rest of you—well, you know."

"What is it?" Nan asked, feeling for a sword that wasn't at her side in automatic reflex.

"Mostly a nuisance, dear," said the eldest of the daughters, looking put-upon. "But it could be unpleasant. If you want to see, peep out from the top of the stairs, but don't go down to the hall. You're considered half-English, as we are, and—well—you'll see."

Now greatly curious, Nan and Sarah went to the top of the stair above the door, and hid in the curtains there, as the sound of raucous singing came from outside. After a moment, she thought she recognized the melody, though the words were so slurred that not even Puck's gift of the language helped her make them out.

"Is that the Mari Lwyd song?" she whispered to Sarah, who nodded. Just then Squire came to the door, with two strong manservants, one carrying a small barrel, and the other carrying a tray of pottery mugs. They were

shortly joined by the eldest son. As soon as the first
verses were finished, they quickly sang in return.

"Instead of freezing,
We'll lead the Mari,
Inside to amuse us
Tonight is Christmastide."

So—there would be no challenge? *Well,* thought Nan,
*Considering how drunk they sound, that might be just as
well.*

But when the door was opened . . . a chill went right
down her back. This Mari had to be the most terrifying
thing she had ever seen that wasn't already a spirit or
some other dread supernatural creature. This was no
half-amusing puppet meant to mock-frighten children.

The horse skull seemed, somehow, to float on its own,
though she knew it was on a pole, carried a good two feet
higher than the man who personified her was tall. The
gray and tattered drape was very, very long, and floated
out behind him, effectively concealing him from view.
The ribbons adorning the skull were old, most were the
red of dried blood, or at least that was the color they
seemed, and there was a wreath of dead flowers about its
ears. The eyes were shining and red, and malevolent;
they reflected the lamplight in a most uncanny way. And
there was nothing mechanical about the way its jaws
snapped. It seemed dead-alive, and if Nan had not
known better, she would have been sure it was some aw-
ful thing brought back to life by magic.

The men of the party, though dressed the same as the
Mari Lwyd group that had turned up before Christmas,
were clearly rougher characters, their costumes shabbier,
and they were very, very drunk. But now that they were
inside, they were not loudly drunk, and somehow that
made them seem the more sinister and somewhat threat-

ening, though they had no weapons on them. At least, none that Nan could see.

But the squire had already begun filling the mugs once the first of them had cleared the door, and passing them out. Nan caught a whiff of brandy; clearly, the squire was taking no chances, he was offering them the best the house could boast.

They filled the hall at the door, and shadows gathered around them, as if there were more of them than Nan had counted. Chills shivered the back of her neck. There was something more to this than just a band of thuggish fellows trying to get drinks out of the squire, and it had to do with that dreadful skull . . .

When the first round had been drunk, a third servant appeared with a goose from the kitchen, still with the feathers on. A short carol was attempted, not very successfully, and the Mari "danced" to it, snapping her jaws at the end of every verse.

There was something entirely horrible about the dead horse, dancing in the hall; it should have been funny, a bunch of thoroughly drunk rogues attempting the same little ceremony that the men of Clogwyn had done. But it wasn't. The shadows grew thicker as the Mari Lwyd danced, the air in the hall grew appreciably colder, and the carol the men sang took on sinister overtones. Nan cast a glance at Sarah. She was frowning, and slipped her hand into her pocket, coming out with the bronze ring. She put it on.

Abruptly, the grisly head swung so that it seemed to be looking right at her.

Sarah's lips moved, though Nan could not hear what she said. The eyes of the Mari Lwyd gleamed for a moment with a red glare that had nothing to do with reflected light.

Then the head shook, as a living horse would shake itself, and the song ended.

"And now," the squire said loudly, "A round to keep you warm upon the road, and the tribute for the troupe!"

"The tribute for the troupe!" the men echoed, and they held out their mugs. Each mug was refilled and a silver shilling dropped into it; mugs were quickly emptied and the shilling pocketed.

"A tribute for the Mari Lwyd!" shrilled someone, and the servant held up the goose.

Quick as a flash the skull dipped and snapped her jaws, and came back up again with the goose dangling from them. The servant stepped back, quickly, trembling a little. It looked for all the world as if the Mari Lwyd had killed that goose herself, and as she shook her head, it was for all the world as if a great and terrible predator had hold of the bird and was shaking it to make sure it was dead. The troupe cheered.

And then, to Nan's immense relief, they began parading out, led by the skull, evidently content. Squire put his back to the shut door, heaving a great sigh, before ascending the stairs with his son to rejoin the party.

"What on earth was that all about?" Nan asked, as Sarah slipped the ancient ring from her finger and put it back in her pocket. "They were—they were not at all like the group that came before Christmas."

"It's a bit of a devil's bargain," Squire said apologetically. "There's two Mari Lwyd troupes, one in Clogwyn, which is made up of plain folk who are good-hearted fellows who are amusing to *pwnco* with, and one in Criccieth who are ... well, they begin the night as good enough fellows, but by the time they get out here, as you saw, they are drunk and rowdy. So we've made a pact with them both. Though tonight is the Mari Lwyd's night, usually, we have the Clogwyn lot out before Christmas, for they'll play with the children and give them a pleasurable fright, but not too much of one. Criccieth is not to come until New Year's, and then after the children are in bed. I *pwnco* with Clogwyn but never with Criccieth . . ." He shrugged. "It just seems prudent."

"Their Mari Lwyd—it seemed different to me," Nan ventured. "Less of a sort of hobby-horse and more something . . . I don't know, it just seemed more unpleasant."

"It's very old, so they tell me. May be over a hundred years old or older. Perhaps that has something to do with it." He sighed. "The ministers and pastors and preachers and priests have begun speaking against these old customs, and though I love them, I tell you, I will not be unhappy the day the good wives of Criccieth tell their men to leave the Mari Lwyd in the cellar and come have a sing at the pub instead."

In that . . . Nan would agree with him entirely.

She whispered to Sarah as they followed him back into the warmth and life of the ballroom. "What happened back there in the hall? What did you see?"

Sarah looked at her soberly. "I am not sure," she said, slowly. "Only that . . . it's not just at Halloween and Winter Solstice that the dead can walk. That skull was . . . inhabited. I was very glad we had Puck's mark on us, and the ring on my finger."

Nan decided that she didn't need to know anything more, and allowed herself to be caught up to learn the steps of a lively dance called Hoffedd ap Hywell, and soon, but not too soon for her, the dark things were driven away into the night shadows with the Mari Lwyd.

16

AFTER Christmas, the only good way of marking the time was by the alternating Sundays and Mari Prothero's increasing size. Dark and snowy days followed bright days, and there were more of the dark than the bright.

Mari felt like a hibernating badger asleep in its den. She sewed and slept and often as not, Idwal coaxed the little Elemental creatures to do the chores she would have done, all but the cooking, that is. Water Elementals could not be coaxed to have anything to do with fire by any means. Rhodri did all the lifting and carrying outside, and she was sorry she had ever thought him feckless, for he was a good and faithful helper and friend. Idwal did the same inside, for it was clear from her girth that it wasn't that she was eating too well, it was that Gethin's "promise" had come to pass and she *must* be carrying twins. Soon enough, that was plain, as she felt four feet a-kicking during the rare times the babes showed some restiveness.

"Is that possible?" she asked Idwal one night. "Could Gethin have some way of . . ." She blushed. "Interfering?"

"He's not the Master that I am, but he holds some secrets only our clan chief has," Idwal admitted. "Those likely have to do with the well-being of the clan, so . . . I would have to say, it is likely."

"He told me, when he was angry with me, *my father was a fool twice over for letting Afanyn choose what babies she'd bear.*" She had thought he was just boasting at the time, but now?

Well, he'd threatened her with twins, so that he could take the one away sooner. And he'd threatened her with boys, so there would be no more headstrong Prothero girls to make him trouble. She obviously didn't know if they were boys, but they certainly were twins.

"I see no problem, my love," Idwal told her tenderly. "So, he has interfered, and you will have two fine boys, and everyone will be pleased. Then if you wish more children, we shall have whatever comes." He laughed. "The only difficulty that I can see is trying to keep track of not one, but two headstrong young boyos with your temper. We shall have some thunderstorms, I expect."

"I don't have a temper!" she objected. And he kissed and teased her, until she admitted, at last, that she did.

She was just grateful that it was spring when she was at her most unwieldy. Counting on her fingers, she reckoned that she would be due about June. And as she grew bigger, and bigger, she began to fervently think that June could not come soon enough for her.

Nan woke up in the middle of the night as a tremendous flash of lightning followed by a wall-rattling crash of thunder rocked the cottage. She sat straight up in bed; a second flash showed her Sarah was doing the same. And they both knew *why* they had awakened, and it was not altogether because of the storm.

"Mari?" Nan shouted over the thunder, and in the other bed, Sarah nodded. Without another word, they both scrambled out of bed and into their clothing.

What they thought they were going to *do,* Nan hadn't the slightest idea—although by now they had assisted at several births in Africa, so at least they were a little better equipped to help so long as everything was normal. But Nan was just afraid that—well, it was twins. And they were Mari's first. And if the little she knew was right, that was very dangerous for mother *and* babies.

They flung their mackintoshes on over hastily donned clothing, and ran down the now-familiar path to the cottage by the sea. The way had never seemed so long, and with every flash of lightning and peal of thunder, Nan was certain that things were going horribly, horribly wrong down at the cottage.

The sea raged closer to the cottage than they had ever seen it before, within mere yards of the door, lashing the beach as if it wanted to get inside. In a flash of lightning she saw that Daffyd had somehow anticipated this; his coracles were safely stowed behind the cottage. They pounded on the door, then Nan wrenched it open before anyone could let them in, sure that they would find Mari in travail, and the men wringing their hands without a notion what to do.

They found themselves, blinking, in a little haven of peace and warmth.

Four lanterns leant their light to the main room of the cottage, Mari lay exhausted, hair limp and lank with sweat, but clearly deliriously happy, in a pile of feather-beds, pillows, and blankets by the fire where Idwal must have carried her. Idwal knelt beside her, giving her a drink from a cup, for both of her arms were rather full. She had a baby cradled in each arm, and both were sleeping. From the sound of things, Rhodri and Daffyd were cleaning up the bedroom, and Rhodri poked his head out to see who had burst in the door, as Idwal and Mari looked up at them and smiled.

Nan gaped. "Ah—" she said.

"Oh, you thought I'd be maundering about without a notion what was to do, eh?" Idwal chuckled. He, too, had been sweating, and from the look of things had been far more able a midwife than either Sarah or Nan would have been. "And just because I am a man, is that it? I am a Master and a Druid, I'll make it known to you, and I have assisted at more births of human *and* seal than I care to tally up." He gestured proudly at Mari. "And here are the new souls. Aled and Aneirin. My sons, these are your guardians and friends, Nan and Sarah."

The babies seemed more interested in sleeping than anything else, although they were probably the prettiest and least-pinched looking babies Nan had ever seen. Both had heads of thick, black hair, pink little faces, and looked absolutely perfect. She went to kneel down beside Mari. "You're all right then?" she asked, reaching hesitantly to touch one rosebud of a little fisted hand with a finger.

"Tired. But glad to have them *out,* at last," Mari sighed, and looked to Idwal. "I think I can sleep now."

"And so you shall." He came and took the babies from her, with a kiss for her and one on the top of each of the babies' heads, and put them in twin cradles—Idwal and Daffyd had finished making the second one just in time. Mari smiled and was asleep instantly.

"When—?" Nan asked, looking up at the Selch.

"It began hours ago. Aled was born when the storm began, Aneirin moments later. It was a very easy birth, but I have been working magics toward that for a month now, and so has she." He grinned. "And you never even thought to ask. Water *is* the birth element, you know."

"Ah, no, I didn't know," Nan admitted sheepishly. "Now I feel like a right fool."

"Don't," Daffyd said, coming out of the bedroom with his arms full of linen. "I was half out of my mind, and I *did* know about the magics. It was bad enough when Afanyn had Mari and her brother. It was worse this time. I just about fretted myself to ribbons."

He went out into the storm and for a moment Nan thought he must still be half out of his mind—but then she realized he was going to hang the linens out in the rain, and let the cold water do most of the work of washing them. She thought about going out to help him, but he was back in soon enough, though soaked to the skin. "Is there anything we can do?" she asked Idwal.

"I would be grateful if the two of you would keep watch, while we finally get some sleep," he said instantly. "It would be a great kindness."

"We would be happy to!" Sarah said instantly. "Grey and Neville will know where we went and they'll fly here at dawn on their own."

"And that will be all that I need to hear," Daffyd said, turning to the ladder and climbing into the loft, which was now his since Idwal and Mari had the bedroom. "I feel as if I had been beaten like a bad dog."

Idwal and Rhodri went to the bedroom, presumably to fall into a similarly exhausted sleep, since the newly-made bed was the only other flat spot for them to fall upon that was long enough to take them. Nan and Sarah looked at each other.

"Well?" said Nan.

"Well, it is a good thing I left that new book here," said Sarah. "And here I was annoyed at myself for doing so." She went to the shelf where she had left it, and picked it up, opening it to the beginning. " 'It was the best of times, it was the worst of times,' " she began.

Mari worked on the nets, the babies beside her, as Idwal drilled her on the ways of telling some of the sea-Elementals apart. Her mind was not on the drill however; she kept looking out to sea until he finally stopped even trying to ask her questions.

"Mari," he said, and snapped his fingers to get her attention. "You've no more mind for this than the babes do. What's wrong?"

"When will Gethin come?" she asked, finally, the question she had been dreading hearing the answer to.

Idwal shook his head. "I don't know. Obviously he'll want to claim one of the babes—"

"And he can't have them! And he can't have *you!*" she exclaimed. "I've no quarrel with one—or both!—of the boys going to the clan, but not when they are babies! Not until they are old enough!" The original Bargain now seemed a terrible one. Give up Idwal and one of her children? Never!

"I have no reason to want to leave you, my love," he said soothingly. "And as long as I am here, Gethin has no call to take one of the boys."

"But what if he *makes* you go?" she demanded.

"I—don't know," he admitted, unhappily. "He is the clan chief. He can command me . . ."

"Well, we will see about that," said Sarah, as she and Nan came around the corner of the cottage, with their usual luncheon-basket and the birds kiting along behind them.

Mari looked from Sarah to Nan and back again with hope and uncertainty. "I know that you know a great deal, and you are my friends. But—the problem is that you are not magicians—"

"No, but we are very good at finding ways out of things," Sarah told her, quite firmly, as she and Nan put down the basket and each picked up a gurgling baby. "We'll find a way out of this. It's logic. Magic has rules, and all we need to do is find the one that will make your marriage binding and permanent, too permanent for Gethin to interfere with."

"For one thing—though I expect Idwal already knows this—I have been told that the Selch are different from the Scottish Selkie. *And* who *is a handsome boy then?*" Nan cooed at the baby who looked at her vaguely and bubbled. "*Aled is a handsome boy! Yes, he is!* The Selkie are seal-spirits that can become human. The Selch are humans who returned to the sea. So that puts a rather different complexion on things."

"How so?" Idwal asked, tilting his head in that way that meant it was curious.

"Because your longing isn't for the sea and your skin, it's for the land and two legs," Nan said. "In a battle between the two, the land will win for you. That is why, I suspect, there are so many Selch husbands and wives choosing to stay with their human spouses, and so few of the Selkie." She put the baby down again, and began unpacking the luncheon, as Grey and Neville landed beside the babies, guarding them from insects. "And that means that any pull that Gethin can put on you, Idwal, will be correspondingly weaker than if you were Selkie."

"So the main thing we have to fight," Sarah said, sitting down with Aneirin in her lap and picking up the conversation, "is the bond of blood between Idwal and the clan. I *think* that is how Gethin will control—"

"And isn't it the clever mortal, then," said a sneering voice. "So sad that you are come to that understanding too late."

There had been *no one* there, not to any of Mari's senses, yet suddenly, there they were, surrounding all of them. Not just Gethin, but two wild-haired, wild-eyed women in primitive skin dresses and nearly a dozen grim-faced men, armed to the teeth.

"Now, since I have two wetnurses, I'll be having the boys," the Selch leader said, cruelly, as two of his men snatched up the babies and handed them to the women before anyone could move. Mari cried out and tried to fling herself at the group, but Nan caught her and held her back. "And I'll be having my Druid as well. Idwal!" He threw a handful of stones at Idwal, who went glassy-eyed and vacant faced. "You will be coming with me now."

Idwal stood up stiffly, and lurched to the side of his chief. Gethin laughed in Mari's face. "You've had your teaching, wench, and you had the husband to your liking. I have the babes. The Bargain is fulfilled. I give you back your freedom and the Prothero luck."

He made a gesture, the sea roared right up to their feet, waves somehow breaking over the Selch without touching the humans—and they were gone.

Mari had nearly gone mad with grief and rage, and it had been all that Nan could do to keep her from flinging herself into the sea and trying to follow. She had finally wept herself into stupefied exhaustion and her father had managed to coax her into bed, promising faithfully that he and the girls would find a way to get Idwal and the babies back.

"Though I haven't a glimmer of how we are to do that," he said, mournfully, as the three of them huddled around the hearth, as much for the comfort of the flames as for the warmth.

Nan absolutely refused to give in to despair. When she thought of everything that *she* had somehow survived to get to this place, she knew that there must be an answer, if only they didn't lose hope and kept looking for it.

"There must be a way," Nan said, firmly. "We just have to find it." She and Sarah looked at each other, and then at the birds, who had been sitting silent till now.

"Old Lion," said Grey, firmly.

Nan and Neville nodded. It really did seem the only place to start. "We'll go back to London and discuss this with Lord Alderscroft in person," Nan said. "If you think you can handle Mari alone—"

"I think I can care for my own daughter," Daffyd retorted angrily, then passed a hand over his face. "Apologies. My temper—no offense meant."

"Has been strained to the breaking point," Sarah replied gently. "No offense taken. In that case, we'll leave in the morning, and be in London well before midnight. Lord Alderscroft will have other Water Masters he can call on, and he can surely advise us. Never forget, Mari *is* a powerful Water Master; she merely does not have the experience that would season her. I think that Gethin is afraid of her. I think he was even more afraid to leave Idwal with her for the two years or so it would have taken for the babies to grow to the proper age to take one, because I think that he knew if he did, she would be so powerful he could never counter her. Remind her of that."

"Meanwhile, we'll see what we can find out," said Nan, standing up, and picking up Neville. "Let her know we haven't deserted her, and whether we find an answer or not, we *will* be back to help."

"I'll do that," Daffyd promised, though his face looked miserable. He could hardly bear to look at the empty cradles.

Nan hated to leave him alone with Mari like this. But what else could they do? It was clear there were no answers here, at least not yet. Mari had descended into a grief so deep that right now grief was all she could see. The Water Elementals would never speak with her or Sarah. And Puck had already said he would never act against his counterpart of the sea. She patted his shoulder comfortingly, and she and Sarah went out into the night.

Mari did not so much sleep as move from grief-ridden wakefulness into a kind of heartbroken paralysis. She couldn't stop crying, though she kept her sobs stifled. She heard what the girls had to say to her da, and although she wanted to cry even more because they were leaving, she knew they were right. But oh, her world was shattered, and the wreckage tossing on the waves, and if she was truly a "powerful Water Master" she certainly felt anything but powerful at the moment. Why, she couldn't even actually follow her love and her babies, because she didn't know where Idwal hid her skin, and without it she could never go beneath the waves to where they were.

She had to hold to hope with both hands, for if she did

not, she knew she would fling herself into the sea anyway, and follow until she drowned. And yet, she could
not see any hope to hold onto, which made her want to
fling herself into the sea even more.

Which would be a *sort* of revenge upon Gethin, for
there would never be more Protheros and the Bargain
would end with Daffyd, but it would be a cold sort of
revenge, and not one she would enjoy.

So she cried until her eyes were swollen and sore, until she could not even think, but merely existed in a kind
of mindless sorrow, and passed into a sort of nightmarish
doze, only to wake and cry more, feeling despair crush
her down into the bed until she couldn't move. When
morning came, she could not be coaxed to eat or drink a
thing, and Daffyd fretted over her. But not only did she
have no appetite, the mere thought of food left her wanting to vomit, though she finally gave in to his pleading
and drank. Then she went back to shadows and weeping,
the grief growing only deeper with each day that
passed—

For with each day that passed in which Nan and Sarah
did not return, she became more and more certain that
there *was* no answer, that they could not bear to face her
to tell her so, and they were never coming back. Gethin
had won all, and she had lost everything she cared about
but her da.

Three days ... then four ... and then came the fifth,
and the fifth brought the storm-crow himself.

Constable Ewynnog had been watching the cottage for
three days now. The girl never came out, and there was
no sign, none at all, of the husband. The first day, he had
been merely suspicious; the second, his suspicions had

hardened, and on the third, he determined that it was time to investigate in person.

Because Daffyd Prothero had a very handsome little cottage, that was, as he understood these things, worth a goodly sum. And the simplest solution to the problem posed by the fact that the cousin would inherit it instead of the daughter would be to marry the cousin to the daughter, then be rid of the cousin. The cottage would go naturally to the daughter, as her husband's nearest heir, without any more interference from other relatives. And a man who had rid himself of a wife would find no great moral difficulty in ridding himself of a cousin and son-in-law as well, particularly not one that was so cordially disliked by the daughter.

Oh there was no proof that Daffyd Prothero had rid himself of his wife, but Ewynnog was mortally certain he had. "A policeman's instincts," he told himself.

Well, Prothero might be clever enough to fool the ignorant villagers, but he was dealing with a trained constable now, and he would find he wasn't able to pull the wool over *Ewynnog's* eyes. Justice would be done. And he had brought the irons with him this time, to see that it was done.

So he marched down to the cottage in a bloodthirsty frame of mind, dropped the irons down beside the doorstep, and pounded on the door furiously. When Prothero opened the door, he shoved his way inside without asking to be let in.

Once inside, a quick glance around only made him more certain that his suspicions were correct. This was no common cottage; this was something on the order of the one the squire had for his friends and special visitors. It was far more than a touch above a common cottage, it was something a prosperous merchant would live in, like the postmaster, and without a doubt it was (in the eyes of a bloodthirsty anarchist of a fisherman at least) worth killing for.

"Where's Idwal Drever?" he demanded, harshly.

"Out fishing," said Prothero, rousing into a sullen anger. "And by what right have you—"

"You're lying," Ewynnog said, just as the girl stumbled out of what he presumed was the bedroom, in clothing that had obviously been slept in, face puffy and eyes red with weeping. "Where's the babies?"

"What—" the girl began, her eyes going wide with shock, as her father shushed her.

"What babies?" Prothero demanded heatedly.

That was enough for Ewynnog, who leapt on the man like a tiger, wrenching his arm around behind his back, and shoving him against a wall. "You lying murderer! I've seen those two babies with my own eyes, and you have two empty cradles right there by the hearth! Where's the father? Where are the babies?" He wrenched Prothero's arm higher in the proper manner, getting a gasp of pain out of him. "Where did you get rid of them? In the sea? Confess!"

The girl shrieked something unintelligible in her coarse peasant Welsh. He ignored her, as he ignored her when she flung herself at him, tearing at his arm with her fingers, crying hysterically, "Let him go! Let him go! He's done nothing!"

He had come prepared this time, in a stout leather coat and leather gloves, so she couldn't tear at him with her nails as these fishwives were wont to do. He had Prothero under control, so he gave the girl a smack across the face that rocked her back, then a shove with his boot that sent her reeling down onto the floor. Since it was obvious he wasn't going to get an answer out of Prothero, he frog-marched the man out the door, the wench screaming and crying after him. He'd left those manacles just outside, and before Prothero could even guess what he was going to do, he'd clapped the man in the irons and grabbed the chain that held the irons to the wrists. His heart sang with the glory of the justice he was doing, and the thoughts of the praise he would get from his superiors. He had a triple murderer!

And best of all, he had timed his arrival so that the villagers would be off doing their work and wouldn't see him bringing Prothero in. He wouldn't put it past them to try to interfere, or even to attempt to free Prothero, and he was only one man; he couldn't hold them all off. He'd keep Prothero safely locked up until reinforcements from Criccieth could come.

"You're coming with me, Daffyd Prothero," he proclaimed loudly, although there was no one to hear but the weeping girl who had followed them out.

"No!" the girl shrieked, and ran at him again, but now he was ready for her, and he gave her another smack across the face that knocked her back. She fell, and sprawled in the dirt on her face. "I am arresting you on suspicion of the murder of Idwal Drever and his children, and I am taking you in."

And with Prothero in tow, the girl crying into the dirt, he started the march back to Clogwyn, a walk made all the shorter by the heady wine of success.

Nan and Sarah were doing their best not to dance with impatience, but it was taking the stationmaster a hideously long time to unload the two bicycles they had brought back with them.

They had not brought them for the sport.

A few days ago, Nan had gotten a horrible feeling that something was wrong. Two days ago, Neville had come chasing after her with her locket in his beak—the one that had sprigs of oak, ash, and thorn in it. Understanding him immediately, she had managed, somehow, to find a fairy circle on the grounds of the school and had dropped all three into the middle of it.

She had been about to declaim one of Puck's speeches, when Puck appeared without it, and had given her the gist of what had happened to Mari since Gethin had taken the babies, so far as Gethin's plans were concerned. Gethin intended Aled and Aneirin never to know their mother, and to set Idwal under a geas that would never allow him any freedom. Puck was angry, but not terribly worried.

"Best to get the advice of the Water Masters, still," he counseled. "The wench is heartsick, but the tale is far from being over. Just tell them what has happened, and get their wisdom. I know what I would advise if this were Earth-creatures, and that might be the same—there are rules for these things, and the folk must abide by them."

"But—" Nan began, about to point out that if Constable Ewynnog noticed that Idwal was gone, there were going to be some difficult questions.

"I came because you called me in distress, but I'm sorting something myself," Puck said. "Now I must be gone." And he vanished straight out of the ring, before she could get another word out.

Far from reassuring her, that only made her more anxious, and she and Neville went straight to Sarah.

Sarah's startled and dismayed expression only reinforced her own alarm. "Of all the times for Lord A to be in London!" Sarah said, looking as if she wanted to curse.

"Some pother or other in the House of Lords—oh *damn* politics! What do we do first? Why did it have to be *now?*"

That was when Memsa'b came in, wanting to know what had them all in a tizzy, and there was explaining all over again.

"Memsa'b, how do we get back there when our tickets aren't for another two weeks?" Sarah cried. "Nothing's arranged, no transport to Gower Manor, nothing! Or do we go up to London and *try* to see Lord Alderscroft? What should we do?"

Memsa'b bit her lip, and thought for a moment.

"Sarah," she said, finally. "Get me your return tickets. I'll have Sahib run them over to the station and get them changed for tomorrow. Nan, there are two bicycles in the shed that Gupta and Agansingh use to get around the grounds. Tell them you are borrowing them, and ask them to take them and put them in the cart. If things are at a difficult pass, you'll need transportation you don't need to wait for. I'll get your traveling things together. Quickly now!"

They all moved—very quickly. Rather than wait on the morning train, they managed to catch the last train into London, and from there, took the earliest out to Wales—changing into a set of bloomer-dresses on the last train to Criccieth. The whole way, they discussed what might be done.

The problem was, as Alderscroft explained, that no one had ever been in quite this situation before, and the one and only Water Master that Alderscroft could find for them at short notice, a Lord James Cliveden Almsley, confessed himself to be at a complete loss. All he could do was to offer them some books of folk-tales as compiled and annotated by Elemental Masters—books that the girls had anxiously gone through, without coming to any actual conclusions.

"Well, the main thing is to make sure that wretched constable—" Nan was saying, when suddenly, Sarah went absolutely white.

"I think we're a bit late for that," Sarah said, voice tight with fury, and pointed.

Nan looked where she was pointing. At the station rain-barrel, which currently contained so many water-creatures that it looked like a barrel of sardines. And all of them were gesturing frantically at the girls, clearly in a state of near hysteria.

"They weren't there a second ago," Sarah said. "I was looking right at the barrel and there was nothing in it but water. Something horrible has happened, and you can bet that Constable Ewynnog is right in the middle of it!"

At *just* that moment, the station-master came up with the bicycles, looking both dubious and a bit disapproving. At any other time they would have paused to soothe his nerves . . . but not now.

Instead, they turned the birds out of their carriers, tied carriers and their own small bags on the backs of the bicycles, thanked him and sped off as fast as their legs could pedal.

The road to Clogwyn had never seemed so long.

17

Nan and Sarah had arrived barely in time to keep Mari—who had gone from hysterical weeping to hysterical rage and actually gotten her hands on a pair of wicked knives and the ax—from going after the constable to murder him.

So far as Nan was concerned, that part was something of a blur. She was certain they had both flung themselves off the bicycles while the contraptions were still in motion, and it was a wonder they both hadn't broken their necks. She *thought* she had probably gone into her Celtic warrior self before it was all over. She *knew* Neville had certainly done his startling transformation into something ever so much more powerful than a large black bird. At least the girl had finally seen sense, and allowed herself to be led back into the cottage. Once there, they brewed a pot of the strongest tea they could manage, made her eat and drink, and when she seemed somewhat sensible again, they told her the little they knew.

Nan expected her to drop straight into despair again, but instead . . . her face took on an expression of calm fury.

"Then we need two plans," Mari said, surprising Nan, and from Sarah's expression, Sarah as well. "We need to get Da away from that constable before anything worse happens, and we need to get Idwal and my babies back. And we need to do both at the same time, or nearly."

"Once we have Idwal and the babies, the constable won't have a crime," Sarah pointed out. But Nan shook her head.

"No, Mari is right," she countered. "We need to get Prothero away from the constable and get him into hiding, and we need to do that first. Now. Otherwise he could be sent to Criccieth or even farther away, and into a proper prison, and we'll have a cursed hard time getting him out even with Lord A's help, because until we can get hold of Idwal and the babies, he's going to be charged with murder. And who knows how long it will take to get Idwal and the children?"

Mari shut her eyes, clearly thinking extremely hard. Then she got up, and poured a bowl full of water and set it on the table. Nan and Sarah couldn't tell exactly what she was doing—they couldn't see the magic—but after several minutes, Mari said out loud, "I know you're lurking, Tylwyth Teg. I'm about to give you leave to do mischief on that human in the blue coat, so you might as well come out."

At first, there only seemed to be an odd little mist on the water, as if it was heated, though of course there was no fire beneath the bowl. But after a moment, an odd little apparition condensed out of the mist; a mostly-naked little wench, clothed in little more than her long green hair and some water-weed, with eyes that danced with malevolent glee.

Oh! said a musical little voice in their heads. *And what is it ever that I can be doing, then? I thought you were going to ask me to fetch home your Selch and his pups, and that I cannot do.*

"The blue-coated blowhard," said Mari, with carefully contained wrath, "has taken my father, as you no doubt know. I will have my father free so that I can spirit him away to safety, and I will have it done with as much trouble and turmoil for the blue-coat, and the least danger and difficulty to myself, as possible. You are the queen of trouble and turmoil, my pretty. What is it that we might be doing, and how can you be in on the doing of it?"

We-ell, a pretty problem ... The spirit grinned. *I do think, though, it may take the very Aspect of Mischief himself to help with this.*

For the first hour, Mari had been too grief-paralyzed to move. For the second hour, she had been ready to cast herself into the sea, and only the fact that she could not seem to get the strength to do so had kept her from going into the waves to drown. She could not see a way out of this. The authorities would never believe her. The best she could hope for was that they would decide that her father had bullied her and done it all himself without her knowledge. He would hang. She would be alone. She would never see her father or her love or her babies again.

What was there to live for?

And with that, she had somehow had the crazed notion that if she had nothing to live for, she might as well die trying to set her father free. She had gotten weapons, and she had started out after the constable, prepared to do her best to cut him up like a salmon, when out of nowhere, like a pair of mechanized angels, Sarah and Nan had come flying down the hill toward the cottage and the sea.

She was still crazily determined to go after her father, but after a little bit of a struggle, and a lot more weeping, some half-coherent explanation and a great deal of tea, she finally, and suddenly, as if waking from a stupor, found herself with a clear head.

She was still aching with grief and despair, but both of those things were pushed to the back of her mind right now. Her da was going to hang. She and Nan and Sarah were the only ones who could save him. Nothing else mattered.

She didn't have *much* of an idea, but she did know this: she had to get her father free. And then she had to go after Idwal. The Water spirits probably would not help her much with the second, but there was at least one who loathed the constable as much as she did, and would likely help her with the first.

So she called up that malicious little creature that had taken such joy in tormenting the wretch. She was mightily tempted to *summon* the Elemental, but that would be a mistake, and she knew it. She *might* get away with such conduct with one of the friendlier Elementals who would understand her and probably forgive her, but the malicious one would resent it, hold a grudge, and do all that she could to undo what Mari needed done.

Of course, offered the opportunity for free rein with Constable Ewynnog, well . . . the malicious one could hardly wait to get started.

She came when called because she was curious. Mari had never actually *called* her before, and she had to have

felt all the grief and despair coming from the cottage.
Perhaps she even knew exactly what was going on; that
wouldn't surprise Mari at all. "You are the queen of trouble and turmoil, my pretty," Mari told her, which made
her preen as if Mari had flattered her. Perhaps, in her
eyes, Mari *had*. After all, she was a small thing, and made
small mischiefs, but to be given such a title implied that
she could do far worse things, and small troubles very
much enjoyed being given an importance far beyond
their true stature.

And when told Mari needed her help with plaguing
Constable Ewynnog, well, it was clear that Mari had just
presented her with her heart's desire.

And oh, how she rewarded such regard!

It was, by Mari's reckoning and by Sarah's pocket-watch,
a half an hour to midnight. The sky was overcast, and
there was a damp bite to the air. Being as it was Saturday
night, and the good people of Clogwyn would be break-
fasting as soon as the sun rose, and in chapel as soon as
they had breakfasted, the little pub, though officially
open until midnight, had closed about ten. There were
not enough hard drinkers or less-than-righteous in such
a small village to warrant keeping it open. This was unlike Criccieth, where the hotel bars *and* several pubs *and*
a population of church-goers (who did not need to put
in an appearance until the scandalous hour of ten in the
morning!) could stay open up until (and sometimes un-
officially after) the legal closing time.

The people of Clogwyn had been asleep in their beds
for two hours at least, which meant there was no worry
about being seen sneaking into the village. In fact, they
didn't need to sneak at all.

Whispering, however, was advisable, as was walking very softly. At least for the three humans. Although Robin Goodfellow had laid an enchantment of sleep over the village, it was a light one, and it was possible that anyone with a touch of magic in him would resist it. The three girls moved carefully; without a lantern it was hard to tell exactly where they were and which buildings were which.

"We could never have done this in Criccieth," said Puck, looking about himself, as if it were broadest daylight. "Too much cold iron. I can abide it, but none else. Here ye be, sweet Sarah; churchyard is right here."

"I'm glad you can see better than I can," Sarah whispered, and gingerly made her way up the little path to the chapel, and from there into the graveyard that surrounded it on three sides.

Nan, Mari, and Puck went on, making for the cottage that the constable had tacked his jail cell onto. When they reached it, they carefully skirted up the street and around to the back, climbing across the hillside behind the row of houses, where the ugly, windowless jut of his addition stood out starkly as the moon finally came out from behind the clouds. Puck gave a little whistle.

Nan managed not to yelp as a tiny faun jumped up from the grass practically at her feet. *How now, Captain?* the faun said cheerfully, giving him a jaunty salute.

Puck chuckled. "How now, spirit? Are you and your fellows ready to play your pranks?"

Not so easy inside, the faun replied. *Iron on the windows, iron on the doors, iron shackles and iron in the kitchen.*

"Then go dancing on the roof, lad, and make all the noise you can," Puck advised. "Tap at the windows, knock at the doors, and like bean-fed goats, make you merry until the human inside cannot sleep! Let's make the fool of this crab-faced manikin, until his neighbors think him mad!"

The faun didn't have to be told twice. He went skipping and dancing over to the cottage, and the closer he got, more other creatures popped up out of the grass and the hedges that divided one yard from the next. Meanwhile, Puck, with a few gestures, laid a spell of deeper sleep on the inhabitants of the houses around this cottage, so that no matter how much noise there was, the neighbors would be ready to swear they heard nothing.

Soon the Earth Elementals and fae creatures were rollicking around and over the cottage like boys turned loose from school early, and as Puck made a further gesture to keep the inhabitants of the other dwellings further away soundly slumbering, his Elementals worked their will on their victim.

The back door flew open, and the constable emerged with a yell in his nightshirt, a cudgel in one hand, looking wildly around for this tormentors.

But of course, there was nothing to be seen. And the night held only the sound of ocean and wind.

The constable searched all over the back yard, then from the sound of things, went out to the street-side door and searched there. He went inside and berated Daffyd Prothero, waking him from the sound sleep that Puck had kept him in, demanding to know if "his conspirators" were behind the mischief. Daffyd protested sleepily.

"What noise?" he demanded. "I was sleeping, hard as it is to sleep in your stone box, without a window! I didn't hear any noise. Maybe you dreamed it. Or maybe the Lord Almighty is giving you a bad conscience for imprisoning an innocent man."

The Constable cursed, and gave over pestering Daffyd. Finally, after another search, he went back to bed, grumbling to himself. The Elementals gave him a few minutes, then began their games all over again.

Four times they stirred him up, with him getting angrier and less controlled each time, waking Prothero and getting cursed for it. There might have been a fifth time, but that was when Sarah reappeared.

"Oh, well done, sweet Sarah!" Puck exclaimed. "And what have we here? Wait a moment, let me strengthen them."

He made a "giving" sort of gesture, as if he was scattering sweets before children, and four disparate figures condensed out of the darkness and night air behind Sarah.

Two were children, one was a woman, and one a man. They looked like chalk sketches written whitely on the dark night. The two children seemed to be in their nightshirts, the woman in the traditional dress of a Welsh woman complete with kerchief and tall hat. The man was harder to see, more like a blurred outline, but it was clear he wore nothing modern. Puck regarded them all thoughtfully. "I remember you," he said to the children, who held each other's hands. "And bad luck to the preacher who frightened you with his stories of hellfire when you were sick five years ago. Come, my sweetings, come talk to the Puck."

"You see who he is," Sarah told them softly, as they hesitated. "Such as he would never harm a child. Go to him."

At Sarah's encouraging nod, the children edged closer, the girl sticking her finger in her mouth. "Now, I am an honest Puck, and I tell you that you've naught to fear," the Land-Ward told them. "Has Miss Sarah explained what we'd like you to do?"

The two nodded silently.

"And will you be so very kind as to do it?"

They nodded again. The girl took her finger out of her mouth long enough to whisper, "Constable is a nasty man. He frighted our mum. *He* should be frighted."

"And so he should." Puck nodded approvingly. "Well then, off you go. Give him a frighting. When you hear Miss Sarah call, come back, and we'll show you the way to leave this dreary place, and I promise, there is no hell-fire waiting for you. Only flowers and sunshine and good things."

The little boy's lower lip quivered. "Our mum has forgot us," he whimpered. "She give our toys to the new baby . . ."

"Ah sweet ones," Puck said, and drew them close to him, somehow managing to embrace them even though they were spirits—and they cuddled trustingly to him after a moment of resistance. "She hasn't forgot you. She would never forget you. But she thinks you are in the good place, waiting for her, and that is why she thinks of the baby that needs her now, and not of the children she thinks are happy and smiling all the day. Believe me."

The boy searched his face, then managed a little nod.

"Now then, go and give Constable a good fright, and come when we call you."

The two child-spirits drifted off through the back of the building, and Puck turned his attention to the woman.

"And you—" he said.

"I have a debt I cannot pay," the woman sobbed. "I wronged Gwyneth Dyas, and her husband left her for me, and he spent all his money on me, and then drowned, and she went on the parish with her babies and they sent her to the workhouse." With every word her sobbing grew louder and choked off her words until finally she could not speak.

"And well it is that you have found yourself at this pass," Puck told her sternly. "And so you, too, are afraid of hellfire? Well we are giving you a chance that few spirits get. You ruined the lives of a man and his wife and their babies. I give you the chance to even the scales, and save the lives of a man and his wife and their babies, and her father to boot. Now, go you into that house, and think on your sins, and weep and wail until we call you back."

Like the children, the woman passed through the wall of the house and entered it. That left the man.

He was dressed in strange, rough garments, and he gazed at Puck in wonder. "Oh Oldest Old One, I have been wandering lost for so many years! The black-robed priests of the White Christ had spread across the land, my kin buried me in strange ground, with strange rites, and there was none to show me the way to the Summer Country—" he said hoarsely, sounding as if he might cry.

This time it was Puck who hung his head. "And the shame be upon me for not doing so," replied the Elemental.

"Nay—nay—opening the way is the work of mortal Druids and the Ladies of the Goddess," the ancient one contradicted him. "Can this little wench with you do that thing? Her thoughts say she can."

"So she can, but we beg a boon of you first," Puck told him. "It is cruel to make you wait and work—"

But again the ghost interrupted him. "I have waited long, long years to pass into the Summerland, what is a night more? And the Selch-kin needs her mate and her babes. I will do this."

And like the others, he drifted into the constable's cottage.

This time, there was no sound from the spirits—at least none that Nan could hear—but it was evident that *something* was going on, because every window in the place was soon full of light, and they could hear the constable rushing around inside gibbering hysterically.

Tis a pleasant music, that, observed the malicious Water Elemental who was suddenly beside them.

"And well done of you, to think we must give the man such wild visions that when he tells of them to his neighbors, they'll think he went mad, and when he tells them to his lords, they'll be sure of it," Puck said warmly.

Oh, well that was the tall wench's thinking as much as mine, the Elemental replied with a shrug of her weed-covered shoulders. *A pretty mind she has for such things. She could work a world of mischief on folk, were she so inclined.*

"Well, it's not the sort of thing I *like* to think up," Nan said, feeling a little guilty, because thinking of ways to torture the constable had been so much fun. It wasn't very Christian of her . . . and she didn't like to think what Sarah's parents would say if they ever heard about it. "I mean, I only do when people deserve it . . ."

Puck made a *tsk*ing sound. "And what is wrong with that? Evil to him who evil does, I say. Be done by as you did, and *someone* has to be doing the done-by." He glanced over at Sarah. "And what are the spirits telling you?"

She had her eyes closed, and her head cocked in a "listening" position. "That he's wedged in a corner behind a chair, and trembling from head to toe. Shall I call them back?"

"Oh yes," Puck nodded, "I think it's time."

More quickly than they had gone, the four spirits came flying back to hover expectantly in front of Sarah. She cast an enquiring glance at Puck, who made a little bowing motion. "Unless I am vastly mistaken, you have a great deal of experience in this now, my pretty wench," he said gallantly. "You began this; let your hand be the one that ends their woe."

Sarah beamed at him, and Nan knew why. Of all the things that Sarah could do, showing spirits how to "cross over" gave her the most pleasure.

She held her hands over her head and a soft light began to shine from them. She brought them down in a double arc, drawing the outline of a pointed door in the air, then stepped a little away from it. The doorway filled with a dim, but welcoming light, and she beckoned to the male ghost.

"Thank you, thank you so very much," she said, her voice full of gratitude. "Go and take your reward at last, for there is Summerland waiting for you, and all those you would meet again."

The man gave a little, glad cry, and rushed through the door. For a moment after he had gone, there was a scent of lupines and violets and grass warmed under the sun.

Then Sarah turned to the woman. "Would you—"

The spirit trembled. "I fear the anger of Heaven," she said, sounding as if she would weep. "I do not see how this balances the scales. Even if I escape the fires of Hell, how could Heaven welcome me?"

"Then take the middle way, and Summerland," Puck said instantly. "Go there and learn goodness. It is in *my* purview and I give you leave to go there, and learn to be better."

The woman did not hesitate, but rushed after the man. This time the scent that lingered was of rue and rosemary and heated earth.

The second of the children piped up in a nervous voice. "Please . . ."

But before Sarah or Puck could say anything, the doorway brightened until it was too bright to look on, and the light shone on the faces of the child-ghosts. The pale, wispy things looked alarmed for just a moment, and then, suddenly, their expressions filled with wonder and joy, and without another word, the elder seized the younger's hand, and they ran through the doorway, laughing. There came a sound of music from far off, and the strong perfume of lilies, roses, and carnations.

And the doorway faded, and was gone.

Puck looked at Sarah with new respect. "Oh *well* done, sweeting."

Sarah looked embarrassed. "I've had a lot of practice," she said, voice trailing off. Mari looked dumbfounded, astonished, and as if she wanted to ask something but didn't quite dare.

Well! If we are all done with our love-feast, will you give me leave to get on *with it?* The acerbic voice of the Water Elemental made them all jump.

Puck laughed, and made another gesture. This time an odd little half-human head popped out of the ground.

"And have you found it? And cleared the way?" Puck asked.

Done and done, said the gravelly voice. *The spring is found, the way is cleared, the path is made. Just let yon water-wench call, and the spring will come.*

The Water Elemental did not wait to be invited. With a grand gesture and a shrill cry, she stamped her foot on the ground.

And water gushed out of the hillside right above the cottage. The air was full of spray and the smell of wet rock and mud, and the sound of water in a great hurry.

You couldn't say that it *flowed* toward the cottage, for that was too tame a word. It was as if a stream in full fury of a spring flood erupted towards the cottage, and in far less time than it took Nan to take it all in, the water had hit the side of the building and plunged underneath it.

It hadn't *really* disappeared, of course. It was just taking the channels that the gnome had cut for it and into which the Water spirit was guiding it.

Right into the cottage.

With a shriek of pure panic, the front door burst open, and the constable, propelled by a rush of water, ran out into the street.

This had, as Nan had hoped, been the last straw. He ran as fast as his legs could carry him, heading—well, she didn't know where he was heading. It didn't matter as long as he didn't come back too soon.

The Water Elemental made another gesture and the water stopped as abruptly as it had started, and Nan, Mari, and Sarah ran for the front of the cottage. The Elemental made a different gesture, and the ground began drying so quickly that by the time they got to the open front door, there was no sign that any water had ever been there. Puck followed at a more leisurely pace.

Daffyd Prothero was beating on the door of the cell, yelling in hysterical fear himself, and Nan didn't blame him, since he'd been awakened by water that had probably been up to his waist, and was locked in a little stone cell with no window and only an iron grate in the door. Furthermore, he had watched the constable, the only man who could get him out, go pelting away as fast as he could. He must have thought he was going to drown.

As Mari reassured her father, Nan and Sarah let him out—easy enough, since the door was only barred on this side and it was a matter of moments to lift the bar and let him out, then drop it back in place again to leave another puzzle for the constable to have to explain. Meanwhile

Daffyd was demanding that Mari tell him what the *hell* was going on, and not waiting for her to actually do so, until finally Mari picked up a pan from the floor that was still full of water and dashed it into his face.

"Now—" she said into the silence. "Da, shut up. You will go with Sarah and this—fellow." Behind her, Puck saluted, and Daffyd stared. "Nan and I are going after Idwal and the babies. We *need* to be able to concentrate on what we're doing without worrying about you going and doing something daft, so you *promise* me, on your life, that you will *stay* with Sarah and Robin and you *won't* leave them until I come to tell you it's all right. Because I won't be rescuing my man only to find my da dangling at rope's end when I return! Do you hear me?"

Daffyd was so astonished all he could do was nod.

"Good." Mari gestured to Puck. "Please take him."

"Wait!" Daffyd shouted. *"Where?"*

"Underhill of course, you daft beggar," Puck said with impatience, while a couple of little gnomish brownies scurried about the constable's cottage, setting things to rights so that he would have even *more* explaining to do. "You know who and what I am! It's the safest place for the likes of you for now."

"But wait—that's—I don't want to come out a hundred years from now!" Daffyd said hysterically.

Puck sighed. "Daffyd Prothero, you and your line is more Selch than mortal. Underhill will have no hold on you, and you'll come to no harm. Enough of your blathering! All of you, join hands!" He seized Sarah's who seized Nan's, who grabbed Mari's, who took her father's—

And in a flash of moonlight and a smell of heather, they were standing on the beach in front of the Prothero cottage. Now Mari took charge again.

"Da, go with Robin. Sarah, can you stay here?"

"Surely," Sarah replied. "No one expects us up at Gower Cottage for days yet. Robin, if anyone comes searching here for Daffyd? Can you hide me?"

"Easy done," Puck assured her. "And Nan too, should that come to pass."

"Nan, have you got the bundle ready?" Mari asked, turning to her.

Nan dashed into the cottage, as Sarah picked up their bicycles, and moved them both into the cover of a bit of canvas and some firewood. "I do now," she declared, coming out with it in her hand. "I just hope I don't get seasick in that little teacup of yours."

"I do too," Mari said somberly, and paused long enough to kiss her father. "Behave yourself, Da. I'll see you soon, with Idwal and the babies. Take him, Robin!"

Before Daffyd could try and escape, Robin grabbed his arm, and they vanished. Sarah went into the Prothero cottage to wake the birds and let them know what was happening. Mari looked at Nan, who nodded back.

"Time to go," said Nan.

18

NAN stood in the cold sea with the water lapping at her ankles and tried not to think too hard about going out on it in a frail little construction of hide and wood and tarred canvas. On the one hand, she did want to help Mari in every way she could. On the other, she really didn't want to be on the open ocean in a tiny coracle. She couldn't imagine how Daffyd Prothero kept the wretched thing from capsizing in good, calm weather, much less in the winter storms he had taken the thing out in. And to cram *two* people into a boat made for one? That was insane.

Well, *nothing* was going to happen unless she could make this next part of the plan work. It all rested on her shoulders at the moment.

So she stood in the surf, and thought on all of the saddest things she could, until finally she landed on the day that her grandmother, the only person who had really cared for her as a tiny child, had died.

And that did it; she felt her eyes starting to burn, she remembered how devastated she had been, how her mother had dragged her away, cursing, and sent her out to beg, and how when she had come back every trace of the old woman was gone and her mother was drinking the gin that selling Granny's pitiful possessions had bought her. Her mother had even sold the little handkerchief-dolly Granny had made for her. That terrible, terrible loss welled up inside, and she let the tears come, counting them as they fell into the sea at her feet, and drying the rest on her sleeve when the number reached seven. Then she took a deep breath, steadied herself and reminded herself that it had been a long time ago, and there was someone else grieving and in need right *now*.

"Rhodri!" she called out over the quiet ocean. "Rhodri! Rhodri! Come to me! Come to me! Come to me!" Threes, always threes; repeating things in triples seemed to be the backbone of much Celtic magic.

For a moment she thought the magic wasn't going to work. Then, as she peered over the moon-spangled waves of the sea, far, far off, she spotted something moving. It neared, as a breeze sprang up and sent the wind from the sea to fan her face, a humped shape moving swiftly through the water, ripples spreading out to either side of it. It heaved itself up into the shallows—showing that the creature was a strong bull-seal—then heaved itself up and up and—

And Rhodri stood there in the moonlight, his sealskin about his shoulders, an approving smile on his face.

"Ah, well done, well thought, well schemed!" he exclaimed. "Not even Gethin can bespell me to resist the power of tears in the sea and my name on the wind! Oh, the sorrow and the pity that your tears were not for missing me, though . . ."

She snorted. He shook his head, but grew serious. "Tell me, what can I do for you? I cannot bring Idwal back, but if there is anything I can do, I will!"

Nan gestured to Mari, who was hauling the coracle down into the surf. "Take us to Gethin," Mari said quickly, tossing the oars into the boat. "Take us to the clan."

"You mean to challenge him, then?" Rhodri said, blinking in surprise. "That's a bold move, my girl."

Mari's jaw set stubbornly. "I do. It is my right, and he can't deny me that much. I won't give up without fighting."

Rhodri shook his head, though not in disbelief. "Well. Well and well. I can do that, I can take you. No matter what our elder says, you are worthy. I will take you to our people. But not, alas," he said to Nan with real regret, "You. You are neither kin nor magician, and are barred from the lands of the Selch therefore."

Nan was torn. On the one hand, she wanted terribly to be with Mari to help. But on the other—

She glanced at the coracle and shuddered.

"It would take a braver woman than I to relish going to sea in that," she admitted, and handed Mari the bundle. "And I would go with you, even so, if I thought there was a chance they'd let me."

"If you were with her, Gethin would use it as the reason to bar you both," Rhodri said flatly.

"It's all right, Nan," Mari replied, and patted her arm. "I'll have to count on Idwal's lessoning and all you and Sarah found for me. And on Gethin still thinking I'm but a weak thing he can disregard."

"All right then." Nan stepped back out of the waves. "Stay brave, and good luck to you."

"Stay safe!" she heard Mari call, as she made her way

back up the beach to join Sarah in the little cottage. And when she turned back to wave goodbye, she saw the coracle moving out to sea, steadily, along a path made by the moonlight on the still ocean.

Mari crouched in the coracle, one end of a rope fastened to the frame, the other around Rhodri's neck. He pulled the coracle effortlessly across the water, as if it weighed next to nothing. The moon was setting, and seemed bigger than she had ever seen it before, as it painted a silver road on the water. Rhodri pulled the boat along that road, silver light enfolding her, growing brighter, as mist arose from the water around her. Soon it was the mist that enveloped her and her boat, and not the moonlight, a softly glowing mist that obscured everything, making it impossible even to see the Selch who continued to pull steadily. Then even the moon vanished, leaving only the glowing mist, and she understood that she was no longer in the world she knew, but in the one that the Selch inhabited, and that somewhere along that path of light she had crossed from her world into one of magic.

Then the mist cleared for a few paces ahead; the boat was no longer being pulled, but propelled on its own. She saw land where no land should be, under a dome of stars so bright she didn't miss the moonlight. The coracle grounded on soft sand, and she took her bundle and stepped out of it. There was nothing to be seen but the mist around her and bright, bright stars in unfamiliar patterns above her.

The mist still surrounded her as she waded to the shore, dragging the coracle behind her by the rope. There was a smell of seaweed and sea-air and wet rock, and not much else; through the mist, within feet of her, she saw the vaguely humped shapes of the sort of rocks that seals like to lie-out on around her, but this stretch of the shoreline, at least, was sand. The coracle might look frail, but it wasn't light, and she strained to get it that last few feet above high tide, as marked by the line of dried seaweed. Only when she had done so did she drop the rope, and try to look about her. The mist still obscured everything, and she took her bundle out of the bottom of the coracle and climbed up on the nearest rock to see if she could get above it.

And that was when it cleared away, all in an instant, and she found herself staring at the enraged face of Gethin, standing on the rocks not thirty feet away from her.

Quick! You must take the advantage! If he speaks first, he can ruin everything!

"Gethin Selch!" she shouted, quickly, before he could get the first word in. "By the right of blood, by the right of kin, by the right of the bond of man and maid, I challenge ye for the bodies, minds, and hearts of my man and my children!" No point in specifying "souls," since Gethin wouldn't have right over those in the first place, and in the second, the legends differed as to whether the Tylwyth Teg had souls at all.

She fumbled into the bundle and brought out the jar that she and Sarah had filled on the directions of the Land-Ward. "Tis something Idwal or any witch could have taught you," Robin had said with a shrug when she asked if this would show his favor to her and get him in trouble with the Sea-Ward. "And once a drop of it strikes him, he'll have to answer your challenge whether he likes it or not." The jar had her tears in it, and herbs, and a little of her blood, and sea-water, and other things. She hurled it at Gethin's feet; her aim was true, it shattered there and some of the contents splattered him, and he jumped back as if he had been burned.

"You cannot deny me my rights!" she snarled. "Pretend it is not true though you will, I am your kin and your clan! The same blood runs in my veins as runs in yours! Deny me, and you deny the Old Ways and your own kin, and you forfeit your right to be chieftain!"

There were more people coming over the rocks, dressed roughly in skins and homespun, hair wild or braided with shells and faded ribbons and holey-stones. They heard her clearly, and began to murmur among themselves, looking askance at Gethin.

Gethin plainly heard the murmurs, and seethed, and his face darkened as one of the men called out, "She's right, Chieftain. Her being here proves she's as much Selch blood as human. She has the rights to challenge by the Old Ways."

"And I've the right to set the conditions," Gethin snarled back. He turned to Mari. "Very well then. I'll set you three Tests. Pass them all, and you'll get Idwal and the babies. But fail them—and you forfeit your life."

Mari felt her heart pound with sudden fear. Forfeit her life? *This* hadn't been in all those stories that Nan and Sarah had read out to her!

Gethin must have seen that in her face, for his scowl turned to a nasty smile. "Oh now, having second thoughts, are we?" he sneered. "I give you leave to be gone then."

"I'm going nowhere!" she snapped back, letting anger drive down her fear—though it didn't stop the pounding of her heart. *What have I to go back to? Da will never be able to come out from Underhill as long as Idwal and the babies are missing.* Oh, she could probably see him now and again, as Robin slipped him out or her in for a visit, but how would she keep herself? The silver hoard under the hearthstone wouldn't last forever. *I can fish, I suppose, for the Bargain was kept and the Prothero luck will still hold, but what's all that when I'm all alone? And even supposing I might find another man one day, and have children, they would never know their grand-da.* She didn't think she could bear being alone for the rest of her life. She could probably find a fisher-boy who would gladly share in the luck, and there were more marriages made for the sake of a little property than for love, but the thought of lying with someone besides Idwal made her ill. *I would always be longing for Idwal and my lost babies. . . .*

That alone decided her. "I set the challenge and I take it!" she snapped defiantly. "Bring your Tests!"

There were murmurs of wonder now among the Selch, and Gethin's scowl deepened. "Very well!" he barked, and gestured to his clansfolk. "Blindfold and bring her to the Trial Ground!"

She did not resist when two of the men came and took her arms, and a woman bound her eyes with a scrap of cloth. For their part, they were very gentle with her, guiding her carefully over rocks, and then on an uneven path. When they were on the rocks, she smelled only the sea and the kelp and the wet stone, but once they moved to the path she began to scent green growing things, the sort of hardy plants that lived on the islands. And then they stopped, and someone unknotted her blindfold, and she looked about her to see what manner of place she stood in.

She was a little surprised to find herself on short salt-grass, in a little hollow, nearly circular, ringed with weather-beaten trees all bent in the same direction from the winter storms. Sitting on the edge of the hollow, just under the trees, were the Selch. Her clan, too . . . and it was odd to think of it, as she turned to look into the faces of people who could have been roaming the mountains of Wales hundreds and hundreds of years ago. Many of them had their sealskins belted about them like cloaks, with the empty-eyed heads over one shoulder or draped over their hair. In the uncertain light, it made for the strange effect of having two heads on a single body, both of them staring at her.

She could *see* the magic all about her, thick as the mist that had surrounded the island; she could taste it in the air, rich and heady, as if all the flowers in the world had been made into a sweet, and this was the aroma pouring out of the pan. She could feel it tingling all of her nerves. *So this is how Idwal lives,* she thought, and wondered how he could bear to be in her world at all, where the power was so thin and weak.

How could my loving him ever compete with such richness? she thought in a sudden burst of terror. *Why would he* want *to come back to me?*

But then, Gethin pushed his way through the seated Selch, with Idwal behind him, eyes cast down, and it was too late for second thoughts.

The Selch-chief looked her up and down, expression closed and cold. "The first test," he said aloud, voice flat and without inflection, "will be the Test of Courage. Here is Idwal, Druid to Selch Seren y Gogledd. You will take him in your arms, and you will not let him go, Water Master. No matter what form he takes, you will hold him, or you will pursue him until you catch him. If he escapes you, then you lose. Only when he cannot change again for weariness will the test be over."

Like the ballad of Tam Lin, was all she had time to think, as Gethin gave Idwal a great shove, sending him into her embrace. She only had time enough to see his eyes, full of love and anguish, and then the magic shivered all around her, and in her arms was not a man at all, but a monstrous serpent.

It was as big around as Idwal, and hideously strong; it thrashed and battered her with its tail, and threatened her with its fangs. She really, truly *hated* serpents, and had ever since she'd seen one devour a little mouse as a child, and fear coursed through her veins like ice water. But she held on, and held on, ignoring the sickly musk of its breath, closing her eyes to the jaws snapping an inch from her face.

Then the magic shivered again, and it wasn't a snake, it was a flaming log in her arms.

She could feel her skin blistering and she *almost* screamed and dropped it. But she remembered through the pain that in the ballad, it had not been a real burning log, it had been an illusion. So she held on, through the pain, when suddenly she heard a voice like the hiss of fire in her ear.

Listen to the magic. Trust the magic. I've told it to lead you, and it is not Gethin's servant. Let it guide you.

Was that Idwal? The pain was incredible, and desperate for any remedy, she just let loose of her reason and did as she was told. *Take me,* the magic said. *I will protect you.* So she seized some of the magic for herself and spun it around herself in a cooling, soothing blanket of the very essence of Water, and her blisters faded and healed even as the log burned brighter.

She barely had time to feel relief when the log writhed in her arms and she was holding some sort of — thing. She wasn't quite certain what it was, but it was covered with black hair, it snarled and stank and raked at her arms with wicked claws. Quickly she formed the magic shields around her into armor that rested just on her skin, and the claws skidded on it without getting any purchase. The beast spat and wriggled and did its best to loosen her grip, but she wasn't going to give up now.

The beast gave a last heave, and suddenly there was a great, slippery piece of ice in her arms. The cold of it struck her like a hammer, and her arms went numb. In a panic, she tried to tighten them, but the ice began to slide loose, so rather than lose it, she dropped to the ground abruptly, still holding as tightly as she could until the cold made her shiver so hard her teeth rattled and she groaned with the pain of it.

And then—

She was holding nothing.

Oh no! she looked wildly about just in time to see a little mouse slipping away into the grass.

She didn't even think; she reacted instinctively, as the magic gave her the remedy, no matter how mad it sounded. *Change!* said that magic. *Change your skin!* And she suddenly knew what this was, another ballad of the "Two Magicians." She heeded the magic again, pulling the magic into herself and changing *herself*—

If he can do it, I can do it. I've been a seal!

She changed, shrinking, falling to the ground as she changed. A heartbeat later, she was the very image of the cottage's wicked cat, and she pounced on the mouse before it could escape, trapping it among her claws.

The mouse squeaked in alarm, and twisted under her paws and—

A fly buzzed out between two of the talons.

In a flash, she became a raven, and as she had seen Neville do in the warm months, she snapped her huge bill at the fly and caught it inside, unharmed. She must have seen Neville play that game with a single fly for

hours, catching without so much as touching a leg, opening his beak, letting it go, catching it again . . .

But Idwal did not remain a fly for long. She felt her
beak being forced open, and though she tried to keep it
shut, she couldn't—and the hare that the fly had become,
kicked her violently away, sending her tumbling backward onto the grass, and ran off.

But she became one of Squire's hunting hounds and
raced after him. Behind she could hear the Selch following. She caught him as he was leaping over a stretch
of water, stream or small river, she couldn't tell which;
she caught him, and lost him as the eel slipped between
her teeth and she splashed ingloriously down into the
water—

To become a fierce pike, that scented the eel in the
water immediately, and was on it, snapping at its tail
though it tried desperately to escape, and in panic, flung
itself out of the water—

Where it transformed to a duck, wings beating frantically to get some height away from the snapping jaws of
the pike that had leapt after it—

And she became a hawk, in hot pursuit of the duck,
talons reaching—

And just as the hawk seized the duck's tail, it became
a fox, turning and snapping at the hawk's head, the two
of them dropping to the ground together in a tangle of
teeth and talons and feathers—

And Mari became a great feather comforter, and enveloped the fox until it stopped changing and struggling.
She felt it become bird, then squirrel, then cat, and knew
he had run out of options and could not escape. He could
not even become fire and burn her up, for she would
smother fire.

Then she felt the magic surge once more . . . and it was

Idwal she held in her own two arms, he limp and exhausted and too weary to move.

The Selch descended on them in a mob, and despite what she wanted, they took Idwal away and set her on her feet again. They were gentle and kind about it though, and one even whispered "Well done, cousin," before the crowd parted and she faced Gethin again.

"Bring the stools," he ordered, glaring at her.

One of the Selch brought a pair of stools and set them down. Gethin took one, and gestured abruptly for her to take the other. She did so, and glad for it, for her legs were trembling with weariness, and if she was not as exhausted by the first trial as Idwal had been, she was not too far off from it.

"The next Trial," Gethin growled, "will be the Trial of Wisdom. We will just see how you measure. I have a horse in my yard, and I never ride him except by the tail." He glared at her in triumph.

A riddle! "You have a pipe, and you smoke it," she answered instantly, now unspeakably grateful for all the riddling games she and her da had played in the long winters, and all the riddles that Nan and Sarah had turned up in all those books of fairy tales.

His eyes widened a moment, then his brows knitted. "And what of the horse I never ride until his back breaks?"

That was one any child knew. "That is your roof, and you ride the rooftree to re-thatch it."

"And the thing I have that grows more hungry the more I feed it?" He was clearly getting angry; evidently this was one trial he had expected to win.

That was not only a riddle, it was the answer to one of the trials of Thor. "That is your fire, the more wood you feed it, the bigger it gets and the more it needs to keep the flames high."

He lost his temper, and leaned forward on his stool. "I have a thing that the whole sea cannot fill!" he shouted.

"You have a sieve!" she shouted back, sitting straight up, and matching him glare for glare.

"I have a house without window or door, but someone lives there!" he snarled.

"You have a fertile egg!" she retorted. That was one the old woman that had taught her to read used to tell. How could he possibly think these were clever? But ... maybe he really did think she was stupid. Or—not stupid, but maybe he thought people weren't interested in riddles anymore, so she wouldn't know them?

"I cut it at both ends and it becomes longer!" He was really angry now, eyes flashing, and he looked as if he was going to lunge up off his stool at any moment and strangle her with his own two hands. He was actually frightening her. *I know the Selch will pull him off, but he could hurt me badly before they do. . . .*

"You are digging a ditch," she said, deciding to act indifferent, and see where that got her. Either it would make him so angry he would give up, or it would calm him down. In either case, it would better than this, because she hated the way he was shouting and edging closer to her, and truth to tell—the way he was making the hair on the back of her neck stand up, it was getting hard to think clearly.

Her indifference either calmed him, or made him think he had to be equally indifferent to impress her or the onlookers; he sat back on his stool. "Thirty-two horses on a red hill; now they stamp, now they champ, now they stand still."

"Your teeth, and you are a lucky man to still have all of them," she said coolly, and surreptitiously took a deep, deep breath of relief that now he was more or less in control of himself.

He ground those teeth audibly, then hunched down on his stool, made his hands into fists, and the battle really began.

He threw literally everything at her. "Cut off my head, I live, cut off my tail, I die." "You're a tree." "I am a lamp that shines over the whole world." "You are the moon." "I am dead and I carry the living." "You are either a boat or a cart, both are made of dead wood and carry the living." And it went on for so long that both of them got hungry and thirsty; he called for water and food, and offered her none, but Rhodri brought her water and some samphire and raw oysters fresh from the ocean that he cut open for her with a flint knife as he sat on his heels beside her stool. She could manage those, she had eaten oysters raw many times in the past although her da had teased her, saying such were for men for reasons he didn't specify. She was grateful for something as familiar as oysters; she could never have done what Gethin was doing, tearing into a raw fish as if he was eating a nice piece of laver-bread. She could have done with a bit of that laver-bread right now.

When he had finished his fish, and she was still chewing on a mouthful of seaweed, he began again. Only now . . . he had changed his tactic altogether. He must have realized that she knew the all riddles that he knew—and as the Trial was to measure her wisdom, he could ask her anything he cared to.

"So," he said. "You are a chieftain. Two women come before you, both stubborn, both claiming the same child. What do you do?"

She knew in that instant that to use the Judgment of Solomon would be a deep mistake here. Firstly, the Tylwyth Teg famously valued children, and often stole them, and to even threaten to cut one in half would horrify them. And secondly, she was supposed to be showing her *own* wisdom here and she rather thought even Gethin and his clan knew the story.

"This is a child and not a baby?" she asked first. "Old enough to speak?"

"Yes, yes," he said impatiently. "What do you do?"

"I let the child choose, taking him away from both women so that he can choose freely," she said, after a moment.

Gethin blinked. He clearly had not thought she would say this. "But why?"

"Because the child will choose the woman that loves him most, and treats him better," she replied, as the Selch murmured among themselves at this.

"But what if he does not choose his real mother?" Gethin demanded.

"Why should that matter?" she replied. "It is better for a child to be with a mother that loves him and nurtures him than one that is his blood-kin but is indifferent to him. Now, a baby is a different matter. A baby cannot choose for itself. I would have set some other test, had it been a baby."

The Selch were murmuring, and it sounded as if it was with approval. Well, they might well be following the tradition of the Tylwyth Teg of the land, and stealing the children of careless, neglectful, or downright cruel parents.

Thankfully, Gethin did not ask her what she would do if it was a baby, because she honestly hadn't an answer except to steal the one King Solomon in the Bible used.

Gethin continued to ply her with hard questions; she answered them honestly, even when the answer wasn't in her favor—

"Suppose," he said, leaning back on his stool and

looking at her through narrowed eyes. "Suppose you win these Trials. Suppose you take Idwal and the children back to the land. And suppose one day your children come to you and say they wish to come to the sea forever? What would you do?"

"I am a mother, I would weep!" she snapped at him. "But I do not own them; they are not my dogs nor my chattel. If that would be what they want, I would hope my tears would move them, but I would let them go!"

"Then why do you fight to keep them now?" he demanded, pointing an accusing finger at her.

"Because they are babies and cannot choose for themselves, or is that so hard a thing for you to accept?" she snapped back. "If you told me 'if you keep them, they will die,' then yes, I would give them up, but I am their mother and I love them more than my own life, and I do not think the women you got to nurse them could love them half so much!"

Well, the last words of that answer did not get so good a response from the Selch, but she wouldn't unsay them. They were the truth, and she remembered what Idwal had told her; a magician must speak the truth or remain silent, but he could not lie.

Especially not here.

Finally when the questions had ceased to be tests of her wisdom and had become mere badgering, three of the Selch stepped forward, and the middle one made an abrupt gesture.

"Enough, chieftain," he said. "You have tested her and she has proved knowledge, wisdom, and her willingness to speak true. You gain nothing more by continuing this. It is time to move on."

She was so grateful for the intervention she nearly jumped up and kissed them. It was impossible to tell what time it was here, for the stars above her had not changed in the least, but it felt like hours and hours had passed.

"One more question," Gethin insisted. He turned to her. "Your world becomes closed to us. There is more cold iron about with every day, even the ships, as you pointed out, are made of cold iron. What would you do on the day when your world brings such pain to your man that he is never free of hurt and harm from morning to night?"

"I—would tell him to go," she said, after a long pause. "How could I claim to love him and demand he suffer for my sake?" She licked her lips. "But if it were possible to go with him, then go I would, and leave everything I know behind to be with him."

If Gethin and hoped to make her look worse in the eyes of the clan with her answer, he had achieved the very opposite. But he had to abide by the will of the rest; with a growl, he stood up, as did she, though her knees were stiff with sitting. One of the Selch took the stools away.

"The last Trial is Love," Gethin said with a smirk. "As you claim you love your man and children so very much, would you know them among a thousand?"

"Yes!" she said instantly. And knew at that moment that he had tricked her.

"Come, then." He stalked out into the mist, and she followed him. The rest of the Selch followed the both of them.

Now what have I gotten myself into?

She discovered soon enough.

19

THE mist blew away from in front of her, and she found herself facing a seal-beach.

As far as she could see, there were seals, cows, bulls, and pups, all stretched out on the sand. She had never in her life seen so many seals; seals sleeping, seals watching her and Gethin, grooming themselves and each other, seals tending their pups, seals doing anything that seals could do except plunging into the surf and swimming off. All of them stayed on the beach, quite as if she didn't matter at all.

"So you would know them among a thousand?" Gethin asked. "Find them."

For a moment she struggled with rage. She wanted to seize a rock and beat the smirk off his face. She wanted to strangle him. How was she going to be able to pick out her babies among all these seal pups? Idwal, she could manage—she had been with him as a seal so many times she knew every detail of him in that shape, something

Gethin was probably not aware of. But the babies? They had no birthmarks, and she had no idea what they would look like as seals!

That blackguard! She thought with rage. *Oh, I hope he loses his skin! I hope no woman will ever go with him again! I hope he loses the thing he cares most for in all of the world!*

If she found Idwal first, could *he* help her?

"Don't think to get your man to help you," Gethin said in a snide tone of voice, quite as if he had read her mind. "This is your task and yours alone."

Could she use her Water Magic? But how? She couldn't think, she felt tears rising up to choke her, and she wanted to throw herself into the ocean in despair . . .

Yes, whispered the magic. *Yes! The ocean!*

The call of the magic held her rigid with shock for a moment. Did the magic actually want her dead?

Then she remembered. Idwal had somehow imprinted the magic here with the will to help her! So, there was something about the ocean that would give her the key to finding Idwal and Aled and Aneirin among all those seals and pups.

The ocean . . .

What if she were another seal?

True, she didn't have her borrowed skin. Nevertheless, she was Selch blood herself, and had she grown up here, she would have a skin of her own. And she had just transformed herself into *how* many shapes here, when chasing Idwal? If she could do that—

I can be a seal. I don't even need the skin that Idwal found for me; I can change into a seal without it—in fact, since I am part of Selch-blood, I can probably become a seal easier than any other shape. And seal-mothers know their own babies, among a thousand . . .

She ran for the ocean, remembering how Idwal had coaxed her into changing the first time. She remembered what it had been like to be a seal, willing herself into the sleek shape, feeling fur instead of skin, a snout instead of a nose, a tail, not legs, and fins, not hands. And she reached the edge of the surf, and plunged under the waves.

And came up, snorting water and shaking her sleek, dark head. She raised her nose to the breeze, trusting her body to tell her what she needed, as she had trusted the wisdom in the skin Idwal had brought her to tell her what to do.

She scented it then. A faint, faint thread that said *mine! My blood! My bone! Fed by my body! My own!*

She scrambled ashore and followed that thread of scent. From time to time she stopped, and called, and waited. There was no answer at first. But the scent grew stronger, and she shoved her way among the other cows and pups, sniffing, calling, sniffing, calling—

And then she heard it. The little bawls that pulled on her heart and sent her onward, deeper into the herd. The scent grew stronger too, making her teats ache with the need to feed her babies, until she was shuffling as fast as ever a seal could move on land, and then found herself scrambling over the rocks and sand in human-shape, with the scent still as strong as ever in her nostrils, and the babies still answering her call, until she found them, and caught them up in her arms, and the moment she touched them, they shivered all over with magic and became human babies again.

She heard a howl of rage behind her, and turned to see Gethin being restrained by several of the clan, as Rhodri picked his way among the seals toward her. He held out his arms.

"Trust me with the pups, Mari," he said, almost tenderly. "I know it is only a mere formality, but find your mate."

And it *was* a mere formality; with her babies found and safe, it was no great difficulty to walk among the bulls and follow her heart straight to Idwal. She knew him without seeing the little wrinkles around his eyes, the scar that a fight had gotten him on his shoulder, and the one where he had gashed himself on sharp rock as a youngster. She went straight to him, and laid her hand on him, and called the magic to her and poured it into him.

With an explosion of joy, the magic burst the bonds that Gethin had put on him and he stood before her and caught her up in his arms as if he would never let her go again.

The coracle was waiting, floating in the shallows, surrounded by mist. The babies were cradled in Mari's sealskin in the bottom of it, and Idwal and Rhodri waited to pull the little boat back to the world she knew. Her kin were gathered on the beach to see to it that Gethin did not work some treachery at the last minute—they had made that much clear, to her, and to him.

Gethin was still chieftain . . . but it was looking as if he would not be chieftain for much longer. The things he had said when she claimed her rights over Idwal and the babies had made a great many, even of his supporters, turn against him.

"It is in my right to close the bounds of our land to you," he snarled at Idwal. "And so I will. Be off with you, and if you regret your choice, know that you only have yourself and that bitch you chose over your clan to blame for your exile."

And at that moment, Idwal gathered himself up and stood toe-to-toe with Gethin, looking quite as if he was prepared to fight. "I am going home, home from the sea, with my wife," he declared. "To *my* home, with *my* wife, and *my* children, who are as much kin to this whole clan as you are, and more!"

Gethin started to raise his hand against Idwal. "Then we will close the door against you! The compact is broken and the Bargain is over! And see how you fare without the Prothero luck!"

Mari stalked up to the both of them, and spat at his feet. "Do so! And we will find another way! Being dependent on those with no gratitude is like getting a herring that is all bone! Away with you! And may *you* have joy of the bed you have made for yourself! I hope it is cold and lonely, for no woman will want a man who is so mean of spirit!"

Gethin roared with anger, and suddenly there was a clap of thunder and a flash of light, and the two of them found themselves sitting in the coracle in the middle of the open ocean.

The ocean was clear of mist and thankfully as smooth as a mirror. No longer were they under unmoving stars; instead, the sun was high in the sky above them.

A seal surfaced beside them and barked merrily. Dazed, Mari recognized Rhodri, and tossed him the rope. He caught it in his teeth, and plunged ahead, and with a jerk, the coracle started moving.

Mari looked at Idwal troubled. "Can he do that?" she asked. "Can he keep you from coming back?"

Idwal laughed, easing her heart. "For no more than seven years, and if he is no longer chieftain, not after that. I do not think that the world will grow so hard to me that I cannot wait seven years."

Comforted, she leaned back in his arms as the little round boat moved surely and easily over the sea, toward home.

Mari worked industriously at mending a net, as her father carefully fastened his precious glass floats to another, and Idwal carved a teething-ring from a bit of whale-tusk. Nan and Sarah had told them they had been gone for two days, and that the constable had been looking for them each day, getting angrier all the time.

"It was wonderful!" Nan had said, her face full of glee. "When he dragged Daffyd to his little prison, as it happened, there wasn't anyone about. I think he might have chosen when everyone was in at supper on purpose, just in case people objected, but he out-foxed himself if that was his intention, because no one in Clogwyn knew he had Daffyd locked up. So when he came to his senses and started shouting about Daffyd escaping, and the ghosts, and noises—"

Mari had laughed until her sides hurt, and nearly did herself a mischief sending the tea she had been drinking up her nose. "They must have thought he had run mad!"

Sarah had nodded. "They certainly did. Well and truly mad. It was the worse for him because there was no stream of water running through his cottage, there were already so many water-marks on the walls from the old leaks that no one could tell there were new ones, and no one had heard anything in the night thanks to Puck. So he came storming down here, looking for Daffyd and Mari, and found the place empty."

"Puck was hiding us, of course," Nan had continued. "And when we thought he might get up to no good in the cottage, we came down the beach. We told him you all had gone off to visit relatives. He wanted to know who, and we pretended we hadn't paid any attention, and when he got nasty, Puck turned up as the dog and ran him off!" Nan described how Puck had harried the constable all the way to the road and they all had laughed until they could scarcely breathe.

The girls had heard that he was going all the way to Cardiff to speak with his superiors, and the lot of them had concocted a plot.

Quite honestly, after their ordeals, all three of them had decided that they deserved a holiday, so Daffyd had left off fishing for a few days and they spent their time resting, eating, mending things, gathering cockles, mussels, and clams from tide pools, and in Mari's case, learning to cook things she had never tried before, since Nan and Sarah went down to Criccieth and brought back some lovely foodstuffs. Rhodri had turned up with a ketch, a little sailing boat with a laid-on keel, big enough to take several people, and was happy to ferry them about. Where he got it, he wouldn't say, but Mari had to wonder if he'd stolen it from the other side, just to tweak Gethin's nose. They didn't lack for their usual fish either, even though Daffyd didn't go out; once the sun was down and they were sure Constable Ewynnog was not going to turn up, Idwal would put on his sealskin and go out, bringing back a fine salmon or some other choice fish. On the first day of their holiday, Daffyd had gone over to Clogwyn to gossip about the pretended visit, let people know they were on a brief holiday, and accept congratulations on the two new grandchildren. He returned laden with currant buns, some fresh vegetables, and good wishes.

And now, at last, when Mari looked up and saw the unusual procession of three carts on the road near the shore, she knew that the constable had returned—with reinforcements.

"The fool didn't even go to Clogwyn first," Daffyd snorted, looking up when he saw her staring at the road. "Oh, he's going to get exactly what he deserves." Mari smiled; her mild-mannered da was all but rubbing his hands with glee. "Idwal, let's you and me go in the house. I want to do this proper."

The men went in; Mari remained where she was, mending the net in the sun, with a baby nicely cradled in a basket on either side of her, a towel over the top of the basket to keep off the sun.

It took Constable Ewynnog and his procession a good long time to make it to the cottage, and he was not in the least aided by the mischievous Elementals of both Water and Earth that were doing their level best to interfere every step of the way. Finally he got to the cottage and marched up to Mari—who did not get up—chest puffed out with importance. "Mari Prothero?" he asked, as if he did not know.

"Drever," she said, shortly, and rudely.

She took him by surprise. Small wonder, since she had never been anything other than shy and possibly dull-witted around him. "Eh—what?" he stumbled.

"Mari *Drever*," she corrected. "*Mrs.* Mari Drever. As well you should know, Constable Ewynnog, since you sat in chapel and glared at me through all three Sundays of the banns." She put down the net, stood up, and planted both her hands on her hips. "And if you have come here to insinuate that my baby boys are bastards, I'll be giving the back of my hand to you, constable or no constable!"

One of the little train of fellow police officers that had accompanied him snickered. The constable turned dark red. "Mari *Drever* then, I am here to summon you to answer for the disappearance of Idwal Drever and your ... two ..."

And his voice trailed off, as one of the twins, roused from his happy nap, complained loudly about the rude fellow who was standing almost over him and shouting—and a moment later, his brother joined in the complaint.

"Mari?" Idwal called from inside. "In God's own name, what is all the noise about?" He opened the cottage door and came out onto the doorstep, drying his hands on a towel. "I think the laver-bread is ready—" Then he pretended to see the convocation of constables in the dooryard for the first time. "Who are you all, and what are you doing, frightening my sons and pestering my wife?"

Constable Ewynnog gaped at him, mouth working like a fish trying to breathe air. The other constables exchanged glances.

"You!" Idwal said, with a fierce frown, pointing at Ewynnog. "I know you! You are that interfering old maid who sat through my banns, scribbling notes as if you thought you were learning something! A fine piece of work that was, and in chapel too!"

"But—but—but—" Ewynnog sputtered. "You were missing! You were dead!"

Now Mari and Idwal looked at him as if he had sprouted tentacles. "When?" Mari asked, finally.

"But I found you here, the babies were gone, you were crying, and—"

"You must have fallen and struck your head; that is the most daft thing I have ever heard anyone say," said Mari crossly, and went over to Idwal, who put his arm around her shoulders. "I never was."

"But I arrested your father! I had him in my cell!"

Ewynnog was spluttering now, and the other constables were moving, not at all surreptitiously, away from him.

"You what now?" Daffyd looked around from behind Idwal. "I don't think so. Mari and Idwal and I took the babies up north to Stromness to meet their kin. His half-brother Rhodri came to fetch us in his ketch—look, there's Rhodri now." He pointed out to sea, and right on his cue, as alerted by Idwal via one of the Elementals, Rhodri sailed into view in his conventionally hulled fishing boat quite big enough to carry half a dozen. "He brought us back a couple days ago."

"Is that so, sir?" asked one of the other constables politely.

"You can ask him yourself; he's anchoring his craft now, he'll be ashore in a bit." Daffyd looked with pity on Ewynnog, who was going red and white by turns, and seemed quite unable to utter a single coherent word now, much less a sentence. He turned back to the constable that had addressed him. "You know, I don't like to repeat gossip," he said in a confiding tone, "But Blue Ruin has been the downfall of many a stout fellow. And if people *will* send a man out alone to find something that can't be found, and keep putting him under terrible strain when he can't find it, you can't blame the poor fellow for—" And Daffyd made a loose fist and put his thumb to his mouth and tipped back his head as if he was drinking from a bottle.

The other constable nodded wisely. Obviously, he couldn't *say* anything without impugning Ewynnog, and by extension, the rest of the constabulary service. But what he did say was, "I am very sorry that we wasted your time, Mister Prothero. There was obviously a grave misunderstanding."

"Quite all right," Daffyd said grandly. "No harm done. We'll just go and have our tea."

"Very good, sir," said the constable, pulling on the brim of his helmet. Then he turned to Ewynnog. "Come along, lad," he said in a condescending voice. "It's clear you were mistaken. Let's just get all this sorted out now, shall we?"

"But they—but I—but—" Ewynnog said weakly, as they surrounded him and more or less herded him back to the carts. "But—but—but—"

Mari heard a peal of hysterical laughter at her feet. She looked down to see the malicious little Water Elemental contorted into a knot of hilarity.

"You know," Daffyd said meditatively, watching the carts drive off again. "That was almost worth getting arrested over."

"I have to say," Mari said, looking at the fish pie, a pie in which half a dozen herring heads were staring up at her from the crust, "This thing is kind of . . . uncanny."

"I promise, and I swear to you," Nan replied, looking up from where she was playing with the babies on the floor, "That is exactly how they make it in Cornwall."

"When you said they called it 'stargazey pie,' I was thinking it was going to look . . . well, not like this." She shoved it in the oven. "I hope it tastes better than it looks."

"It does," Sarah assured her, and laughed at Grey, who was playing peek-a-boo with Aled by flipping a cloth over his face, then whisking it off. The baby found this hilarious. "But I warn you, the Cornish say that the reason that the devil never comes there is because he is afraid a Cornish housewife will make him into a pie. I don't think there is a thing in the world that the Cornish haven't tried to stuff into a crust."

Mari laughed. "Oh, I am going to miss you two so much!"

Nan scooped up Aneirin and stood up, going over to hug her friend and handing Mari the boy with the same motion. Mari sat down and cuddled him. "Oh, you won't miss us that much. You'll have Rhodri here. Pish-tush, probably before too long, you'll have far too many Selch here for comfort. Just because Gethin barred Idwal from going to the clan, he's not going to be able to bar the clan from coming to Idwal."

"That's true," Mari replied, looking up from her baby. "But they won't be you."

"Well then," Sarah told her, with a smile. "We'll just have to keep coming back to visit."

Mari heaved a great sigh of relief. "I was afraid we were too backward for you," she confessed. "After all, we don't have all the things there are in London."

"Oh, like air you can't breathe?" asked Sarah. "We'll just have to make sure the Old Lion thinks it's important enough for us to come see how you are doing now and again."

"Well, he should, for all he's a heathen English lord," said Daffyd, kneeing the door open so he could bring in the things he had traded for in Clogwyn. "After all, there's two Water Masters here. And from the look of it—look at that little lad a-gurgling at the sprite there!—there's like to be four before very long."

Mari glanced down at the baby she held, who was, indeed cooing and gurgling at the kindly water-sprite, who was playing in the kitchen barrel and making fountains for him. "Oh—" she gasped. "He's never done that before!"

"That'll be important enough!" Nan said with a huge grin. "Problem sorted!"

"All right, my loves, time to go to Criccieth for the train. Rhodri's got the ketch unloaded so there's room for you and the birdies." Daffyd hugged Nan and Sarah as if they were his own daughters. "Off you go, and come you back as soon as you can."

The girls picked up the carriers, and the birds jumped onto their shoulders. Everyone agreed it was safer for the birds out of the carriers than in, at least while they were on the water. There were hugs and kisses all around, and a little basket of laver-bread pressed on them for the journey "for you won't get it anywhere but here!" and then they were gone, and Idwal and Mari were alone in the cottage except for the babies, watching the ketch sail down toward Criccieth from the doorstep.

"How long do you think they'll keep coming to visit?" Mari asked, missing them already.

Idwal put his arm around her. "As long as we are here," he said, sounding quite certain of it.

"And how long will we be here?" she asked—something she had not dared to ask until this moment, even though the question had been eating at her ever since Gethin had asked her what she would do if the world she knew became too painful for Idwal to bear.

"Well now . . . as long as your da is alive, for I'll not leave him alone, and he won't take to the sea," Idwal said easily, which made some of the knot of fear in her chest loosen. "And as long as Gethin bars us, which will be seven years at least."

"But—" she ventured.

"But—" he stayed her words with a kiss. "We are not barred from other clans. And Gethin can rage all he wants, the Selch are not one body; so should need drive, we can find shelter with other Selch or even Selkie."

A little more of the fear ebbed.

"But I'd rather not." He held her close. "True it is that the power is thick and pure on the other side of the barrier. But there are other things in the world than power, or why do you think the little ones like yon sprite stay? Perhaps one day, it will be too hard to live in this world, and on that day you and I and all our family will come away. Or perhaps not." He shrugged, and she felt the last of her fear melting with his love. "But until then, dear love, and dearest friend, you can truly say that we are in our proper place, doing our proper work; guarding the world, doing what needs doing, home from the sea."

MERCEDES LACKEY

The Elemental Masters Series

"Her characteristic carefulness, narrative gifts, and attention to detail shape into an altogether superior fantasy." —*Booklist*

"It's not lighthearted fluff, but rather a dark tale full of the pain and devastation of war, the growing class struggle, and changing sex roles, and a couple of wounded protagonists worth rooting for." —*Locus*

"Putting a fresh face to a well-loved fairytale is not an easy task, but it is one that seems effortless to the prolific Lackey. Beautiful phrasing and a thorough grounding in the dress, mannerisms and history of the period help move the story along gracefully. This is a wonderful example of a new look at an old theme." —*Publishers Weekly*

"Richly detailed historic backgrounds add flavor and richness to an already strong series that belongs in most fantasy collections. Highly recommended." —*Library Journal*

To Order Call: 1-800-788-6262
www.dawbooks.com